Praise for *The S*

"The queen of high-ten
a twisted tale that v
Sunday Times

"*The Stolen Sisters* is one wild read! Buckle up for twists and turns that I for one never saw coming . . . I would put *The Stolen Sisters* to the top of your TBR pile."
Amazon Reviewer, 5*

"With great skill, Jensen slowly unveils the well-hidden aspects of all three characters and propels the book to a moving and convincing conclusion."
Daily Mail

"An absorbing, twisted, dark and emotional rollercoaster that will appeal to fans of psychological thrillers. I could go on for hours about how much I LOVED this book but I want you all to go out and experience it for yourselves. My FAVOURITE book from Louise Jensen yet!"
Amazon Reviewer, 5*

"A fast-paced, suspenseful thriller with unforeseen clever twists and turns to keep the reader captivated until the very last page."
Candis

"I think I will be suffering a little bit of a book hangover now I've finished this one. Definitely worthy of the full five stars."
Amazon Reviewer, 5*

"Twisting, turning, breathless ride to the end."
Woman & Home

Louise Jensen is a global No. 1 bestselling author of psychological thrillers. Louise has sold over a million copies of her books and her novels have been sold for translation in twenty-five countries, as well as being featured on the *USA Today* and *Wall Street Journal* bestsellers' lists. Louise was nominated for the Goodreads Debut Author of 2016 Award and the *Guardian*'s Not the Booker 2018. *The Gift* has been optioned for TV and film.

When Louise isn't writing thrillers, she turns her hand to penning love stories under the name Amelia Henley. Her debut as Amelia Henley, *The Life We Almost Had*, is out now.

Louise lives with her husband, children, madcap dog and a rather naughty cat in Northamptonshire. She loves to hear from readers and writers and can be found at www.louisejensen.co.uk, where she regularly blogs flash fiction and writing tips.

Also by Louise Jensen

The Family
The Gift
The Sister
The Surrogate
The Date

Writing as Amelia Henley

The Life We Almost Had

The Stolen Sisters

LOUISE JENSEN

ONE PLACE. MANY STORIES

This novel is entirely a work of fiction. The names, characters and incidents portrayed in it are the work of the author's imagination. Any resemblance to actual persons, living or dead, events or localities is entirely coincidental.

HQ
An imprint of HarperCollins*Publishers* Ltd
1 London Bridge Street
London SE1 9GF

This edition 2021

1
First published in Great Britain by
HQ, an imprint of HarperCollins*Publishers* Ltd 2020

Louise Jensen asserts the moral right to be identified as the author of this work.
A catalogue record for this book is available from the British Library.

ISBN: 978-0-00-847839-1
Walmart Exclusive: 978-0-00-851289-7

MIX
Paper from responsible sources
FSC™ C007454

This book is produced from independently certified FSC™ paper to ensure responsible forest management.

For more information visit: www.harpercollins.co.uk/green

This book is set in 10.6/15.5 pt. Sabon

Printed and Bound in the UK using 100% Renewable Electricity at CPI Group (UK) Ltd, Croydon, CR0 4YY

For Finley Duffy
Who always has the best ideas…

Part One

Chapter One

Carly

Then

When Carly looked back at that day the memory was in shades of grey; the trauma had sucked the blue from the sky, the green from the freshly mown grass. She had sat on the back doorstep, the coolness of the concrete permeating through her school skirt, the late-afternoon sun warming her bare arms. Carly remembers now the blackness of a beetle scurrying down the path before it disappeared into the soil under the rose bush. The stark white of the twins' socks, bunched below their knees.

Inconsequential details that later the police would jot in their notebooks as though Carly was somehow being a great help but she knew she wasn't, and worse than that, she knew it was entirely her fault.

It had all been so frustratingly normal. Leah and Marie had shrieked in mock disgust as Bruno, their boxer, bounded towards them, drool spilling from his jowls. But their screams then still carried an undercurrent of happiness, not like later when their cries were full of fear and there was nowhere to run to.

The things that have stayed with Carly are this.

The way her fingers gripped the cumbersome Nokia in her

hand as though she was clutching a secret. Her annoyance as she angled her screen to avoid the glare, never dreaming that soon she would be craving daylight.

Fresh air.

Space.

The pounding in her head increasing as the girls bounced a tennis ball between them across the patio. The way she had snapped at the twins as though it was their fault Dean Malden hadn't texted her. Of all the things that she could, that she should, feel guilty about, she had never forgiven herself that the last words she spoke to her sisters before they were all irrevocably damaged was in anger rather than kindness.

Although in truth, she had never forgiven herself for any of it.

'Shut up!' She had roared out her frustration that the first boy she loved had shattered her thirteen-year-old heart. Crazy now to recall that she once thought the absence of a text was the end of the world. There were far worse things. Far worse people than the floppy-haired blond boy who had let her down.

Her younger sisters turned to her, identical green eyes wide. Marie's sight trained on Carly's face as she chucked the ball for Bruno. Carly's irritation grew as she watched it fly over the fence.

'For God's sake.' She stood, brushing the dust from the back of her sensible pleated skirt. 'It's time to come in.'

'But that's not fair.' Marie looked stricken as her gaze flickered towards the fence.

'Life isn't fair,' Carly said, feeling a bubbling resentment that at eight years old the twins had it easy.

'Can you fetch our ball, please, Carly?' Marie pleaded.

'Fetch it yourself,' Carly snapped.

'You know we're not allowed out of the garden on our own until we're ten,' Marie said.

'Yeah, well I'm in charge today and I'm saying you can. It's not like we live in a city. Nothing ever happens in this dump.' Carly was sick of living somewhere so small where everyone knew everyone else's business. Where everyone would know by tomorrow that Dean Malden had rejected her. 'Be quick and shut the gate *properly*.'

She turned and pushed open the back door, stepping into the vast kitchen that never smelled of cakes or bread. It never smelled of anything except freshly roasted coffee. Carly clattered her phone onto the marble island and yanked open the fridge door. The shelves, which were once stocked with stilton and steak and that had groaned under the weight of fresh fruit and vegetables, were woefully bare. There was nothing except a shrivelled cucumber and some out-of-date hummus. It was all right for her mum and stepdad out for the evening at yet another corporate function. They spent more time on the business than with their children nowadays, although Mum had assured her it wouldn't be for much longer. She'd soon be at home more but in the meantime it was left to Carly to sort out tea again. She had loved her half-sisters fiercely since the day they were born, though sometimes she wished Mum still paid the retired lady down the road to babysit, but since Carly had turned thirteen, Mum felt that she was responsible enough.

She sighed as she crossed to the shelf above the Aga and lifted the lid from the teapot. Inside was a £10 note. Chips for tea. She wondered whether the money would stretch to three sausages or if they should split a battered cod.

Minutes later the twins tumbled into the kitchen.

'Yuck.' Leah dropped the tennis ball coated with slobber into the wicker basket where Bruno kept his toys.

'Wash your hands.' Carly checked her phone again.

Nothing.

What had she done wrong? She had thought Dean liked her.

Marie perched on a stool at the breakfast bar, swinging her legs, the toes of her shoes thudding against the kick board. How was Carly supposed to hear her text alert over that? Marie had her chin in her hands, her mouth downturned; she hated being in trouble. Carly could see the way her lip trembled with upset but she couldn't help yelling again.

'Shut. Up.'

Marie slid off the stool. 'I… I left my fleece in the garden.'

Carly jerked her head towards the door in a go-and-get-it gesture before she clicked on the radio. The sound of Steps flooded the room. Marie paused and momentarily their sisterly bond tugged at them all. '5, 6, 7, 8' was one of their favourite songs. Usually they'd fall into line and dance in synchronicity.

'Let's do this!' Marie flicked her red hair over her shoulders and placed her hands on her hips.

'It's childish,' Carly snapped although inside her shoes, her toes were tapping.

'It doesn't work unless we *all* do it.' Marie's voice cracked. 'We *have* to be together.'

Carly pulled the scrunchie she'd been wearing like a bracelet from her wrist and smoothed her long fair hair back into a ponytail. The twins got into position. Waited. Carly reached for her phone and tried to ignore the pang of meanness that flitted through her as the smile slipped from Leah's face. Marie's small shoulders rounded as she headed back outside.

Minutes later she raced back in, socked feet skidding across the tiles, tears streaming down her freckled cheeks. 'Bruno's got out. The gate was open.'

'For God's sake.' Carly could feel the anger in her chest form a cold, hard ball. It was one of the last times she ever allowed herself to truly feel. 'Who shut the gate?'

Marie bit her lower lip.

'I did,' said Leah, slipping her shoes back on.

'You're supposed to bang it until it latches, you idiot. You know it's broken. Three times. You bang it three times.'

The girls pelted into the garden, calling the dog's name.

Marie hesitated at the gate. 'Perhaps we should wait—' Under her freckles, her skin was pale. She'd been off school yesterday with a stomach ache and although she'd gone back today, she didn't look well. Carly knew she should ask if she was feeling okay but instead she shoved her roughly into the street. 'It's your fault, Marie. You search that way.' She pointed down the avenue lined with beech trees.

Marie grabbed Leah's hand.

'No,' Carly snapped. 'Leah can come with me.' The twins could be silly when they were together and she had enough to worry about without them getting into trouble.

'But I want—' Marie began.

'I don't *care* what you want. Move.' Carly grabbed Leah's arm and led her in the opposite direction, towards the cut-through at the side of their house, which led to the park.

It all happened so quickly that afterwards Carly couldn't remember which order it all came in. The balaclava-clad face looming towards hers. The forearm around her neck, the gloved hand clamped over her mouth. The sight of Leah struggling against arms that restrained her. The scraping sound of her shoe as she was dragged towards the van at the other end of the alley. The sight of Marie, almost a blur, flying towards the second man also clad in black, who held her twin, pummelling him with her small fists.

'Stop! You can't do this! Don't take her. I don't want you to take her!'

The soft flesh compacting against hard bone as Carly bit down hard on the fingers that had covered her mouth.

'Run!' she had screamed at Marie as the man who held Leah grabbled to find something of Marie's he could hold on to, clutching at her collar, her ginger pigtails, as she dodged his grasp.

'Run!'

Chapter Two

Leah

Now

Dread crawls around the pit of my stomach. It's impossible to ignore the urge to run back into the room. I push open the door and step inside. The kitchen is exactly as I left it, not surprising as I am the only one home, but nevertheless I twist the dial on the oven three times to make sure that it's off, despite knowing that I haven't cooked anything today.

Safe.

I have to keep us all safe.

My compulsions are worsening again. If I was being kind to myself I'd think it's not surprising considering what I've been through, what I've yet to face over this coming week.

I'm rarely kind to myself.

But still, I remember what happened the last time everything got out of hand. The build of pressure. The loss of control. Despite the scrutiny I'll be under over the next few days, I have to hold it together this time, if not for me, then for George and Archie.

The silver-framed faces of the three of us at Drayton Manor Park beam down at me from the dresser. Archie has inherited bits of both of us. He has my fiery red hair but instead of being poker-straight it's curly like George's dark mop would be if he didn't keep it so short. Unlike George's hair, Archie's always smells of the apple shampoo I wash it with each night and as I recall the familiar scent, momentarily I allow myself to relax, until an incoming text lights up my phone.

I need you.

I tell myself I can just say no, but anxiety rises as quickly as Archie's tears do when he's overtired.

Calm yourself.

I force my eyes to travel around the room and name three things to ground myself.

Archie's cuddly toy Labrador curled up in its wicker basket, a fake bone between its paws. He's forever begging for a puppy but I can't cope with the thought of a real dog.

George's sheepskin gloves on top of the microwave; he always forgets where he's left them.

A canvas print of three girls holding hands on a golden beach. I don't know who they are but when I saw it hanging in the window of a local gallery I stood there for the longest time, unsure whether it made me feel happy or sad. For three years it's hung on my wall and I still feel a flurry of emotions when I catch sight of it. I still can't unpick what they are.

Calm.

A second message buzzes.

It's important.

I can just say no.

But I won't.

I can't delay it any more. Peeling off my disposable gloves I snap on a fresh pair and gather my keys and my mobile. On the doormat is a business card from a reporter with *Call me* scrawled across it.

I won't.

At times like these I wonder why I've never moved away from this small town I grew up in, where everybody knows who I am and what happened to me. I think it's partly because there's no getting away from it. Once you've been global news there is no fading into anonymity. It only takes one person to post a sighting on Twitter or Facebook and your face is everywhere again. The public like a game of hide-and-seek even though I don't want to play. There's also a comfort in being surrounded by familiar faces. Strangers still terrify me. The main reason though, if I'm honest, is because staying so close to where it happened is a form of punishment and deep down we all feel in some way responsible.

We *still* blame ourselves.

Although I'm late, I'm in no hurry to get there; part of me knows what she'll want to talk about and I don't think I can face it.

I'm careful as I drive, headlights slicing through the gloom. The dark skies give a sense of early evening rather than mid-morning. We're barely into autumn and it already feels like winter. I'm mindful of the traffic, peering into cars, wondering who's inside and where they're going.

If they're happy.

Everyone in the town was more vigilant after our abduction.

The community was pulled together by threads of horror but over time they… not exactly forgot but moved on. Or tried to. Eyes that once looked at me with sympathy became filled with annoyance as another anniversary summoned a fresh batch of true-crime fans, pointing out the house we grew up in. Our old school. The swings in the playground our parents once pushed us on – higher-higher-higher. It's where I now take Archie.

I'm almost halfway there when I notice the fuel gauge is nearly empty. Inwardly, I curse. George was supposed to fill my car up last night, he knows I find it difficult. I can't bear the smell of fumes. I was sure he'd gone to do it while I gave Archie his bath and read him a story but I must have been mistaken. He probably got caught up in another long work call. The hours he's putting in at the moment are ridiculous but I'm lucky he's working so hard towards our future, even if we don't always want the same thing.

It's tempting to go home but I'd still have to refuel before picking Archie up from nursery so I indicate left and pull into the forecourt of the BP garage. The instant I step out of the car the smell of petrol invades my nostrils and I have to swallow down bile.

My hand is shaking by the time I replace the pump and go and pay.

The cashier is busy with another customer and as I wait I impulsively pick up a KitKat for Archie and a Twix for George. I don't snack, preferring proper meals. My debit card is already in my hand, ready to tap it on the reader, but I've gone over the contactless limit and so I stuff the card inside the machine. Out of my peripheral vision I notice a white van pull up alongside my car. Flustered, I enter my pin number incorrectly twice before I remember what it is.

A man with spiked black hair steps out of the van. I've never seen him before. He's young. Younger than me, and he looks happy but still, that doesn't mean he's not dangerous, does it? We all wear a mask sometimes, don't we? I'm guilty of it myself. The calm mother, the carefree wife. That's unfair. I'm being hard on myself again. I've had periods of months – years even – when I've almost, if not forgotten what I've been through, come to terms with it. Learned to live with it, I suppose, like the patches of eczema that used to scab my skin when I was stressed. Oddly my skin has been clear since my rituals became all-consuming. My mental health plummeted and my physical health problems disappeared almost overnight.

'You can take your card.' The sharp tone of the cashier's voice tells me this is not the first time he's asked me. I mumble a 'thank you' to him, an apology to the van driver standing behind me, whose eyes I do not meet. I hurry outside.

I'm just passing the van when I hear a thud coming from inside. I hesitate, ears straining. There's nothing to be heard except the steady thrum of traffic coming from the main road but still I cup my hands and peer through the driver's window.

'Oi!'

I jump at the noise and try not to cower as the driver jogs over to me. 'What do you think you're doing?' His manner as spiky as his hair.

'Do you have anyone else in the van?' I ask.

'What's it gotta do wiv you?'

I keep my gaze steady, waiting him out.

'No. Just me.' He jabs his key into the lock but before he can climb inside, we both hear it. The shuffling coming from inside his vehicle.

'I'm DC Ross,' I lie. 'Do you mind if I take a look, sir?' I stride to the back of the van with a confidence I don't feel.

'I've told you there's no—'

'Then you won't mind showing me, will you?'

Tutting, he unlocks the back doors. My heart races as he yanks them open. I make sure I'm not standing too close. There's a delighted yelp as a white Staffie with a dark circle around one eye launches himself at his owner.

It's just a dog.

I back away, feeling his glare on me. Flustered, I get in my car and start the engine, gears crunching as I pull back out onto the road, breathing heavily. I'm edging forward at the T-junction, waiting to turn left when I catch a flash of the profile of the driver who slides past me in a black car, indicating right.

It's him.

The man who nearly broke me.

I'm frozen to my seat, neck rigid, willing my eyes to take a second look.

I catch him again as his car turns into the traffic. I'm not as certain as I was a few seconds ago that it *is* him. The jawline is wrong. A horn blasts behind me and in my rush to move forward I stall my car. I'm trembling as I twist the key to fire the engine to life once more.

It *can't* have been him.

It's impossible.

As I pull forward, I imagine him in his cell. The thick iron bars that contain him.

It's the anniversary that's made me so skittish, I know. Twenty years. It's been almost twenty years.

I'm in a state by the time I pull up outside Marie's flat. Noticing Carly's car is already there doesn't calm me.

Soon we'll all be in one room.

Three sisters.

Nothing good happens when we're all together.

I can just say no.

Above me the grey clouds break apart and rain lashes against my windscreen.

It feels like an omen. A sense of impending doom.

Chapter Three

Carly

Then

It felt like fate that something terrible would happen because she'd behaved like such a bitch. Acid coated the back of Carly's throat. She swallowed her sickness back down. She had to be strong for the sake of the twins. They would be terrified.

She was terrified.

It had all happened so quickly. She could still feel the arm around her throat, another around her waist as she was manhandled into the van, struggling to get free. The catch on the door scratching against her cheek, tearing her skin. The scream that ripped from her throat as she saw the second man following, dragging the girls.

'Run!' Carly had shouted as she kicked out again, but she knew that even if one of the twins could wriggle free, they wouldn't leave the other.

The arms restraining Carly hefted her from her feet, shoving her roughly into the back of the van.

'Help!' Carly's voice growing hoarse.

That was when she saw a glint of silver. A sharp point pressed against her neck. Instantly the bottom fell out of her world, her body slackened. She had to stay alive for her sisters. Carly forced herself to be passive as her hands were wrenched behind her back. She was shaking so violently that the rope being twisted around her wrists chafed against her skin. Tape was smoothed over the lips she had thought an hour ago Dean Malden would be kissing. She was placid as her ankles were bound. A blindfold snatched away her last glimpse of the sun. She was astonished that something like this could happen in broad daylight. She felt a jarring against her arm. Heard the thud of the twins being shoved next to her and listened helplessly to Leah crying and Marie pleading,

'This is a game, isn't it? Please. This isn't real.' Marie's small voice a squeak.

But the real games were being played in the park just metres away, the cheering of a goal drifting through the hedgerow, and Carly knew that whatever *this* was, it was deadly, deadly serious.

Still, she thought someone would have heard them, would swoop in and save them at the last minute. All her storybooks ended well and it had never really occurred to her that sometimes there might not be a happily ever after. That was until the door slammed shut, the engine roared and she crashed onto her side as the van pulled away.

The stench of petrol in such a confined space was overpowering, along with the stink of body odour. At first Carly thought it must be coming from the men until she felt her shirt sticking to her back with sweat and she realized it was emanating from her. The smell of her own fear.

It was hot. Bumpy. She swayed, unable to use her tethered hands to steady herself. She tried to breathe deeply to calm down but each time she inhaled the tape across her lips prevented air from entering her lungs. Her chest burned painfully. Her nostrils flared as she drew in short, sharp bursts of air until she felt dizzy. The knot from the back of her blindfold dug into her skull.

One of the twins was whimpering, the other frighteningly silent and it was the silence that scared Carly the most. The girls had been nothing but noise since they'd been born. Laughing. Crying. Playing. Chattering away in their twin language that no one else understood. Carly planted her heels on the floor, her ankle bones rubbing uncomfortably together, and dragged her bottom, weaving forwards, slow and uneven – a spider missing legs – until her feet reached something that could have been a body. She shuffled herself around, her hands groping until she connected with another hand. A frightened cry and then long fingers gripping hers. Piano-playing fingers. She thought it must be Leah.

Carly moved again, fumbling around until she located Marie. She was still. Too still. Afraid, Carly pressed against her wrist, willing a pulse to jump beneath her fingers. She blinked back tears of gratitude as she located the slow and steady thump. She wouldn't allow herself to cry.

She had taken the twins out of the garden and got them into this.

She *had* to get them out.

Thoughts jostled for attention as Carly tried to process what had happened. Who had taken them and why, but nothing made any sense. Part of her clung desperately to the vague hope that it was a prank. The programme her parents liked to watch where unsuspecting members of the public were fooled – but the blood streaming from a gash in her cheek told her it wasn't a joke. On TV, the tricks were unexpected, funny. Never cruel.

She rubbed her face against the wall of the van, trying to dislodge her blindfold. Each time they drove over a bump her head smashed painfully into the hard metal but still she persisted until at last she felt the material begin to slide.

She could see blurry shapes. She waited for her eyes to adjust.

The space was compact, dark. Only a small amount of light spilled through a grimy opaque window that led to the cab. Two figures sat shadowed in the front. Just two. Carly felt a flicker of hope. Although the twins were small, together they outnumbered the men. They had a fighting chance if only she knew what was planned for them. Where they were going.

She shifted her weight. If she could get close enough to the partition without being spotted she might be able to hear their conversation over the growl of the engine.

Always have a plan was her dad's motto.

She might only be thirteen but they shouldn't underestimate her.

Progress was slow as Carly rocked herself onto her knees. Using her toes for balance she moved her legs apart, waddling forwards, trying not to fall as the wheel dipped into a pothole. The engine grew louder as they gathered speed. They must have left town. A lump rose in Carly's throat as she thought of the distance they must be from their house. Her pink flowery bedroom she was nagging her mum to decorate now that she was a teenager, her canopied bed she had loved at six but now found embarrassing. The twins' mermaid room they insisted on sharing, stupid because their house was big enough for a bedroom each. Their cuddly toys lined up on the bed. Carly's bears were stuffed at the bottom of her wardrobe. Still part of her, but not quite.

Focus.

She forced her left knee forward again as simultaneously the van flew over a bump. She toppled over, her face slamming against the floor. Stunned, she turned to the side, the tape that had covered her mouth hanging off. She spat out blood and a tooth, her nose hot with pain. She thought it might be broken.

She drew her knees to her chest and lay curved like a comma. Not a full stop. Not the end.

Her watch *tick-tick-ticked*.

Ten minutes? An hour? She'd lost all concept of time. She'd lost all concept of herself; a mass of pain and blood and fear, her cells skittering around her body as adrenaline flooded her system.

Fight or flight. She'd learned about it at school.

Determined, she dragged herself up onto her knees once more.

Another lurch. Wheels dipping in potholes. She was back on her side, juddering over rough terrain.

A slowing.

The crunch of the handbrake.

A momentary silence as the engine cut out.

Carly summoned all of her strength and drew her knees in before kicking both feet as hard as she could at the side of the van over and over. Screaming for help until her throat burned raw.

Someone would hear her.

They had to.

She squinted in the brightness as the door yanked open. She was dragged by her hair.

'You're a feisty one,' a voice said but it didn't sound angry, more amused. Her blindfold was retied tightly around her eyes.

Too tightly. 'That's better. Three blind mice, three blind mice,' he sang.

Carly could feel eyes on her. She clamped her lips together hard as he stretched another piece of tape across her mouth. She wouldn't cry.

Her breath left her body as she was slung over a shoulder as though she weighed nothing.

She breathed in. Listened. Committing what she could to memory so later she'd be able to tell the police, her parents, everything she knew, for she had to believe there would be a later.

The smell of soil. A farm? The sound of rustling. Leaves?

Inconsequential details that would never make up for her putting the twins in danger.

It was wholly her fault.

The man began to walk, Carly curved over his shoulder. Again a comma, and that thought gave her strength. Not a full stop.

This wasn't the end.

Chapter Four

Leah

Now

There's a crackle when I jab the intercom with my finger and before I can speak, there's the click of the front door releasing its catch. I hadn't replied to Marie's text but she hasn't asked who is at the door. She doesn't need to – she knew I'd come. The door sticks. I shoulder it open and the letterbox falls at an odd angle, like a slipped smile. I try to stick it back in place but it's missing a screw.

The stairwell always smells of wee. I spiral my way to the third floor. Flat nine. Remembering her doorbell doesn't work, I lift the knocker, which is ginger with rust, and let it fall, thumping my arrival. The vibration causes flecks of black paint to drift to the floor. Instantly, the door is yanked open, Marie's arms wind around my neck, engulfing me in a cloud of the perfume she's always worn, something woody. Nothing like the floral scent our mother used to wear, or still does wear perhaps. I wouldn't know, it's been so long since I've seen her. I return Marie's hug, feeling the sparrow lightness of her jutting bones. She's lost so much weight, it almost feels like I could snap her in two. She steps back and clasps my shoulders while she studies me. The bracelets that glitter on her wrists jangle as she twists me from side to side.

'You look good.'

'So do you. Are you okay?' What I really want to ask is, *are you drinking?* – but I don't. The whites of her eyes are tinged pink but that could be because of the tears we all shed at this time of year. I can't smell any alcohol on her and that's a good sign. There was a time we wouldn't have to ask each other how we are. She used to know exactly what I was thinking. She felt what I felt, but over the years she has become a stranger to me, almost. What we went through brought us all together and then pushed us apart.

'Carly's here.' She gestures me inside and as I squeeze past her I realize she hasn't answered my question. Is she okay? Are any of us?

I make my way into the tiny kitchen that smells slightly rotten, as though the bin needs emptying.

Carly's leaning against the old-fashioned gas cooker, fingers flying over the keypad of her phone. As soon as she sees me she tosses her mobile onto the worktop and pulls me close to her and for a few seconds I lose myself in her embrace as though I hadn't last seen her a couple of days ago. Carly is the one I'm closer to now. She's the one who stayed while Marie travelled the country, choosing draughty theatres over a proper home. Chameleoning herself into different characters, all of them as beautiful and as damaged as her. There are no happy ever afters in the dark productions she takes part in.

I shuck off my coat and unwind my scarf, piling them on top of Carly's denim jacket.

'I'll make some tea.' Marie fills the kettle as though this is just another social visit. My eyes meet Carly's and she raises her eyebrows.

'I've brought my own cup.' I pull a mug wrapped in plastic from my bag and pass it to her. I'm poised to defend myself but she doesn't ask what's triggered my contamination OCD this time (although it's probably obvious), or how long it's been going on, and I'm glad. I'm not here to be judged.

A phone rings, the sound coming from the top of the fridge.

'Do you want me to get it?' I'm nearest.

'No!' Marie reaches for her phone and switches it off.

'You didn't have to do that. It might have been a job offer?'

'It wasn't. There's some biscuits somewhere, Leah. If you can find them.'

I rummage around on the worktops, looking for snacks I will not eat.

Marie's flat is as chaotic and cluttered as her life. Washing-up piled in the sink. Every surface messy. Tubes of half-used make-up litter the small table in the kitchen where she eats her meals for one, a box of L'Oréal hair dye pokes out of the overflowing bin; it's the complete opposite of my minimalism. Once my twin and I shared everything but now we don't even look the same, I think, taking in her newly bleached hair, cropped close to her head. I still keep mine long. Although I'm only twenty-eight, threads of grey are weaving into my natural red but I'm determined not to start colouring it. Every few minutes Marie runs her hand over the back of her neck as though reassuring herself that her pigtails are gone. That no one can grab them again. It's as though she wants to be somebody else – somebody different – and I understand that, I've felt it too. But we can't run away from ourselves, can we? The things we've done. Years of therapy have taught me that.

'Is Archie okay?' Carly's face shines as she mentions her nephew. It's such a shame she's never allowed anyone to get close to her. She's never had a family of her own. *It's too much responsibility*, she had said once when I'd asked her if she wanted children.

It took her a long time for her to be able to look after Archie. 'I can't,' she had said when we had first discussed the possibility of me going back to work. I had taken her hands in mine.

'I trust you.'

She had shaken her head. 'You shouldn't.'

'Well, I do. George and I both do and… Carly, I couldn't trust anyone else.' There was no way I could leave Archie with a stranger.

'What if…' She had squeezed her eyes tightly closed.

'We can't live our lives by what-ifs.'

She had looked at me then with such a disbelieving expression on her face.

'Okay,' I had conceded. 'I see the irony in that but I am trying. Try *with* me. You adore Archie.' From the second she had first held him at the hospital and he had wrapped his tiny fingers around her thumb she was lost to emotions she just couldn't fight.

'It's *because* I love him I can't do it.'

'It's *because* you love him that you can.'

Now, Carly picks Archie up when I'm working at the insurance firm in town, processing policies for the fears that keep people awake at night – theft, death, illness, but I know these things aren't the worst that can happen. Not by a long way.

'Archie's fine,' I say over the sound of the kettle boiling. 'I was mortified earlier though because all the other kids were already sitting in a circle when we got there. *Sorry we're late*, he shouted. *Mummy couldn't get in the bloody bathroom because Daddy was doing a big poo*. That child.' I shake my head as though I'm despairing but we all know I'm not. Archie is the light of my life. 'You must come and see him, Marie.' I try not to sound critical that we see her so infrequently.

'Yes. Sorry, I've been busy.'

'Doing what?' Carly asks. Marie was sacked from her last role for turning up drunk five minutes before she was supposed to go on stage. That was six months ago and she hasn't worked since. She said it was the kick she needed to give up drinking and focus on the future.

'This and that,' she says vaguely. Her mouth gapes a yawn. There are dark shadows under her eyes. She's not sleeping well either.

'Something keeping you up at night. Or someone?' Carly asks.

Marie doesn't answer but her neck flushes red. She's keeping something from us.

'Marie, are you seeing someone?'

She doesn't deny it, instead she busies herself splashing milk into mugs and fishing out teabags with a spoon. I don't repeat my question. If Marie doesn't want to tell us something, she won't. She leads us through to the lounge, sweeping piles of magazines from the sofa onto the threadbare carpet. A stick of incense on a stand on the windowsill billows smoke. The scent is cloying. Momentarily it crosses my mind that she might be masking the smell of booze. I steal a glance around the room, searching for empty bottles stuffed into corners, lipstick-stained tumblers, but there's nothing. My eyes meet Carly's and she shrugs. I know she's thinking the same as me. I set the chipped plate stacked with Tesco basic digestives on the table.

'So—' Marie beams a smile that doesn't reach the rest of her face. Her lipstick has stained a patch of her nicotine-yellow teeth crimson.

'I can't do it this year,' Carly cuts in. 'I just can't.'

The atmosphere, already heavy, thickens. I take a sip of my tea, trying to recall whether Marie had rested the teaspoon on the draining board before she fished out my teabag.

'I know it's difficult this year—' Marie's knee jiggles. She tugs her jumper down over her hands.

'It's difficult every bloody year.' Carly pushes her hair away from her face. Her sleeve rides up, displaying the comma she has tattooed on her wrist.

She's right.

Each year around the anniversary of our abduction Marie's always desperate to rake it over. Unwilling to let the dying embers of our trauma crumble to ashes.

It wasn't as bad as we thought, was it?

It's made us into the people we are today.

It's as though she wants to make it into something else, something different.

She can't.

I don't know why, perhaps it's the only way she can handle it. We all cope the best we can, Carly not allowing herself to love anyone new, me with my routines.

'But…' Marie continues as though Carly hadn't spoken. 'It's twenty years and I've been approached by a journalist—'

'We've all been approached by journalists these past few months.' That was a given; THE SINCLAIR SISTERS – WHERE

ARE THEY NOW? I don't like the direction the conversation is going in.

'She wants us to go on TV to mark twenty years. It'd be live, of course, that only gives us a few days to prep—'

'Absolutely not,' Carly says firmly.

'I know you don't enjoy being in the spotlight, but I'll take the lead. You don't have to say much as long as you're there,' Marie says matter-of-factly. This would be her starring role, us her supporting cast. 'Leah?'

'There's nothing worse I can think of than going through it all again.'

I can just say no.

'You said yes last time,' Marie says.

I shift uncomfortably in my seat. We were offered a book deal around the tenth anniversary. Carly and I weren't interested but Marie had begged, said the exposure might kick-start her career and we so wanted her to succeed. My therapist at the time thought it might do us good to share our story. Take away the stigma and the shame that we feel; that *I* feel, at least. She thought if we spoke about it exclusively to one source it would stop the vultures picking over the rest of our lives. We could finally move on. The publisher introduced us to a ghost writer. All we had to do was meet him a few times while he recorded our stories on a dictaphone and that was it. Six figures each. We weren't expected to write a single word ourselves.

'The book deal was years ago,' I say to Marie. 'Things are different now. I've Archie to think about.'

Archie starts primary school next September and I don't want to be playground gossip any more than I already will be. The headteacher is the same one Marie and I had when we were abducted. Some of the other parents will be kids I shared classrooms with, but the advantages of having him go to the same school that I went to is knowing the layout, the routines. If I needed to get to Archie quickly, I could.

'I don't want to stir up bad feeling,' Carly says. 'I don't want the community to think we're blaming them for not being vigilant.'

'I agree with Carly.' The locals look after their own. I don't like the thought of them watching me on TV. I won't make my life a media circus again. I've no reason to. 'Besides, going over what happened again—'

'It's not just that,' Marie pushes on. 'The network wants to know what long-term effects it's had on us.'

'Nothing. We're fine. Now.' Carly lightly runs her finger over her tattoo as her voice cracks with emotion. I sit there, palms damp in my gloves.

'I'm not fine,' Marie says quietly. 'My career is… well, I'm resting at the moment and honestly, I could do with the cash. Couldn't you?'

It's true my bank account could do with a boost. I hadn't touched a penny of our advance until I met George. I paid for our house, although he insisted the deeds were in my name. He hadn't wanted anyone to think he was after me for my money. I remortgaged the first time to start him up in his own architectural firm and then again because his income isn't what he'd hoped for – no one is building with the economy in the state it's in.

'I make a living,' Carly says. With the publishing advance she could have afforded a small house in our area but she bought a flat instead. It doesn't have a garden. With the remaining cash she trawled the charity shops looking for bargains that she later sold on eBay. This is how she gets by, that and the small wage I pay her for childminding.

'Well, good for you. I ploughed everything into funding that tour of the supernatural play.' Marie had had high hopes but nobody had understood the plot. 'The TV people have offered us a ridiculous amount of money if we can tell them something that's not in the book.'

'We can't tell them anything they don't already know.'

'Yes, we can.' Marie swallows hard. 'We can tell them the truth.'

Chapter Five

Carly

Then

Tell me who you are, Carly screamed inside her head, but the man carrying her over his shoulder couldn't hear her. He strode on, strong and purposeful. She tried to identify her environment from the sound his footsteps were making.

Crunching.

Snapping.

Carly was certain they were walking across dried grass. Twigs. The woods? She could hear the whisper of leaves. The creaking of branches. But not enough for a forest. They were somewhere overgrown, at the very least. The breeze was welcome against her sticky skin but she wished she didn't have tape around her mouth so she could breathe a little deeper. She couldn't hear the second man following them and her dread at being separated from the twins, combined with the bumping sensation – each tiny movement causing her head, hanging upside down, to knock against the man's back – sloshed nausea around her stomach. Carly swallowed hard. She hoped she wouldn't be sick, she had no way of spitting it out. Fear that she might choke became her overriding emotion. Her skin once again clammy as her heart raced so faced the world spun. If the man abruptly put her down, she would fall.

Calm.

Carly thought of Leah and Marie. She had to keep her wits about her. The first opportunity she got, she needed to be able to run. To locate a house, flag down a car, find an adult who would help them. It was the thought of a grown-up taking charge that made Carly's eyes burn with tears. She was only a child. Thirteen. She didn't know what she could do. How she could possibly overpower a grown man, but she must. Right now, she was all the twins had.

She inhaled slower. Deeper. The smell of nicotine infused the man's coat – and something else? Something earthy.

They still must be in bright sunlight because behind Carly's blindfold her eyes flooded with red – the colour of staring at the sun too long.

The colour of blood.

The man slowed. Stopped. The hand holding Carly's calves withdrew but she could still feel the weight of his fingers and it took her a second to realize she could move her legs. She bent her knees, drawing her heels back up to her bottom before driving her feet forward, her toes slamming into his chest. She braced herself to fall. Prepared to spring to her feet, stumble forward. To run whether or not she could see where she was going.

The man barely moved as she repeatedly kicked him.

He didn't scream with pain, but inside Carly there were enough screams for the both of them fighting to be released.

A jangle.

A click.

A creak.

The hand returned to her calves and they were moving forwards again but this time it felt different. Instead of a crunch there was a clump-clump-clump. The sound of boots on a hard surface. The breeze kissing her skin wafted away.

They were inside. It smelled old. Musty. Unused and unloved.

Carly's fear increased. She couldn't pinpoint exactly what she was afraid of but she knew that without the possibility of someone stumbling across them – the potential of someone helping – the man could do whatever he liked.

The air inside felt thick and heavy. Somehow she knew they were alone in this building.

However much noise she made, there was no one to hear her.

Again, the man hesitated. Terror gripped Carly tightly as she imagined the next step forward would take them on a descent into a cellar. She'd had an unnatural dread of underground spaces since she'd watched *Psycho* with her dad last year, pretending to agree as she laughed along with him at how dated it was.

But Carly's heart had hammered against her chest. She knew fear was amplified in the grey spaces between the black and the white.

The man's fingers clutched at the back of Carly's jumper. She was pulled away from his shoulder, which suddenly, inexplicably, now felt warm and safe and somewhere she wanted to stay. Her legs dangled helplessly until she was set down upon a soft surface. Not a staircase.

A mattress?

Vomit rose once more.

She swallowed, once, twice, unable to dislodge the painful

lump in her throat, instead clenching her jaw so tightly that her temples began to pulse.

Don't touch me-don't touch me-don't touch me.

She had seen the news. She knew what sometimes happened to girls.

Her body began to shake and she told herself it was just that. A body. A shell. Not the essence of her real self, which was buried somewhere unreachable. If someone had to be hurt it was better to be her rather than Leah or Marie. They were only eight. Babies really. Still at primary. She was older. She could cope.

Although she knew she couldn't. Already something inside of her was cracking and breaking apart.

Don't touch me.

He didn't.

It took a beat for Carly to distinguish his retreating footsteps from the thump of her heart.

She lay rigid, scarcely breathing, ears straining.

Nothing.

There hadn't been a sound of the door closing and yet Carly sensed that he was gone.

She threw her weight onto her side. The mattress stank of urine but she rubbed her cheek against it until she found the corner. Again and again – a cat batting its head, desperate for affection – Carly chafed her face against the hard seam until her skin was sore. With painstaking slowness, her blindfold began to slip.

Eventually the scrap of material had fallen from her eyes, across her nose. Carly's nostrils were now covered, her mouth still taped shut. She couldn't breathe. She shook her head in desperation until the blindfold fell another half an inch.

She could see.

Her eyes scanned the concrete floor coated with dust and rubble, the walls sheathed with graffiti. Something creaked behind her. She yanked her head around so fast her neck cricked, half-expecting to see Norman Bates' mum in her rocking chair, but it was a tree outside the barred window dipping against the wind. The room wasn't empty but Carly scarcely noticed her surroundings. Piles of rubbish, a cardboard box. She didn't check to see if there was anything there she could use to escape with.

She didn't have to.

The door was wide open.

She shuffled her body much the way she had in the back of the van – a snake shedding its skin – until she reached the wall. Carly drew herself onto her knees, then onto the balls of her feet, until she was standing. Her legs felt like the lemon jelly the twins loved so much. It was the thought of her family gathered around the table, eating dessert, that gave her strength. She almost believed she could smell citrus rather than the stench of damp and neglect. Carly began to jump – a sack race without a sack. Steadily, determinedly, momentarily pausing after each movement to regain her balance. She fell into a rhythm.

Jump.

Thud.

Jump.

Thud.

Into a corridor with multiple rooms to her left and right, doors hanging woefully from rusted hinges. At the bottom, a staircase with a makeshift ramp propped against the stairs. A battered skateboard on its side, missing a wheel. Cool air hit the back of her neck. Carly turned. The front door was swinging open.

Open!

Frantically she made her way towards it, as fast as she could.

Perspiration slicked her skin. She thought she could perhaps wriggle her wrists free of her binds if she tried but not until she was outside.

Not far now.

Her muscles trembled with effort. She moved more slowly, not covering the same distance as she had moments before.

Come on, Carly.

The twins cheering her name during sports day. The finishing ribbon in sight.

Jump.

It was so hard to breathe. She longed to tear off the tape, open her mouth wide and draw in air. Soon. Soon she would be free. At home. Snuggled on the sofa with Bruno and Leah and Marie.

Jump.

Dried grasses crunched beneath her feet as she landed. She'd made it.

She was outside, dizzy with effort. Dizzy with relief.

She heard two voices. Her muzzy head couldn't make out what direction they were coming from.

Her head spun to the left; another building, windows smashed, spray paint colouring the brick. On its flat roof, a traffic cone. To the right; a clutch of bushes.

Which way should she go?

She needed to move.

Now.

Chapter Six

Leah

Now

'What do you mean *tell the truth*?' Shock jolts through my body. 'You mean about me?' I can't believe Marie would betray me. Her eyes, the same green as mine, look at everything but me.

'You've got to be fucking kidding me.' The booming anger in Carly's voice fills the room. 'Telling everyone that Leah left the gate open won't help anyone.'

'I did leave it open, though.' By some unspoken agreement afterwards we'd all claimed we couldn't remember who closed the gate, that it must have blown open.

'So? It doesn't matter—' Carly says.

'But it does.' It's something I've never let go of. 'If I hadn't…'

'If. If. *If*. We've all got a million ifs and not one of them makes any difference.' Carly drops her head into her hands.

'I didn't mean tell the truth about the gate,' Marie says but it doesn't comfort me. The gate is the tip of the iceberg really in all the things I've done wrong. Got wrong. Under the surface lurk far darker secrets. As reluctant as I am to be on TV, it occurs to me that if we did share our side it might stop other journalists digging into the past, trying to create their own story. If anyone uncovers what I did a few years ago I could be prosecuted. Lose Archie. Panic is a heavy weight on my chest; I tap my fingers three times against my knee and try to breathe through it.

'Leah?' Carly slides across the sofa and drapes an arm across my shoulder. 'You're okay. You're safe.'

'I didn't mean—' Marie crouches before me and rests her hands on my knees.

'What *did* you mean? The truth?' I am desperate to know. If she didn't mean me, then what?

'We're not doing it, Marie.' Carly squeezes my shoulders. 'I don't want to and Leah… Well, just look at her,' she says but not unkindly. Once more, I am the youngest, the one they need to protect. If only they knew what I was really capable of. Again, my breath catches in my throat. Sweat trickles off my top lip, coating my mouth with salt.

'I'm sorry, Leah.' Marie rests her head on my lap. I begin to stroke her hair, as I would Archie's. The feeling calms me.

The silence settles around us, we are all lost in our individual thoughts. Twenty years is a huge milestone and the lead-up to the anniversary has been worse than usual. I've changed my mobile number countless times but journalists still call at all hours. Notes are pushed through the letterbox because I refuse to answer the door when I'm not expecting anyone. Business cards – *Call me* scrawled on the back – are left under my windscreen wipers. It's awful, I know, and I'm ashamed to admit it, even to myself, but I long for something to happen that will deflect the attention away from us until next week slides by. A collapse of the government, a celebrity death. I know it's horrible but still, it's been a slow news month and the papers have pages to fill. How deep will they dig?

'What *did* you mean, Marie?' I ask again.

'I don't know really. Just a different angle.' She pushes herself to standing and stamps her feet. 'Pins and needles. Anyway, sorry I've upset you, Leah. Both of you. I just wanted—'

'The cash?' Carly says wryly.

'It wasn't only about money. I spoke to our publisher recently and book sales have picked up this year, interest is high again. Our royalty statements should be pretty healthy this time. I just wanted… closure, I suppose. Forgiveness.'

'What do you need forgiving for?'

She shrugs. I study the emotions that pass over her face, she's always been so hard to read.

'Marie?'

She begins to cry. 'It's always been my fault.' She furiously swipes her eyes with her sleeve.

'It hasn't!' I stand to face her. 'Look at me.' I rest my fingertips on her cheeks. The dampness of her tears seeps through my cotton gloves. I had never heard her openly blame herself. I knew she carried it still – that was apparent from the whisky on her breath, the shiny red tinge to her skin – but I thought that was trauma. Shock. Not guilt.

'It was down to me.' She takes a long, juddering breath.

'I can't bear it if you blame yourself.' I can feel my own tears building. 'I hate that this whole thing has driven us apart. I need you, Marie.' I rest my forehead against hers. 'Sometimes I feel I've lost you,' I whisper.

'You'll never lose me,' she says. 'But it *was* me that threw Bruno's ball over the fence. If it wasn't for that—'

'Enough. This is precisely why we shouldn't do the interview,'

Carly says. 'We each think we're at fault and maybe it's time to let it go. *All* of it.'

Carly's right. We all blame ourselves. Twenty years on and we all *still* blame ourselves. Marie for throwing the ball over the fence, me for not shutting the gate properly and Carly for taking us with her to look for Bruno. We've heard a million times that it wasn't our fault. Our parents repeated it endlessly when we first came home, as did the police officers, the therapists we've tried and discarded over the years – but hearing something is different to feeling it. Guilt is corrosive. It eats away from the inside out. We paint on smiles and it looks like we're coping but we're not, not really. I don't think we ever will. Two years, twenty years, it still feels the same. I know we weren't the first children to be snatched and we won't be the last, but the *why* – I can never get my head around the why. How different our lives would have been if we had never been taken. But I can't allow myself to think that way. If I had a different life I might not have George and Archie.

'It *is* time to let go. Twenty years of suffering is twenty years too much. That's why I thought opening up might help. It wasn't all about the money,' Marie says. 'Although God knows, I could do with it.' She gestures around her tiny flat. 'But it's been a lot to carry, hasn't it? Sometimes I feel I'll snap under the weight of it all. I don't know how you both cope, living in the same town full-time. At least I get to leave, go on tour.'

'But you always come back,' I say quietly.

'I come back for you two,' Marie says. 'And it's hard. Every bloody time I drive past *that* place. How can you bear it?'

'I think it's easier, staying. Everyone knows us and what we've been through but because of that everyone protects us – or tries to, at least.'

There was a shift in the town when we had finally been found. The streets, once filled with kids kicking footballs, racing around on bikes, were empty. In supermarkets mothers would tightly hold on to their children's hands. Cars jammed up the residential roads around the primary school. Nobody let kids walk anywhere. There was a sharp decrease in independence for the kids. A sharp increase in fear for the parents. And guilt. Neighbourhood Watch groups were formed and Mum had said they were full of the 'if only we'd all been more vigilant' and the 'there but for the grace of God go I' brigade.

It's all changed now of course, but nobody has really forgotten and it's because the community felt they had let us down that they close ranks when reporters ask for snippets of 'What are the Sinclair Sisters really like?' gossip. If we moved away people would still find out who we were and we wouldn't feel as… safe, I suppose, although I don't think any of us have ever felt completely safe since before we were snatched. It wasn't only our physical selves that were taken away but our innocence and our inherent naive faith that people were good and adults could be trusted.

'At least here I know that no one will ask me out,' Carly says.

'I wish you'd meet someone,' I reply. Carly, more than anybody, deserves to be happy.

'I can get you not wanting kids,' Marie says, 'But… you must get lonely.'

'Not really. I've got you two. And Archie and that's enough for me. Imagine falling for someone and they turned out to be… bad. You never know who to trust, do you?'

I know what she means. Monsters walk among us and sometimes they look like you.

Sometimes they look like me.

The conversation stutters again. Carly wipes away tears that are streaking her cheeks. I want to tell her that letting George into my life was the best thing that ever happened to me. That she too can learn to allow someone in – but I think of the secrets I carry inside and outside of my marriage and I know that would make me a hypocrite. Who am I to give life advice when I am making such a mess of mine?

'You should speak to someone, you both should.' I'd tried to get them to see my last therapist. Francesca. I had connected with her in a way I hadn't with those who had come before her. She seemed to genuinely care, spending more time with me than she was obliged to, making sure she understood our family's dynamics. She even helped explain to George what was happening mentally to me a few years ago and because of this he tried his best to support me through it. Love me through it. Of course I didn't tell her everything, I've never told anyone *everything*. I haven't seen her for months but I know what she would advise us to do right now. 'Francesca says—'

'No offence, Leah,' Carly says. 'But we're indoors and you're wearing gloves. I love you but you're the least sorted of us all.'

'I don't want to hurt you, either of you,' Marie says. 'I thought it might help. Really. Not just sharing what happened but talking about how we've felt, I suppose, since.'

'We can do that without an audience,' I say.

'I guess,' Marie says. 'It's just that with an interviewer present I thought we'd all be more... in control of our feelings, I suppose.'

'Feelings. Everyone's obsessed with feelings,' Carly says. 'I was coming out of Tesco's last week when a journalist showed me a picture of the grave and asked me how I felt about it now. I told them I felt nothing. Nothing. I wish now I'd told them I felt glad.'

I tell Carly that I was shown the same photo too. The cemetery where one of our abductors was laid to rest. His plot a tangle of weeds. Unkept and unloved. No flowers, no sense that anyone ever visits. They probably don't. I don't say that, unlike her, I felt something when I saw it. In fact, I felt everything: sadness, remorse, anger, regret and relief. I had felt relief that he, at least, couldn't hurt anyone again. But he hadn't acted alone.

Our rare openness of a few moments ago vanishes. The air chills and I know we are all thinking the same thing.

'He's due out of prison again next year.' Carly doesn't speak his name. None of us do. I've tried but the letters twist and tangle and form a ball in my throat.

Him.

The air chills.

'Let's talk about something else.' Carly lifts her mug and gulps coffee that must be cold. 'Tell us how Archie got on with his first swimming lesson, Leah.'

'Oh God.' My cheeks colour thinking about it. 'The instructor sat the kids down before they even got wet and asked them the things people worry about when they go swimming so he could set their minds at rest. One little girl said she worries she'll swallow some water. Another that the pool would be too deep and she wouldn't be able to touch the bottom. Archie said… no. Archie *shouted*, "My mummy worries about wearing a costume because her bum is wobbly and her legs look like orange peel." Honestly…' I shove Carly. 'Shut up. It wasn't funny. Everyone stared at me.'

'Ooh, did the instructor want to see your bum as proof? Was he hot?' Marie waggles her eyebrows.

'I thought you had a new man, Marie,' Carly teases her.

'It's early days. It's complicated.'

'Actually, the instructor wasn't bad,' I say.

'Don't let George hear that!' Carly laughs. 'You'll ruin your perfect marriage.'

'Nothing's perfect,' Marie says and the atmosphere that felt lighter moments before feels heavy once again.

Nothing *is* perfect. My marriage the least of all.

I start when I check the time on my phone. It's almost time to collect Archie. An email alert tells me my parcel has been delivered. I jump to my feet.

'I have to go, George will be...' *home to discover my secrets.* I finish my sentence in my head. Really, he's the last person I want to see after last night but I can hardly avoid him.

'George will be what?' asks Marie.

'I just have to go, that's all.' My tone is sharper than intended, but then fear has the ability to harden; a soft stomach filled with knots, a tightening of the chest, muscles tense and solid.

The set of a jaw.

A clenching of the fist.

Chapter Seven

Carly

Then

Carly's fist would often dangle a toy above Bruno the boxer's head, until he'd hurl himself at her in a bid to reach it, his body slamming into hers, surprisingly heavy and solid. That's the way her body felt now as she gathered her energy to jump again.

Heavy.

Solid.

As though her blood had been removed and replaced with stone. She was so tired it was almost impossible to move but she had made it outside. She *had* to keep going.

She was almost at the corner of the building. Strands of her blonde hair worked free from her scrunchie, trailed in front of her eyes. With the tape covering her mouth, she couldn't huff it away. She wished again her hands were free.

Voices.

Louder now.

Carly took two quick jumps and stopped, shielded by the side of the building. She peeked back around the corner. The men were striding towards the front door, each carrying a twin over their shoulders as though they were weightless. As though they were nothing. The gold crosses the girls wore around their necks inverted like a sign of the devil as they dangled upside down. Not that her family were religious but the twins had discovered early Madonna.

'I don't know why you're so fascinated with her,' Carly had said just weeks ago as her sisters had chewed gum and loaded their wrists with bangles. 'She's been around forever.'

'So had Marilyn Monroe when you plastered your wall with her posters,' her stepdad had kindly pointed out. That was true so, instead of laughing at the twins, Carly helped them draw thick black lines under their eyes and crimp their hair when they played dress-up.

Now Leah's hands – which had donned black lace gloves – were clenched into tight balls as she struggled to be free.

Marie was listless. Hanging limp.

Carly faltered. Her head urging her to move, her body crying out for a rest, and her heart? Her heart wanted to bound back towards the twins and reassure them it would be okay, but that was a lie.

Even then she knew that none of them would ever be the same again.

Think.

The men had disappeared in the building. In seconds they would realize she was gone. They'd know she hadn't got far with her wrists and hands still tied. They'd expect her still to be blindfolded.

Carly had to move, but where should she go?

Her eyes scanned the area. There was a tank decorated with purple, pink and yellow spray-painted flowers, its gun pointing to the ground as though it was hanging its head in shame. Giving up hope. A water tower rose towards the sky. To her right was a larger building, ivy desperately clinging on to the crumbling stone columns that flanked its entrance. A sign that once hung straight and proud – NORCROFT ARMY CAMP – dangled vertically from a single rusted chain. She knew where she was now. An abandoned military training ground a few miles from town. She remembered Mr Webster, her teacher, projecting photos from his laptop onto the whiteboard of how the base used to look before it crumbled to dust while waiting for planning permission for a housing estate that never seemed to come.

Once during a sleepover at Nicola Morgan's house her brother had shone a torch under his chin and told the terrified girls how he'd broken in one evening with his friends. He said they had seen with their own eyes the wailing, bloodied officers – soldiers missing limbs – who haunted the camp. It wasn't until Leanne Patterson started crying that he backtracked and admitted that once you'd made it past the high, barbed-wire fences there was actually nothing worth coming back for.

No reason for anyone to come.

Carly drank in the sight of the small concrete building opposite, noting that the windowless and doorless structure looked like a face with empty eye sockets and a mouth eternally screaming. She saw how a beam of sunlight bouncing off the steel gate in the distance glowed fiery orange. She heard two birds chirping a conversation only they could understand, like Leah and Marie's twin language.

Inconsequential details.

It wasn't until Carly felt a hand on her shoulder, warm breath on her neck, that she realized she had lingered too long.

She hadn't escaped.

She wondered if subconsciously she hadn't wanted to.

The man lifted Carly from her feet, gently this time, none of the frenzied grabbing and pulling there had been before and she let him carry her back to her sisters, watching the rise and fall of his Dr. Martens boots as he walked.

This time, after placing her on the stained double mattress, he knelt next to her on the filthy floor and began to unpick the knots that bound her wrists.

'What the fuck?' the second man growled. Through the slit in his balaclava Carly could see the hairs of a thick black moustache tickling his pale pink lips.

The first man, Doc – as Carly called him in her head after his Dr. Martens boots – didn't reply but continued working at the rope until it slackened. Her fingers tingled as she flexed them. Her eyes met Doc's through the slits in his balaclava and for a split second she felt an unspoken message pass between them but she couldn't quite decipher it. Nevertheless, some sixth sense told her not to try and fight him. She didn't want to risk being separated from the twins again. Instead she knew that she should wait. That he wouldn't hurt her.

The second man, though? Moustache. She wasn't so sure.

Doc stood and brushed grey dust from his knees and this small act gave her hope. If he cared about dirt he wouldn't leave them here in this grimy room. The sun barely filtered through the thick bars at the window. Sour air clogged her nostrils, making her mouth taste of wee. But he did leave, trailed by Moustache. As Moustache strode towards the door he scratched the back of his neck. His balaclava rose and Carly saw the tattoo of an eye. She shuddered. Even when he wasn't facing her, he was still watching her.

She was left here for the second time that day but this time the door slammed shut although the men were still there, outside the room. Carly could hear their voices, one loud and angry, the other speaking more slowly and calmly.

Terrified, her eyes scanned the room. There were no other exits. No other way out.

They *had* to get out.

Carly tore off the tape that covered her mouth and before tackling the binding around her own ankles she reached across to her sisters.

'I'm going to untie you both,' she whispered, eyes darting fearfully to the door. On the back of the wood someone had sprayed a clown's face, a shock of orange hair and a bright red nose, his mouth stretched into a macabre grin. She gently eased the tape from Marie's mouth, millimetre by millimetre, not wanting to pull at her skin.

'Now for your blindfold. Leah, I'll get to you in a minute. Marie, are you okay? Say something,' she whispered but Marie's lips remained clamped together, too scared to make a noise.

Once she had uncovered Marie's eyes, Carly could see they were glazed with shock. 'It's okay. We'll be home soon.' Carly started on the ropes tying Marie's hands but her shaking fingers couldn't unpick them.

'Shit.' She leaned forward and tried to work the knots free with her mouth. The rope was bitter and strands of thread stuck to her tongue. She was only making it worse. Frustrated, she began to try and rip the rope apart, grunting with the effort, until finally it began to give.

'Quick. Pull your hands free.'

Marie shook her head fearfully.

'Marie. Quick.' Carly was as careful as she could be but had to yank the rope over Marie's hands to free her, wincing as she saw the red welts left in its wake. Carly turned her attention to Leah. 'Shh.' Carly removed the tape covering her mouth. 'It's okay. I promise.'

Soon they were all untied.

Free, but not.

There was one last angry shout from the corridor outside and then the sound of bolts sliding closed.

One.

Two.

Three.

Three bolts for three sisters.

It was then the screaming started.

Chapter Eight

Leah

Now

While I'm fetching my coat from Marie's kitchen I collect Carly's denim jacket. I know she won't stay here without me. There are often awkward silences when we're all together nowadays and those silences can be deafening.

'Sorry to rush off,' I say to Marie. 'And sorry about the TV thing. If you need some money?'

It's a genuine offer although I've no idea what I'll do if she takes me up on it. Each month end we're practically stuffing our hands down the back of the sofa, fishing out a few meagre coins along with Archie's Lego bricks and sweet wrappers, so we can afford milk. George's architectural practice is floundering. My part-time job doesn't pay much, it's more for my mental health, to get me out of the house. It gives me the semblance of being able to function normally among other adults. I'm reluctant to increase my hours because I don't want somebody else picking Archie up from nursery every day, even if it is Carly. I think being a mother is the most important job of all but I do feel I should be doing more to help financially. When Archie starts school next year I'll be able to work nine to three every day, which will take the pressure off George.

'Thanks but I'll be okay. The theatres will be scheduling their next quarter shows after Christmas and I'm sure something will turn up. I won't starve.'

'In the meantime, get that new man of yours to take you out to dinner.' Carly gives a hollow laugh. She doesn't offer to lend Marie any money. One too many times in the past we've pushed notes into her hand, knowing that she'll drink them. Knowing that we'll never get them back.

'Carly, do you want to stay and have a bite to eat?' Marie puts a hand on Carly's arm. Her bracelets jangle. She seems jittery at the thought of being on her own. 'I've no plans tonight. I haven't got much in but...'

'I've got to go, sorry.' Carly pulls a face, quickly hugs Marie and steps outside. I am left with my twin. Our relationship is strained but it's still a wrench to leave her. It always is. 'I've forgotten my mug,' I say.

'I'll go and fetch—'

'Don't. You can give it back to me another time. Let's not leave it too long. Come and see Archie?'

'I'd love to. It would be good to hear how he's getting on rehearsing for his first nativity. I could perhaps give him some tips.'

I kick myself for not mentioning Archie's starring role in his nursery's production. Carly must have mentioned it before I arrived. It was something he had in common with his aunt, it might have made the conversation flow a little more easily. 'He'd like that. George would love to see you too.'

'I don't... I...' Marie's face reddens. 'Perhaps we could take Archie to the park, you and me?'

'Okay but...' I hesitate, unsure whether to mention Marie's

last meeting with George; she had turned up on our doorstep late at night – steaming drunk and rambling about all men being bastards – but I have to. It's obviously still playing on her mind. 'It's all forgotten, you know.' The last thing I want to do is embarrass her, so I wrap her tightly in a hug. Her brittle blonde hair is rough against my cheek. 'I love you,' I whisper into it.

'I love you too,' she says. 'I will see you soon. I promise.' She offers her pinkie. 'Cross my heart.'

I find myself smiling, linking my little finger through hers, seeing through the layers of her dark make-up down to the freckles dotting pale skin. Skinny jeans may have long replaced the white knee-length socks that had always bunched around her ankles but I see the child that still exists inside. I let my inner eight-year-old come out and play and we chant:

'A pinkie promise can't be broke
Or you'll disappear in a puff of smoke
This is my vow to you,
I'll keep my promise through and through.'

Carly rolls her eyes at us – 'You two are so lame' – falling back into her too-cool-for-school role. For the first time in a long time we feel united, slipping seamlessly back into our identities. I feel that as I leave Marie it won't be for long. I turn to wave as I reach my car and she mouths she'll see me soon.

And I believe that she means it.

Archie launches himself at me – you'd think it's been four weeks instead of four hours since I last saw him – but I don't mind. I feel much the same. Each time I say goodbye to someone my stomach gives a series of tiny flips like the jumping beans Marie and I used to hold in the palms of our hands. It doesn't settle until I see them again. Rationally I know that Archie is safe at nursery. That I always collect him at one o'clock unless I'm working and then Carly is always there, but that doesn't stop me worrying.

I zip up his coat, covering the Weetabix crusted to his Thomas the Tank Engine jumper that my wandering mind had missed that morning.

'Let's get you home, mister.'

'Is Daddy there? He said he'd have lunch with me today.'

'I know! He should be.' The fact that George is popping home to eat with Archie means he'll likely be working late tonight. I stretch my face into a smile as I strap Archie in the car, trying not to worry about what might be waiting for me if George is home.

As I drive, Archie chatters incessantly, his words falling out in a rush. 'Mum, a policeman came to visit today.'

'Why?' I ask sharply, already fearing the worst as I grip the steering wheel. A child has gone missing. There's been a stranger hanging round the nursery gates. That happened last term and I kept Archie home for a week. George says I have to loosen my hold on him as he gets older but I don't think there's anything wrong in trying to protect him. An image flashes into my mind of my mum at the police station when we were finally reunited. 'I'll never stop blaming myself.' She had wiped tears from her cheeks. It's a big responsibility having a child, isn't it? As joyous as it is watching them grow, it's also equally terrifying.

'The policeman taught us about being safe when we cross the road,' Archie says. 'We have to hold our grown-up's hand. That would be you or Daddy. And then look left and right and not step off the pavement until the green man says it is okay but

I said I've never seen a green man and the policeman said he's not actually a man at all so it's silly he's called one, isn't it, Mummy?'

'Yes.' I take one hand off the wheel and use my glove to mop my damp brow. A routine visit, that's all. Nothing is wrong.

'And we can only cross the road when it's straight and not on a corner because we are little and the cars can't see us but, Mummy, cars can't see us because they don't have eyes. I think the policeman was a bit bonkers bananas, don't you?' He screams with laughter.

I think policemen are many things: brave, resourceful but also sometimes painfully slow. There's a process they have to follow, rules. I get that, but sometimes the wait for justice can seem endless and sometimes you have to take matters into your own hands. I feel sick as I meet Archie's innocent eyes in the rear-view mirror.

We drive past the cemetery. I don't look. I can't look.

George's car is already on the driveway. The knot in my stomach tightens, along with my chest.

I lift a wriggling Archie from his seat and carry him in front of me like a shield. He kicks his legs, desperate to get down and walk.

'Hello!' I shout down the hallway that smells of strawberries thanks to the diffuser on the windowsill. 'We're home.' My shoulders are concrete but I keep my voice bright and breezy. I'm not sure whether George knows so I brazen it out.

'I'll fix us some lunch...' I trail off as I enter the kitchen. See the brown box on the worktop.

The open brown box on the worktop.

George stands next to it, a knife in his hand. I can tell from the set of his jaw that he's angry.

He's angry again.

Chapter Nine

George

Now

George is furious with himself. He knows it's guilt that drives him home at lunchtimes as well as a desire to see Archie. He isn't treating his wife well, and it pricks at his conscience each time he sees her, and yet when he does spend time with her, he can't help snapping at her as if everything wrong is down to her and her alone. And there's such a lot wrong, it seems impossible to think he can ever put it right. Does he even want to? He loves his son, he really does. And his wife? He thinks he must still – that's why he still hasn't made a final decision – but it's a question he asks himself endlessly.

George is home earlier than usual. On the street is a car he knows belongs to a reporter. He stalks over to it and tells him again to piss off before he calls the police.

He shouts, 'Hello,' as he steps through the front door although he knows nobody will answer and not just because Leah's car isn't on the driveway – there's something different about the atmosphere when Archie's not present. Even if he's asleep the space somehow feels lighter. Happier.

George hasn't been happy for a long time. He hopes he and

Leah will be able to talk calmly later. He had tried so hard to repress his anger last night but nevertheless it had spilled out anyway. He needs to apologize. Throughout their marriage it seems he is always saying sorry. It's Leah's day off but he can't remember if she said she had plans today. They only half listen to each other nowadays. Hear what they want to hear.

He tosses his keys onto the worktop, his eyes skimming the kitchen. It's tidy. Clean. At first glance you wouldn't guess a lively four-year-old lives here. There are no Lego bricks strewn across the floor. No stick-man pictures clinging to the fridge with magnets. George frowns. He was sure there were displays of Archies 'art' on the baby-blue Smeg a few weeks ago. The only reason Leah would have taken them down would be to make the fridge easier to wipe clean and the thought of this makes his stomach plummet.

He can't go through it all again.

George pops a cappuccino tab in the Tassimo machine and while the coffee bubbles into his mug he gazes at the photo of them all at Drayton Manor. He remembers it well. It was a couple of years ago and Leah was going through a good patch, which meant *they* were going through a good patch. After the event they never talk about – just before she fell pregnant with Archie – he had thought they'd never have any sort of normality again. That the woman he fell in love with had vanished for good, but then she had started seeing Francesca and everything changed. She'd visited so many therapists before but Francesca had been different. She hadn't looked at them with sympathy in her eyes. Or with the horror he had seen before as Leah began to roll out the story of her childhood. Instead, she had said she wanted to focus on the future. To help them all move forward as a family. And she had. For a time.

The click of the machine pulls George's eyes away from the photo but the image is forever imprinted on his mind. The three of them crammed on a tiny caterpillar rollercoaster. Archie's arms thrust high in the air. George's arm looped around his wife and son's shoulders. But it's Leah's hands he remembers the most. Skin bare on the safety bar that rested against their laps. Her eyes clear and bright, no hint of concern about germs. No distress at touching the place other hands had touched. He remembers how proud he was that she hadn't pulled out one of the antibacterial wipes she carries in her handbag and wiped the metal down. He remembers how much he loved her then, and now? His heart is torn in two.

George isn't proud of himself. He never thought he would be *that* man. The one in four who supposedly have affairs. But she had caught him at a vulnerable time. Leah had turned him away once too often; her fear of becoming pregnant immense. Archie was an accident, although ultimately a happy one, but Leah spent the pregnancy is a state of constant anxiety about giving birth in a hospital. The germs. The risk of infection. Although they had hired a birthing pool and set it up in their lounge, Leah had known there was a risk that medical intervention might be needed, and she had been right. Archie was breech. The midwife wasn't happy with the way Leah's labour was progressing. George had had to drive them to the hospital, Leah sobbing all the way. Screaming when they entered the ward because he hadn't brought the kit she'd assembled containing her antibacterial spray and hand sanitizer. Her gloves. It took Leah months to recover from the trauma. She kept Archie away from mums-and-tots' groups because of the risk of illness and became so distressed when George had taken him anyway, that he had never tried again. Gradually, though, she'd relaxed into her role.

Being a mum doesn't come easy to her, he knows. It's not only the germs, it's the constant fear that something might happen to Archie. Something bad. He feels this himself as a father. The nagging worry that the outside world is too big, too harsh for his precious boy. He thinks this is probably true for most parents, but of course for Leah everything is heightened because of what she's been through. Still, he had hoped as Francesca gradually lifted some of the heavy burden of fear Leah felt that she would want another baby – George had always dreamed of having a large family – but she was adamant she could never go through it again. Her heart couldn't take it, and as a result his heart was half-empty.

Was.

George takes his phone out of his pocket and calls Marie. It rings and rings and he pictures her in her chaotic flat, shifting junk as she hunts for her mobile. Running her fingers through her hair while she tries to remember where she last had it. Hair that Leah says used to match hers, but Marie changes its colour all the time. There's no hiding from those green eyes though and sometimes when Marie looks at him, it's like looking at Leah and then the guilt kicks in. She's so much like his wife, and yet equally different. Her answer service kicks in and he rings off. Tries again but she doesn't pick up.

The sisters have been through so much, he doesn't want to come between them. It's suffocating to think that he could make their relationship, or break it. That his actions will have such a profound effect on all their futures.

During a therapy session Francesca had told him he had

a 'rescuer identity'. A need to be needed. A desire to save and he believes that to be true. He remembers the first time he met Leah there was something about her that brought out his protective instinct. She had a fragility about her that made him fall instantly in love. It was weeks of gentle courtship before she began to open up to him, tentatively at first, but then her story rushing out as though she couldn't possibly contain it for one more second. She had wept as he held her shaking body against his, but what she didn't know was that he was crying, too, for all that had broken her – but he believed then that he could be the one to put her back together, and he thought that he had. However, since that terrible time with the police a few years ago and the questions and the suggestion that perhaps Leah should be committed for her own safety – for *everyone's* safety – it feels so temporary. The good periods may stretch for longer with Francesca's help but he's always on tenterhooks, waiting for Leah to shatter again. Wondering if he has the strength to hold her together once more.

The doorbell rings. A cardboard box is thrust into George's arms. He carries it through to the kitchen and slices through the brown tape. His shoulders tighten as he stares at the contents. This will set everything off again when Leah comes home. He can't pretend he hasn't seen *this*. The thought of another row is almost too much to bear.

They'd fought last night. He says 'fought' but there were no raised voices – he didn't want Archie to hear his parents arguing and he never shouted because Leah was jumpy, easily frightened – but it was there in his body language. The furling and unfurling of his fists despite knowing he'd never use them. In the set of his jaw.

His anger.

'Show me,' he had demanded.

Leah had played with the cuff of her gloves. 'It's too sore.'

'You're lying.' He knew she was wearing gloves again because she was slipping backwards, not because of some non-existent eczema. Why couldn't she just be… the word *normal* sprang to mind. George felt instantly ashamed, and then furious again, and then helpless.

Why wasn't he enough for her? Why wasn't all of this enough for her? A home of her own. A family.

Her past was horrible and twisted and awful but she'd come through it, and yet it was still with her. In every guarded smile. In every single one of her bloody rituals.

He had known it was inevitable when the first journalist approached them several weeks ago.

The anniversary.

The fucking anniversary.

He'd be glad when it was all over and they could all move forward with their lives.

A fresh start.

George picked up his handset and rang Marie again.

This time she answered.

Chapter Ten

Leah

Now

George puts the knife down on the worktop next to the cardboard box and opens his arms just as Archie bowling balls into them. 'Have you had fun at nursery?'

'Yes!. I talked to a *real* policeman!'

George raises his eyebrows and I give an almost indiscernible shake of my head. The police were nothing to do with me. Not this time.

'Have you ever met a real policeman, Daddy?'

There's a beat before George says, 'Yes,' but unlike Archie, there's no excitement in his voice, just an underlying sadness and regret and again I think about all I have put him through since we have been married. The endless interviews. The detectives. The psychiatrists. The whispers that I should be sectioned despite me being adamant that I knew what I had seen. What I had witnessed.

Throughout it all he had never left my side, holding my hand. Promising me that he wouldn't let them take me away. That he could look after me.

He believed me. He believed *in* me.

The lies came later.

My lies.

His.

Last week I found our bank statements and it is all worse than I'd feared.

'We're fine. We're managing,' George had said. 'I'm working my arse off to get us back on track.' That much was true, at least. He is always networking, trying to bring in new business. It's not fair the burden falls to him. Especially when I can't give him the one thing that he wants.

Another child.

He has always been the one desperate for a sibling for Archie. I've been reluctant to agree. Truth be told, I'd been horrified when I found out I was pregnant with Archie, as I'd been so careful. George has stopped asking me for another baby. I hope it's because we can't afford one right now, because the thought that he might still want a large family – but not want one with me – is almost too much to bear.

I look at him across the kitchen, my handsome husband with his mop of dark hair and blue eyes that look permanently worried. He is slipping away from me. For a split second I wonder how much money the journalist had offered Marie. What we would have to say to generate enough interest to rocket our bank account from red to black, but I dismiss it instantly.

There are things I will never tell no matter how high the stakes.

'How's your morning been?' I ask George as I lift the box from the worktop. He puts Archie down.

'Go upstairs and wash your hands while Mummy and I make you some lunch.'

'Okay, Daddy. I'll fly.' Archie stretches his arms into wings and zooms around the kitchen twice before he thunders upstairs.

George takes the box from me and puts it back down. 'What the fuck, Leah?'

I swallow hard. 'You shouldn't have—'

'I *knew* you weren't coping.' George tips the box onto its side and out spills bottle after bottle of antibacterial cleaner, hand wash, disinfectant wipes. Disposable gloves.

'I… I am…' I'm coping because of the contents of the box, not in spite of them.

'You're not. You haven't got eczema again at all, have you?'

I stare miserably at my gloved hands. 'No.'

'You need help.'

'It's because of the anniversary.'

'I know.' His voice is quiet. His expression despairing. 'I know how difficult it is for you. All of you. But remember the last time? I can't go through it again, Leah. I'm not putting Archie through it. If you need to go and stay somewhere—'

'A psychiatric hospital? I'm *not* mad.'

'I'm not saying you are but you need specialist—'

'I'll ring Francesca. Make an appointment.'

She had helped before. She was the one who came to the police station and fought for me when they wouldn't let me go. She explained the truth to them, however implausible it had seemed. My pulse accelerates as I remember the disbelief etched on their faces. The suspicion. She managed to persuade them I was innocent.

That time, I was innocent.

'George? I said I'll ring Francesca.'

'Okay.' There's such weariness to that one word. He doesn't follow it with 'when?' or 'call her now' and I know what he is thinking.

'I know she's expensive but Marie says we're due some large

royalties. I can cover the cost. Soon the anniversary will have been and gone and everything will be back to normal, I promise.'

'You can't put a price on mental health,' he says. 'Do you want me to come with you?'

'Thanks. I'll see what she suggests.' I flash him a smile that he doesn't return.

After a silent sandwich – even Archie is subdued, picking up on our tension – George disappears into his study.

'What shall we play with, Archie?' I ask.

'Are your hands too sore to play trains, Mummy?' He studies my face.

My throat swells as he looks at me with concern. 'I'm never too sore to play with you, Archie.' Not a direct lie, but not the truth either.

Archie scampers upstairs, returning minutes later, his thick winter gloves covering his hands.

'Now we're the same.'

I blink back tears as I watch him struggle to push the carriages around the track, hating myself, and loving him more.

It is just Archie and me for dinner. George is heading out again. After we've eaten, Archie asks if he can go and watch George get ready. He loves it when George smothers his chin in shaving cream, a Father Christmas beard.

I settle myself in front of the TV, channel-hopping, trying to find something upbeat – there are far too many crime series on. Channel 4 is halfway through an episode of *Come Dine With Me* but I watch it all the same.

My mobile trills its old-fashioned telephone ring. Anxiety cackles in my ear when I see where the call is coming from.

Why is he ringing me? But I know why.

For a split second I think about not answering, but I know if I don't he won't stop trying. Each time I change my number I text him my new one but he rarely has cause to use it. Now he must have something important to say and he'll be determined to say it.

I don't want to hear it.

My toes scrunch inside of my slippers.

I don't want to hear it.

The urge to run away is immense.

I don't want to hear it.

I will myself to think of Archie upstairs.

Calm yourself.

I search the room for three things to ground myself with.

Chocolate-brown cushion with pops of orange flowers.

Green spider-plant on the windowsill.

The side lamp with its warming buttery glow.

Calm.

My phone falls quiet. I stare at my screen, waiting for the voicemail icon to pop up.

It doesn't.

The ringing starts again, demanding attention. I mute the TV and peel off one of my gloves so I can swipe to accept the call but, rather than imagining germs, it is his words I can feel already crawling over my skin regardless of the fact he hasn't yet spoken.

'Yes?' I don't bother with hello. This is not a social call.

'It's Graham.' His Scottish accent is broad although he hasn't lived there for years.

'I know.' Although 'Graham' still seems too familiar. Chief

Inspector McDonald is the name that flashed up on my phone. He's retired now but I still can't address him by his Christian name. Whenever I hear his voice I'm that eight-year-old girl once more, frightened and confused. Cowering in the brightness of the police station, the light and noise a stark contrast to the quiet darkness I'd been rescued from. My arms wrapped around my father's neck – me on one hip, Marie on the other, while Chief Inspector McDonald – Graham – assured us, 'I'll find the bastards who did this, I promise,' and my mother sobbed into a tissue, a bewildered Carly pressed against her side.

'How are you?' he asks although he'll know how I am.

'Fine,' I say but we both know that I'm not.

We're so horribly British, that it comes next, the idle chit-chat about the weather.

'It's brass monkeys out there, I can't feel my hands,' he says.

'I know. I couldn't spread the butter on Archie's toast this morning because it was solid.'

We play I'm-colder-than-you tag for a few minutes more.

'Leah.' I know what's coming even before he confirms that I am right. There's no other reason he'd be calling me. Part of me thinks I should say it first, take some control, but my mouth is desert dry, the words stuck to my tongue. I hear his breath in my ear.

Please don't tell me.

The sound of a chair leg scraping against the floor.

Please don't tell me.

The spark of a lighter. A draw on a cigarette.

Please don't tell me.

But then he does. He *has* to.

'He's out. He was released yesterday.'

He doesn't speak again and I think it's because I'm screaming but then I realize the sound I'm making is only in my head because I can hear Archie call, 'Bye Daddy,' followed by the slam of the front door.

Graham allows the words to settle for a moment more before he says, 'Time off for good behaviour.' He makes a noise that could be a laugh or a snort or something in between because we both know there has never been anything good in his behaviour, but still they keep releasing him.

He's out.

I am gripping the handset so hard my knuckles are white and my fingers ache.

He's out.

Last time he was released he had ignored the condition of his parole stating he couldn't come anywhere near me, Marie or Carly. It was such a relief when he was arrested again after the police had uncovered what else he had done while he'd had his freedom restored. He's been gone for a number of years since and, although I knew he wouldn't be locked up forever, this still feels like a slap in the face but then it proves I was right, wasn't I? I *had* seen him this morning as I'd pulled out of the petrol station.

Twenty years.

Happy anniversary.

Without thinking about how rude I am being, I cut the call. My fingers hover between the contacts in my favourite list. I ring Carly first.

'Hey, Leah. What's up?' Her voice is thick with tears. It's been a hard day for us all at Marie's flat. For a moment I hesitate, not wanting to make her feel any worse.

'He's out.' It's all I need to say.

She sharply draws a breath.

'Who told you?' she asks.

'Graham.'

'Not Mum?'

'Of course not.' Our relationship with our mother is complex. 'Do you think she knows?' Would the police be obliged to tell her?

'Dunno. Should I call her?'

'Do you want to?'

'Not really, no.'

'Then don't. Anyway, there's nothing she can do and we need to tell Marie first. Speak to you later.'

I hang up, not waiting to hear her thoughts on his release. Her reaction will be the same as mine: outrage, sadness, fear.

Marie's phone rings and rings. I will her to hurry up. Her answer service kicks in. I cut the call and try again with no luck.

She definitely said she didn't have any plans that evening, that she was staying in.

In between bathing Archie and putting him to bed I try her again.

Still, she doesn't answer.

My stomach churns with worry. When I was young I came down with tonsillitis unbeknown to Marie, who suddenly lost her voice, despite not feeling ill.

Twin instinct, Mum used to call it.

My thoughts cast back to that room – our prison – when I had thought she was going to die. I knew it then and I know it now.

Something is wrong.

Very wrong indeed.

Chapter Eleven

Carly

Then

Leah released another bloodcurdling scream and, before Carly could react, she tore over to the door, rattling the handle with both hands.

'Come back! Let us out!'

Marie shouted, 'Stop it, Leah. You'll make them cross.'

Leah turned to Carly, her eyes wide and disbelieving. 'They… they've left us here.'

'It's okay.' Carly forced out the lie. 'I'm going to get us out.'

'How?' Leah waited for an answer and when she didn't get one she turned back to the door. Hammering on it with her small fists. 'Help.'

'Shh.' Carly grabbed her wrists. 'Stop that. Give me a second to think.'

Panic tightened in Carly's chest, forcing her to draw in deeper breaths. The putrid smell was unbearable. Carly covered her nose with her sleeve while she stalked around the room.

It was small.

Oppressive.

Graffiti scrawled over the walls.

Ten frantic paces long and six paces wide.

One locked door.

One barred window. The tree outside tap-tap-tapping against the metal bars as pain tap-tap-tapped behind Carly's eyes. She wondered if she had concussion from where she'd banged her head in the van. She'd seen that happen once on *Casualty*.

What would happen to the twins if she wasn't here to protect them?

Carly pulled at the bars as hard as she could but they were concreted into place. Oddly they weren't weatherworn or rusty, but shiny and new. It was a slow dawning. Carly realized with horror that they had been fitted recently, either for them or for someone who had been held here before.

This wasn't random, it had been planned.

Why?

Had they been kidnapped for a ransom? Her stepdad was always featured in newspaper and magazines with his business. He and Mum were often out at work functions – 'networking', he called it. Drumming up business. She didn't fully understand what he did, despite his patience in explaining it. His clients were all companies with money who paid him to build online campaigns to get the public to contribute to fund the manufacturing of new products. It seemed crazy.

'Why can't the companies just pay for their own stuff?' Carly had asked.

'Why risk your own money, if someone else is willing to pay? Besides, some of these big names genuinely can't afford to pay for development in this economy but they can't admit they're in the red. If consumers knew there was any sort of risk of the company folding, they'd avoid them like the plague. Too worried about their guarantees being void or not being able to cash in gift vouchers.'

'So it's tricking them.'

'Not tricking them, no. Creating a buzz is a win-win for everyone. The manufacturers get their product launched with minimal risk, and the consumers feel a real part of something. Everyone gets something out of it.'

It was confusing but it paid well. Their house was the nicest in their street. If the men demanded money Carly knew her parents would give it to them. That had to be it, didn't it? But what if it wasn't?

The girls had been brought here for a reason.

Carly just didn't know what.

She closed her eyes.

She didn't want to know.

Think.

Tap-tap-tap, said the tree.

Hurry-hurry-hurry.

Carly raced back to the door. Twisted the handle.

'It's still locked,' Leah said.

'I *know* that.' What Carly didn't know was what they – what she – was going to do. Panicked, she ran her fingers down the side of the door, feeling for the bump of the hinges. Could she unscrew them somehow and remove the door? There didn't seem to be screws visible and Carly wondered if the door needed to be open in order to see them. She rattled the handle again.

Think.

Desperately, she scanned the room. The mattress took up much of the floor space. Broken glass littered the grubby grey floor; the fluorescent tubes had been wrenched from the ceiling and smashed. There was a heap of rubbish that looked like the bonfire her stepdad had mounded in the garden last year. Carly remembered the strike of the match, the flames that licked higher and higher until the guy the girls had made was alight. His legs, his torso. His face.

Was that what the men had planned for them?

She couldn't breathe. The thought… The thought of being trapped in this room, toxic smoke filling the air, filling their lungs. The relentless heat.

They would burn.

Suffocate.

Die.

Carly stumbled over to the window as though smoke was already seeping into her lungs. She grasped hold of the metal bars, thankfully cool and not scorching hot. Lifted her feet from the ground.

Come on.

She wasn't heavy enough to yank them from the window.

'Girls. Come and help me.'

Leah slipped her arms around Carly's waist, hanging from her like an infant monkey. Carly's shoulder sockets screamed with pain, her clammy palms slipped, as the sisters tumbled onto the hard concrete ground, into a puddle of stagnant water that had pooled under the window. It stank.

'I want to go home.' Leah clung to Carly, the tips of her fingers digging into the already-bruised flesh of Carly's arm.

'We're going to go home.' Carly stood, and helped Leah up. Both of their skirts were sodden. 'Why didn't you help us, Marie?'

'We can't get out,' Marie stated the simple truth.

Leah began to cry.

'It's okay, though.' Marie stroked her twin's hair, the way she had calmed Bruno the night fireworks lit up the sky behind their garden. 'It's a game. Isn't it?'

Marie's eyes met Carly's and there was both question and fear in them.

'Yes,' said Carly eventually. Marie had the right idea. Leah was born only twelve minutes after Marie, but she'd always seemed much younger – the one they needed to protect with her endless worries. It was better to lie and calm her. 'It's a game.'

'But I don't want to play.' Leah sobbed harder.

'If we don't all play, we can't all stay together,' Marie said.

'What do you mean?' Leah wiped her nose with the back of her hand.

'I mean…' Marie hesitated. Indecipherable emotions slid across her face – she had always been so hard to read – before she masked them with a half-hearted attempt at a smile. Forever the fearless one. Always trying to make her twin feel better. 'We have to be good. Brave. We're together, that's the main thing.'

'Might they split us up? Who are they? Don't let them take me away.'

'I won't,' Marie said firmly. 'Cross my heart.' But Leah still looked terrified until Marie curved her little finger into a hood and offered it to her twin.

'A pinkie promise can't be broke

Or you'll disappear in a puff of smoke

This is my vow to you,

I'll keep my promise through and through.'

'See, it'll be fine!' Carly took a deep breath to steady her voice. 'Marie's right.' She glanced at Marie. 'We'll treat it like a game. A mystery. We're good at solving those, aren't we?' It wasn't too long ago they'd created invisible ink. If only lemon juice could help them now. 'Let's make a plan.' She crunched over the broken glass and perched on the mattress. It was filthy but safer than the floor. She patted the space either side of her. The twins huddled against her. 'Right. I don't know who took us, or why, but there's two of them. Doc—'

'A doctor?' Leah asked.

'No, but I call him that because of his boots, and Moustache is the other one. They haven't hurt us yet so I don't think they will.' Carly crossed her fingers behind her back.

'Look.' Leah pointed with a shaky finger. On the wall, in jet black aerosol, the words, *You're going to die.*

'That isn't aimed at us,' Carly said. 'Look how many other things have been written.'

'*Run.*' Leah read another.

'I meant names and stuff. It's vandals. Some of the kids at school have been here. Nobody is going to die.'

Think.

They fell silent.

Think.

Suddenly it came to her.

A plan.

'Marie, we need you to pretend to be ill.'

'Why?' asked Marie.

'Because you're the best at acting.' Marie had a confidence Carly could only wish for. Last Christmas she'd played Annie. Mum had styled her red hair into a mass of ringlets and she'd stood centre stage, belting out 'Tomorrow' without a hint of self-consciousness.

'I know I'm the best. Acting is easy. You just pretend. I meant why should I look ill?'

'That way I can call the men and they'll think you're really sick. If they're worried you might die they'll have to take you to hospital. There'll be police there.' Carly thought but she didn't know. There were always policeman chatting up the nurses on *Casualty*.

'No,' said Marie. 'It's better we stay together. Besides, they won't hurt us.' She tried to form it as a statement. Carly knew she was trying to reassure Leah but there was still a tinge of doubt to her voice. This was the first time in her eight years Marie had caught a glimpse of how harsh the world could be and Carly didn't blame her for not wanting to accept it. 'They didn't mean to scare us, did they, Carly?' Marie raised her eyebrows and tilted her head towards her twin.

'Of course not, but—' Carly began.

'There you go, then. I won't leave Leah.' She linked her fingers through her sister's. 'Or you,' she added as she caught sight of the expression on Carly's face.

'Marie—'

'No, Carly! Besides, they wouldn't believe it if I was suddenly ill.'

'It wouldn't be much of a stretch.' Carly gestured to the piles of rubbish littering the graffiti-daubed room. 'It's filthy here – there'll be germs crawling all over the place, probably enough to kill us.' Carly shuddered.

'We could *die* of germs?' Terror was thick in Leah's voice. Her eyes rapidly scoured the floor as if searching for germs scurrying around.

'Not really.' Carly wished she could take back her words. Leah had a tendency to worry about everything.

‘Nobody’s going to *die*,’ Marie said. ‘It’s a game. That’s all. Pretend. We stay quiet and don’t make a fuss and we’ll be home before we know it. Right, Carly?’

‘Right.’ Carly tried to lift her mouth into a smile but she couldn’t. In truth she didn’t know if they’d ever go home, and even if they did, the thought of what they might have to endure between now and then was utterly horrifying.

Carly felt sick. Dizzy. The lump on her head throbbing.

Think.

She was all out of ideas and worse than that, her bladder was uncomfortably full. Again, her eyes travelled across the room, hopefully looking for a toilet.

‘I need to wee.’ She stood.

‘Are you going to knock on the door and ask?’ Marie said.

‘Don’t go out there without us, Carly,’ Leah begged.

‘I’m not. I’ll…’ She was hot with humiliation. ‘I’ll go over there, by the corner. You two face the wall.’

The twins did as they were told. Carly’s fingers reluctantly hitched up her skirt and dragged down her pants. At first she couldn’t go, too scared the men would come in and see her exposed. She closed her eyes and pictured the waterfall they’d visited a few years ago in Wales. The roar of the water, the surge of the current. Hot splashes splattered her legs as she released a stream of urine.

‘I’ve finished,’ she said quietly.

‘It stinks of wee now,’ Leah said.

‘It stank of wee anyway.’ Carly was horribly embarrassed. She needed to find something to soak it up with. Careful to avoid the broken glass, she crouched down beside the pile of rubbish. There was a large cardboard box she could tear apart.

Carly pulled it towards her, expecting it to be light and empty. Instead it was heavy and full. Sealed with brown tape.

Carly felt dread settle heavily in her stomach before she'd even opened the box.

Before she had seen what was inside.

She somehow knew it would be bad.

Very bad.

Chapter Twelve

George

Now

George closes his eyes momentarily. He can't concentrate on his breakfast meeting. Has no appetite for the full English in front of him despite the bacon being crispy and the egg yolks sunshine-yellow and runny, just the way he likes them. Guilt has eradicated his appetite. No room for food in his churning stomach.

'George, do you agree?'

'Umm. Yes. Absolutely.'

He tries to smile. Tries to pay attention but on each attempt to focus, his thoughts drift back to Leah. Were they too broken to fix? George doesn't know. He doesn't know if he wants them to be. In sickness and in health, George had promised, and it wasn't that he hadn't meant it, more that he never envisaged there being so much of the sickness. The minute he had opened the parcel yesterday and had seen the array of cleaning products, he knew. He just *knew* she was slipping backwards and it shamed him to admit that there was a split second when he had stood, rooted to the spot, with the thought that he could run away flickering across his mind. Never come back. Start a new life, one with love and laughter and happiness. But he couldn't force his legs to move. He had too much to lose, but if he stayed, everything to gain.

'George?' The client stabs the last piece of sausage onto his fork with more force than necessary. George knows he'd been asked another question.

'Sorry. I... My wife is unwell. I think I need to go. Sorry.' He opens his wallet to throw some cash on the table but it is empty. Instead, he pulls out his credit card, hoping it won't be refused.

'It's okay. I'll settle up. You get home to your wife.' The man sitting opposite him softens. George knows he has a family too, but that doesn't always mean anything, does it? Families can cheat and lie. Betray each other in an instant.

He should know.

The needle on the fuel gauge hovers close to empty. He fills the tank with diesel and remembers he had forgotten to fill Leah's car when he had promised to. Ashamed he'd let her down again, he picks up some yellow and orange flowers from the reduced-price bucket. The roses in the bouquet are browning and shrivelled but if he plucks them out the other flowers are fresh.

He hasn't seen Leah since their row yesterday. They had eaten their lunch in silence. Even Archie had been quiet, chewing his crusts without complaint, finishing his carrot sticks before asking for a cookie. George doesn't want him growing up in an atmosphere – it isn't fair on anyone. Is having two unhappy parents under the same roof better for a child than being shuttled between argument-free homes? He just doesn't know. Not that he can afford a second home, he is barely managing the first, sinking all his money into the mortgage on a property that's not even in his name. That's unfair, though. Leah didn't have a mortgage before he'd wanted to set up a business. She'd believed in him enough to take on a job purely so the bank would give them more funds than they could feasibly afford to pay back. It wasn't irresponsible money-lending but a calculated risk. They have plenty of capital. The house is worth much more than they owe. Even so, he feels the bank is just biding its time. Waiting to snatch their home away.

As he had hugged Archie goodbye before heading out for the evening, he pretended that he was saying goodbye after a weekend visit and leaving his boy for a week, just to see how it felt.

It hurt.

The clock in the hallway had displayed midnight by the time he returned. The *tick-tick-tick* of its hands seemed to reprimand him.

Liar-liar-liar.

He had hesitated. His foot on the bottom step, his fingers lightly resting on the bannister. He couldn't climb into bed with his wife, not smelling of another woman's perfume. Not when the smell would be so familiar to her. Instead, he had spent a restless night on the couch.

George doesn't call out as he enters the house, he doesn't quite know what to say. How to sound. The TV is on in the lounge, Archie cross-legged on the floor and glued to *Shrek*. George frowns. Archie hadn't seemed unwell when he'd kissed him goodbye early that morning and by the way he is dipping his hand into a bag of Pom Bears, crunching the crisps, he probably isn't ill. Instead of disturbing him, George wanders into the kitchen, in search of his wife. Leah is sitting at the table, studying something on her laptop.

For a moment George drinks her in. The way her soft hair hangs like a glossy sheet down her back, the sun through the window picking out natural golden highlights among the red. She really is beautiful. A one-of-a-kind gasp-in-surprise when she walks into a room type. Except she isn't a one-off. Marie is almost identical although she has entirely different hair. An entirely different personality. His sister-in-law intrudes into his thoughts far more frequently than he'd like nowadays.

As George crosses the kitchen he can see Leah is watching the press coverage from her original case on YouTube. He feels a mixture of sadness and anger that their boy is alone in the lounge while Leah has again stepped into the past.

'Hi.' George ignores the way she flinches when she became aware of his presence.

He holds out BP garage's finest peace offering. 'Are you okay?' he asks, although she clearly isn't. Her eyes are bloodshot and red-rimmed as though she's been crying for hours and he wonders if he's been the cause of that or if it is something else.

Hurriedly, Leah slams the lid of the laptop down with her gloved hand before opening it again slightly. She repeats this ritual twice more, lightning fast, all the while unable to look George in the eye. It takes seconds and a casual observer might not have noticed, but George feels panic rising.

Threes.

He hadn't realized she was quite so bad.

Again.

She pushes the computer angrily away. George feels she's pushing *him* away. He feels alone, not like last night with arms and legs wrapped around him. Soft breath and warm moans in his ears.

'Why isn't Archie at nursery?' he asks.

'He's out' is all she says flatly and at first George is confused. Archie is out? What does that mean? But then she says, 'Graham McDonald called to tell me,' and he realizes why she was watching YouTube.

Watching *him*.

He's out.

'I couldn't face leaving the house. The thought of him out there.' She stares out of the window with wide eyes.

'He was always going to be released sometime,' George says, but his voice is thin. The memories of what happened last time he was released are still raw. Then he had desperately wanted to save Leah. He knows he should feel the same now. George reaches for his wife but she leans sideways on her stool, away from him. Instead, he crosses to the sink to wash his hands. Afterwards, she allows him to hold her but her body is stiff.

'We can't let this affect Archie. You can't keep him inside forever. He needs to go to nursery. You have to go to work. You can't let that… *that man* be the ruin of you. I bet he hasn't given you a second thought. Any of you. Leah, you can choose to—'

Quickly, she pushes him away. 'It seems we *all* have choices to make. I saw Marie yesterday. You'll never guess what she said?' Damp patches form in George's armpits. He doesn't know what he should say to that, what he could say, and so he says nothing. Has Marie given away their secret? He doesn't think Leah would have kept quiet about it for twenty-four hours if she had. Infidelity isn't something his wife would forget to mention. Besides, Marie would have warned him, wouldn't she?

'She's been approached by a journalist.'

'We've *all* been approached by journalists the past few weeks.'

Even George. He'd felt sick at first as the man in the coffee shop had leered at him as he pushed his card into George's hand. *What's it really like living with a Sinclair Sister? Does she have trust issues? Issues with men?* George knew what he was asking and he had wanted to throw a punch until the man hit him with a figure his paper was prepared to pay. 'Fucking scum,' George muttered but he was still staggered at the money on the table.

'I say journalist, but it's TV. A live show.'

George tries to rearrange his features into one of surprise, as though it's the first time he has heard this.

'They want *a new angle*, apparently. I guess the fact he's out there again, gives it a new angle.' She laughs bitterly.

'What do Carly and Marie think of the TV idea?'

'Marie's all for it. She thinks it will be healing. Get everything out there once and for all and lay it to rest. She thinks we'll be left alone then.'

'Maybe she's right?' George says cautiously. 'You have nothing to be ashamed of, Leah. None of you,' he says although he knows Marie should feel ashamed.

Does feel ashamed.

'Marie says she wants forgiveness. Don't we all?' She sighs.

'Yes,' George says softly. Sometimes he thinks he wants to be found out but Leah doesn't ask him what he needs to be forgiven for and he wonders – not for the first time – whether part of her knows. Whether she really believes he has so many evening meetings. 'Maybe meet with the producer and talk it through? It could be good for you. Good for us.' George purposefully doesn't mention the huge fee he knows is at stake.

'Carly hates the idea. Last night I rang her and she was crying and that was even before I told her the news. This morning when

I called she could barely pull herself together long enough to talk. It's too much, him being out so close to the anniversary. I can't get hold of Marie either. I rang her about a million times last night after Graham called. She said she was going to be home all evening but she didn't pick up. I thought I saw him yesterday, you know.'

'Graham?' George can't keep up with the way her mind is fragmenting.

'No. Not Graham,' she says impatiently and George knows exactly who she means.

She thinks he's coming after her like before.

It's happening. It's happening again.

'Leah.' He takes her hand. Wishing he could feel skin instead of cotton. 'You have nothing to hide.'

'You don't understand…'

'I do.' He squeezes her fingers. 'I know what happened to you back then. I know everything about you.'

'Nobody knows everything about anyone,' she says darkly.

George knows he has made a promise to Marie. He knows the approaching twenty-year anniversary is landsliding it all back, threatening to bury them all completely.

George knows more than he should.

He knows what's to come.

He shakes away all thoughts of running away.

He doesn't want to arouse suspicion.

Chapter Thirteen

Carly

Then

What was in the cardboard box?

Carly scratched at the brown parcel tape that sealed it with her nail until the end lifted but still she didn't dare rip it off. Her heart kicked against her chest. Her stomach spun around faster. She had assumed the smell of decay was from years of neglect, from the rubbish, but what if it was coming from the box? What if it held the remains of something… or someone? It wasn't large enough for a person, unless they'd been chopped up, but that only happened in movies, didn't it? She thought again of *Psycho*. Of Norman Bates' dead mother rocking in that chair.

'What are you do—'

'Stay over there,' Carly ordered her sisters.

Think.

She needed to be brave and find out what was inside but Carly didn't feel brave. She felt small and scared and she wanted to go home.

'Is there something in the box?' Marie asked.

Something.

Someone.

'I... I don't know, Marie.'

'Why don't you just—'

'Shush a minute.'

Think.

The cardboard was stiff and dry. It hadn't been here for as long as everything else. There was no blood seeping from the bottom of the box. What if it contained, not unimaginable horrors, but something useful? A torch perhaps. The prospect of this excited her not just because it would be dark soon and they'd have light, that was secondary to the desire for a weapon. Carly could picture herself hiding behind the door. Feel the weight of the torch in her hand, the force in her shoulder as she brought it down on Moustache's head. Hear his screams. Smell his blood. She wasn't usually one for dark thoughts but then this was not a usual situation. Her mind hopped. If not a torch then maybe tools. Something she could use to slice through the metal bars.

She *had* to find out.

Carly glanced out of the window and then across to the door. No one was watching except the graffiti clown with his wide staring eyes, but still she felt uneasy.

Her hands shook as she tore off the tape. She quickly shuffled backwards, half expecting a swarm of rats to rush towards her or a plague of insects, but there was nothing. Carly inched forwards again, taking care to avoid kneeling on the shards of glass.

'Oh.' Out of all the things she had been expecting, it wasn't... *this*.

'What's in there, Carly? Can we see?' asked Marie.

'In a sec.' Carly rummaged through the contents, her hope sinking as she interpreted what they meant. The box had been left here for the girls, Carly had no doubt.

What was in store for them she still didn't know but she *did* know that they wouldn't be going home yet.

There were multiple bags of Spicy Tomato Snaps, the green dragon grinning his toothy grin from the front of the packet. Carly normally loved them but she shoved them out of the way, disinterested. Underneath them lay a couple of bags of blackcurrant liquorice sweets and several cans of cherry Coke. There was also a pink blanket, soft and fleecy, still with its tags, and somehow Carly knew that Doc had put that in there, and oddly a small teddy bear, his arms outstretched, red knitted jumper riding over his rounded belly. This kindness seemed at odds with the way they'd been so brutally snatched from their lives that Carly began to cry.

What did they want with them? It was all too much.

The tapping of the tree outside grew louder. The room grew smaller. Carly cried harder, fighting for breath as the ceiling pressed down.

She crouched low. She couldn't breathe.

'Don't cry, Carly.' Her sisters rushed to her side and each draped a thin arm around her neck, pressing their warm bodies against hers, and this made Carly's tears flow faster.

'The bear doesn't want you to be sad.' Leah reached for the teddy from the box and waved him in front of Carly's face.

'It will be okay.' Marie stroked her hair. 'I promise. We'll be home soon and then we'll go on holiday.'

'Where to?' Leah asked.

'Disneyland probably,' Marie said.

Carly knew it was wishful thinking. They were supposed to go to Florida last year but it had been cancelled because Dad was too busy with work and, although he promised they'd go away at half-term instead, they didn't end up going anywhere.

'See. Don't cry, Carly. We'll be on a plane on the way to meet Mickey Mouse soon,' said Leah even though she was terrified of flying. This small act of bravery led Carly's lungs to loosen. Oxygen began to flow around her body. The burn in her chest started to subside. She couldn't give up. She *wouldn't* give up. But while she waited for an idea to hit – the perfect plan to get them home – she could distract her sisters. Distract herself.

'Let's play a game while we wait to go home.' She led her sisters over to the mattress and they settled down. Carly wiped her eyes with her sleeve. 'We each have to name something in the room alphabetically. You start, Leah.'

'Animal.'

'There isn't an animal!' Marie said.

'There's a bear.' Leah was cuddling the soft toy from the box.

'If you can have that, I'll have *A teddy* for my A,' Marie said. 'Carly? Your turn.'

'Annoying sisters,' Carly said but they all knew she didn't mean it.

'Now. B. Umm… bed! Kind of.' Marie patted the mattress.

'Broken glass,' Carly offered.

'Bars,' Leah said flatly and Carly clapped her hands, drawing her sister's gaze away from the window.

'My turn to go first, C.' Carly looked around the room. 'This is harder.'

'Not for me!' Marie shouted. 'Carly!'

Carly rolled her eyes. 'Okay, I'm going for carpet.'

'There isn't a carpet!' Marie shoved Carly.

'There's a dust carpet!'

'That would be D then, silly. Pick something else.' Marie's

eight-year-old logic was often skewed. How she rationalized things was often a source of amusement at home.

'Okay then... crisps. Your turn, Leah.'

'Clown.' Leah began to cry. 'I don't like that clown, Carly. He's watching us.'

They all stared at the graffiti on the back of the door. The clown's eyes did seem to be fixed on them, his stretched mouth laughing.

'I don't want to play any more.' The brief moment of lightness was gone.

'Do you want some crisps?' Carly remembered she hadn't given the girls their tea. She rubbed her fingers together, still feeling the paper of the £10 note smooth against her skin, almost tasting chips drenched with salt and vinegar.

'I'm not hungry.' Leah lay on her side and began to suck her thumb. She hadn't done that since she was three.

Time dragged. It felt like days since Carly had sat on her back step after school and felt the heat of the sun on her skin. The room was chilly with its bare walls and floors. Outside the last burst of sun streaked the sky orange as it began to dip, and Carly knew they'd grow even colder. One blanket wasn't enough for them all.

Leah hugged her knees to her chest. Carly could see the goosebumps on her arms.

Marie sat cross-legged, spine rigid, staring at the door that never opened. Carly shuddered. That clown gave her the creeps too.

'Come on.' She stood and stretched out a hand to each sister. 'Let's warm up.'

'How?' Marie asked but she was already standing.

Carly raised her arm above her head and mimed spinning a lasso – '5, 6, 7, 8' – the way she should have done in the kitchen earlier that day.

Tentative at first, the girls' singing grew louder, stronger, as their feet shuffled across the concrete, hands on their hips. Momentarily it seemed to Carly they could have been somewhere else. Back at home with Bruno barking and jumping up, doing his own dog dance. Carly's voice faltered as she swallowed down a hard lump that rose in her throat as she wondered what might have happened if she hadn't been such a bitch earlier and had danced with the twins when the song had come on the radio. That four-minute delay might have made all the difference. The men might have given up searching for someone to take. Or it could be different girls trapped here right now. Instantly, Carly felt like a cow for wishing this on somebody else and she pushed away the part of her that whispered *better anyone else than you*.

She sank onto the mattress, too emotional to carry on. 'I'm out of breath. You girls take over.'

Marie and Leah exchanged a look before breaking out their best Madonna. Carly had heard them sing 'True Blue' a million times before, sometimes with lips coated in Mum's red lipstick, a beauty spot drawn below their left nostril with an eyebrow pencil, and usually it irritated her but here it sounded sweet and pure, the twins placing their hands dramatically over their hearts as they declared true love. Would they live through this to find their soulmates one day? Carly thought of Dean, she might never see him again. The twins slipped seamlessly between the songs they'd choreographed in their bedroom. Marie's fingers sought out the cross around her neck, lifting it as she sang 'Like a Prayer'. Leah's hand felt around her own throat. 'My cross! It's gone!'

'It must be here somewhere.' Carly remembered the gold glinting in the light as Leah was carried in.

'We'll find it,' Marie dropped to her knees.

'Be careful of the broken glass,' Carly joined in the search but it was fruitless. 'I'm sorry, Leah. We'll get you another one.'

Leah nodded. Carly could see she was upset but she didn't complain. 'Do you want to sing something else?'

Leah shook her head. 'I'm hungry now.'

Carly was surprised to find that she was too.

'Let's have some Snaps while we wait for Doc and Moustache to bring us some proper dinner.' There wasn't nearly enough food in the box to keep all three of them going for more than a few hours and this gave Carly hope that the men would be back soon.

The sisters licked spicy tomato crumbs from their fingers and fizzed open cans of cherry Coke.

And waited.

They waited for dinner. They waited for a light.

But nobody came.

They all felt it, the creeping claustrophobia that built as dusk fell. Gloom casting shadows into the corners of the room, across the ceiling.

'I want to go home, I want to go home.' Leah's voice dripped with hysteria. 'I want to go home!'

She raced over to the door and began beating against it, screaming, 'Let us out. Help us.'

Carly and Marie rushed over to Leah's side but rather than trying to calm her they too began thumping the door.

'Let us out. Please. Somebody help us.'

The clown laughed and laughed at their panic. The whites of his eyes, his teeth, the last visible thing as darkness swallowed the girls, feeding on their fear.

It was pitch black.

Still they screamed.

Still nobody came.

Chapter Fourteen

Leah

Now

There is somebody in our garden.

I peer anxiously out of the window into the gloom, my fingertips resting on the glass, eyes searching for shadows.

Blood whooshes through my ears and rising above that, the steady thump of George's footfall on the stairs.

'Archie fell asleep halfway through *The Stick Man*. I put on my best voices too. I think… Leah? Are you okay?'

'I thought I heard something,' my voice wobbles. 'And when I looked outside there was…'

Movement.

Him.

'I can't see anything now, though.'

George stands by my side. 'Just because they've released him doesn't mean you need to feel—'

'I know.' I don't *need* to feel unsafe, but I do. That man has ruined my life. When he was contained in a prison cell, guarded by officers, I could almost, almost pretend he didn't exist. Now he's back out there somewhere. He could be one hundred miles away.

One mile away.

Staring at me right now.

I have no way of knowing.

'Are you going out tonight?' I ask.

'I did say to a client…' George begins. I meet his eyes and his gaze flickers to the flowers he had given me, which now sprout from a bright yellow jug on our coffee table. 'Do you want me to stay here, Leah?'

'Yes, please,' I say, adding hurriedly, 'it isn't because I'm scared to be alone.' *It's partly because I'm scared to be alone.* 'It's… I'm worried about you, George.'

A flicker of surprise passes across his face. It's horrible it's such a shock to him that I've been thinking of something other than myself, my sisters, the anniversary. Despite everything, I love my husband with all my heart and it seems he has lost sight of that. We have both lost sight of that. I sit on the sofa, patting the space next to me.

He cautiously settles himself. 'I'm… okay.'

'I miss you. Archie misses you. We miss our family movie evenings.' *Finding Nemo* and buttery popcorn. 'And our games nights.' Hungry Hippos while Archie was awake and once he'd gone to bed, cards. Red wine and cheese and crackers. Olives. Folk music streaming through the Bose. Dylan urging 'Don't Think Twice' as I arranged my cards into suits and tried to second-guess what George would be collecting.

'It's been… hard.'

I think he means I've been hard, but I wait for him to elaborate.

'The business isn't doing great,' he says eventually. 'I'm doing all I can but… I'm sorry, Leah.' His eyes are sad, bordered with fine lines that hadn't been there months before. When was the last time I had really looked at him? There is a groove on the bridge of his nose, wrinkles forming on his forehead. Each one of them telling the story, the story of us.

'You've nothing to be sorry for.' I know I have a hundred apologies to make to a hundred different people and even then, it won't be enough. I hate the way I've made him cross lately – wearing the gloves, restarting my rituals – and I hate the way he has to fight to keep his feelings in check for fear of upsetting me. I only pick up on his anger from his body language, never his voice. I've let him down.

'I've let you down…' His voice cracks, along with my heart. I can't let him stagger under the weight of our family alone any more. It is breaking him apart. Emotions flicker in his eyes and I know how conflicted he is. It must be awful to leave your warm house, on cold nights, to schmooze with clients when you'd rather be reading a bedtime story to your child. Snuggled up on the sofa with your wife. Knowing that whatever you are doing, it still isn't enough. I have it easy, the one who stays home in the evenings. Who works part-time. That's one thing I can change, right now.

'Lionel's offered me extra hours because Carol's leaving.'

'I don't know, Leah. I don't think you should.'

'Because you're the man?' George is quite traditional sometimes.

'Because of Archie. Carly's great helping out but how would you feel if she were always the one picking him up? Do you really want to work full-time?'

'No. But if I need to, I will. I'll do everything I can to help, you know, with money,' I am lying to myself. Lying to him. The TV production company are offering enough to obliterate our debts but I can't sell myself that way. The thought of it makes me feel sullied. 'We'll be okay.' Another lie, but sometimes we tell ourselves the things we need to hear, don't we? As though our words can make it so.

'Yeah.' He shuffles closer, puts his arm around me. I rest my head on his shoulder. We sit in a silence that is companionable rather than awkward.

I must have dozed off because the slam of a car door rouses me. Within seconds I am on my feet, peeping out of the window again.

'Let's go to bed,' George says behind me. His breath hot on my neck.

Upstairs, I stroke George's face with my fingers, feeling the rough stubble beneath my skin. I never wear gloves in bed. It's my safe place. The feel of him around me, on me. In me. It's the one place I forget. His lips are dry as I push mine against his, which are slow to move in response. My thumb dips under the elastic of his boxers. He catches my hands in his. Raises them to his mouth and kisses them. 'I'm so tired.' Rejection stings but I understand.

'It's been good to talk, though, hasn't it?' I ask.

'Yes. Leah?' There's a beat. 'I miss you too, you know. You have a choice to spiral backwards or to move forwards. To not let your past define your future. You get to decide, no one else.'

Turning this over, I coil my body around his, wishing I could draw in his strength. He is right. Anniversary or not, I can't, won't let *that man* break me. If I did, he'd be breaking us. George. Archie.

Tomorrow, however scared I feel, I will drop Archie off at nursery and go to work. Ask for more hours. Step up to my responsibilities. I am an adult now, not the scared eight-year-old girl I once was, however much I still feel her presence inside me with every decision I make. Everything I do. For me. For my family, it is time to move on. Perhaps there is something in Marie's words. Twenty years of suffering is twenty years too much. In a few days the anniversary will be over. But I can make it lose its power now. Like throwing water over the wicked witch and watching her shrivel. Forging a normal life will be my bucket of cold water.

Enough.

I can cope now, I can. Even if it is the fear of George slipping away from me, fear of losing something, someone else, that has made me determined to do more. Be more. I won't let another family fall apart. Not when I can stitch our fraying threads back together.

I fall asleep.

It's still dark. A noise wakes me. I lie motionless. My body rigid. Fingers gripping the duvet.

Waiting.

My eyes scan the room. The digital clock shouts 6 a.m. in neon green digits. There's a warm orange glow emanating from the plug-in night light by the door. Archie thinks it's funny we have one too. He thinks it's so we're the same as him but what he doesn't know is that I hate the way the night-time swallows me, the suffocating blackness. The fear that something bad, someone bad, will spring out of the shadows.

I know that sometimes they do.

There's nothing to be heard except George's breath rattling in his throat. Slowly, my hands relax.

My pyjamas are damp with terror. In my nightmare I had taken Archie to the circus but we were the only ones in the Big Top, the smell of sawdust rising from the empty ring as we took our rickety front-row seats, fluffy pink candyfloss balanced on sticks. The lights went out, Archie had whimpered.

'It's okay,' I had whispered but my heart was pounding. The urge to run immense.

Brightness had filled the tent but only for a second but that second was enough for me to see it. The clown. The lights began to strobe and each time they flashed on, the clown's face loomed closer and closer. His smiled his slashed red grin, sharp teeth dripping with blood.

And that was when I woke.

There's a circus coming to the meadow in town in the new year. We won't go. We never do.

I know I won't get back to sleep now and so I roll onto my side and gently push George onto his. His snoring stops. I wrap my arms around his waist and press my cheek against his back.

When I get up, Archie is still starfished in his racing-car bed. The mountain of cuddly toys he adores have slid onto the floor in the night, as they always do. There's a panda, a sloth, a tiger. I've never bought him a traditional teddy.

I never will.

The belt on my dressing gown hangs loose and I tighten it as I pad down the landing, relishing the thought of a quiet cup of coffee in a house that will soon be filled with noise.

I see it as I soon as I reach the bottom of the stairs. My feet sinking into the pile of the carpet. My heart sinking into my stomach.

A white envelope on the mat. The noise that woke me must have been the letterbox. It's too early for the postman. I don't want to pick it up.

I don't want to open it.

Somehow I know that whatever is in the envelope has the power to shatter my already shaky resolve to be more.

There's one word written on the outside:

Leah.

I don't want to open it.

Where I had felt cold moments before, I now feel hot.

My fingers slips under the seal, the paper rips.

I don't want to open it.

The world shifts beneath my feet as I read what is scrawled on the paper inside.

I'm still standing there when Archie thunders down the stairs demanding Weetabix, orange juice, a kiss.

I'm still standing there when George sidles up behind me, reading over my shoulder, seeing those two words that shift and blur and move in and out of focus.

The innocuous words that sound like a warning.

FOUR DAYS.

Chapter Fifteen

George

Now

It was George who gently removed the letter from Leah's fingers. George who settled her on the sofa before retreating to the kitchen to fill the ginormous hole Archie declared he had in his tummy, with milk-soft cereal and sweet-sticky toast.

Four days, the letter had said.

Four days until it will all be over. But then there's next year. The year after. Thirty years. Forty. The milestones stretch out before him, a long path of unhappiness.

Is he doing the right thing?

He has never felt more conflicted. Last night for the first time in ages he'd felt closer to Leah. They were still a long way from being happy but a token bunch of forecourt flowers and taking the time to talk, to listen, was a start. He owed it to her to try, didn't he? He owed it to his wife to be honest and true. Look at the state one letter had left her in. For all her bravado last night, George knew she wasn't strong. She'd be easily broken. The thought of having to pick up all the pieces and glue her back together once more made his chest feel tight. He doesn't know if he can, not again.

But she needs him right now. He should spend more time at home. For Archie's sake as much as anyone's.

George understands what Marie wants from him, but he just can't give it to her. Not yet.

Is it too late to call the whole thing off? Would Marie forgive? Forget?

'Leah,' he crouches beside his wife and pushes a coffee into her hands. 'It'll be a journalist trying to scare you into talking. Everyone's looking for a headline. It'll be okay.'

'Do you promise?' she asks him the impossible.

He closes his eyes against the memory.

Arms and legs wrapped around him. Soft breath and warm moans in his ears.

But it wasn't real. *This* is his real life. Morning sun gathering strength, shining a halo over the table where Archie is dabbing up crumbs with his fingers. Strawberry jam smeared around his mouth.

This.

Isn't it?

He doesn't promise it will be okay.

He can't.

Chapter Sixteen

Leah

Now

Four days.

I've called work and told them I'll be late. George offers to drop Archie off at nursery on his way to work. He reassures me again that he'll remind the staff to be mindful of security, to call if anything out of the ordinary happens. I wave them goodbye out of the window, wearing a bright smile that hurts my face to hold. My hands had touched the letter. I've washed them repeatedly until my skin is pink and sore but I can't wash the words away from my mind. They feel dark and dirty.

Four days.

I pace the living room – treading the same path over and over – a zoo animal.

Trapped.

Watched.

Carly rushes up the driveway. I open the door to usher her inside, as she's trailed by the shouts of a reporter who has been loitering outside our house all morning.

'Carly! Is it true he's out? How do you feel?'

Carly says to me, 'How does he fucking think I feel?' She

slams the door behind her. Her face is pale. Eyes tinged pink. Although I only saw her two days ago, she seems smaller. Thinner. Shrinking under the weight of the past or shrinking away from the present. Perhaps both.

She doesn't sit or take off her coat. Instead she smooths out an identical letter onto the kitchen table, which is still lemon-cleaner-damp from where George had wiped away the remnants of Archie's breakfast. Although my fingers are now encased in gloves, I don't pick the piece of paper up.

'What do you think it means?' I ask when what I really want to know is who does she think sent it but I'm scared that her answer will match the one that is marching around my head.

Him.

'I… I don't know.'

'It sounds like a warning.' A warning of what, I do not know. Nothing could be worse than it was twenty years ago, but as I catch sight of the photo of George, Archie and I at the theme park I know that things can be unimaginably worse. 'Do you think Marie got one too?' She must have. 'I still haven't managed to catch her on the phone to tell her.'

He's out.

'Leah. Breathe.' I feel Carly rubbing my back. Suddenly the breath that had been stuck in my throat bursts from me. I sink heavily onto a chair.

'It's happening again.' The eight-year-old inside of me begins to cry.

'It isn't.' She falls back into big-sister mode. 'It's probably just some crackpot – you know how people get and there's been extra media coverage this year.'

'George thinks it's a journalist trying to create a story.'

'There you go then.'

'Do you believe that?' Her eyes won't meet mine. I know she doesn't believe it any more than I do.

We take my car, since Carly's car is full of parcels and her latest charity-shop finds. I don't feel entirely safe behind the wheel. I don't feel entirely safe anywhere.

Marie doesn't answer the buzzer. I rattle the door handle as though it might suddenly open.

It doesn't.

The letterbox is striped with duct tape from where it had fallen off last time I came and I can't open it to peep through.

'She's not here,' Carly says.

'We can't just leave. I want to make sure she's okay.' Not passed out drunk on the floor.

Carly stamps her feet, her breath billowing a cloud. 'Right, well…' I look at her expectantly but before she can come up with a plan, there's a click. A man with a beanie pulled low over his head rushes past us without acknowledgement. Carly thrusts her foot in the door before it can properly shut.

'Looks like we're in,' she says.

Our feet pound against the concrete stairs. We reach the top floor. My heart is thumping but it's not just exertion making it race. It's fear.

'Marie?' I knock on the door but my gloves muffle the sound and so Carly raps with her knuckles instead while my fingers spider-crawl across the top of the door frame, hoping that it's still there.

It is.

'Spare key.' I slot it in the lock while Carly rolls her eyes and mutters about security.

The smell hits as soon as I open the door.

'Marie?' I call into the stale air and dust, somehow knowing that she won't answer.

There are only four rooms and it doesn't take us long to conclude she isn't in any of them.

'Something is wrong.' I know it deep in my gut. The mug I had left here two days ago is still on the coffee table. Still half-full of grey tea. The plate of biscuits I had carried through, stale.

Back in the kitchen I see the washing-up piled in the sink is exactly as it was, crusted baked beans line a saucepan, the frying pan coated with burned egg.

'It's as though she left after our visit and never came back.' Momentarily I cover my nose with my hand. The overflowing bin is pungent. 'I'm going to check the bedroom.'

I really don't know what I'm checking for as I yank open drawers and rifle through Marie's belongings. It feels as though I'm intruding as her underwear, black and lacy, spills out onto the floor; the sort of things I've never worn, even before I'd had Archie. There isn't a wardrobe, the room is too small for that, but there are clothes piled everywhere; on the rickety chair by the window, on the bed that clearly hasn't been slept in. It's impossible to know whether anything is missing. My stomach convulses as I realize I no longer know my twin well enough.

'I've found something!' Carly shouts from the kitchen. I hurry back through.

'Look.' She thrusts a notebook towards me. On the top page is scrawled in Marie's handwriting: *Stand-in for lead. Broken ankle. Leave tonight. Six-week run!* Circled around each sentence are flowers and hearts. I remember the way her schoolbooks were always covered in doodles.

'So she's just… gone?' I shake my head.

Carly shrugs. 'It seems that way.' She looks as upset as I feel.

'But it was only a couple of days ago we saw her. We got on so well. She promised she'd see more of us. Archie.'

'If she got a call for work we can't blame her for taking it. Remember her phone kept ringing while she was here? We know she needs the money.'

'She's left her washing-up. The mugs in the lounge.' I open the fridge. There's a half-empty carton of milk and some drying ham. Two cans of cherry Coke. The sight of the logo makes me feel ill. How can she bear to drink it? To remind herself? Or is she punishing herself? Still, punishing herself.

'Perhaps we all deserve to be punished,' Carly says quietly. I must have spoken my thoughts aloud.

I slam the fridge shut. Slam the door on my memories but the lid springs open when I am faced with fridge magnets of Mickey Mouse, Donald Duck, Pluto with his lolling tongue. We never did make it to Disneyland. Archie is longing to go but even if we could afford it, I'll never take him.

'Did you find anything else?' My gaze is drawn to the worktops. 'A four-day letter?'

'No but ours only came today. She must have left pretty soon after we did because she doesn't seem to have made any food since we were last here.'

'But she must have got one. It doesn't make sense.' I scan the room again. Nothing makes sense.

'Maybe he tried but the letterbox downstairs is taped up and he can't get upstairs without being buzzed in.'

'*He?*' It's not just my paranoia, she's thinking the same as me.

'She. They. Whoever,' Carly says unconvincingly.

'Don't you think it's odd she didn't let us know she was going?'

'She doesn't usually.'

'Shall I call Mum?'

The question surprises me as it pops out of my mouth and my surprise is mirrored on Carly's face. We don't really see or speak to Mum although Marie still does. A trauma is like a magnet. It has the ability to pull a family together or repel them apart. Our parents are divorced. I don't think any of us speak to Dad since he left Mum. They blame each other, blame themselves, blame us. Blame is a game we pass between us like a parcel and the one left holding it has to peel off another layer of the lie. Nobody wants to be left holding the truth.

Although I hadn't wanted to speak to Mum straight after Graham had rung me, this time is different. This time instead of imparting news I need answers. I hold my mobile out to Carly – there's no way I'm taking my gloves off in this filthy kitchen – and she swipes through my contacts and presses Mum's number. Neither of us are expecting her to answer, but she does, her voice tinny over the speaker.

'I know what you're going to say,' she says sharply. She hasn't even said hello.

'You don't,' I cut in quickly. She'll be expecting this to be one of my usual anniversary phone calls when I call her crying, sometimes drunk – the only time of year I allow myself to be out of control – asking her why she allowed us to be taken. I'd never, never let anyone take Archie. It's part of the job as a mother, isn't it? To protect. I don't meet Carly's eye. She doesn't know about my phone calls. I don't know if she makes them herself. 'I'm calling about Marie. Do you know where she is?'

'No.'

'Do you know the name of her current agent?'

'I thought she'd been dropped again?'

'Are there any friends you can think of that might—'

'She hasn't got any friends. You girls—' I hear the spark of flint as she lights a cigarette, a long inhale. She never smoked. *Before*. 'You girls used to be enough for each other.'

My eyes water as though I have smoke in them.

'I've got to go, Leah. I can't do this.' She cuts the call. I want to redial and ask her what she can't do. Cope with the prospect that again, she doesn't know where one of her daughters is.

Carly closes the keypad and hands my mobile back to me. 'Let's go.'

'I wanted Marie to know. That he's out there again.' Now there's six weeks until she comes back. She'll miss the anniversary. In a way I'm envious. Rather than putting the spare key back on top of the door, I slip it into my pocket as we leave.

Something draws my eye as I'm starting the car. I try to speak but I'm too frightened. Instead I clutch Carly's arm.

It's him. Through the teeming rain. The face of my nightmares on the opposite side of the road. He spots that I've noticed him, turns and rushes away. Climbs into a black car. The same sort of car I'd seen after I left the BP garage.

He was watching us go into Marie's flat.

Had he followed her?

Had he taken her?

Is he coming for us all?

I have to know. My foot squeezes the accelerator. I yank the wheel and we lurch into the traffic.

'Leah! Slow down.'

Instead I speed up. I can't risk losing him.

The blare of a horn. The screech of brakes. Carly screaming my name, 'Leah!'

The oncoming bus.

Chapter Seventeen

George

Now

George feels safe and warm, cocooned in loving arms and a warm quilt. The rain drums against the window of his sanctuary. His mobile buzzes angrily, skittering across the bedside cabinet.

Leah.

He's tempted to ignore it. He knows she'll be agonizing over the letter, wanting to go over it again and again. She always finds it impossible to let things go but then doesn't everyone to some extent? Clinging on to lives that don't quite fit any more. Living in a skin that feels like someone else's. The phone quietens. For a minute he worries that it wasn't Leah's anxieties that would have poured down the handset if he'd answered, but that something is wrong with Archie. He calls the nursery to check his son is okay.

He is.

George tries to summon up the feeling of a few moments ago when he felt both the protected and the protector. It had been a long time since he had felt that way, life with Leah was a one-way street. But sometimes the rescuer needed rescuing too. He tunes in to the pitter-patter against the glass. Feels her soft body curve against his. Her hand dipping low again. He closes his eyes and tries to relax. Even if Leah looked for him she couldn't find him. She has no idea of this address.

His mobile sounds again. It seems louder now. A swarm of angry bees, impossible to ignore.

'You'd better answer, it's *your wife*,' she says.

'Don't say *wife* like that, as though she's a stranger to you.' But perhaps that's the only way she can cope. Theirs is the ultimate betrayal.

He swings his legs out of the bed and sits up, turning his back on the crumpled sheets that smell of sex.

He says a cautious hello. He can feel his frown deepening, gouging lines in his forehead as Leah garbles down the phone while he bites his lip, keeping the words he really wants to say safe in his mouth.

'I'll be with you in fifteen minutes.' George cuts the call and reaches down to retrieve his boxers from the floor.

'She thinks he's back. That he sent the letter,' is all he says.

'Well, she would do. I said—'

'She's at the police station.'

He rapidly pulls on his clothes. Going to the police is something neither of them wanted. There are a lot of things neither of them wanted. A lot of things they crave, too.

How is he ever going to sort this whole mess out?

It's slipping out of his control.

Chapter Eighteen

Leah

Now

At the police station, my breath is wild and out of control. I fight to slow it down. Carly sits rigid beside me. We haven't spoken to each other since we got here. Since I nearly crashed the car trying to follow him. My hands twist in my lap. Already I cannot wait to rip these gloves off and scrunch them into the bin.

The foyer is light and bright but I see germs crawling everywhere. The dirt of a thousand crimes. The squalid remnants of scores of criminals marched through in metal cuffs and with steely stares. My chest tightens again. Sometimes I still feel my hands are tied, ankles bound. Eyes and mouth covered.

I cannot breathe.

Insects crawling between the layer of skin and denim that clads my thighs. In my ears, scurrying sounds.

I cannot gulp down air.

'Let's go,' whispers Carly but her voice is thin, buried under the scuttling legs that fill my mind. I brush at my arms, as though brushing away creatures, but when I look at the floor it is empty save from the dog-ends and ash despite the large NO SMOKING signs.

Oh, those warning signs can carry the threat of incomprehensible dangers.

Behind the desk the officer watches me, a worried expression on his face. 'You *can* come through—'

I shake my head. I cannot answer. The room starts to spin. I'm not going anywhere or saying any more than I already have until George is here.

Calm yourself.

Three things. Name three things.

Orange plastic chairs, tethered to the floor.

A notice stating abuse will not be tolerated.

Fluorescent light tubes stretching across the ceiling.

Calm.

When George finally arrives I launch myself into his arms. His suit is damp but I don't care as I press myself against it as though I can melt into him. Meld into one substance. One person. Somebody else. Somebody stronger.

We are led through to a small room and introduced to PC Godley, who offers us a drink. My throat is dry. I'm desperate for water but I won't allow myself to drink out of one of their cups. I swallow hard.

'Mrs Morgan, do you have the letter on you?'

'No. But I can bring it in. You can check it for fingerprints—'

'Unfortunately that's not as simple as it sounds.' He pulls a face. 'It's a question of resources and no crime has been committed.'

'It's a crime to threaten someone!'

'But *four days* isn't an actual threat.'

'It feels like one.'

'Look. I understand this is a difficult time for you. Twenty years is going to bring out the crackpots and true-crime addicts. You know from previous experience it's not unusual to get letters or 'ave things left on your step. Crank phone calls. I wouldn't expect anything less with the recent exposure. I bet you're plagued by journalists at the moment?'

I nod.

'I wouldn't put it past one of them to 'ave sent you the letter. Trying to drum up some new angle.'

'But Marie is *missing*.'

That's one irrefutable fact he can't ignore.

'But you found a notepad, in her house—'

'Flat.' Hasn't he been *listening*?

'Which implies she's been offered the lead in a play? And this was written in her handwriting?'

'Yes.'

'And it's not unusual for her to travel and not let you know when she's going, or where.'

'We're not as close as we should be.' Now I feel like I'm on trial – charged with being a terrible sister. 'But I *know* something is wrong.'

'I think Miss Sinclair has done the right thing, getting away. You should consider it too until the anniversary is over. No one will likely bother you then.'

'Until the next one,' I mutter.

'There's no evidence of anything untoward in Marie's flat? The front door was secure. No signs of struggle? No signal there's anything actually wrong. Other than your *feeling*?'

'I saw him,' I say quietly.

Nobody speaks.

'I saw him,' I say again, louder now. 'It was the second time and both times he was in a black car.'

'So you said earlier, Leah.' He turns to Carly. 'But you didn't see him, you say, Carly?'

'No,' Carly says. 'Sorry.' I don't know whether she is apologizing to him or to me. I had clutched Carly's arm, pointing in horror the second I'd spotted him, but rain was running down the windscreen like soup, stretching the outside world. Everything distorted. By the time my trembling fingers had managed to jab the key into the ignition and swish on the windscreen wipers he had disappeared. Then we had nearly been crushed by that bus when I'd tried to find him.

'I've read your notes about the last time he was released. What you claimed 'appened. What the medical professionals recommended for you.'

I close my eyes. I knew it would come to this. Then, they had believed me at first. They don't believe me now. With my history, they won't. It all feels so fruitless. My throat swells hot with frustration.

'Look,' George says firmly. I slip my hand into his. Grateful he, at least, is on my side. 'Can you tell us where he's living, put Leah's mind at rest that he's not in the area?' His questions shatter the faith I had that at least my husband would believe me. I can tell by the way Carly has shifted nervously in her seat since we got here – avoiding eye contact – that I haven't convinced her either.

'I'm sorry, I can't share that with you,' we are told.

Carly has driven my car home, so she can pick hers up and collect Archie from nursery. George is taking me to work. I hadn't wanted to go. The thought that he is out there – that he knows my address – makes my stomach spasm with nerves, but PC Godley's voice echoes loudly in my mind: *what the medical professionals recommended for you*. I was nearly sectioned. If it wasn't for George and Francesca fighting my corner, I probably would have been. It seemed awful enough at the time, but then I didn't have as much to lose. I didn't have Archie. If creating the illusion of a semblance of normality is what I need to do to keep my life together – my family together – then I will. But I *did* see him. I know I did.

Heart FM pelts out cheesy hits but I'm only half-listening until I hear a song so familiar my heart skips a beat.

'5, 6, 7, 8,' and it's not just a reminder; it seems like a message from Marie. But what?

George pulls up outside my office and cuts the engine. The radio is off but the song carries on playing in my head.

'I think it's the right thing for you to be at work. To take your mind off everything.'

I don't answer. In my mind I'm singing and dancing, one of the Sinclair Sisters when we were free. When we were happy.

George sighs before he gets out of the car. We walk into my office together.

'Hi.' Tash's smile freezes and then slips when I don't return it. 'Are you okay?'

'I'm fine.' I try to kiss George goodbye but he turns his head so my lips connect to his cheek rather than his lips.

I head towards my desk, wondering what I'll tell Tash, if anything – I know she'll worry. She's my closest friend, my only friend in the world. I was the youngest here until she joined us four days a week. At the Christmas party we had crossed the line between colleagues and friends after weeks of making small talk. We'd had watched – with mutual repulsion – as Barry from accounts sucked the face off Janet in sales.

'There must be a huge increase in births in the autumn after all the drunken office hook-ups the winter before,' Tash had shouted over Kylie Minogue wishing she was lucky. 'I can't think of anything worse than having something drooling at your tits.' She shuddered.

'Babies are—'

'I wasn't talking about a baby. I was talking about Barry.'

I'd laughed. It felt loud and unnatural, but good. It felt good.

'I never want kids,' Tash said unapologetically, not caring about being judged.

'Me neither. Obviously I've Archie and he's a complete joy but I couldn't go through it again.'

'Why not? Not that I blame you.'

It was refreshing to meet someone who didn't want a family. The mums at Archie's nursery were always obsessing over weaning and potty training and speculating on the perfect time to create a sibling. Tash… well, Tash just didn't care. Whether it was the alcohol, or the sharing of confidences, I had found myself blurting out, 'I worry too much that something will happen to him.'

'I think all mums worry about that, don't they? That's why I'm never going to reproduce. I'm too selfish.'

'They don't worry as much as me. But that's what being thrown into the back of a van and kidnapped does to you. It makes you paranoid.' My voice had been breezy, high with vodka but my palms were sweating. I didn't usually share but there was something about Tash I wanted to emulate. Her directness. Her fearlessness.

'Yeah, don't you just hate it when that happens at the end of a good night out? I reckon Janet's heading that way with Barry. What does he drive?' She'd cupped her hands around her mouth. 'Run, Janet, run!' Then turned to me, laughter dying on her lips as she studied my face. 'Fuck. You're not serious, are you? Kidnapped?'

I'd nodded. Took another swig of my drink. My eyes stung with tears. 'I don't know why I said that. I don't usually tell anyone.'

'Well… No… It's not really a conversation opener.'

'You really didn't know?' I had asked. Tash had shaken her head. 'You can't have grown up around here then. I'm the cautionary tale. The one parents wheel out to stop their kids breaking curfew. Running riot.'

'No, I'm not from here. I moved because I wanted to leave home and couldn't afford city rent. Anyway…'

I'd waited for her to say she was going to the loo, to the bar, to mingle – anything except stay here with me. But instead she'd asked, 'Do you want to talk about it?'

'No.' I drank deeply once more. 'I was eight.'

'Fuck' was all she said and that was refreshing. No false sympathy or platitudes. Just… fuck. It pretty much summed everything up.

'But I can't tell you anything else.'

'Of course. You don't have to.' Tash had drained her glass and pulled a hip flask from her bag.

'I was with my sisters. It was my fault, really. I hadn't shut the garden gate properly and our dog ran out. We chased him and there were two men and…' I inhaled deeply through my nose.

'Van?'

'Van.'

'Fuck.'

'So… I have… issues.' Then the music changed to S Club 7. Opening up had made me feel lighter. Wanting to reach for the stars. 'Dance?' I'd asked her.

'Yep.' Tash had stood and smoothed down her impossibly short skirt. 'Leah. What you've been through, it's—'

'Shitty?'

'Shitty. But—'

'Honestly, Tash. No more tonight.' Even then I'd known there would be other times. That she would become somebody I could talk to. A friend.

'Okay. But remember. However bad things have been – get – it could be worse.' She'd jerked her head towards Barry flailing his arms in the centre of the dance floor; an octopus being electrocuted.

'Yeah. At least I'm not Janet,' I'd said.

Over the past three years I've seen Tash frequently out of work. She's met both Marie and Carly.

'They don't have families of their own?' she had asked beforehand.

'No. It makes me really sad not be an aunt,' I'd shared. 'But I think the stress if Marie or Carly fell pregnant would drive me crazy. The thought of them going into hospital, putting themselves at risk. Not to mention the endless anxiety the thought of trying to protect another life would bring.'

'It makes you really ill, doesn't it? The worry?' She had understood I didn't experience concern in the way other people might. My fears are crushing. They have broken me before now. If it weren't for George…

We talk for hours, often at my house, because her flat is poky and cold. She and George get on well, although he generally disappears after dinner to 'leave you girls to your gossip'. But she hasn't come round these past few weeks.

I miss her.

I settle myself at my desk, squirting the surface with antibacterial cleaner and wiping it slowly, before cleaning my phone, although nobody uses the handset but me. When I've finished I cross the room to toss the cloth into the bin. Through the door I can see out into the reception area. George is still here, huddled by the door with Tash. They are both exchanging whispers, wearing the same harried expressions as though they are facing a mirror, not each other.

Hesitantly I step forward. Oddly it feels like I am intruding even though I know they are talking in hushed tones about me.

'We can't tell her. Not yet,' George says. 'She's too fragile.'

'It's so hard keeping secrets – I feel like a total bitch,' Tash says.

'You're anything but.' Briefly George lays his palm on her cheek.

'If we're not careful, she'll guess,' Tash says.

I hurry back to my desk, feeling sick. Again, PC Godley's words boom: *what the medical professionals recommended for you*. Are they planning an intervention in case I relapse? The thought of who they might make me see. Of where they might take me is terrifying.

When my best friend comes and takes her seat opposite me I turn my face to the wall to avoid her questions. So I don't ask any of my own.

Chapter Nineteen

Carly

Then

It was morning. The girls had been imprisoned for an entire night. Through the window Carly watched as dawn brushed its pink-and-orange fingers over the sky. The world was so beautiful, she had never realized. She wondered whether she would ever get to enjoy it again. Tears leaked from behind her eyes. She didn't wipe them away, not wanting to disturb the twins, who were still sleeping. Her heart hurt as she gazed at their pale faces. Their small hands, dark purple bruises staining their skin. Carly's own hands throbbed from banging them against the door. Her head pounded, gums ached where she'd dislodged a tooth. Her knees were sore, the cut on her cheek raw. Every single muscle in her body was as hard as one of Bruno's bones. The twins had taken up most of the room on the mattress and all night Carly had balanced on the edge, fearful of toppling onto the hard, dirty floor. The blanket wasn't quite large enough to stretch over them all. Carly had tucked it around the shoulders of the twins and lay shivering, not only with cold but with terror.

What were they going to do?

Think.

The sun rose higher, pushing through the bars and creating stripes on the drab floor as it burst thought the pastel colours, painting the sky a cornflower blue. The clown on the back of the door grinned.

'I fucking hate clowns,' Carly muttered.

'You said the "F" word,' Leah whispered.

'I fucking hate him too,' Marie said.

'I didn't know you were both awake.' Carly was mortified. She already thought she'd be blamed for getting them into this mess. If the twins started swearing at eight years old she'd be in even more trouble. She rose to her feet. Stalked around the room again and again. Ten paces long, turn. Six paces wide, turn.

Think.

Panic clutched at Carly as she inhaled the stifling air. They couldn't stay in here another day. Another night.

Ten paces, turn. Six paces, turn.

Let-us-out. Let-us-out. Let-us-out.

The words were inside Carly's head, inside her mouth, inside the room.

'Let us out. Let us out. Let us out,' she yelled as she pelted towards the door. All three sisters began thumping to be free again. Screaming. Fists pounding against the clown's face. His nose. His mouth. His eyes.

It didn't take long before they tired. Weak from lack of food. From the surges of adrenaline that rushed through their veins before ebbing away.

'My tummy hurts.' Leah slunk back to the mattress.

'Mine too,' Marie joined her twin.

'It's because we're hungry.' Carly dully made her way over to the box. Snaps and Coke for breakfast. They were running low on food. Surely the men would come back today. The thought was terrifying and reassuring in equal measure. She was sure they'd find out why they had been snatched but did she really want to know? There was a cruelty to Moustache she could sense. He was like Stephen at school who bullied the younger kids, stealing their lunch and their branded sports kit. Punching them in the stomach for fun. Stephen's friends hung around him because they were intimidated. Was that why Doc was with Moustache? She thought he had a gentle side. The softness of the blanket, the teddy bear with his fluffy coat and rounded tummy, which made him 'totally cuddleable', according to Leah.

If Doc came on his own they might have a chance. She could, perhaps, talk him into letting them go. Carly had watched her mum persuade Dad to do things he didn't want to do with the right words, a smile. *You twist me round your little finger*, he would say. Could she do that to Doc?

If he comes without Moustache.

If.

If.

If.

In the meantime, Carly scanned the room again; they were stuck. Trapped. Again, panic swooped low, clutching Carly around the throat. There wasn't enough air in the room. She *had* to get them out. Her feet tingled as she clumped around the room. Examining every single millimetre of the wall for the umpteenth time. Running her hands over the cold, slimy surface, feeling for something under the graffiti. A hidden exit. A loose brick.

Something.

There was nothing. Carly stared up at the ceiling until her neck ached. Why wasn't there a hatch, an air vent?

Anything.

'I need to wee, Carly,' Leah said in a small voice.

Carly jerked her head towards the corner, averting her eyes, unfairly cross with Leah. The stench in the room was already unbearable.

She couldn't breathe.

Ten paces, turn. Six paces, turn. A lion in a cage.

Waiting.

Waiting.

Waiting.

Time ticked past painfully slowly. Intermittently, Carly had doled out sweets. They had hardly any food left, and only one can of Coke that they were sharing.

'Small sips only,' Carly had warned. Although hunger pangs cramped her stomach, she knew they could survive days without food. Not without any liquid, though. It was only the second time that day she had needed to wee and her urine stank – she was becoming dehydrated.

Carly pulled up her pants and turned around to see the telltale bulge of a blackcurrant liquorice sweet in Marie's cheek. 'For God's sake. I *told* you not to have any more.'

'I'm starving,' Marie said.

'We're all starving. Did you *steal* a sweet too, Leah?' Carly spat out the word *steal* like it was the worst thing you could do and she thought perhaps stealing was. Not sweets though, but children.

Leah shook her head. Carly believed her, she was always the one who followed rules. Horrified when she had caught Carly forging Mum's signature on notes so she could get out of doing PE.

Carly gave Leah a sweet, it was only fair. She hesitated before she took the last one for herself, untwisting the purple wrapper, placing the hard shell of blackcurrant that would soften into liquid on her tongue. 'God, I'm so sick of these. I'd kill for a Big Mac.'

'Ooh, Carly. You have to broaden your palate.' Marie perfectly imitated her father. Carly clutched at the chance of a moment of lightness.

'Remember when Dad ordered scallops for me in the Maldives and I thought it was some sort of berry on top but it was caviar?' She pulled a face.

'Fish eggs!' Marie squealed. 'You ate the actual eggs of an actual fish!'

'You can't talk. What about the frogs' legs you had in Cannes?'

'I liked them.' Marie rubbed her tummy. 'They tasted just like chicken. Don't you wish you'd tried them, Carly?'

Since her mum had married her stepdad, holidays in damp, rented caravans and chicken nuggets for tea had been replaced with trips to Monaco and roasted game. Carly was grateful her mum was happy and her new dad was so generous – she'd never even met her biological dad, but though her stepdad treated Carly exactly the same as his biological daughters, sometimes she missed the old days. She'd only been small but she remembers she and Mum eating dinner with their fingers in front of *The Simpsons*, just the two of them. Her mum had never said as much but Carly thought she missed those days too. Sometimes when her stepdad was out and the twins were in bed she would wink at Carly and dig out a bag of chicken nuggets and chips she had hidden at the bottom of the freezer.

She would shake them onto a baking tray and while they were cooking Carly would retrieve the bottle of ketchup hidden at the back of the fridge and squirt it into bowls. They would snuggle up on the sofa, their hands dipping chips into the red sauce and Carly thought sometimes that was when she was happiest. It wasn't that she didn't love her sisters, because she did, but the ritual was something that was just hers and Mum's. TV and junk food in their pyjamas. She preferred it more than dressing up and eating the miniature meals she had tried at Michelin-starred restaurants. The twins loved all the fancy food but then they'd been brought up on it. Even at their tender age the twins could sit without fidgeting through a five-course meal, always using the right cutlery.

'Carly!' Marie nudged her and Carly realized she hadn't replied. 'I *said*, do you wish you'd tried frogs' legs? They tasted like chicken.'

'I'll tell you what tastes like chicken,' Carly said.

'What?'

'You! Carly pounced on her sister and raised Marie's arm to her mouth, pretending to chew on it like Bruno would a squeaky toy. Leah squealed and dived on Carly, tugging at her until Carly turned her attention to Leah, tickling her until she screeched with laughter that bounced off the walls and returned to their ears loud and shrill.

'You taste like poo,' Marie said to Carly, a wicked glint in her eye. She sprang to her feet and Carly played along, chasing her around the room, dividing her attention between the twins, swiping at both, but purposefully catching neither.

'Stop!' Carly held up her hand. Marie launched herself at Carly's legs, still in the game.

'Shhh.' Carly was deadly serious. 'Do you hear something?'

An engine.

A door slamming.

Footsteps.

Someone was coming.

Oh God. *Someone* was coming.

Was it help or was it *them*?

Fruitlessly Carly looked around for somewhere to hide the girls. Why had they been talking about bloody food when they could have been building a barricade from the rubbish and mattress. Something to shield them from immediate view. In her mind she imagined Moustache stalking around one side of their hiding place while they crawled out from the other end, ran through the open door...

'Carly, I'm scare—'

'Shhh.'

From outside a voice, barely decipherable.

Fear pin-pricked Carly's skin.

The *pound-pound-pound* of boots on concrete.

A muttered, 'I'll take care of it.'

Them. It was *them*.

Terror rose in Carly's throat as she listened to them growing closer and closer.

And then...

The sound of three bolts sliding open.

Chapter Twenty

Leah

Now

Archie and I eat alone. George has another meeting. Am I being selfish by not doing the TV interview? The money would mean George wouldn't have to be out all hours but the thought of exposing myself in front of viewers for cash seems sordid and dirty. Not much of a step up from one of the webcam channels Tash caught Barry watching at work, one hand stuffed down his trousers, when he thought the office was empty.

'Do you have to go out tonight?' I ask.

George hesitates. I can see he is torn.

'Sorry,' I try to smile. 'You go. I'm just worried about Marie and—'

'Marie will be fine. It's not as though she hasn't disappeared before. She's resourceful. Please don't worry about her, Leah.' He brushes his lips against mine. 'Have you made an appointment with Francesca yet?'

'No. But I will. I know I'm not… easy again. But it's not an easy time.'

'I know.' He shrugged on his coat. 'I'll try not to be too late.'

After I've bathed Archie and put him to bed I sit on the landing outside his bedroom, spine pressed against the cold wall, listening to him chattering to his soft toys. Telling them that it will be his birthday soon and he'll be five.

'I'll be almost a grown-up but I'll still cuddle you,' he says.

Loneliness engulfs me at the thought of my baby growing, slipping away. Archie will be starting school next September and this only seems a step away from him leaving home. I pad downstairs. The lounge is too quiet and so I settle myself in the kitchen with a coffee, the soft hum of the fridge company of sorts. I'm edgy. It's natural I will be, but I know there's more to my inner turmoil than anniversary anxiety.

Marie.

Again, I try her mobile. Again, I leave a message.

Where is she? Something is wrong.

I call Tash, wanting to talk everything through with someone impartial. Carly's as emotional as I am at the moment.

Tash doesn't answer.

I have to try and find Marie.

Carrying my coffee, I make my way into George's office. His computer glows as I shift the mouse, Google already loaded. I open a new tab and search for theatres. For the next couple of hours I ring around, asking if they have a production running for the next six weeks. If they know of an actress who has broken her ankle. If they've heard of Marie.

Drawing a blank, I try drama companies next and although I reach a few people who know Marie, who have worked with her in the past, none of them know where she is right now.

Despite the police believing she's gone on tour, I'm not convinced. There is somewhere I could go for answers. The thought leaves a dragging feeling in my stomach but tomorrow, however anxious it makes me, I have to try.

It's late. My eyes are stinging. I close the webpage and then decide to shut the computer down altogether. It's gone eleven and George won't be working any more tonight. One by one I close the tabs, until I stumble across something that shakes me to my core.

George.

Why has he been searching for *this*?

A lump rises in my throat. I reach out and touch the screen lightly with two fingers as though I am touching his face.

As though I am asking why he has betrayed me.

Chapter Twenty-One

George

Now

George's conscience pricks at him. He can't sleep. Leah was already in bed when he crept through the door at eleven thirty, silent and ashamed. Next to him she breathes slowly and evenly. It's not her usual sleep pattern; there are no whimpers, no tossing and turning, and he wonders if she's faking it.

He wonders if everyone is faking something.

This morning, after he had dropped Leah at work following the burning shame of sitting in front of police officers who knew her history, he had gone home and googled. Read the results with a heavy heart. He was so engrossed in the things he had found out, he was running late for his next meeting so on a whim he decided to skip it and instead had called in to Francesca's clinic. Had sat in her waiting area to catch her between appointments. She was surprised to see him.

'Sorry, this will only take five minutes,' he had said apologetically. 'It's important.'

She had led him into her office. He didn't take a seat.

'I think I should action a Power of Attorney,' he had blurted out.

Francesca's face had fallen into shock. 'What's brought this on?'

'Leah's relapsing. She says she's going to make an appointment to see you but I don't think she has?' George asked.

'I can't disclose patient details, George. You know that.'

'But would you support me? Be prepared to say Leah has diminished mental capacity?'

'How can I possibly say that? I haven't assessed her.'

'But you know her really well. You know us both. You remember what happened the last time?'

'Of course I do. Who could forget that but—'

'She's heading the same way again. I'm sorry to suddenly spring this on you. I've only just looked into it and I was passing and... well. Cards on the table. I'm scared. Leah was so close to being sectioned before and where would that have left me, financially? I'd have had to cut down on work to look after Archie and I wouldn't have been able to access Leah's royalties or her accounts. Not to mention the fact the house is in her name.'

'But she wasn't sectioned,' Francesca had said. 'We uncovered the reason behind her behaviour and...'

'I know.' George ran his hand over his chin. 'But I'm beginning to wonder whether she would have been better off... Whether she might be better off...'

'George, I don't like where this conversation is going. I can't condone you considering institutionalizing your wife. Besides, she's no longer a patient of mine. What you're asking is unethical and—'

'Sorry... it's just the anniversary.' George felt hot. Too hot. He loosened his tie and undid his top button. 'It's Archie I'm thinking of, that's all.'

‘My next patient is waiting.’ Francesca had said quietly. George had slunk back to his car.

He’s never going to be able to sleep. George thumps his pillow. Leah mutters and rolls over.

He wants to shake her awake. Unburden himself.

‘It’s so hard keeping secrets,’ Tash had tearfully said, earlier.

He reaches for his mobile and texts her.

It’s hard for me too x

Chapter Twenty-Two

Leah

Now

I'm thinking of getting up and making Archie's breakfast when he bursts into my bedroom and cannonballs himself onto our bed. George heads into the bathroom. The sound of him sliding the bolt across the door is akin to the sound of someone running their fingernails down a blackboard. I don't know why he's started locking it. There's only the three of us in the house. I hear the spurt of water from the shower, the gurgle of the pipes. The quiet tones of his voice; I wonder who he is talking to this early but I don't think about it for long because Archie says, 'Mummy! Can I wear my fire engine socks today? I like the blue Power Ranger best. When are we going to have green jelly again?'

'When am I going to get a good-morning kiss?' I tickle him in the ribs and he shrieks as he kicks his pyjama-clad legs, his hair tousled with sleep and dreams.

My legs feel leaden as I cross to the door, Archie's arms wrapped around my neck as I carry him like a baby monkey. I'd tossed and turned much of last night as beside me George had done the same. I've almost made my mind up that I won't go into work today but when I reach the bottom of the stairs there's another envelope on the mat. I set Archie down. He zooms into the kitchen, his arms stretched sideways as he makes the noise of a plane.

I scoop the letter from the mat. Before I even open it, I know what it's going to say.

Three days.

I peep out from behind the lounge curtain into the street but it's empty. Dull. The morning sky grey and bulging with cloud. Suddenly home alone is the last place I want to be. I want Archie to be safe at nursery behind the locked gate and the door with the access code. I want to be in my office among people, outside of this cul de sac, outside of my own head.

My phone rings – Carly's photo flashes up. It was taken during a picnic at the park with Archie. She's smiling as she watches him kick a ball. Her skin is tanned – it's the only time the faint scar on her cheek from the cut she sustained in the van is visible.

'I've got another letter,' she says as soon as I pick up.

'Me too.'

'What should we do?'

'I don't see what we can do. If we go back to the police they'll say it's some crackpot or journalist again.'

'Are you going to work?'

'Yes. Are you okay to collect Archie?'

'Yes. Leah…' Her shallow breaths drift down the line. The catch of tears in her voice. 'We have to stay strong. It will all be over soon.' She's a million miles away from the image on my phone of the laughing girl. Almost as though fate cruelly let me glimpse into the life she could have had.

'Three days,' I say grimly before I hang up.

*

Tash is already at her desk. As soon as I settle into my seat she crosses the room. 'The photocopier is buggered. I've rung the repair company and somebody will come out today.'

'Okay.' I stifle a yawn.

'And Janet has called in sick so there aren't any morning papers.' Lionel, my boss, still provides a selection of newspapers for his staff. He hasn't quite grasped yet that we can all read the news online.

'Did you get another letter?' She perches on the edge of my desk. I make a mental note to disinfect it again when she stands up.

'How do you know about the letters?' I hadn't spoken to her much yesterday. I hadn't spoken to anyone much.

'George told me yesterday.'

'What else did George tell you?' I can't help snapping, recalling the conversation I had overheard. My suspicion he might want to section me.

'Leah! George asked me to keep an eye on you, that's all.'

'Sorry.' I quickly gather myself. 'I would have told you about the letter but George thinks a journalist must have sent it to stir things up, but if he's talked to you he must believe that—'

'He didn't give the impression you're in any danger.' She second-guesses what I'm thinking. 'More that he's worried about you. We both are. We know how… fraught you become this time of year and twenty years is quite a big deal.'

'It'll be over soon,' I say.

'Three days.'

I flash her a look. 'Why did you say that?'

'Because there are only three days until the anniversary, aren't there?'

'God, sorry. Yes. I got another letter that said *three days*. It's rattled me but I'm okay.' I force a brief, tight smile. 'They'll keep on coming until the anniversary, I suppose.' I keep my voice low, not wanting anyone else to hear. 'You haven't told anyone else about the letter?'

'Of course not. The only gossip here is Barry and Janet and the amount of time they spend in the stationery cupboard. You must be going… I've noticed…' Tash raises her hands and wiggles her fingers.

'It's eczema.' I place my gloved hands on my lap, out of sight under my desk.

'You don't need to bullshit me, Leah,' she says.

'I know.' This time my smile comes naturally. 'Let's have a night out next week when all this is over.'

'I'm not sure I can afford it.' Tash fiddles with a button. After a beat she asks, 'Have you decided what you're going to do about Lionel's offer? It's just that if you don't want the extra hours I could really use them.'

'I thought you liked having Fridays off?'

'I did. I do. I could just use the extra cash right now.'

'Is everything okay?' She looks pale. Dark rings under her eyes. I can't remember the last time she came over to dinner. It's not easy to talk in this open-plan office.

'I'm fine,' she says.

'Good. Look, sorry, but I think I might have to take those extra hours.' I feel awful but I was here before her. 'George's business isn't going so well and—'

'I thought you'd be raking it in with your book?' She looks shocked as the words blurt from her lips. 'I didn't mean… God, sorry. I thought George was stressed yesterday but I assumed…'

'You thought it was just because of me?' I shake my head. 'It's probably a mixture of everything.'

My phone rings, it's Lionel.

I lift the receiver, and hold it slightly away from my head, taking care not to let the plastic touch my ear or mouth.

After a brief conversation I put the handset back in the cradle three times before I let it go. 'I need to go out and run a few errands.' I open my drawer and pull out the company's bank card. 'Want anything, Tash?'

'You could pick up the newspapers while you're out and a Mars bar… two Mars bars. I've already eaten my lunch and it's only ten thirty.'

I'm jittery while I'm out. Constantly looking over my shoulder, worried I'm being followed. I take a few extra minutes to ring the nursery and make sure Archie is okay, before I ring Carly and double-check she's picking him up although she hasn't once let me down.

In the newsagent's I pick up a couple of papers and flick through them, making sure there's no mention of me. There isn't this time but I know in three days there will be.

Three days.

'There's no stories on you girls yet this year,' the elderly man behind the counter tells me as I'm paying. 'I remember when it happened I didn't believe it. I thought, *this is a safe place. Who'd come to our small town and do something like that?* Now it's everywhere, terrorism, knife crime. I sell the newspapers but most days I wish I could bloody burn them. I said to our Joan—'

'I've got to go.' I scoop up my purchases and hurry from the shop.

Back in the office I tuck the bank card back in my drawer and take the papers into the staffroom. The stench hits me before I enter the room.

Grease.

Salt and vinegar.

The thought of fish and chips makes my stomach roil, I can't even walk past a chippy. I'm furious. We have a 'no hot food' policy at work. I grip the papers in my hand, ready to toss them onto the table but on the formica top is the remnants of somebody's lunch. The white paper bag stained with oil, with a few crispy batter bits still inside. The bag is resting on creased sheets of yellowing newspaper, the way chips used to be wrapped. I don't want to touch it but I can't leave it there where it will breed bacteria, attract flies. I'm about to scrunch up the newspaper, when I see it.

The photo.

Carly, Marie and I the day we left the police station after being missing for days. Our parents' faces taut and worried as they tried to shield us from the photographers. THE SINCLAIR SISTERS FOUND. I feel I might faint. The heady smell of the chips and the onslaught of memories making me dizzy, I force myself to take a closer look. It's dated almost twenty years ago. Under the first sheet is another story. First kidnapper found dead, the second still at large.

Who has done this?

I scrunch the whole lot together and dump them in the bin.

Who has done this?

I run out of the kitchen, and bump into something hard and solid.

Someone.

I take in the tool box in his hand. My eyes rise to find the PHOTOCOPY REPAIR badge on his boiler suit. And finally his face.

His face.

He's found me. Come for me. I knew that he would but shock still torrents through me.

'Please…' I back away, holding my hands up to protect myself. 'Please…' I say again as he steps forward. My throat tightens. I can't say anything else. Can't scream. Instead, I turn and run. I'm back in the past running, running, running for my life.

Stupidly, I'm heading deeper into the building, away from the front door. My feet thudding against the hessian carpet. I can't feel my body properly. I feel like I'm floating. Should I stop and ring the police? I round the corner and steal a glance behind me. I can't see him.

But that doesn't mean he isn't coming.

To my left is the toilets. I slam through the door to the Ladies, praying he won't risk following me here.

This time it is me sliding the bolt across the cubicle door.

Chapter Twenty-Three

Carly

Then

The second Carly heard the bolts slide open on the other side of the door she had ushered the twins behind her and stood, legs splayed, hands ready to fight.

The door remained shut. The clown laughing at them.

Think.

'Yeah, I know.' The voice, Doc's, spoke again.

A pause.

Carly glared at the clown. Hatred curdling in her stomach.

'I said I'll fucking take care of it,' Doc growled.

Silence.

Carly realized he must be on the phone. Moustache wasn't with him but what had Doc promised to take care of?

Oh God, she was so, so scared. Her legs barely supported her.

The clown flashed her one last grin as the door began to swing open. Doc stalked inside. Carly wondered if he could hear the galloping of her heart. Smell the sourness of the girls' urine in the corner. Her humiliation made her brave.

'What do you want?' she demanded of him, knowing that

if it were her sisters he had come for she would die before she let him take them.

'I've brought you some things.' He held up a white plastic bag before setting it down.

'I don't mean now, I mean why are we here?'

'There's some more of those crisps and…'

'We don't *want* fucking crisps.' Carly was furious. 'We want to go home. We want proper food. We're starving. A hot meal. The girls are only eight.'

'My teacher said we need vitamins and minerals to grow,' Marie said.

'LET US GO!' The words rocketed through Carly's throat, leaving a burning sensation in their wake. Doc turned to leave.

You twist me around your little finger, her stepdad had said to her mum. She tried a different tack.

'Please. I know…' she began gently. Waiting until Doc faced her before she spoke again. 'I know you're a good man. I can tell. You don't want to hurt us.' It took gargantuan effort for Carly to smile. 'My parents have money. Lots of it—'

'I can't let you go—'

'But we're children.' Carly kept her voice soft. 'You don't want to scare children, do you? I can tell—'

'Look. Don't be scared. It'll be okay, I promise. I'll see what I can do about proper food.'

He was softening. She had seen it in her dad before her mum gave one last push for the thing that she wanted.

'We won't tell anyone if you let us go. You're kind. I can tell,' another forced smile. 'You're not like that other horrible man—'

In a flash Doc dropped the bag onto the floor and left, slamming the door behind him.

‘No!’ Carly screamed, hurtling across the room as fast as she could. ‘Don’t leave us!’

But he had.

‘Come back. Come back.’ The girls screamed, hammering on the door until Carly felt the skin on her hands split, blood trickling down her wrists, her forearms.

‘Stop,’ she told the girls. ‘He isn’t coming back.’ She felt oddly numb, not quite able to process she had asked an adult for help and he had walked away. At a loss as to know what else to do, she crouched and looked inside the carrier bag he had left.

Again Spicy Tomato Snaps, bags of blackcurrant liquorice sweets, cans of cherry Coke. Even Marie, who was always particularly fond of fizzy drinks and snacks, shook her head.

‘Isn’t there any water?’ she whined. At home Mum could never get Marie to drink water, she was obsessed with sweet cordials and fresh juices. Fizzy drinks.

‘No,’ Carly said. ‘I’ll ask him to bring some bottles next time he comes.’

‘What if he never comes back?’ Leah asked.

Carly handed her a bag of crisps.

Hours passed.

‘I said I’ll fucking take care of it,’ Doc had said.

It?

Their ransom? Arranging to sell them.

It?

Killing them? Was he going to… No! She wouldn’t let her mind go there. Dean Malden was supposed to be the first boy to touch her and the girls were babies.

It? It? It?

She turned over theories while the clown laughed at her.

I know. He said. I know what's going to happen to you.

Carly was exhausted from thinking. From feeling.

Lethargically she trudged around the room. Too restless to sit. Too weary to tug at the bars at the window. Too weak to rattle the door handle.

Too tired to scream.

To shout.

To cry.

'Shall we do some dancing?' Marie asked. Carly felt ashamed. She should be the one trying to lift the mood.

'I'm too hungry to dance.' Leah sucked her thumb.

'What about... What about "I spy"?' Carly cast her eyes around the room. *P is for prison.* 'Or...'

'I'll tell us a story.' Marie patted the mattress in between her and Leah. Carly padded over to them and lay in the space on her back. The twins nestled into her.

'Once upon a time,' Marie began in the voice she used for school plays, 'there were three sisters who found themselves in terrible danger. They—'

'The sisters are us, aren't they?' asked Leah.

'I'm not telling. If you keep interrupting I'll stop.'

'Sorry.'

'Anyway, they came face to face with two dragons and they could have run away but they knew they had to make their family proud of them so they were brave and...'

Daylight was fading. Sleep swiped for Carly and she kept pushing it away, only hearing fragments of Marie's tale of triumph where somehow the girls turned into princesses and won medals for courage. Eventually Marie's voice grew smaller, her breathing deeper until at last they all slept.

Carly was disorientated as she woke to half light, unsure whether it was the same day. Although her arms were numb, she lay still, not wanting to wake the girls either side of her who were using her shoulders for pillows. She gazed out of the window until she was certain the sun was rising, not setting.

They had been here another night.

A solid mass of melancholy lodged in her throat. What if they really were here forever? There was no prince riding on a white charger to rescue them but there had to be people looking for them. Their parents. The police. Maybe even Dean Malden. Why were they taking so long to find them?

A tear trickled down Carly's cheek. She turned her head to the side, away from her sisters, and then she saw it, by the door.

A blue carrier bag.

It definitely hadn't been there before.

Somebody had been in the room. The thought that the men might have stood over them while they were deep in exhausted sleep was chilling. She could have woken to find one of the twins missing. Both of them missing.

Why hadn't she used the rubbish to build some sort of early warning signal by the entrance so anyone coming into the room would dislodge it and alert the girls to their presence? She must do that before tonight. She was already resigned to the fact they wouldn't be getting out of here.

She tried to summon up some hope but she felt oddly detached as though this was all some weird dream and she was watching herself from high above, staring at the bag, while the clown stared at her.

She was so thirsty.

There could be water in the bag.

Slowly, she inched out from between the girls. Crawled over to the door. She reached inside the bag and pulled out a tightly wrapped package, grease stains seeping through white paper. A faint smell she recognized.

'Chips?' She looked questioningly at the clown. He didn't answer. She was so parched her tongue was thick. Perhaps he hadn't heard her. 'Chips?' she said again, cautiously unravelling the paper, staring in confusion at the thick slabs of potatoes until they danced in front of her eyes. She popped one onto her tongue.

Cold.

Greasy.

Delicious.

'Girls! Wake up.' Carly was delirious as she unwrapped the rest of food; a sausage, a huge piece of cod, a pie. The twins stumbled over to her, rubbing sleep from their eyes. They didn't carry their breakfast back over to the mattress. They didn't talk. Instead, they squatted among the dust and the rubble and the broken glass, and shovelled food into their mouths with both hands, looking fearfully around them as they chewed, half-expecting someone to burst in and take it away.

After eating, Carly dozed again. Waking to the sound of Marie crying.

'I don't feel very well.' She splayed her hands over her stretched stomach.

'You'll be okay.' Carly yawned, soothing her sister's hot forehead with her fingertips, her tangled fringe damp.

Although her skin was slick she was shivering. Carly covered her with the blanket and wished she had a bottle of water. Suddenly, violently, Marie began to vomit, coating the blanket, the mattress, herself. She retched again and again.

'It's okay.' Carly looked around for something to mop up the mess with but anything absorbent they had already used for their makeshift toilet in the corner. 'It's probably the same bug that kept you off school with stomach ache.'

'I don't think it's that.' Marie shook her head.

'Well, perhaps you ate your food too quickly. It'll pass.'

'Maybe it was poisoned,' Leah whispered.

'It wasn't poisoned,' Carly said.

'How do you know? Marie's the only one who ate sausage.'

'It definitely wasn't poisoned.' Carly tried to keep the doubt and the worry out of her voice. She glanced frantically at the clown. The graffiti on the wall.

You're going to die.

'Carly…' Marie didn't often cry.

'Shh. The food was fine. It could be anything making you ill. The shock of eating so much, your tummy isn't used to it.' Carly felt her own stomach cramping as they'd eaten. 'Eating with dirty fingers.'

'It's the germs.' Leah looked around fearfully. 'You said the germs would make us ill. You said the germs could *kill* us.' She frantically wiped her hands over her skirt as though dislodging an army of invisible insects.

'It's fine. Marie is fine, just a little sick. Tell Leah a random fact, Marie.' Marie retained snippets of useless information, recalling them the way she did at home would make her feel better and cheer Leah up, Carly was sure. She waited for Marie to speak.

Kangaroos can't walk backwards.

You fart on average fourteen times a day.

Hippopotamus milk is pink.

But she didn't. Carly searched through her memory banks for something she could share.

'Hey! Did you know that fingernails grow quicker when you're cold?' Sometimes Carly painted the twins' nails a frosted pink.

'Then I guess our nails will get really, really long here.' Leah drew her knees up to her chest. 'If no one finds us our nails might fill the room.'

Carly knew she'd picked the wrong fact. 'But they'd be good for picking your nose!' She waited for one of the twins to say something gruesome about accidentally spearing your brain and pulling it out through your nostrils, but they didn't.

Carly fell into silence, using the blanket to clean up as best she could but the mattress was a mess.

Everything was a mess.

It was difficult to gauge the time. Outside, the rain hammered down. The sky was a dark grey. There was a sense of foreboding in the air.

'Are you feeling any better?' Carly pressed the back of her hand against Marie's forehead, the way her mother did to her when she was ill. She wasn't quite sure what she was feeling for – how hot was too hot? Mum always said it was as good an indicator for a fever as putting the thin tube of mercury under your tongue. 'Because Mum is literally in the title, ther-mom-meter,' she would laugh. Carly wished she were here. She'd know what to do.

'No. I'm… I'm sorry, Carly.'

Carly dropped her hand. If Marie did have a temperature there was no medicine to give her. 'It's not your fault.'

'It's all so awful. I…' Marie closed her eyes.

'You can't help it.'

'Carly, I…' Marie trailed off as she began to throw up again. Her face was green.

'Shhh.' Carly didn't know what to say to make her feel better. Carly had vomit over her fingers, her own mouth flooding with saliva at the smell. She looked hopelessly around the room for anything that might help her but there was nothing.

She had never felt more helpless.

'Help!' she screamed. 'We need help!' She needed a grown-up. She needed her mum. Her stepdad.

Marie stopped vomiting.

Stopped crying.

Talking.

Her stillness, her silence was even more terrifying.

The girls huddled together. *Help*, Carly called again but it was only in her head. Nobody was coming.

Nobody.

All she had was the clown and a wall of scrawled words.

You're going to die.

Panic shook her hard.

They were *all* going to die.

A noise?

Again the sound of sliding bolts. This time Carly didn't stand. There seemed little point. Her energy had gone, her fight too.

'I've brought something that will help you,' Doc said as soon as he stepped into the room.

Chapter Twenty-Four

Leah

Now

The photocopier repair man… it's *him*.

Panic slams into me. My chest so tight I cannot cry.

I am so, so scared.

Calm yourself.

Three things but there's nothing to see in this toilet cubicle.

My breath comes too quickly. I don't want to touch anything but dizziness forces me to stretch out my hands and steady myself against the walls.

Calm yourself.

The flush handle.

Cistern.

The PLEASE WASH YOUR HANDS poster on the back of the door

Calm.

But calm is a million miles away. I'm trapped here in this small space with *him* outside the door.

Again.

The contents of my stomach rise, splattering the bowl of the loo. The smell takes me back until I am kneeling in the filth of that dirty room, terrified my twin was going to die. Terror pulses deep in my gut. I've touched the toilet seat with my gloved fingers, my sleeves. My skirt has brushed the tile floor. I want to rip off my clothes and burn them. Scrub my skin until it's pink and raw.

The door swings open. I press my hands over my mouth to suppress my scream before I remember where my hands were resting just seconds before. Revulsion strokes me with its filthy fingers.

I whimper.

'Leah?'

I can't answer. I'm frozen.

'Leah? Please, what's going on? Jesus, have you chucked up? Christ, the smell is making me gag.' I hear Tash retch.

Slowly I stand, brushing the germs from my knees, invisible insects from my skin.

Scuttling. Scuttling.

The floor of the cubicle sharply shifts. I stumble.

'You'd better let me in before I kick this door down and don't think that I can't. It's me or Jim the rep and he needs a new hip.'

That sliding bolt. I can't stop shaking.

'Is he gone?' I whisper.

'Who, Jim—'

'The photocopy guy?'

'Yes. Why—'

I push past her. Grab my bag and coat.

Run.

The streets are busy. I see him everywhere, walking into the chemist, punching numbers into the cash point, loafing at the bus stop.

I've left my car behind, knowing it will be quicker on foot, knowing that parking would be a problem when I get there, but without its steely casing and locking doors, I feel vulnerable.

At last I hare into the right street. Thunder up the steps and push against the front door. It's locked.

'Francesca!' I bang on the door, not caring if she's with another patient. 'Francesca!'

It's been so long since I've been here, I wonder if she still rents this as office space but the plaque by the doorbell tells me she does. She might have a day off. I pull out my mobile to see if I can find her home address online when I hear footsteps behind me. I swing around. It's Francesca and for a second I am so relieved I can't speak.

'Leah?' She looks wary, afraid. I must appear as though I've gone mad. Sweat streaming down my forehead, my hair wild and cheeks burning.

'Please help me,' I rasp. With one last worried glance over her shoulder, she ushers me inside.

While Francesca makes tea we both know I won't drink as I haven't handed her my own mug, I wash my hands three times in the bathroom before shaking them dry and pulling on a fresh pair of gloves. My clothes feel vile, my skin filthy, but it's the best I can do for now.

'It's back,' I say as soon as she returns to the room.

'Your contamination OCD?' Her eyes flicker to my gloves.

'All of it.'

She gives a sharp intake of breath.

'Look, Leah, I don't know if I'm best placed to treat you any more.'

'It's back.'

'I can recommend a colleague—'

'It's back,' I say again, before I follow up with a 'please' filled with desperation. 'I know I stopped coming and I ignored all of your messages asking me why. I'm sorry but I was feeling so good. I wasn't even wearing the gloves any more. It was silly to stop treatment and ignore you but... but I thought it was over and I wanted to put everything behind me – but now...' my voice breaks, 'he's out.'

'And you think you've seen him?'

'Yes.'

'And have you?'

I swallow hard and think carefully about my answer. 'I don't know... It *felt* real...'

Francesca sips her tea. The clock ticks.

And as I wait for her answer, I remember.

It was a few years before Archie was born. My mental health always plummeted around anniversaries, Marie's drinking escalated, Carly became a virtual recluse, relinquishing her regular charity-shop expeditions and replacing them with buying things on eBay, hoping to take better photos, write better descriptions, sell them at a higher price. Graham had called to let me know he'd been released again and my OCD skyrocketed. Not just the contamination side but my rituals too. Everything having to be done three times, everything taking three times as long. I'd already been seeing Francesca for a while – her support along with George's was just about keeping me upright, just about keeping me together – but the news that he was out there once more sent me plunging into an abyss that I just couldn't scale.

The first time I thought I saw him I was terrified. The police wouldn't do anything, couldn't do anything. He hadn't approached me. Hadn't threatened me. It wasn't a crime to be walking down the street. I felt exposed and alone in a world that felt shaky much of the time anyway. Marie tried to hide in the bottom of a bottle of Jack Daniels while Carly hid indoors. Home felt like the safest place until I opened the door to a pizza delivery man, and it was him. I screamed and he ran away. This time the police visited him but he whipped an alibi from his hat and with sleight of hand he was free. It was me who was trapped. I saw him everywhere, documenting it all in a diary while George took me to the station again and again until they arrested him for stalking. I hadn't known they were holding him and when I went to file another report about him coming to my house – this time wearing a post office uniform – it was me who was arrested for wasting police time. He was in custody, they told me. Currently in a cell in this very building. It was impossible that the postman had been him 'unless he's bleeding Houdini' I was told sarcastically. I cried. I wouldn't admit to lying because I hadn't been. I stuck to my story over and over until at last I was released into the freezing car park. A light mist swirling around my ankles, breathing in damp. There was a figure by my car, waiting.

Him.

I screamed and screamed until the officer who had interviewed me had raced outside and escorted me back to the small interview room.

'Please.' I looked over my shoulder. 'He's following me. Please.' Why wasn't I being taken seriously?

'I don't know what game you're playing but…'

I threw another glance behind me. It was definitely still him. Still following me.

My legs were shaking so hard I collapsed. A duty doctor was called who verified that the man by my car – the man who followed me back into the station – was Detective Inspector Lansford. He had wanted to make sure I was okay.

I wasn't.

It was impossible to pull myself together. To change my story. I knew what I had seen, and I had seen *him*. The doctor recommended I was sectioned for my own safety and George was called. He raced to the station, having picked up Francesca on the way, and it was she who had saved me. Confused by my garbled stories of being stalked at my therapy sessions, and my subsequent charge, she'd been researching and she realized I had Fregoli Syndrome.

'Freg— what?' the officer dealing with us asked scathingly.

'Fregoli Syndrome. It's a rare neurological disorder. There aren't a huge number of diagnosed cases but there are thought to be a high number of undiagnosed cases.'

'And what is it exactly, this Fregoli?'

'It's a delusional disorder in which the sufferer mistakenly believes that a person present in their environment is a familiar person in disguise. Leah might see his face, or she might get a sense that it is him masquerading as someone else. It is very real to her. She believes wholeheartedly that he is persecuting her.'

'I've never heard of this.'

'As I said, it's rare but we believe if more health professionals were aware of it then the number of diagnoses would increase. I believe a proportion of cases where people report they are being stalked could be because they have Fregoli.'

'And you can just… catch it?' He steps backwards as though I am contagious.

'There are several known causes. Leah hasn't sustained a head injury but she suffers with other mental health issues, which can cause an onset of Fregoli. For instance, Leah has contamination OCD, paranoia and panic disorder. Every incident where Leah claims she is being followed is very real and very frightening to her. She thinks she sees his face everywhere, or sees him disguised as other people, but it's not him.'

'Right…' You could see the officer was having a hard time believing her. 'If Leah is sectioned she can be treated and—'

'I believe sectioning Leah will be counter-productive. She'll still see his face or think he is disguised as a nurse—'

'She might think he's a woman?'

'It's possible, yes. She'll think he's clever enough to carry that off. If she's sectioned she will have the added trauma of being in a locked ward with no familiar faces and no way to escape. She needs medication and therapy, but not to the extent of drugging her to an almost vegetative state. She needs to feel safe.'

'I don't know. It all sounds fuc— so *unbelievable.* No offence.' He looked at me and then turned quickly away as though I might cause his face to change. 'And this is one of them newfangled mental health thingies we're supposed to be sensitive about?'

'It's not new.' Francesca didn't show any hint of impatience. 'The first diagnosed case was in 1927. A theatregoer was convinced that two of her favourite actresses were disguising themselves as other people and following her. Her theory was… disproved,' Francesca said carefully, not adding that the theory was disproved after the lady attacked a stranger, thinking it was one of the actresses, as I found out later. 'The condition was named after Leopoldo Fregoli, who thrilled Victorian theatregoers with his quick-change act. Look. You can discharge Leah into my care. I'm confident I can treat her. Once the anniversary is over, the pressure will be off anyway and it will likely disappear as quickly as it came on. You do all know what she went through as a child.'

'Yeah.' This time his voice was softer, he probably had children of his own. 'Okay. You can take her home. But she better not be back in five minutes reporting she's seen him again.'

I didn't but ironically, he did approach me – all three of us – wanting to apologize. We didn't accept, didn't care if he'd 'turned over a new leaf'. Not long after, he was arrested again. Boomeranged back to his cell.

Now, my drifting thoughts are interrupted by Francesca's voice.

'Feeling real doesn't mean it is real. You know that, Leah.'

'I know but the timing... Me seeing him the day after he was released – and I didn't know at the time he *had* been released. The twenty-year anniversary.'

'Where did you see him?'

'I was coming out of the BP garage.'

'Walk me through it. Where were you coming from? Going to?'

'I'd come from home. Marie had texted and asked me to go round. I was cross because George had promised he'd fill the car up but he hadn't. You remember the smell of petrol always reminds me of being in the back of the van?'

'I do.'

'I filled up my car and I was paying and there was a white van,' I pause, trying to decide whether to tell her I thought the van had someone trapped inside. That I made the driver open the doors, but I don't want to appear any more paranoid than I probably do already.

'And he was driving the van?' Francesca prompts.

'No. He was in a black car. He passed me as I came out of the garage.'

'So you were already in an emotionally heightened state because you were on your way to see Marie. You'd seen a white van, which of course is distressing for you, as is the smell of petrol. On a scale of one to ten, how certain are you it was him?'

'I wasn't,' I admit. 'I thought he was still in prison but I saw him again the next day, outside Marie's flat.'

'Did he approach you?'

'No. I was in the car with Carly and it was raining. He was on the street.'

'Did Carly see him too?'

'No.'

'But you saw him clearly? Through the rain?' She studies me.

'Well, no but I had a really strong feeling.' I reach to tuck my hair behind my ears. My hands are trembling.

'It's okay, Leah. You're doing great.' She gives me a second. 'Have you seen him anywhere else?'

'Today, at work. He was the photocopier repair man. He chased me.'

'He chased you?'

'Yes.' But had he run after me? 'Well, I ran away from him. I think he came after me. I don't know. That's it anyway. Just three times. So far.'

'If your Fregoli has returned, there will likely be many more instances of you spotting him.'

'I know. I don't want to go through it again. I can't put George through it again. Thinking he's everywhere I turn. Not knowing what is real and what isn't. Please. Will you help me again? I have to know if this is all in my head. I've been getting letters. Hand delivered. If it's him he knows where I live. Where Archie lives.'

'That must be frightening.'

'The police think it's a crank.'

'You've been to the police again?' She doesn't sigh but she doesn't have to.

'Of course I have. I'm being threatened.'

'What do the letters say?'

'Four days. Three. It's a countdown to the anniversary. Who knows what might happen then? The police don't class it as an actual threat but it feels like it.'

'Is there anything else I should know, Leah?'

I hesitate. I haven't told her I think he's snatched Marie. I want her to agree to take me back as a client before I tell her that.

'I don't think there's anything else,' I say. If I tell her about the old newspapers in the staffroom she might not believe me and I don't have them to show her as proof. The reappearance of Fregoli is one thing but I can't have her questioning my mental capacity. She – teamed with the police – could section me and I have to be around to protect my family. No matter what everyone says, I'm not convinced it isn't him I'm seeing, but without her help I'll never be sure. I'm not certain it's the Fregoli Syndrome playing tricks on me. Hiding in plain sight, they call it. With my medical history he could be standing right in front of me and I'd have no way of knowing if it was actually him or someone else and I was just seeing his face.

Unless he hurt me.

Three days.

The letters sound like a warning.

And although I know with my track record no one will believe me, I do think he has come back to hurt me.

Three days.

And there's only me who will be able to stop him.

'I'll help you,' she says eventually. 'But not now. I've a client due in ten minutes.'

We fix up an appointment. 'Go straight home and get some rest,' she says as she sees me out.

'I will, once I've picked up my car,' I promise but it's a lie. I'm not going home but I can't tell her where I'm going.

She wouldn't approve.

Chapter Twenty-Five

Leah

Now

I'm steeling myself to knock on the door. It is after lunch but all the curtains are drawn. There's no telling if Mum is here. This isn't the home I was born in – but the council house we'd moved to after her divorce from Dad. We all left years ago and I thought she'd move but she's stayed local, even though Dad didn't and sometimes I wonder why. She doesn't have much of a relationship with us. She doesn't have much of a relationship with anyone. The town had judged and found her guilty of lacking the skills a mother should have. The ability to keep her children safe.

My memories of my childhood are divided into a definite before and after. An invisible glass wall separating the people we were from the people we all became. Sometimes, in my dreams I'm pressing my face against that glass wall – the way Bruno pressed his nose against the patio doors, his breath fogging the glass – watching the versions of us who were happy and healthy and loved.

Mum would sit on the edge of my bed and brush my hair one hundred times before doing the same for Marie. She treated us exactly the same. I can't quite remember whether Marie and I insisted our clothes, our shoes be identical, or whether our parents, delighted with having twins, tried to mould us both into the same person. We didn't mind though, me and Marie were closer to each other than anyone else. Carly's relationship with Mum was different. There were evenings when Dad was out and Marie and I were in bed when we'd creep downstairs to beg for a glass of water, another story, a cuddle, to find Mum and Carly nestled together on the sofa in front of the TV, fingers dipping chicken nuggets into thick ketchup.

Mum loved us all – of that I've no doubt – but she loved Dad the most of all. Her eyes shone whenever he walked into a room. They always kissed each other hello and goodbye and held hands when we strolled around the park with Bruno. Often I wonder what life would have been like if it wasn't for that single, horrifying event that changed the shape of our future. Would we be one of those families who ate Sunday lunch together each week? My parents kneeling on the floor playing with grandchildren in the way they hadn't always had time to play with us?

Would we be parts of a whole rather than fragmented pieces of something that will never again fit together?

In the days, the weeks, the months that followed our abduction, Mum and Dad veered between sadness and anger. Tears and rage. Once I'd wandered into the kitchen to find Mum sobbing, 'I'm their mum. I should have protected them, I've let them down,' while Dad hissed, 'And you think *I've* let them down too? Just say it.'

They kept us cooped up. Not wanting us to even play in the garden alone. I'm not sure whether they were scared we'd be taken again or scared we'd be interrogated by one of the many reporters who still trailed after us wherever we went. Probably both.

My parents' glittering life crumbled. Our childhood was unpicked in the tabloids. How had we been raised? Why had Carly been left alone to feed and take care of her two young sisters? How often did my parents go out? It was a carousel of blame and scrutiny and it makes me dizzy just thinking about it now. How would I feel if my relationship with Archie was dissected? The entire country seemed to blame my mum until she became a shell of the parent she had been. Old photos of her laughing would appear in the paper captioned, *Face of loving mother?* She began to leave us to our own devices – mine and Marie's hair becoming matted and tangled, as though she didn't trust herself to do things properly. That's what I like to think, anyway, that it wasn't that she didn't care. She just didn't know how to be a mum any more when she'd failed so spectacularly in the eyes of the world. She and Dad divorced. She began to drink. We'd find vodka bottles hidden everywhere. In the laundry basket. The freezer. The cupboard under the stairs. It's probably where Marie gets it from.

When the publisher approached us before the ten-year anniversary we wanted to tell Mum face to face. Carly, Marie and I had sat on the threadbare sofa, the bars of the electric fire glowing bright, the coffee table devoid of tea and biscuits. She never made us feel welcome.

'We're going to write a book. Our story.'

'Absolutely not,' Mum had said.

'They want our version, now that we're adults,' Marie was twitchy, picking at the skin around her fingers. We hadn't realized then that she was drinking or how bad it was, anyway.

'And what will you say?' Mum stared at Marie until she looked away.

'We won't say anything bad about you,' Carly said.

'But that's what they'll want to know. Christ, there's enough already out there about how you were neglected, left to fend for yourself, how you had the worst mother in the world.'

'Nobody thinks that,' I said.

'Don't they?' She studied Marie again.

'Look,' Marie said. 'Maybe most of the facts are out there but we've never talked about… the details, I suppose. The food we were given. How frightened we were.'

'I thought Marie was going to die,' I said.

Mum stood up. 'It seems you've made your mind up so if you don't mind, I've got things to do.' She gestured to the door.

Marie filed out first, followed by Carly. I hesitated, Mum's eyes were full of tears. 'This isn't a betrayal of you, Mum,' I said quietly. 'It's about us and what we went through.'

She gave a single nod of her head. 'You know if I could change the past – if I could go back to that day and be there, looking after you all – I would.'

'We don't blame you,' I said.

She didn't answer.

Although Carly and I weren't keen on talking to the ghost writer, we'd already signed the deal and received the advance. We tried to keep our parents out of the book as much as we could but naturally there was much curiosity surrounding our family dynamics.

Around six months after the book came out Marie received a short note from our father after years of no contact, saying he thought the book was fair and thanking us for portraying

Mum in a good light – *it's brought me much sadness that the stress drove us to divorce*, he said and that stung. He didn't even ask how we were. We didn't reply. As far as I know, Mum has never read the book. When we received our first royalties I slipped a wad of notes in a blank brown envelope through her letterbox and I think my sisters likely did the same. Blood money, I suppose. Mum had always struggled financially and no matter what had happened in the past we still had a desire to help her. She never acknowledged the money.

It's an odd relationship, mother and daughter. Although we rarely see her and she never makes an effort with us, I know that Marie still visits her sometimes and Carly rings her on her birthday and at Christmas. She's never met Archie, or expressed any desire to, and that makes me incredibly sad. Despite the life I have forged for myself, the family of my own, there is some deep-rooted need for her love. For her approval. But she is the one who distanced herself from us. She made her choice as I have made mine.

Although my stomach skitters with nerves, I need to see her now. Ask her face to face if she knows where Marie is. She was so cagey on the phone.

The street stinks of blocked drains. Even with my gloves on I am reluctant to touch Mum's gate, which is flaked with paint and rust. Her front garden is a mess. The scant flowers pushing their way through the choking tangle of weeds hang their heads in shame. A far cry from the days Mum had a gardener. As I think of our old garden my anxiety rises as I remember that day.

The excited barks of Bruno as Marie and I tossed the ball. Afterwards our beloved pet had been found roaming the streets but we didn't take him back and often I wonder whether he found a new family. Whether he was happy.

I am still lost in memories when I hear Mum's voice behind me.

'What are you doing here?' No *hello*. No *how are you?* But it's a shock, I know. I'm sure she's been steeling herself for my usual anniversary phone calls, not a visit.

'Let me.' I reach for one of the laden bags she is carrying but she twists it away from me and waits for me to speak. She isn't about to invite me in then.

'Steak?' I spot two pieces of rump nestled on top of a bag of leafy salad. 'You must be doing okay?' My parents used to eat steak every Saturday night. No matter how I feel about her, I am glad she can afford to treat herself.

'I need to get this lot in the fridge. Did you want something?' she asks as though I am just passing, despite knowing I both live and work over twenty miles away. Momentarily I am lost for words. I'd at least have expected her to ask how her only grandchild is but then I remind myself Mum is not a typical grandmother. There is no knitting of terrible jumpers and baking of calorie-laden cakes slabbed together with jam and buttercream. If I'm being kind, I can put it down to the fact she's frightened to love again. Frightened to properly feel. I can't imagine how terrified she must have been with her children missing but still, rationalizing her reluctance to get to know Archie, understanding it, doesn't make it any easier to bear. Sorrow expands in my throat.

'I'm worried about Marie. Do you know where she is? Please tell me if you do.'

'I told you, I don't know where she is.' She looks me directly in the eye and it is me who shifts uncomfortably.

'Is there anyone you can think of who might?'

Mum shakes her head. Her hair is dark brown and shiny – she's covered up her grey. Being kind to herself – I wish I could do the same. Her shoulders are sagging under the weight of the shopping. She glances at her door and I know she's eager to be inside. To get away from this conversation that is both awkward and painful. A stark reminder of how separated our family has become.

'I thought she'd gone on tour?' she asks.

'That's what the note she left said, but what if someone made her write it?'

Mum gives a half laugh. 'I don't think anyone can make your sister do something she doesn't want to and don't you ever believe that they can. She's *always* made her own choices.'

'He's been released from prison again.' The swerve in conversation causes her to blink rapidly but she doesn't speak. 'Say something!'

'You can't keep living in the past, Leah. He has no interest in you. He didn't try to hurt you last time, did he?'

My muscles tighten across my upper back.

'Well, did he?' she urges.

'No.' I give her that. At least she's making some effort to make me feel better.

'You have to forgive. Move on.'

'Forgive? Do you forgive him for what he did to us? All of us? Mum don't you remember how close we all were… before?' My emotions stream out of me. I'm ashamed of the longing in my words. Why can't everything just be like it was?

'I can't keep apologizing, Leah. You're a mum now. I'm sure you're doing the best you can for your boy, the way that I did for you girls, but sometimes… Sometimes our best isn't good enough, is it? With all the good will in the world, we can't always protect our children—'

'I wish you had. Protected us,' I say quietly and I feel something inside of me release. It's been so long since I tried to talk to her about it all, perhaps it's not too late to salvage our relationship.

She nods. 'I wish you could forgive me.'

I want to tell her that I want to forgive her and that has to be a start but while I'm searching for the right words she tells me she needs to go in and unpack her shopping.

'I could help?' I offer.

'It's okay, Leah,' she hesitates. There's something on her face I can't quite read. 'Try not to worry. Marie *will* turn up.' She doesn't add 'like a bad penny' but the connotation is there. It's not only on my doorstep my twin has turned up drunk in the past.

'Right,' I say. There's a beat. 'I'll be off then.'

I walk back down the street towards my car. I turn. Mum is still standing outside her door. Still gripping her shopping, a sad expression on her face.

Something catches my eye, drawing my gaze upwards. I think the bedroom curtain twitched but I can't be sure.

Chapter Twenty-Six

George

Now

George pulls onto the driveway, feeling a flicker of relief that Leah's car isn't here. He's shattered and can't take another discussion about the letters. The sightings she thinks she's seen. His overriding emotion at the police station yesterday should have been sympathy for his wife, instead it was embarrassment. How stunned PC Godley was when he'd read Leah's notes. His confusion as he tried to process that Leah was convinced that many people were masquerading as one man. PC Godley's expression had flickered between disbelief and amusement. George had wanted to hit him.

It brought it all back. The last time, before her diagnosis. The frequency with which his wife had cried that she'd been followed again. His frustration the police wouldn't, couldn't do anything. His fear that something awful was going to happen to Leah. His anger at his inability to protect her. He felt he was failing as a husband. As a man. The utter helplessness as he got the call advising him that Leah was being detained under the Mental Health Act. George was incredulous as he was told Leah had accused their postman of being her tormentor when in fact the man she feared was already in custody – and then to mistake a detective inspector for him. Was she deliberately lying? The terror radiating from her trembling body as he held her close against him felt genuine.

George had driven straight to Francesca's. Although she was with a patient, she came as soon as George told her Leah was being held. On the way she'd filled him in on what she now believed. That Leah had Fregoli Syndrome. He'd tried his best to empathize. His wife had a mental illness, but it was a lot, on top of the constant cleaning, the constant rituals, the constant worry. It was wearing. Unfairly, he'd felt cross with her as though it was all her fault, but of course he knew it wasn't. It wasn't his either but he was also affected. Leah didn't seem to realize this. Her world seemed to then centre around herself, Marie and Carly, and then later Archie. George felt he was always on the periphery looking in. Part of her life, but not.

George finishes his phone call and then wipes his call history before he heads inside.

Archie is perched at the breakfast bar with Carly when George gets home, crafting unidentifiable animals from plasticine – a pink giraffe with a neck so long its head trails dolefully by its feet, an orange elephant with flapping ears, larger than its body. The kitchen is warm and cosy. Smelling of coffee and toast. George kisses Archie hello, and then wipes the remnants of strawberry jam from his son's mouth with his thumb.

'Do you want another cup?' George asks Carly as he pours himself a mug of the syrupy coffee.

'No, thanks. Another mug and I'll be climbing the ceiling.'

'Like Spider-Man!' Archie shoots invisible webs from his wrists. 'Uh oh – it's the Green Goblin.' Archie leaps from his stool and races around the kitchen, fighting something only he can see.

We're all battling something hidden, thinks George.

Carly, always the practical one, whips a large tablecloth from the drawer.

'Quick.' She scrapes the chairs across the floor and drapes the cloth between them, a makeshift tent. 'The Green Goblin won't find you in there, Spider-Man.'

Archie clambers inside and Carly follows him on her hands and knees. Not a second's hesitation while she deliberated when the floor was last cleaned. No noticeable flinch as she places her palms on the tiles.

'You're so resourceful,' George laughs. It amazes him how different the three sisters are. One he hugely admires, one he loves and one… well, he doesn't know how he feels right now.

Carly crawls out of the tent and passes Archie a couple of chocolate fingers.

'Superheroes need to keep their energy up. I'll see you tomorrow.'

'Stay,' George asks. The realization he doesn't want to be alone with Leah sits uncomfortably on his stomach.

'I can't. Little man has worn me out.'

Carly's eyes are shadowed with deep violet rings. None of them are sleeping properly.

'Leah shouldn't be long.'

'Really, I need to go.'

'Are the letters scaring you?' he asks, suddenly worried about his sister-in-law. Moments ago he'd been mentally berating Leah for not considering his feelings and he was guilty of doing the same with Carly, but she always seemed to be the one who copes.

She might have chosen not to have kids of her own but who's to say she would have done anyway? She doesn't have a crutch that George can see, no alcohol or rituals for her. And yet these past few days seem to have shrunk her.

Twenty fucking years. It's enough to break anyone.

'Not scaring me… just… I don't know. I feel angry, I think.' She tilts her head to one side like a bird waiting for a crumb. 'Yes. Angry and disappointed and… I just want it to be over now. I need it to be over now.'

'Three days,' George says.

'Three days,' she whispers.

It doesn't sound long. Less than a week. Seventy-two hours. But empires had been torn apart in less. Lives left in pieces.

'What did you think about the TV offer?' George can't help asking as Carly pulls on her coat. The colour bleaches from her already pale face.

'There are things…' Carly's breath hitches and she takes a second to compose herself. 'There are things that are too awful to comprehend. That should never be shared.'

George nods. He knows all about things that are too awful to comprehend. He's guilty of them himself.

George knows all about secrets.

Chapter Twenty-Seven

Leah

Now

The two-day letter is on my doormat when I tumble downstairs after a sleepless night. It isn't a surprise but it fills me with dread all the same. Two days. Two days until what? I am almost willing the next forty-eight hours to thunder past so I can get it over with, whatever *it* is. The anniversary or something else.

Something worse?

I slip the letter into my pocket like a secret – the empty chocolate digestive packet after I'd binged, stuffing biscuits down to suppress my rising fear.

'Morning,' George pads barefoot into the kitchen. 'Did you get another letter?'

'No, nothing today.' I'm thinking of the Power of Attorney search he'd done online. I need to show him I am coping but we both know that I'm not.

He studies me, a surprised expression on his face almost as though he expects me to keep receiving them until the anniversary. 'You can talk to me, Leah, about… about anything.'

'I know but I think the letters have stopped. We can get back to normal.'

'That's good.' He offers me a tight smile. 'I'm going to get dressed.'

After breakfast I drop Archie at nursery with a kiss, telling him that Aunty Carly will pick him up later. I can't tear myself away from Archie until I see his favourite nursery nurse, Rebecca. I remind her again about security and she reassures me again she will notify me of anything unusual.

'I'll see you this evening,' I say as I leave. We'd missed Archie's parents' evening last night because of George's meeting but Rebecca has offered to see us tonight instead, which is really good of her on a Friday.

Before I leave I hang Archie's coat on his peg in the small cloakroom where the children's trays are. I ease Archie's open. There's a picture inside of three large stick people, and one small one. Archie has labelled them *Mummy, Daddy and Aunty Carly*. It pains me to see that whenever Archie depicts his family Marie is always missing. By stick-Archie's feet is the dog he so desperately craves. I shut the drawer. I'll go through Archie's work this evening with George. Archie is the lynchpin that holds us together and this might make us feel closer.

I head straight to my first formal appointment with Francesca since I'd turned up crying on her doorstep.

'I wasn't sure if you'd come.' She sits upright, spine straight. The warmth that used to coat her words when I was a patient before has disappeared. She doesn't sound cold exactly, just professional when before I felt we were edging towards being friends. I wonder if it's hard for her. Building relationships and then watching them crumble.

'I'm sorry I just stopped coming before without letting you

know. I really thought I was better, that I didn't need you, but it was rude of me not to let you know,' I tell her again.

'It often happens. Clients get to a point they feel they don't need therapy and medication any more but don't seem to recognize it could be *because* of the therapy and medication that they are feeling better. Anyway. Moving forwards. Have you seen him again?'

'No.'

'That's a good sign, Leah.'

I don't answer, instead I unscrew the lid from my water bottle and take a sip.

'And the letters?'

I hesitate. I'd lied to George but I need to talk to someone. 'Yes. I've had another. So has Carly.'

'And Marie?'

Again, I stall for time, looking out of the window. Weighing up the benefits of being honest; I want to feel better – against the negatives; if my mental capacity is called into question again I want my notes to show that I'm rational. But the police already know about Marie and I'm horribly worried about her.

'Marie is missing.'

'Missing?'

'Yes. She… I don't know. After the first letter arrived me and Carly went to see if Marie had one but she was… gone.'

'When you say gone—'

'Her flat was exactly as we'd left it two days before. Our drinks and biscuits still on the table.'

'I assume you called her.'

'Yes, but she isn't answering.'

'And you've no idea where she is?'

'She'd scribbled something on a notepad about a tour but... I don't know. She's done this before but, with the anniversary and the notes and me thinking I saw him outside of her flat, it feels... wrong. The police aren't worried. There's no sign of a struggle. But... I don't know what to think. George says Marie is resourceful and not to worry.'

'I'm sure he's right,' Francesca says. 'And...' She glances down at her notes, her pen scratches against paper. 'How are things with George?'

I search for the word. 'Strained.' A pang of sadness spears my chest. 'He's upset I'm wearing these again' – I waggle my gloved hands – 'and he's... scared, I suppose, that I'm going to spiral back to the stage where I won't let Archie out of my sight. But he's trying to understand. He brought me home a bouquet of flowers and we've been talking... or trying to. It isn't easy. Perhaps I should bring him here for a couples session?'

'I don't think it's the right time for that. Let's get you feeling more in control first, shall we?'

'Yes. Please.' In control is exactly how I want to feel.

After I've left Francesca's with a clutch of CBT exercises to try at home, I drive to Marie's, letting myself in with the spare key. Nothing has changed. She hasn't been back. I conduct a more thorough search this time and find some old flyers for productions she has been in. I google the companies that produced them but most are no longer performing. I call the ones that are but no one has heard from her. I lock up as I leave but before I go I knock on her neighbour's door. It cracks open and an elderly woman peers out.

'Hello.' I smile brightly. 'I'm Marie's sister, Leah.'

She looks blank.

'Marie? Your next-door neighbour.'

'Her wiv the hair that changes colour all the time?'

'Yes. I was wondering when you'd last seen her?'

'I mind me own business, luvvie. I ain't seen her, not for a few days.'

'Have you noticed any visitors?'

'As I said, me duck, I keep meself to meself. Noticed you the other day, though. And there was a blonde girl.'

'That's Carly, my other sister. Anyone else?'

'There were a man. Later that day. But like I said—'

'A man?' A chill feathers its way down my spine. 'What did he look like?'

'Couldn't tell you, duckie. I don't take much notice. He were tall though, with dark hair, and he hadn't bothered to shave. In my day a suitor—'

Him. She has described him.

'And have you seen Marie? After the man came here?'

'No. But then, I'm not one for being in other people's business.'

Don't overreact.

There's no evidence that Marie left her flat unwillingly. Lots of men are tall with dark hair, George included. He could have been anyone. A delivery driver. A salesman. It could have been anyone.

But I know it wasn't.

He's back.

At home I am desperate to tell Carly what Marie's neighbour has said but she looks terrible: bloodshot eyes and her voice is hoarse.

'I'm sorry,' she says as soon as I walk into the kitchen.

'Don't be silly.'

'I'm not... I don't know what I'm doing.' She's making a sandwich for Archie but she stares at the butter as though she's never seen it before. I slip the knife from her hand. 'You look awful. Get yourself home and tucked up in bed.'

'But it's your parents' evening tonight. I'm so sorry.'

'You can't help it.' Her eyes fill with tears and I know she feels she's let me down. 'I'll ask Tash to babysit.' I usher her to the door.

'Two days, Leah.' Her voice cracks. 'In two days it will have been twenty years since... since...'

'Carly, it will be okay.' I offer my sister a reassurance I don't feel but I know when you're feeling unwell everything is magnified and why shouldn't I be the strong one for once? The one to look after her. 'Go home.'

She looks so small as she climbs into her car. I watch her drive away before I head back into the kitchen and disinfect everything before throwing away the loaf of bread she had touched, giving Archie cream crackers for lunch instead.

I slick confidence over my lips and paint my cheeks happy before zipping up my red skirt. I'd heard that the colours you wear can reflect your mood. I can at least look brave, even if I don't feel it. Coming out of the bedroom I hear Archie shriek with delight. Then the slosh of water.

I poke my head around the bathroom door. Archie has smeared a foamy bubble-bath beard over his chin. The scent of apple shampoo lingers in the air. 'We need to leave in about twenty minutes.'

'Can I come?' Archie asks for the hundredth time.

'Sorry. It's just for grown-ups.'

'But it's *my* nursery.' His expression changes in a millisecond. He's tired and on the brink of tears.

'I know, and your teachers will tell us how brilliant you are and then at the weekend we'll get you a treat.'

'A puppy!' Archie lifts his hands in the air. Bubbles drift to the ground and pop.

'Not a puppy, no.' I can't bear to look at his disappointed face.

'Parents' evening.' George shakes his head. 'At four years old.'

'It's to talk about his transition to school,' I say although I feel there's nothing that can prepare me for that.

'But I—' Archie begins and I cut him off with 'Tash is coming to read you a story – that will be much more fun.' Tash always gives the characters accents.

'Tash is coming here to babysit?' George frowns.

'Yes. She'll be fine.' George used to say Tash was so much fun but irresponsible. But I wouldn't trust her with Archie if I thought she couldn't cope.

'I thought Carly was coming?'

'She's unwell.'

Before George can respond the doorbell peals. I run down the stairs, checking out of the lounge window to make sure it is Tash before I answer the door.

'Hey, Leah.' She hugs me hello.

'Thanks for coming. Have you had a good day off? Done anything nice?'

Her cheeks flush as she shrugs off her coat and I make a mental note to turn down the heating before we leave. 'No. Nothing. You look fab! If I didn't know any better I'd think you guys were sneaking off on a romantic date night.' She raises her eyebrows.

'Just the nursery. I thought I'd make an effort, though.' It's silly, I love Archie more than anything, but there is a part of me that feels everyone is judging me. Seeing me as the imposter I feel I am. How can I possibly be a good mum when I can't always look after myself?

'Where's your gorgeous husband?' Tash asks next.

'He's getting Archie ready for bed.'

'He's so good with him. You don't know how lucky you are.' Tash trails me into the kitchen.

'Now, you will be okay, won't you? If there's any problems call me. Or George. Or the nursery—'

'I'll be too busy snorting cocaine off your coffee table to notice anything wrong.' She catches my stricken expression. 'Relax.'

I try to smile, flick on the kettle. 'Coffee?'

'I thought if I shared a vodka with Archie he'd sleep better—'

'Tash.' My tone is sharper than I intended.

'Sorry, Leah. You know I'm only joking but it's probably the last thing you feel like with the anniversary. It's my defence mechanism.'

'Defence against what?'

'I don't know. Ignore me. My moods arc all over the place at the moment. Archie!' Tash crouches down as a damp Archie snowballs into her open arms.

'George.' Tash raises her face and meets his eyes. There's a beat before he says, 'Tash.' He pats his pocket for his car keys. 'Come on, Leah. We're going to be late.'

We perch on too-small grey chairs, our feet resting in patches of glitter that I know are impossible to clear up. The smell of Play-Doh is mingled with glue and something sweet. Biscuits, perhaps. George's knees are bunched to his chest as Rebecca heaps praise on Archie. We are obviously doing something right. Despite my fears and rituals, we are told he is happy and sociable. There are no concerns at all about how he might settle at school. I will be the one who has trouble adjusting.

'If you want to go through his tray while I clear up?' Rebecca says.

For the first time in days I feel something close to relaxed as I head into the familiar space, confident my boy is doing well.

George folds himself onto a wooden bench, head craned forward to avoid the coat hooks that dot the wall behind him.

I reach for Archie's tray, pull it towards me.

When I see what's inside I can't stop screaming.

Chapter Twenty-Eight

Carly

Then

'I've brought something that will help you,' Doc said as he stepped into the room. He lifted up a carrier bag. 'Magazines to pass the time. I'm not sure what you girls like. There's a *Beano*, and a fashion one and...' he wrinkled his nose. 'Has someone been sick? Is everything okay?'

'No.' Carly's voice cracked under the weight of her tears. 'Everything is *not* okay.' She raised her head, met his gaze. 'Marie needs a doctor, please. She's really ill, I... I don't know what to do. I've nothing to clean her up with. Please. You have to fetch help.'

'I can't—'

'Can't or won't?'

'Kids get sick all the time.' Doc sounded uncertain, as if he's not used to children.

'Marie doesn't. This place is filthy, it's not even fit for animals. If she dies, it's on you.' Carly heard Leah take a sharp intake of breath but Carly couldn't reassure her. She didn't believe Marie had anything serious, she was already looking much better but... *You twist me around your little finger.* She had to have one more try. The atmosphere was heavy with Carly's expectation, Doc's silent deliberations. She remained quiet. A game of chess – it was his move.

'I'm sure… No one's going to die.'

'Are you positive?' Carly's gaze didn't waver. 'If you can't let us all go, take Marie to a hospital, *please*. Can you really live with yourself if she doesn't make it out of here alive?'

'No… I… This isn't what…' Doc stepped forwards and then backwards. 'Look, it's not up to me. I'll go and ask.' He rushed from the room.

Carly heard the door slam behind him. The sound of Doc's boots drumming against the concrete corridor, growing fainter and fainter. But the bolts? She hadn't heard the bolts.

For a split second she was frozen in indecision before the blood roared in her ears. This could be their only chance.

'Get up.' She stood, tugging at Marie's arm.

'But I'm tired—'

'Get up. We're getting out of here, but we have to go. Now!'

'Away from the germs?' Leah rose to her feet, taking Marie's other hand and pulling. 'Come on, Marie.'

Carly felt a pang of guilt. Marie was washing-powder white. Angry violet bags were carved under her eyes. Vomit crusted down her school shirt. But if they didn't go now, go quickly…

Tap-tap-tap, said the tree on the bars.

Hurry-hurry-hurry.

She rushed the twins over to the door. The handle was cool and hard in Carly's hand; it creaked as she twisted it. Her eyes met the clown's in panic.

Let us out, she silently implored.

You'll be back, he grinned.

Slowly, slowly she cracked opened the door. Her breath hitching in her throat each time the hinges squeaked. Her heart felt as though it might burst out of her chest as she spotted Doc at the bottom of the corridor, leaning against the front door frame, smoke pluming from his cigarette. He had his back to them as he spoke on the phone, his voice low and urgent. Carly knew he must be asking Moustache if he could take Marie to a doctor. It wouldn't take him long to say no – he was obviously in charge – but Doc's voice was insistent. It was almost, almost as though he was on their side.

Carly raised her index finger to her lips, warning her sisters to be quiet as she led them out of the room, turning away from the front door. Carly first, Marie's fingers tightly around hers, Leah third, one hand holding her twin's, the other clutching the bear in the red jumper. Ducks in a row, waiting for the hunt. To the left and right were rooms. If they hid in one of these they could be trapped, easy to find. At the other end of the corridor, the stairs. There was a chance Doc could turn around and spot them before they made it there. But even if they reached them, the wood could be rotten, the stairwell collapsing before they had climbed to the top – and if they did reach the second floor, what then?

She only had a split second to make a decision.

Think.

Carly led her sisters through the doorway to the room next door to theirs, the terror in her throat growing with every step. The room was smaller than theirs; the graffiti on the walls here was oddly beautiful. A woman riding a unicorn, long pink hair flowing behind her. The floor was littered with empty aerosol bottles, crumpled foil, syringes. A crumpled sleeping bag in the corner. Outside the wind howled, the rain blew through the empty window frame, puddling on the floor. Here, there were no bars.

The girls crunched over broken glass as they hurried across the room.

Carly linked her fingers together, her hands forming a step. She nodded at Leah, praying she didn't protest it was too high, she was too scared, she didn't want to be first. With a quick glance at Marie, Leah placed her foot in Carly's hands, and allowed herself to be hefted upright, until she could scramble through the gap, dropping to the outside with a thud. She reached back through the open space and quickly helped Marie out.

The front door slammed. Doc's footsteps echoing down the corridor.

Hurry-hurry-hurry.

Carly's pulse accelerated. They had minutes, perhaps only seconds, before he discovered they had gone. She threw a leg over the window and hurled herself outside. Grabbing the twins' hands she dragged them away from the building. It was stupid to stay out in the open. They'd be spotted almost straight away. The nearest building, the one with the NORWOOD ARMY CAMP sign was only a few metres away.

'Oi!' Doc roared.

Hurry-hurry-hurry.

They sprinted to the building. Pounded up the five steps leading to the entrance.

Carly wondered how many soldiers had felt as terrified as she was as they were summoned into the main building to receive their orders, hear their fate. Despite their uniforms, their weapons, they were only flesh and bone, just like her. Everyone was fallible. Expendable.

Not everyone got out alive.

You're going to die.

The space was vast. A curved wooden reception desk directly opposite the entrance. *Welcome* spray-painted in thick black letters, alongside a coarse skull and crossbones. Carly briefly considered the stairs before ushering the girls to their left. They rushed through the corridor into a larger room. Clouds of dust rose around their ankles. In here was a large cinema screen, miraculously still suspended from the wall. Multiple wooden benches were upended, their legs broken off. In the centre of the room was a pile of ash and soot. This was where the briefings were held. Carly shuddered. The soldiers would have felt the same fear as her. Neither knowing if they'd ever see their families again.

There was nowhere to hide.

Hurry-hurry-hurry.

'Come on.'

But Marie was swaying on her feet, drained and wan.

'Just a bit further.' Carly half-dragged her sister through the next corridor, which opened up into something Carly recognized from Mr Webster's class.

The ballroom.

There were three large holes in the ceiling where the chandeliers had been yanked down. Glittering shards of glass blanketed the floor. She remembered feet dancing across plush carpet that now lay in shreds, some of it burned, the red pattern dull, the cream part filthy.

In the middle of the room, a huge pile of empty boxes,

wooden pallets, faded floral curtains, as though someone had gathered the rubbish for a bonfire.

Outside, the sound of an engine, squealing tyres, brakes, a slamming door.

'Where the fuck are they?'

Moustache had arrived.

Chapter Twenty-Nine

Leah

Now

Beetles.

Archie's tray is crawling with beetles.

Instantly I am back in the cold and the damp and the dark. Insects in my hair, my mouth. Sharp feet scuttling over my skin. One plummeting down my throat, meeting the scream that rose.

The smell.

The sound.

The knowing they were there but unable to see them in the blackness.

Now I can see, in the light, bright cloakroom. The tray has slipped from my fingertips. The beetles scurry over the shoes that I will feel compelled to throw away.

'Leah!' George pulls me away, back into the classroom as Rebecca runs towards us.

'What's happened?' she asks, a worried look on her face as her eyes flicker between me and George. I don't answer.

I can't.

My body is here but my mind is back in Norwood. Back in the place that was worse than the room we were first held captive in. The place with scratching rats and glowing eyes. My vision tunnels until all I can see is a pinprick of light, and then nothing.

'I am so sorry.' Rebecca can't stop apologizing. We are in the staffroom. She offers me a glass of water. I shake my head. I can't hold it in my hand that still shakes violently and anyway, I wouldn't be able to drink from the glass. 'It's the damp. We've had a problem with insects coming in now the weather's turned. There's a small hole they scurry through. Someone's coming out next week to have a look.'

'It's not your fault.' George assures her again.

'Sometimes the children hide their snacks in their trays too. It doesn't help...' She looks mortified.

'Honestly, don't worry. Leah, are you okay to stand?'

I'm not sure of the answer but still I nod.

George helps me out to the car.

He pulls out of the car park and I shrink in my seat. Night has drawn in and every approaching car looks black. We don't talk, the Nineties radio show a low drone.

Steps begin to sing '5, 6, 7, 8'. I wrap my cardigan tighter, convinced it's a sign that I'm right. That he's somehow been to Archie's nursery and planted those filthy beetles in my baby's tray. I should have asked if there were any visits from the maintenance men today.

We're almost home. The engine thrums as we wait at the traffic lights by the newsagent's. There's a man in dark clothing and it isn't until he lights a cigarette that I see his face.

'Stop!' I shout just as the light has turned amber and George has accelerated. He slams the brakes on. I rock forwards, the seat belt slicing into my chest.

'What's wrong?' George asks.

I twist my head around. There is nobody there but I know what I saw.

I know what I *think* I saw.

'Did you really see him?' Francesca would ask but it's feasible I have, isn't it? He's out there somewhere. It isn't the Fregoli, I know it. But I've been certain before and I was wrong then.

I am the boy who cried wolf. Nobody will believe me until it's too late.

'Nothing,' I mutter. George tuts.

The second we step through the front door, I am taking the stairs, two at a time, desperate to know that Archie is here. That he is safe. He's sleeping. Hair sticking up at angles, arm draped over his cuddly lion. I kiss my index finger and press it against his forehead.

By the time I come downstairs, Tash has gone.

'She didn't say goodbye? Did she seem all right?'

'Yes, just tired. We didn't know how long you'd be upstairs. I'm going to catch up on some work.'

I have showered and scrubbed my skin until it is raw and bundled the clothes I'd worn this evening into the machine and put them on a hot wash. In the black bin outside I stuff my shoes. I'm making coffee when my phone beeps an unknown number. I warily open the text.

You look nice in that red skirt.

It's as though I have been punched. I double over the sink, phone clutched in my hand.

He is watching me. Was he loitering outside the nursery,

watching my reaction through the window as I pulled open Archie's drawer?

Immediately I think I must call the police. They can't dispute this new evidence, here in black and white, but then I read the text again.

You look nice.

A compliment, they will say.

Nothing threatening. No crime has been committed.

But I can feel in my gut there's only a matter of time until one is.

He is clever, this I know from before.

I have to be smarter.

Chapter Thirty

Carly

Then

The second Carly heard Moustache arrive she dragged the twins across to the pile of rubbish in the centre of the room.

'We have to outsmart them. We have to hide.'

The girls burrowed into the centre of the pile. Pallets and boxes began to slide. Carly caught them before they could make a sound. Arranging the debris over the twins until there were no visible limbs or red hair or tell-tale pieces of clothing on show, Carly tried to carefully slither on her belly after the girls but instantly a crate dislodged with a clatter.

Carly held her breath. She heard a shout. Footsteps heading in her direction. Quickly, she lay on the floor, moulding her body around the edge of the pile. She dragged an off-cut of carpet across herself – it stank. She imagined it was crawling with bugs. Her skin and hair began to itch. Real or imagined insects skittered across her skin. Crawled into her ears. Her nostrils. Her mouth. Tiny feet brushed the hairs on her arms. She suppressed a whimper, resisting the urge to scratch. She felt too conspicuous, exposed, in the middle of the room, but she also hoped that was what would prevent them remaining undiscovered.

Hiding in plain sight.

Carly tried not to think about anyone tossing a match onto this makeshift bonfire. She tried not to think about the flames dancing around that effigy of Guy Fawkes she and the girls had made last year. She tried not to think of anything except home.

Safety.

Warmth.

She waited.

Outside, the rain beat against the flat roof. The wind howled through the broken windows. Footsteps slapped against the concrete floor.

'This place is incredible.' She recognized Doc's voice. 'Can you imagine the history—'

'You'll be fucking history if you don't find them. I can't believe you—'

'Yeah, I know. They can't have gone far though. One of them was really sick.'

'You'd better fucking hope they haven't.'

They grew louder. Closer. Through a sliver of a gap where the carpet met the floor Carly could make out boots. A rush of heat swept up her body from her feet to her prickling scalp.

Please keep still, girls. Please keep still.

Another step, Doc's foot brushed against the carpet covering her, dislodging a cloud of dust that tickled her nose. She was going to sneeze. She could feel it building.

Building.

Building.

Filling her nostrils. Her mouth automatically opened.

Please, no.

Millimetre by millimetre she raised her hand until she could press her index finger underneath her nose, her heart skittering as the carpet shifted. She prayed no one had noticed. She prayed it wouldn't slide off her completely.

The rain drummed.

Her heart drummed.

Moustache's footfall drummed.

'They ain't here. Let's check upstairs.'

Silence, but not relief. The second she could no longer hear them she heard a soft crying but before she could comfort the girls, shush them quiet, she realized it was coming from her. She tried to swallow her tears back down, but she couldn't.

To their credit the twins didn't speak, didn't move. It took Carly several minutes to compose herself, pushing her fingertips hard against her eyelids. Breathing deeply through a nose that was clogged with snot and dust.

'Are you both okay?' she eventually managed to whisper.

'Yes,' Leah's reply was small.

'Marie?'

'I feel really sick again.'

Carly wasn't surprised, even she fell ill with the stench of damp and urine and soot.

'Try to be still for a little while longer and when we're sure they've gone, I'll get you out.'

'My legs want to move,' Leah said.

'Imagine they are,' whispered Carly. 'Imagine we're singing along to Steps and dancing. Close your eyes and hear the music. Feel your feet move. We're at home safe, in the kitchen. Ready? 5, 6, 7, 8.'

In Carly's mind the girls moved in unison, lips synching along with the lyrics, feet instinctively knowing which way to turn. It was comforting to know that Leah and Marie were playing the same scene inside their heads, as though they were all watching the same movie. It was odd but, although they were pinned in place under a pyre, Carly felt a strange sense of freedom.

It was the pins and needles that finally forced Carly to move. Slowly she peeled back the carpet, eyes darting around the room. She couldn't see the men.

She couldn't hear them.

But that didn't mean they weren't close.

She had never felt so scared. Was she just making it worse for them all if they were caught? Would they be tied up again? Gagged. Blindfolded. No longer able to see the horrors but imagining them instead. The worst things happened in darkness. That was where nightmares raged and demons loomed.

Enough. Carly focused on the now. She just wouldn't allow them to be captured again.

'I'm going to get you out now, but be quiet.' Carly lifted slats of wood and carefully placed them on the ground, removing a large piece of damp cardboard that fell to pieces in her hands. She reached for Leah, knowing she was more scared than both of them, but Leah shook her head. 'Get Marie away from the germs first.'

Marie's skin was tinged green, the whites of her eyes streaked pink. As soon as Carly helped her out she sank to the ground as though standing was too much effort. Leah was next, still clutching the teddy bear, its red jumper now streaked with white dust.

'Do you want to cuddle teddy, Marie?' she whispered to her twin. 'He's very brave.'

Marie shook her head.

'We're going to get out of here,' Carly promised. 'We'll run as fast as we can and—'

'I don't think Marie can run very fast right now.' Leah had her arm draped around her twin's shoulder. 'If you want I… I could go. I'm quick and…' Fear sparked in Leah's eyes and she swallowed hard. 'I could find help. I could try anyway. Couldn't we, teddy?' She raised the bear, pressing him against her heart.

Carly deliberated. Should one of them go for help? She glanced out of the open window. The sky outside was definitely fading and not just because it was storm grey either. Night was beginning to draw in. She'd be the obvious choice. Faster. Calmer. But how could she leave her sisters?

'Thanks, Leah, but we'll stick together. It'll be dark soon and we won't have to worry about moving so fast. They won't be able to see us.'

'But we won't be able to see where we're going,' Leah said logically.

'No, but we'll have the moon to guide us. It'll be fine, I promise.' But the lie tasted as sour on her tongue as the urine and the stale vomit tanging the air. 'Let's go and sit in the corner. We'll hear them if they come back in and we can hide again.'

They huddled against the wall and played 'I spy' to pass the time. Nerves bit at Carly's stomach. They'd almost covered every object in the room when Carly became stuck on Leah's 'something beginning with *S*.'

'Sick.' Marie pointed to the front of her shirt.

'Nope,' said Leah.

'I give up,' Carly said.

'If you do you're the loser.' Leah made an *L* shape on her forehead.

'What was it?' asked Carly.

'It was chandelier.'

'That begins with a C,' Marie said.

'Doesn't.'

'Does too. It's a *ch* like chef.'

'Don't believe you. It's my turn again.'

'It's no one's turn,' Carly said. It was too gloomy to see. 'It's time to leave.'

The girls hands instinctively sought out each other's. They crossed the room, retracing their steps to the entrance. They stood in the open doorway, rain pelting against them. It was blacker than Carly had thought, the moon barely visible behind the clouds.

'Ready?' she asked but it didn't matter whether they were or not.

They didn't have a choice but to step out into the unknown.

Chapter Thirty-One

Leah

Now

George and I glare at each other. He wants Archie to go on the nursery trip as planned and I am adamant he can't.

'Please, Mummy. Please.'

'Leah,' George's voice a warning.

'No.' I turn away so he can't see my tears. The one-day letter crinkles in my dressing-gown pocket. I haven't even opened it.

'You can't stop him going because of… last night.' George's voice drips exasperation. He thinks it's the beetles that are stopping me taking Archie to nursery, when in fact it is the man who had put them there.

'But I want to go, Mummy.' Archie slams his beaker on the table. 'We're going on a minibus and I wanted cheese dippers for my packed lunch.' The proposed outing to the nature reserve to gather things for an autumn table has been the source of much excitement.

'You could go on the trip with him?' I offer George a compromise. I don't want to let Archie out of my sight but I know how disappointed he is. The outing had originally been diarised for a couple of Fridays ago but due to staff illness had been rescheduled for today. I'd hoped that, now it was taking place on a weekend, George would be free.

'I've got to work.'

'It's Saturday,' I hiss.

'All the more reason for Archie to get out and have some fun.'

'One more day,' I say to George. 'Why can't you give me one more day and then it will all be over…'

'Until next time,' he snaps. 'I have to know you're capable of looking after Archie, Leah—'

'How dare you even insinuate I'm not!'

'But we can trust Rebecca to look after Archie.' The connotation is that he does not trust me. Years of dealing with the anniversary, tiptoeing around my triggers and the horrors of the past has taken its toll on George. It has taken its toll on us. He's right although I am loath to admit it. Even after tomorrow it won't be over. It will never be over.

'Please, Mummy, please, Mummy, please Mummy.'

'No!' I shout and Archie bursts into tears. 'I'm sorry.' I rush over to him and wrap him in my arms.

'If Mummy *won't* let you go on your trip' – George doesn't say *can't* and in this moment I feel as resentful of his lack of understanding as he is of my foibles – 'then perhaps she'll take you to the park and you can gather some things to take in on Monday.'

'Yes! Park. Park. Park.' Archie's tears instantly dry.

'Please come?' I ask George.

'I'm sorry. I've really got to go to this meeting. Can you manage, Leah?'

Power of attorney. Diminished mental capacity.

'Yes.'

As soon as George has left I call Carly to ask if she can come with me but I can barely hear her. Her voice almost gone. On a whim I ring Tash to see if she fancies a walk but she tells me she has an emergency dentist's appointment for a throbbing tooth.

I am on my own.

'Mummy, too fast!' Archie tries to wriggle his hand free of mine but I hold on tightly as we march past the newsagent's where I had seen *him* last night on the way home from parents' evening. As the road widens I begin to feel a little safer. There's more traffic. Pedestrians stare at their mobile phones as they somehow weave around each other. There are several dog walkers, leads gripped in hands.

The park is busy. There's a pang of nostalgia as I eye the baby swings. Remember lifting Archie who stretched his pudgy arms towards me. Gently patting his bottom to see how full his nappy was. Now he tries to run towards the play equipment. I pull him back.

'We're here for the nature table, remember?'

'Just a little, tiny go on the slide.' He presses his thumb and index finger together before opening them a fraction. 'One small go?' he asks forlornly.

'One,' I say. Although I feel unsettled here, I felt equally unsettled at home. At least now there's safety in numbers, I think, as I glance around at the other mums. Archie thunders up the steps, no careful climbing for him although he does at least hold the handrail. He whizzes down and the joy on his face breaks through my agitation.

'Go on,' I say before he can ask for another go. After the slide it's the roundabout. The climbing frame. It's here he falters, not yet brave enough to climb higher than five rungs, not appreciating that the slide he loves is even taller. 'Shall we go find some leaves and stuff?' I ask.

'What stuff shall we find?' He slips his hand into mine, tired now. I'm glad I let him run off some of his energy in the playground.

'Treasure?'

'Pirates?'

'Parrots?'

We play our word association game while Archie gathers leaves, twigs, stones and pine cones. He heaps them into my hand. I should have brought a bag to put them in, my jacket doesn't have pockets and they'll get crushed in my jeans. I glance around. There's an old lady to my left, waiting while her dog cocks his leg up a tree.

'I'm going to ask that lady if she'll let us have some poo bags,' I say. Archie doubles over in laughter.

'Poo! For poo! We're having a poo!'

'Shh.' The lady is watching us now. I cross over to her and explain what I need and why. She holds open a bag while I tip Archie's discoveries inside and then she gives me another.

'Archie.' I turn, pleased that we have a spare bag to fill. 'Archie?'

There's a sick feeling in my stomach as I scan the spot Archie was standing in. It's empty.

'Archie!' I shout but there is no 'Mummy' to let me know he is nearby. There are no footsteps.

'Archie!' I scream again.

Three steps away. I was only three steps away, but in the brief seconds I was talking to the lady he has vanished.

Chapter Thirty-Two

Carly

Then

Carly wished they were invisible. Out in the open she felt horribly exposed. Driven by the wind, rain lashed into their faces. The sky a dark, angry grey. Night was drawing in quickly.

'Where do we go?' asked Leah. Underneath the desperation that dripped from her voice nestled a thin layer of hope that her big sister would know what to do.

Carly frantically looked around as though the way out would suddenly materialize, like the Tardis. She wished she'd paid more attention to Mr Webster's class when he'd shared the photos of the base. She could vaguely remember him highlighting the main building on the aerial view but she couldn't remember which direction the town was in. They walked – more slowly than Carly would like but they were all weak, Marie most of all. Carly kept her eyes trained on the ground, seeking out footprints, tyre tracks, anything that might lay a Hansel and Gretel trail and lead them back the way they had come in. But the earth was slippy with rain and anything that might have been visible once had been washed away. One leaden foot in front of the other, progress was painfully slow. Carly could hear the laboured breathing of Leah and Marie. Fleetingly she wondered whether they should have waited until morning. At least in the ballroom they'd been dry but they'd had nothing to eat or drink and Carly knew they'd have less energy than they did right now.

The weather was vile, fog swirling around them. Carly imagined they looked like three small ghosts wandering around the base, and again she thought of the tales of dead soldiers. She held the girls' hands a little tighter.

'Look, there's a bigger building.' Carly urged the girls forward. 'Perhaps it's…' Her stomach plummeted to her feet as she took in the wonky NORCROFT ARMY CAMP sign. They'd walked around in a circle.

'Girls!' All three of them froze as Moustache's voice sliced through the storm. 'Come out, come out, wherever you are,' he sang.

Lightning flashed. Leah screamed. She'd always been scared of storms. Carly clapped her hand over her sister's mouth.

'Over there!' Doc shouted.

'Run,' Carly growled. She shoved Leah between her shoulder blades before grabbing Marie by the wrist, forcing her feet to move. 'Run!'

They tore through the long grass that snatched at their socks and their skirts until the blades thinned and they were slip-sliding across mud. Thunder rumbled as mutinous black clouds sucked the light from the day. Mist swirled around their rain-soaked bodies. The smell of damp earth invaded Carly's nostrils.

'Oh, girls!' Despite their sprint, the voice didn't sound any further away. If anything it was nearer.

They ran again. The buildings were scarcer, looming out of the fog as though ready to snatch at the girls, but Carly led her sisters around them. They needed to find the fence. Climb it if they couldn't locate the gate. Once they'd reached the road she would flag down a car. Someone would stop and help, ring their parents. Her longing for her mum and stepdad was painful.

She stole a glance over her shoulder. Two yellow lights trained on the ground bobbed behind them. Her spirits dampened as she realized Moustache and Doc were following the imprints of their shoes in the mud.

'Faster,' she urged Leah and Marie but they were tired, their short legs unable to put enough distance between them and their hunters.

Abandoning her search for the fence, she ushered her sisters over to the nearest building. They had to find somewhere to hide until the rain stopped and the ground dried.

'Inside.' She shoved them forwards. 'I'll be back in a minute.'

Ignoring Leah's soft cries and Marie's protest that they had to stay together, Carly dashed forward, all the while seeking out the torchlight, gauging how much time she had before they were found. When she couldn't risk going any further she dropped to her knees and wrenched off her school shoes, stuffing her hands inside of them. She ran the flat soles over the squidgy mud, obliterating their earlier footprints. Inching backwards, the cold rain streaming into her eyes, blowing into her mouth, she pressed her shoes down as hard as she could, over and over as the torchlight grew nearer and nearer. They were dangerously close now. If it weren't for the fog they'd be able to see her.

'Come out, come out, wherever you are,' came the cry again but this time the voice wasn't travelling. Doc and Moustache had reached the end of the footprint trail and Carly could sense their confusion.

'Split up.' One light went in the wrong direction, the other headed straight towards her.

Carly's chest tightened with fear. Frantically she swept her arm back and forth, all the while retreating. She couldn't leave any footprints, she just couldn't.

She could hear the sound of boots now, squelching through the mud. He was almost upon her. Certain she'd be seen she held her breath as she sidled backwards again.

Behind her, pressing against her socked feet, a wall. She'd reached the building. Keeping low, she scrambled inside.

Safe for now, but for how long?

Arms wrapped around her, her sisters' small bodies trembling with fear, as Carly stood, her eyes straining to adjust to their surroundings. With the small amount of moonlight trickling through the patchy roof, she could just make out a rusting sign: DANGER. RISK OF CONTAMINATION.

Darkness loomed ahead but she couldn't risk staying in the doorway. In the absence of footsteps she knew the men would soon turn their attention to the buildings and this was the closest one.

Suddenly lightning flashed again, briefly illuminating the twins. Before Leah could scream Carly dropped her shoes and pressed her hand over Leah's mouth.

'It's okay. Count and see how far away the thunder is,' she whispered. It's what her mum would have said.

'One. Two. Three.'

Thunder boomed and as it faded another noise took its place.

Whistling.

And the calmness, the ordinariness of that sound was the most frightening thing Carly had ever heard. Swiftly she located the twins' hands and pulled them forward to the next room.

Hide.

They had to hide. In the eerie light she hurriedly took in their surroundings. On the wall were two metal doors. One said SHOES the other CLOTHES. Above them somebody had spray-painted, *Abandon hope all ye who enter here.* Carly shuddered as she realized they were in the Gas Decontamination Chamber she'd learned about. There was nothing else in the room. Nothing to take shelter behind.

'Quick,' Carly whispered, moving on.

The next room was full of showers. She remembered seeing this in Mr Webster's photos but then they had curtains over the cubicles. Now they were empty, pipes ripped from walls. Mounds of debris clogging the drains. Carly backed up against a wall, felt slime coat the backs of her legs.

'Here!' came a shout. 'I've found some shoes.'

Carly cursed herself as she ushered the girls through a doorway into another empty room. Where could they hide? Her panic rose as they crossed a corridor. Here the roof was whole. The blackness was absolute. Carly released the girls and fumbled against the walls until she found a doorway.

'Quickly.'

They fell into the room, a slash of sky visible above their heads. On first glance in the dim moonlight this room appeared empty too but then Carly spotted a flat metal trolley on its side. She darted forward but as she crouched behind it she realized there wasn't space for them all. Her eyes slid around the room, resting on rows of lockers on the walls – some were gaping black holes where their doors had been wrenched off, but some were intact.

'In there.' Carly shoved Leah inside.

‘Please don’t shut me in here, Carly. I’m so scared of the dark. Please…’

Carly ignored her sister’s whimpers and closed the door.

Footsteps grew closer.

‘Your turn.’ Carly lifted Marie to a locker with a door and when satisfied she was hidden she searched for another intact one she could hide inside.

It was high.

Too high. Carly couldn’t reach.

The footsteps echoed in the corridor they had just crossed.

Carly’s hands stretched above her head as her socked feet scrambled for purchase. Her arms were on fire as she attempted to hoist herself up, before plummeting back to the ground.

‘Oh, girls.’

Almost whimpering, certain she’d be discovered, she tried again and this time she gained enough thrust to launch herself forward, until she was inside the locker. Carly was poised to curl herself into a ball but instead found there was a depth to the space that hadn’t been evident from the outside. She rolled onto her side and found she could stretch out her legs.

It dawned on her then that these weren’t lockers for possessions at all. They were built to house bodies.

They were in the morgue.

She could smell it then. Death. Despair. She thought of the things Nicola Morgan’s brother had boasted he had seen. The spirits of limbless soldiers. Bloodied officers. She imagined them laying where she now lay.

Abandon hope all ye who enter here.

The blackness settled over her, choking her. Carly’s heart beat loudly out of her chest. So loud she was sure it would draw the men to them like a beacon.

Footsteps.

Carly clamped her hand over her mouth to trap the whimper that threatened to escape.

'*Three blind mice, three blind mice*,' Moustache sang. '*See how they run*.'

The nursery rhyme turned her blood to ice.

But even more chilling was what came next.

Chapter Thirty-Three

Leah

Now

My bones are ice. Eyes frantically searching for the flicker of Archie's red coat as I scream his name. My brain trying to make sense of what is going on.

But I know.

He has been taken.

Just as Marie, Carly and I were snatched all those years ago.

Just like Marie has been again. I knew *he* had got to her and now he's got to Archie and… Oh God. I don't know where to look first. There are too many bushes obscuring my view. Trees looming ominously. *He* must have been hiding. Watching Archie and me. Waiting for the opportunity to make his move.

I have to call the police. George. I unlock my mobile but it slips through my fumbling fingers and drops to the ground. Sobs escape me as I pick it up.

Hurry.

'Are you okay, dear?' the lady with the terrier asks, tentatively placing her hand on my arm.

'My son. He's gone. He's…'

'Isn't that him just there?' She nods her head to my left. I turn.

Archie!

My heart sings. I am giddy with relief.

'It's such a worry when they're that age and they run off.' The old lady's voice fades to nothing as I see what Archie is carrying in his arms and I know he didn't run off at all. He was lured.

'Where did you get that?' I snatch the bear from his arms. The teddy's arms are outstretched. A red knitted jumper rides up over his rounded belly.

It's the same.

The trees around me sway.

It's exactly the same teddy.

'I found it behind the bush over there. Can I keep him?' Archie pleads.

'I think another little boy or girl has dropped him and they'll probably be missing him,' the old lady says. Why can't she just shut up? Go away. Give me space to think. I know another child hasn't dropped this bear. I know that from the gold cross that is looped around his neck.

My bear.

My cross.

My nightmare all over again.

I throw the bear as hard as I can and we watch as it somersaults through the air before sprawling onto the soft earth.

'Mummy?' Archie is scared. Scared of me. I want to tell him that I'm not the one he should be afraid of but instead I scoop him onto my hip. Automatically he winds his arms around my neck.

I have to get him home. Just because he wasn't taken this time, doesn't mean he won't be.

That I won't be.

That Marie hasn't been.

Run.

My feet crunch against leaves. I weave in and out of trees, seeing shadows everywhere. Sensing eyes on me. There are too many places to hide. Panic builds and builds, my heart bursting out of my rib cage, legs pumping of their own volition. If I stop I'll fall. But I'm not stopping.

Run.

The playground is almost deserted now, the mums have taken hungry toddlers home for their lunch. In my peripheral vision I see something dart towards me. I spin around, pressing Archie's face into my shoulder, shielding the back of his head with my palm but it's only a Labrador bounding towards me, tail wagging, tongue lolling. In my mind he morphs into Bruno.

Run.

The gates loom. I sprint through them. I should feel safer on the pavement with the traffic and the pedestrians and the row of houses with their neat front gardens, bottle-green lawns and white picket fences, but I don't.

A black car approaches. I try to shrink Archie and keep him hidden. It doesn't slow as it reaches us, the driver doesn't glance our way.

I'm tiring.

My arms burn in their sockets from the weight of Archie. My hip throbs where he balances on the bone. My legs are growing weaker.

Another black car.

Another.

Run.

Eventually my street. My house. I am thundering down my driveway, keys already in my hand.

Safe.

For now.

*

Archie is sleeping. His eyelids keep fluttering closed as I tucked him in bed for his afternoon nap, before snapping open.

'Why couldn't I keep the bear, Mummy?'

'Because it belonged to someone else.'

Now I wish I'd brought it home. Examined it properly to see if it was mine.

I sit on the landing outside his bedroom – a lioness guarding her cub – and take deep breaths before I can start on the phone calls I need to make.

'Mum?' I say as soon as she answers. 'What happened to our things from… you know. Our clothes. The jewellery we were wearing. Do you have them?'

'No. They were taken for evidence and I didn't want them back.'

I cut the call and ring Graham.

'Leah.' He sounds tired.

'Is the evidence still being held?' I blurt out before Graham starts with his small talk. 'My cross that was found afterwards, the—'

'Not after all this time. No. I think your personal effects went back to your mum.'

'She says they didn't.' But then, even if she didn't want anything to do with our book, she might have sold our possessions to the true-crime fans when she was short of money after the divorce.

'What's this about?'

'He's… he's doing things.'

'Like what?'

I hesitate.

'Off the record, Leah.'

I recount everything that's been happening. He won't tell anyone, I know. He must have been approached a thousand times from journalists wanting an exclusive from the officer in charge of the case, and he's never once talked. 'I'm so scared, not just for me but… Marie.' My voice cracks. 'Just because she's taken off before doesn't mean she has again. Can you help me?' I ask when I've finished.

'I would if I could, but—'

'No crime has been committed,' I finish his sentence for him.

'No.'

'Can you at least tell me where he is living?'

'You know I can't tell you that, Leah. Look, last time you thought he was after you, he wasn't. I know you'll never forget what happened but he has no reason to come after you now, does he?'

'Revenge?'

'For what?'

'For getting caught and spending years in prison.'

'Possibly but it doesn't feel right.'

'There's something else.' Something I've never told anyone. 'Off the record?' I check.

I hear the flint of his lighter spark. 'Okay.'

'After he was released for what he did to us I… I was a mess. You remember? I thought I saw him everywhere.'

'But it was your illness.'

'Fregoli, yes, but after that had come to light and the police knew not to take any sightings that I reported seriously… he… he *did* approach me.'

'You could have still—'

'I couldn't. I was so close to being sectioned, Graham. I knew that no one would believe me.'

'I would have believed you, Leah.' He sounds disappointed in me. 'Did he threaten you?'

Briefly I think about lying, but Graham has shown faith in me, and I have to put the same trust in him. 'He didn't... he didn't threaten me, or try and hurt me. He... he tried to apologize. I freaked out. I couldn't cope with the thought that he might keep trying to contact me. No one would have taken me seriously if I had told them. I... I was desperate, Graham. Desperate and angry... and scared.'

'What did you do, Leah?' His voice has hardened. He already knows.

'I don't want to go into who or how – I won't implicate anyone – but... I paid someone to frame him. I just wanted him back behind bars. I wanted to feel safe.'

'Don't. Don't tell me things like that. I might be retired but morally—'

'Morally? *He* doesn't have any morals.'

'Two wrongs don't make a right. Did you think about the implications? Other people getting hurt?'

'Yes. I was clear no one was to get hurt. I only had a few thousand pounds. It's not like—'

'Don't try to justify this. What you've done is a serious crime. You could go to prison.'

'I know that but I couldn't bear the thought of him out there. Couldn't just sit around, waiting for him to do... *something*.'

'I can't condone—'

'I don't expect you to. Are you going to report me?'

I wait. Listen to Graham drawing on his cigarette.

'I don't want us to speak of this again,' he says eventually.

'Of course. But you do see this gives him a motive.'

'How would he have known it was you?'

'He knows somebody had set him up, and who hates him more than me, Carly and Marie? Who fears him more? *Still* fears him more than us? I'm so frightened, Graham.'

'Are you *sure* you've seen him?'

'Yes. I might have had Fregoli before but it's different this time, don't you see. The teddy—'

'It's not unusual to find a lost toy in the park.'

'Wearing a cross?'

He doesn't respond.

'Please, Graham. You said a minute ago if I had told you back then that he'd approached me you would have believed me – now you're doubting me too. I just need to know if he's local? I'm going out of my mind here.'

Neither of us speak. Seconds tick past.

'Leah, I can't tell you if he's local. I can't tell you where he lives. I can't tell you not to go to the Dog and Duck for a drink.'

Graham puts the phone down without saying goodbye, before I can say thank you, but he's told me all I need to know. The minute George is home from work…

The power has shifted in my favour. I know where to find *him*.

One day.

Fuck tomorrow. This is where it will end.

Today.

Chapter Thirty-Four

Carly

Then

'*Three blind mice, three blind mice.*' Carly shrank away from the words. She could almost picture Moustache's pale pink lips moving, the thick black hairs above his mouth shifting and settling. '*See how they run.*' His voice grew louder.

A slam. A palm against metal. Moustache was hitting the lockers. Again a slap, a cracking in her ear. Lying on her side, Carly felt the vibrations rise through her hip, trembling down her spine.

He knew.

She clamped both hands over her mouth now to contain the scream that was building. Tears leaked from her eyes.

Please be quiet. Please be quiet. She sent a silent message to Leah and Marie. She was surprised Leah wasn't openly sobbing and, despite her fear, her desperation, she felt a sense of pride that neither of her sisters had given their hiding place away. They were all in this together. A team.

A family.

A creak. The rusty hinge on the door of the locker next to hers protested as it was opened. She cowered in her metal coffin, feeling the whispers of all those who had lain here before, almost their final resting place. Please don't let it be hers. She drew her knees upwards, that comma again. Not a full stop, please not now.

She had tried so hard to get them out of here, but it wasn't good enough. She wasn't good enough.

At primary school in assembly the kids had recited the Lord's Prayer. Carly would parrot the words, not thinking too deeply about Jesus and God. Not caring, if she was honest.

She cared now.

Dear God. Carly began to pray. Her lips moved, but the words solely in her head.

Please.

Please.

She pictured herself in her bedroom, sprawled on her bed, Bruno snoozing next to her, his paws twitching as he dreamed. He must be missing her. Her parents would be fraught. Would she ever see them again?

'They're not upstairs.' Doc spoke now, breathless as though he had been running. 'Christ, what was this? Some sort of hospital?' There was a crash as he kicked the trolley.

'A morgue, I think,' Moustache said.

'It's as creepy as fuck. I've had enough of this place—'

'I don't give a shit,' Moustache snapped. 'We stay until we find them. We don't get the girls, we don't get paid. If they're not here they could have made it out by now and then we're fucked. The road is only a few metres away.'

Bitter disappointment crawled through Carly's veins. They'd been so close. If it weren't for the fog they would have spotted the fence.

'Let's have another scout around outside then, but if we don't find them soon we'll have to go. They could have flagged down a car, someone could be calling the police right now...' Doc's voice grew fainter and Carly slumped with relief. They were gone.

The urge to burst out of her hiding place prickled at her goosebumped skin but Carly forced herself to remain where she was, to make sure they really were alone. As she waited she turned their words over in her mind. *We don't get the girls, we don't get paid.*

She had thought that this was a kidnap and they had demanded a ransom from their parents but perhaps the men were planning on selling them to someone else? Either way there was a plan for them. Carly needed to get her sisters to safety before it was put in place. *The road's only a few metres away.*

It was knowing this that gave Carly the strength and courage to gently push open the door to her locker, wincing at the creak. Moustache and Doc believed that she might have flagged down a car and asked for help and so she too must believe that she could. Determinedly, she unfolded herself from the small space, toes wriggling to chase the pins and needles away from her socked feet. As she dropped to the floor she drew a deep breath, fetid and repugnant, but the air still fresher than it had been inside her steel casket. Hurriedly, she released her sisters, shushing them as she helped them out.

'We're almost out of here,' she whispered. 'We're right by the road and once we find it we can go home.'

'Will Mum and Dad be cross?' The whites of Marie's wide eyes were bright in the silver moonlight that pushed through a gash in the roof.

'Of course not,' Carly said. 'They'll have been horribly worried but this hasn't been our fault, any of it.' But even if that was the truth it felt like a lie. She blamed herself endlessly. If only she hadn't let the twins play with the ball in the garden, if only she had been the one to shut the gate.

If only, if only, if only.

'Come now.' Marie and Leah both slipped a hand inside hers, their palms slick with fear. They padded across the room. The rain slipped inside the building and puddled on the ground, but Carly barely noticed as her socks absorbed the water.

They were going home to dry socks. Dry clothes. Food.

Love.

At the doorway she hesitated. Which way? If she turned left she could lead them out the way they came in, but was that the way the men had gone? Unlike the other buildings Carly hadn't seen any windows that they could climb out of, which was a shame. But they could fit through spaces the men couldn't. Carly didn't know if there was another exit and she didn't want to waste time searching. She retraced their steps, all the while her chest painfully tight, her throat clogged with the scream she kept trying to swallow back down, but her mouth was so dry. They were tantalizingly close to freedom but still light years away.

'We're nearly outside,' she whispered and the thought was both terrifying and reassuring. Fingers tightened around hers as they passed through the corridor where the roof was intact – the blackness swallowing them – and then they were in the shower block. The shower heads bent towards them cackling – *you'll never escape-you'll never escape*. For a split second the room was bright with fluorescent light. Soldiers in the showers rinsing off blood, stumps where their arms should be, crimson water trickling towards the drain…

Carly whimpered.

'Are you okay?' Marie's whisper yanked Carly back to the now where there were no wounded soldiers, no blood, but the fear – the threat of death – was just as real as though it had hung suspended in the air for years, waiting to be reignited.

Waiting for them.

'Move.' Carly's panic lent her feet a sense of urgency. If she had to spend another minute in this place the strands of the past would reach out and wrap around her neck, slip down her throat, trapping her here for eternity. She wouldn't become a ghost.

A full stop.

She was a comma.

This wasn't the end, although in that moment it felt like it.

Abandon hope all ye who enter here.

They were almost at the exit. She could make out the door.

And that's when it happened.

Her shoeless foot landed on something sharp and cutting.

The pain sliced through her skin.

She screamed.

The distant shout told her she'd been heard.

They were coming.

Carly sobbed openly now.

Abandon hope all ye who enter here.

Her eyes slid from the graffiti to the hatches – CONTAMINATED SHOES, CONTAMINATED CLOTHES.

They could fit through spaces the men couldn't.

She released her sisters and sprang forward. Her hands closed over the round metal handle, felt the roughness of the rust as it crumbled. She yanked as hard as she could.

'Come on.'

Her slippery palm lost its grip.

'Come on!' She tugged again. It didn't move. She tried the next hatch, waited for the feel of hot breath on her neck, a hand to clamp on her shoulder, fingers to squeeze her throat. 'Open!'

A sudden pop. She fell backwards as the small door opened, shockwaves of pain ricocheting up her spine. She scrambled to her feet. They were almost out of time, she knew.

But Leah had already sensed what she was about to do. Was already offering a leg up to Marie, who was protesting, 'No. No. We have to stay together.'

'Fucking move!' Carly shouted, her fingers gripping Marie's school jumper and hefting her off the floor, shoving her through the gap. Leah was easier, desperate to follow her twin whose screams were fading. The bear she'd been clutching tumbled to the floor but Carly didn't stop to pick him up.

'Oi!'

The men clattered into the room. Arms outstretched to grab her. Without hesitating Carly hurled herself through the hatch head first.

She was plummeting down the chute into darkness.

Into fiery hot pain.

Into nothing.

Chapter Thirty-Five

Leah

Now

I have shed my usual jeans and T-shirt in favour of smart black trousers and a white shirt, wanting to look capable and in control, even if I don't feel it. Each time my confidence abates, I recall how it felt when I believed Archie had been snatched earlier and my resolve hardens. The second George comes home I am going to the Dog and Duck to see if *he* is there. If he is I'm going to warn him that he's gone too far. He ruined my life and I sent him back to prison the last time he was out.

Tit for tat.

I would set him up again if it weren't for Archie. Now I have too much to lose. Nothing is comparable with what he put me through. We're not even by a long way but it has to stop. When he was a threat to me I was scared. Now he's involved my son I'm furious. The teddy had brought it all back. Not only the child I was then, but the child I had been before. The one who laughed and danced and didn't know what if felt like to feel afraid. I want to be her again. I am stepping out of the quicksand of my past and planting my feet firmly in the present.

George's car pulls onto the drive. I gather my bravado and my keys. I am out of the door before he is in it.

'Where are you going?' he asks.

'Tash's.'

Worry pinches the bridge of his nose into a crease.

'Don't go to Tash's, Leah. Stay in and we'll—'

'I'll be fine. I *am* fine.' I zap my car open and climb inside. While the engine turns over I retune the radio, searching for a Nineties show but the songs are all unfamiliar to me. Too modern.

Instead I call up Spotify- and Bluetooth-courage into my car.

'5, 6, 7, 8.'

Carly and Marie are with me. Together we will end this.

The Dog and Duck is on a main road and I have to park around the corner. I hurry to the entrance, my heart racing as I step across the alley next to the pub, remembering the arms that snatched me. My terror as I was dragged away from my twin. My helplessness as I watched Carly being roughly shoved in the back of the van. I am sinking once more. A figure moves in the shadows. I glance down the gloomy walkthrough. Graffitied on the fence is a clown. *The* clown. His shock of orange hair and menacing grin unsettling me they way it did in *that* room. I dash into the pub. Throwing open doors that clatter my arrival.

The barman glances at me before turning his attention back to the football on the widescreen TV. It's gritty underfoot as I walk to the bar. The smell of chips lingers in the air. Now I'm here I don't quite know what to do. My nerves scream for a vodka but I haven't brought my own glass. Even if I had, I wouldn't be able to drink anything here. Despite the overpowering stench of cheap toilet cleaner, the place looks as though it hasn't been cleaned for years. Still, I can't stay if I don't spend some money so I approach the scratched bar, avoiding leaning my forearms against the surface.

'Excuse me.'

The barman doesn't acknowledge me.

'Excuse me!' My voice echoes around the empty room.

'Whoever you're looking for, I haven't seen them. Don't know them.' He meets my eyes with a stare that chills me.

'Sorry? I don't know...' This isn't going as I planned. How does he know I'm looking for someone? Does he know who I'm looking for?

'Copper, ain't you?'

'No.'

'You look like one.'

I should have kept my jeans on.

'I'm not. I'm...' I think quickly. If I ask if he knows that man, Simon – for the first time in a long time I allow his name to pop into my mind, a testament to how strong I feel right now – then he might text him. Warn him I am here and there's nothing like the element of surprise.

Let me go. Let Marie go.

There are a row of brass pumps tagged with beers named after wildlife. I order a pint of Badger's Black Brew, registering the barman's surprise. He raises his eyebrows again as I count out coins with gloved hands before I drop the money into his open palm, avoiding contact. I choose a rickety chair near the window so I can see anyone approaching. My knee jigs frantically up and down.

Calm yourself.

Three things.

A *Who Wants to Be a Millionaire* quiz machine.

The green baize covering the pool table.

Stainless steel stools with black leather seat pads guarding the bar.

Calm.

I wait.

The traffic whizzes by. A number of pedestrians. None of them are him. Rather than bringing me down, I find this thought cheery. Last time Fregoli led me to believe that he was everywhere. Now I can count on one hand the number of times I have caught sight of him. It has to be real, doesn't it?

The football has finished. The pub now half-full. The jukebox plays 'Bat Out of Hell'. I make a deal with fate. *If you play Steps next I know I'm in the right place.*

'Crazy Nights' plays instead.

I glance at my watch. Archie will be in bed by now. I feel wretched that I haven't kissed him goodnight. I wonder what I'm doing here. Whether I should go home.

But then I see him.

He's heading towards the pub, drawing on a cigarette, smoke pluming from his nostrils.

It's him.

The age doesn't fit. He looks older. Greyer. But it's definitely him.

My senses are in overdrive. Conversations roar around me. The smell of hops is nauseating. Adrenaline floods my body. I'm torn between fight and flight. I want to run. I want to run and never look back. I screw up my eyes, the image of Archie is painted on the inside of my eyelids, his arms around the bear.

Be brave, Leah.

I open my eyes, the street is empty. I turn my head. He is standing next to the table, looking at me with an odd expression on his face.

Without thinking what I am going to do, I leap to my feet. He turns and runs. The hunter has become the hunter.

'Stop!' I cry. Not knowing what I will do if he does.

The doors crash open as he thunders outside. He is pelting down the street but he's not as fast as me. Not as fit. All the hours spent running after Archie are paying off. He throws a glance over his shoulder, expression turning to panic when he sees how quickly I am gaining on him.

'Stop!' I shout again, stretching out my arm. My fingers brush against his back.

It's the blast of horn that alerts us both to the car that is hurtling towards him.

Honestly, I cannot say whether I grabbed him to pull him back or to push him forward but somehow he is sprawled on the road in line with the oncoming traffic.

My thoughts skip from horror to fear to a morbid relief that now it really will all be over.

Chapter Thirty-Six

George

Now

George sits at the kitchen table, moonlight pooling through the window as he nurses a nightcap. He can't believe that tonight an innocent man could have died. Not quite so innocent. He was a drug dealer and thought Leah was a copper chasing him. He was lucky the car didn't kill him. At least a broken pelvis will keep him off the streets for a while. But still. After the police brought Leah home and told George that she was in shock, he knew he should look after her but he couldn't help asking what she was thinking.

She couldn't answer. Couldn't tell him why she was in the pub when she said she would be with Tash.

She's lying.

He's lying.

The thought that the man could have been killed chills George again. He sips his whisky to warm him. Perhaps he should rethink his plan but it's all in place.

Tomorrow.

Chapter Thirty-Seven

Carly

Then

Carly prised open her eyes, squinting as a brilliant white light poured through her.

Was she dead?

Chatter.

Laughter.

Music.

She blinked, once, twice, three times until the blur veiling her sight slipped away. Everything fell into sharp focus.

To her astonishment she was in the ballroom, but not as it had appeared when they'd hidden there earlier, with the soot and the ashes and scattered broken glass, but how it was in Mr Webster's photos. The vibrant red and cream carpet lying smooth over the floor. The three chandeliers suspended from the ceiling, their light creating rainbows through droplets of crystal, long before they were wrenched down and stamped on until they smashed.

'*We'll meet again...*' Vera Lynn promised. All around Carly couples danced. Around her, through her. She didn't know if they were the ghosts or if she was. The handsome men in their high-waisted trousers and frock coats, pinned medals glinting as they spun around women in pencil skirts and hats, beautiful in their matching uniforms and matching smiles.

Happy. Everyone was happy.

'Carly.' Someone was calling her and she wondered whether it was the boy ladling punch with the cropped blond hair and the brilliant blue eyes. He couldn't have been much older than her. Perhaps he wanted to dance with her. She felt a hand slip inside hers but the boy hadn't moved. Carly was confused.

'Wake up.'

But Carly didn't want to wake up. She wanted to stay here where everyone was hopeful.

She wanted to feel hopeful.

Carly felt tears slide onto her cheeks. She wondered why she was crying.

If ghosts could even cry.

'Is she dead?' she heard.

She wanted to tell the boy she wasn't dead, she was here and whole and she wanted to dance with him, but tears dripped again and Carly knew it wasn't the boy who was whispering. It wasn't her own tears she could feel.

'I'm okay,' Carly reassured her sisters but as she tried to sit up, feelings returned hard and fast. Pain in her head, her foot. The tang of blood in her mouth. She wanted to spit it out but didn't want it to land on Leah or Marie so she swallowed it down. Felt it travelling down her throat, swishing around her empty stomach. She retched.

After taking a couple of deep breaths, she asked, 'Are either of you hurt?'

'I think I've twisted my ankle,' Leah said.

Marie began to cry. 'This isn't a game, is it?'

'If it is, we're going to win.' Fuelled by the courage Carly had witnessed in the ballroom, she forced herself to sit and then to kneel. The soldiers had faced far worse than she had. Where would the country be today if they had given up? 'We're getting out of here.' Acid rose in her throat as waves of pain battered her skull each time she moved. 'We need to look for a way out. We don't have much time.'

'But I can't see…'

'You can feel, with your hands. There must be a handle. Something.' Carly remembered Mr Webster telling the class the decontamination chamber had been built when there was a real threat of gas attacks. He had told them about the chutes where any clothing that might be contaminated would be stuffed but he hadn't said what would happen after it had toppled into this small space they now found themselves in. There had to be a way to empty it surely, or did they just burn it? Drop a match through the hatch. Carly looked up fearfully as though she might see fire, her panic raging.

'Carly! I've found something.' Marie was excited, she was always so desperate to please.

'Good girl,' Carly said, shuffling around on her knees, arms splayed out before her until she found her sister.

'Here, on the ground.'

Carly tightened her fingers around a metal ring and pulled as hard as she could. It didn't move. A chink of light caught her eye. She looked up. Someone had cracked open the hatch.

'No,' she moaned as she rattled the handle again.

'*Three blind mice, three blind mice*,' Moustache sang softly.

Slowly. She couldn't hear Doc and she knew he'd be trying to find another way to reach them.

Despite the freezing temperature, she was boiling. She wiped her face with her sleeve.

'Grab hold of me and pull as hard as you can.' Carly grasped the ring, tighter now, with both hands, her sisters' arms wrapped around her waist.

They pulled and pulled until pain seared in Carly's shoulder joints. She felt her body might tear in two as the combined weight of the twins dragged her backwards.

Carly clenched her fingers harder. She wouldn't let go.

Suddenly the trapdoor swung open, sending the sisters tumbling like dominoes.

Sobbing, Carly felt around until she found one of the girls and without hesitation she dragged her over to the hole and shoved her down into the blackness. Whatever was down there couldn't be any worse than being trapped in this tiny space with Moustache still singing above them. It made Carly's stomach contract to realize that he was relishing the chase. Wanting it almost.

'*See how they run. See how they run.*'

'Carly, I…'

'Move,' she snapped, cutting off Leah's protests that it was too dark, she was too scared. She propelled her into the unknown, after Marie, then she scrambled after them both.

The tunnel was low. Damp. The stench was cloying. Their progress was slow at first. Carly felt around with her hands as they moved, terrified there'd be more to the tunnel than they knew. Different routes. The danger they might spend eternity lost in an underground maze was terrifying and something she didn't want to be responsible for. Something *else* she didn't want to be responsible for. Intermittently there were larger openings shooting off the main strip, which didn't seem to lead anywhere, almost as though they were passing places but Carly didn't understand why.

'I think this is the right way. If we keep going straight, we have to come out somewhere, eventually.' She crossed her fingers as she spoke. 'As fast as you can.'

Carly could hear Leah softly crying, the shuffle of the twins as they crawled, and something else.

Rats?

It seemed to take forever, palms pressed into dampness, knees sinking, but in reality it couldn't have been more than five minutes before the tunnel grew wider, and then she saw it.

Pale light.

The moon. Carly nodded her head furiously, affirming to herself that yes, they were nearly outside.

A sharp blow to the nose, sprang tears to Carly's eyes.

'Why have you stopped?' she whispered crossly to Leah, trying to shove her forwards again.

'Marie can see Doc's boots. He's out there.'

Carly felt angry. Helpless. Scared.

'Back up,' she hissed. She retreated, patting the walls, desperately trying to locate one of the pockets they could hide in. Her heart hammered in her chest. She knew if Doc crouched down and shone his torch in the tunnel it was all over.

At last found what she was looking for. She shuffled back even further, ushering the twins inside the cramped space, before she curled herself around them. A comma once more.

They waited.

From outside a shout.

'I've found something! An opening.'

A light sweeping left to right in the tunnel. Carly screwed her eyes tightly closed.

Please don't spot us. Please don't spot us.

And then darkness.

Silence.

'Has he gone?' whispered Marie.

Carly wanted to scream, 'I don't know. I don't have *all* the answers.' She knew that was unfair, but still. She didn't know what to do.

'I think so but let's wait a while.'

She pressed her fingertips over the walls, over the low ceiling. She found something smooth and hard, a large stone. They weren't too far from the outside. Could they burrow out a different way? Potentially Doc and Moustache were waiting at the exit, ready to grab them when they emerged. If they could slip out somewhere else they'd have a chance to reach the road.

Was it silly to try to dig? Could she somehow cause the tunnel to collapse? But knowing that freedom was so tantalizingly close drove Carly to prise her nails under the stone and drag it out of the damp earth.

Suddenly they were all screaming as a deluge of insects poured down on them. Tiny, sharp feet scuttling over their skin. One fell in Carly's open mouth. She gagged as she flicked it off her tongue. They were crawling over her scalp, tangled in her hair. Slipping down the neck of her shirt. She could feel them everywhere, but she couldn't see them. She screamed again as something hard and solid rammed into her eye. The elbow of one of the twins who were flailing their arms. She slapped at her shoulders, pushing down on hard shells.

Beetles.

She tried to calm herself, tell herself she wasn't scared of them but no matter how violently she smacked them away, they wouldn't die. She could still feel the movement of their legs. Hear them scurrying manically under them, above them, on them.

They stank.

Her head was spinning, panic dulling her senses so she didn't instantly notice that the space she was in was now bigger. Emptier. The twins had crawled back out into the tunnel. She could hear Leah screaming as she headed towards the exit.

'No, wait.' She knew the men could easily have heard their cries. Be waiting to grab them. But the girls didn't slow and she had no choice but to follow them.

Chapter Thirty-Eight

George

Now

George slips out of the house while Leah and Archie are sleeping. His mouth is still sour with last night's whisky.

As he climbs into his car he receives a text. Tash. He calls her via his hands-free system.

'Are you okay?'

'George.' Her voice is thick with sobs. 'I can't do this any more. I can't keep lying to Leah. She's my best friend.'

She's my wife, George thinks and he does nothing *but* lie.

'It won't be for much longer,' he promises before he pulls into the car park of the greasy spoon to see the man as he'd arranged.

'Here.' George hands the man an envelope stuffed with notes and in return reluctantly takes the box. It feels as heavy as George's heart as he hefts it into his car. The plan had felt so right, but now it feels so wrong. But he is committed.

There is no going back.

Chapter Thirty-Nine

Carly

Then

Carly burst from the tunnel after her sisters, resigning herself to the fact that hands would grab her. Drag them back to the oppressive room that stank of blocked toilets and vomit.

But there was nothing.

She rose to her feet, all the while brushing her hands against her body. Shaking out her hair. She could still feel the beetles on her.

Thought she would always feel the beetles on her.

Shc usually loved the rain, felt it made everything smell clean, but now there was only the stench of insects in her nostrils. She shivered, her clothes soaked through.

'What do we do?' asked Leah.

Carly wanted to lie down on the floor and cry. She wanted to give up, but that wasn't an option. She was the big sister but she felt so shaky, her legs like spaghetti.

She spun a slow 360, eyes searching the gloom, but it wasn't until the cloud passed across the moon lifting the darkness that she saw the glint of the fence. It was close.

So close.

'Listen.' She crouched onto her haunches and gathered her

sisters to her. 'You've been so brave but I need you to be brave a little longer.'

Her sisters nodded. Their faces edged in silver light.

'Over there is the fence. We're going to run as fast but as quietly as we can. If the men come back – if one of us gets caught – we don't stop. We don't go back.'

'But—' Marie began.

'No buts. If we're separated it will only be until one of us reaches help and then all of this will be over.' Carly felt guilt scrunch her insides. Marie was sick and Leah had hurt her ankle, but if she went at their pace, there was a danger they'd all get caught. At least this way there was a chance she'd make it and she'd fetch help more quickly. She was determined if she left them, it wouldn't be for long. 'We'll soon be home.'

'With Mummy and Daddy.' Leah perked up.

'Yes. And Bruno. Cross my heart.' Carly curved both her little fingers and hooked them around the twins' pinkies:

'A pinkie promise can't be broke

Or you'll disappear in a puff of smoke

This is my vow to you,

I'll keep my promise through and through.'

'We're going home.' Carly's voice was steadier this time. 'Are you ready?'

'Yes,' they said, but their voices were small.

'Run!'

Carly's feet flew over the rough ground. She didn't slow. Didn't stop to check how far behind Marie and Leah were.

She threw herself at the fence. Twisted her fingers around the wire, shook it hard. It was too high to climb and besides the top was razor wire.

Quickly she moved on. Her eyes scanned for a gate but instead of the exit she'd tumble through, open and conspicuous, she found something better.

A hole.

She dropped to her knees and clawed through the undergrowth, the sharp edges of wire scraping against her back, until she was through and could stand once more. She took a precious second to seek out the twins. They hadn't yet reached the perimeter, their arms around each other. Carly wasn't sure who was holding who up. Carly waved until she was sure they had spotted her and then she turned and scrambled up the bank, slip-sliding backwards, driving herself forwards once more.

And there it was.

A road.

The road.

She nearly wept, but instead threw herself into a ditch and it was there she waited until Marie and Leah popped their heads over the bank like meerkats. The sisters were reunited once more. A team. Carly was glad. No matter how much they needed her, she knew she needed them too.

The road was barely a track, and Carly's spirits dipped as she wondered how frequently it was used, but she told herself to stay positive. Even if they didn't meet any traffic the road had to lead somewhere. Somewhere there would be a phone and a police station. Warm, dry clothes, and a sense of safety. Somewhere they could wait for their parents and that thought made her both nervous and excited. Although she'd told Marie they wouldn't be angry there was a doubtful voice inside her head, wondering if they might blame her. If her stepdad would hate her for putting his daughters at risk, but that was silly. He'd never made her feel any different, any less. Their parents would be overjoyed to see them, all of them, she knew.

'Keep low and follow me.' Carly crawled along the verge, her hands slapping against wet grass, her knees slipping. 'If Moustache and Doc appear, lie flat and keep still.'

She couldn't hear them. Couldn't hear anything except the rain beating against the tarmac and her own frantic heart. Her eyes searched the darkness for yellow beams of torchlight but there was nothing.

Had they got away? Carly dared herself to hope.

Progress was slow. Her back ached. Her head hurt. She stole a glance behind her at Leah's face deathly pale in the glow of moonlight. Carly could see she was in pain but she hadn't once complained about her ankle.

Eventually they came to a fork in the road.

Which way?

There wasn't a tell-tale glow of lights from houses, or the blue flickering light from TV sets.

Left or right? Right or left?

There was so much at stake.

Before Carly could make up her mind she saw two spots of light in the distance.

'No.'

She shook her head as though she could make them disappear but then she realized they were travelling too fast to be torchlights. They were headlights.

A car.

Lightning cracked.

Carly felt adrenaline course through her as she cast one last look around for the men, but they were nowhere to be seen.

She staggered to her feet and stumbled into the middle of the road, waving her arms.

'Help! Help!'

The rumble of thunder masked her thin cries. Leah and Marie joined Carly in the middle of the road, the air full of their desperate pleas.

'Stop! Please!'

For a second the car seemed to accelerate before it stopped. Its hazard lights winked as it hugged the verge.

Carly shielded her eyes. She couldn't see who was driving.

Both doors clicked open.

Were they safe now?

Chapter Forty

Leah

Now

Today is my first thought as the sun glaring through the curtains prises open my eyes. My head is fuzzy. There's a bitter taste in my mouth, almost as though I have a hangover. It's not alcohol causing bitterness to rise in my throat though, but the memory that last night I had almost chased an innocent man to his death.

I'd been so sure it was him but it was my Fregoli again deceiving me. I am no longer sure what I think. I no longer trust myself. My only hope is that everyone else is right. It's some crackpot sending the letters and everything else is just in my imagination.

The teddy bear is a coincidence.

The cross, though? That can't be as easily explained.

I roll over, stretching my legs out in the empty space George should be.

By the end of today this will all be over.

Until then I am not going out. Archie and I will snuggle up on the sofa and watch *Peter Pan*. *The Incredibles*. *The Jungle Book*.

We'll be safe, I tell myself. Safe.

It is then Archie lets out a piercing scream.

Chapter Forty-One

Carly

Then

Two women were in the car that had stopped. Now, the sisters clung to each other on the back seat while the women asked them for their names. Carly couldn't answer. Leah and Marie wouldn't. Strangers were once just people they didn't yet know, now they were to be feared.

'Taken' is all Carly could say.

'Taken? What have you taken?' The women exchanged a glance.

'Taken.' Carly began to cry.

'My God.' One of the women leaned towards Carly and placed a hand on her knee. Carly flinched from her touch. 'Are you the Sinclair Sisters?'

'The girls that were abducted?' the other woman said. 'You've been headlines in every single newspaper and on all the TV channels. Not just in the UK but worldwide.'

Carly cried harder. Leah and Marie also burst into tears.

'It's all right. Everyone's been looking for you. There's been alleged sightings of you up and down the country, and abroad but… my goodness. You're here. You're okay.'

'Please...' Carly hiccupped out breaths. 'Take us home.'

'Your poor parents will be so relieved. We're not far from a police station so—'

'Quickly.' Carly looked out of the windows fearfully. 'Before they find us.' The women exchanged hurried whispers before they pulled away.

Despite the fan blasting out heat, and the tartan blanket draped over their knees, Carly couldn't stop trembling. The heat magnified the smell of the dried vomit on their clothes, the urine on their socks. She swallowed down bile.

Every pothole, each flash of lightning and rumble of thunder made her jump.

As she tried to stem her tears she was aware of the woman in the passenger seat twisting around, asking her if they'd been hurt, who had taken them, telling her that they were now famous, but Carly couldn't look at her. Couldn't tear her gaze away from the window. Rain slid down the glass. The trees shadowed against an iron sky. In the distance, darker shapes, the buildings from the RAF base. Carly couldn't bear to see it but she couldn't turn away either.

The car slowed, indicators *tick-tick-ticked*.

In her peripheral vision Carly caught a movement. She turned her head.

It was him.

Doc.

She inhaled sharply. Her throat was clogged with fear. She couldn't draw air in or force words out.

He was so close. If he hurried he could wrench open the door and grab her.

She felt hot and cold. Sick. Unable to react.

His eyes found hers and there was something in them that Carly thought she had seen in him before.

Sympathy?

Regret?

He nodded once. The car began to move again. They were leaving him far behind but nevertheless he would always stay with Carly. In her nightmares, in her head.

She twisted further around in her seat, her palms against the window.

He was gone.

Once they reached the police station it all became a blur, as though Carly was, at last, allowing herself to switch off, allowing somebody else to take charge.

'The Sinclair Sisters.' A crowd of police officers grinned at them as though they had personally found them. 'You've caused quite a fuss.'

'Am I in trouble?' Carly whispered, knowing it was all her fault. She should have taken better care of her sisters.

'Of course not!' A lady with a white pixie cut and pink cheeks spoke kindly. 'I'm Angela and I'll stay with you until Mum and Dad arrive. Let's take you somewhere more private while we wait for them. It won't be long until the vultures find out that you're here.'

'Vultures?' Marie asked.

'Tabloids,' the woman said.

'Do tabloids eat dead people like vultures?' Marie looked confused.

'Yes, they like to pick over bones. Don't you worry, my darling.'

They were ushered into a room and wrapped in blankets. Next to Carly, the radiator was blasting out heat but still she couldn't stop shivering.

'Are you hurt?' Angela asked.

Carly shook her head, 'But Leah twisted her ankle and Marie has been vomiting.'

'We'll be getting you all checked over by a doctor when your parents are here, but first let's get something sweet inside of you.'

Flimsy polystyrene cups of hot chocolate floating with clumps of powder were pushed into their freezing hands. Leah and Marie drained their drinks, not waiting until they had cooled. Carly couldn't touch hers, her stomach a mass of worry. She didn't know how to explain herself. She couldn't make sense of how it all happened. One minute she was texting Dean while the twins were playing and then… Carly began to cry again. How could her parents ever forgive her?

The twins were on their third hot chocolate when the door creaked open. Her parents rushed inside. Leah and Marie ran over to their father and scrambled up his legs like monkeys climbing a tree. 'Thank God. Thank God.' Her stepdad balanced a twin on each hip. Carly's mum cupped her face.

'Do you hate me?' Carly asked.

'Hate you? No! If anything, I hate myself. I should have been at home with you all. This *wasn't* your fault.'

The twins wriggled free and pulled at Mum and then all three girls were encircled in arms, Mum and Dad holding them too tightly, whispering 'sorry' over and over again in their hair. Carly sagged against them as she realized they didn't blame her, they blamed themselves. It felt like they melded together as one. Carly couldn't tell where her family began and she ended.

And there, in the small room with the plain walls and the harsh fluorescent light, Carly felt like she was home.

'Mr and Mrs Sinclair?' The voice melted the glue that held them together and they fell apart. 'Can I run through what's going to happen now? I'm Chief Inspector Graham McDonald.'

Dad scooped up the twins again.

'We will find the bastards, I promise you that,' said Graham in a thick Scottish accent while Carly's mother sobbed into a tissue.

It seemed to take forever before they were ushered out of the back entrance of the station to avoid the reporters, but still as they were driven past the front of the building cameras clicked firework-night flashes, rapid and bright. Questions were shouted. Outside of their house were news vans. Neighbours stood on steps in their dressing gowns, breath billowing in the frigid night air. It was chaotic and overwhelming and Carly couldn't wait to be inside, but once back in her bedroom she found it unfamiliar and unsafe.

For weeks afterwards the twins would creep into Carly's room after darkness fell, sneaking into the canopied bed she'd found embarrassing before she'd been taken but now she was thankful for the wispy white voiles she could draw around them. Shut out the world. The sisters would cuddle up together and Carly was thankful for the company. She couldn't bear to be alone even if Leah had started wetting the bed and in the early hours, Marie's arms and legs would thrash, as though she was running or fighting off an attacker. Carly herself would wake in the middle of the night, her sheets drenched with sweat, and for a nanosecond she'd wonder if it had been some awful, terrible nightmare. Then her tongue would prod the gap in her mouth where her tooth had been knocked out in the van on the way to Norcroft. Her parents had tried to persuade her to go to the dentist. Reassured her that he'd be able to fix it so you'd never know, but she hadn't wanted to – wanting that physical reminder to never again become complacent.

Often she'd sense she was being watched, catch sight of a shadow the other side of the voiles. Fear would stab her chest until she peered around the material to see it was her mum watching them, as though she was concerned they would disappear again. In the day Mum often touched the girls, reassuring herself they were really back. A hand on their arms. Fingers brushing the hair away from faces. But she never asked them questions, as though she was afraid to hear the answers. Not wanting to know what her children had been through – but it was there in her eyes, the wondering what the men had done to them. The tentative questions that Carly brushed aside. She couldn't bear to talk about it. She wanted to tell her the men hadn't done anything to them but she knew that wasn't true. Physically they might be unharmed but mentally, emotionally, Carly knew they would never be the same again. Any of them.

Each day there was talking. Endless talking. Adults with hard eyes and soft voices asked them to draw their feelings. Countless photos of tattoos were slid across the table in front of her until Carly identified the eye on the back of Moustache's neck. The police knew who he was. Although he'd fled his last known address, they found his brother, Doc, in his flat, hanging from the bannisters. Inexplicably, Carly felt sad when she learned this. They reassured Carly's parents that they were confident they'd catch Moustache, that they shouldn't worry, but they did. Her parents seemed to have shrunk since the girls had been snatched. Lines of worry were etched into their faces. Carly caught a whispered discussion between them about moving abroad, somewhere remote, but Carly knew for certain that however far they moved away Moustache would be able to find them if he wanted to.

Three blind mice, three blind mice.

Reporters still camped outside their home. They couldn't go to the park, they didn't go back to school for ages. Prisoners. Still prisoners. When they did have to venture out, a crowd closed around them, microphones thrust towards mouths, cameras held high above heads, relentless click-click-clicking. The police would form a barrier with their arms and demand everyone clear some room, give them some space. They'd hold hands, Carly, Leah, Marie, her mum and stepdad – a family united – and rush, heads down, never pausing to give a comment.

See how they run. See how they run.

Mum made their favourite meals, macaroni dripping with cheese and chicken stuffed with garlic butter, but Carly's appetite didn't return.

'Can't you just forget it's happened?' Mum asked wearily.

'Forget?' Anger flared in Carly's stomach.

'I don't mean forget but… it's like you're punishing yourself. Punishing us. We need to try and put it behind us. All of it.'

'You don't know what it was like.' Carly gripped the edge of the table so tightly she feared her fingers would snap.

'I know but I do know that I can't go back and change things for you, however much I want to,' her mum said. 'I'm trying to make it up to you, Carly. Make everything normal again. Please. Try and eat. You know you love my apple crumble.'

But Carly pushed her bowl away. Everything tasted of Spicy

Tomato Snaps and blackcurrant liquorice sweets. She stalked across the kitchen. Her mum had fetched a glass as Carly lifted a bottle of cherry Coke from the fridge, watching as her daughter fizzed it open and tipped it down the sink, trying to understand, but not.

As much as her mother smothered her, her stepdad was the opposite. Out of the house at all hours. Tense and angry when he was home. Constantly calling the police station for an update. The phone clutched tightly in one hand, his other hand shaking a fist indicating what he would do to the surviving kidnapper if he ever got hold of him. He would jab off the TV if anyone put it on – the sisters were still featured on every channel. Their scared, pale faces stared out from newspapers. Hordes of cuddly toys were delivered, postmarks from all around the world. Brightly coloured cards depicting balloons, houses, champagne – with messages of *welcome home*; *congratulations!* Mum put them all in the bin. Once Carly had fished one out, which read, *If you don't accept Jesus into your lives your girls will be taken again.* Her family weren't religious but that night Carly had knelt at the side of her bed, hands clasped together and prayed.

The only people Carly could bear to spend time with were the twins. They became a unit of three, bound together by their trauma. It was Carly they turned to for bedtime stories, Carly they handed their hairbrush to each night. Her sisters were all she wanted. All she needed. Carly screamed at her mum so many times to leave her alone, little by little she began to comply. Mum retreated into herself. Her skin seemed to hang off her frame. Her eyes bloodshot, black bags hanging beneath them.

Why couldn't the police find Moustache?

Carly shut everyone out. Ignoring the unread texts on her Nokia, even the one from Dean Malden. He didn't seem important any more.

All the time, there was that awful knowing twisting in Carly's gut. Moustache was still out there.

It all felt too much, but it turned out that was the lull in the storm.

It's incomprehensible that being abducted wasn't the worst part at all.

What came after they were rescued was far, far worse.

Chapter Forty-Two

Leah

Now

Archie screams again. My body responds before my mind properly processes what I am hearing. I am rocketing down the stairs, towards the noise, but his screams have now morphed into something else.

Laughter.

I fly into the kitchen, Archie is kneeling on the floor, giggling as a puppy licks his face.

'No.' I back away. Wondering if I'm still dreaming.

'Before you start—' George holds up his hands. 'If we hadn't taken him in, he'd have been put down and Archie's been asking for a puppy forever.'

'No.' I can't seem to think of anything else to say.

'What happened to you wasn't Bruno's fault,' George says gently as though he has read my mind. 'You can't keep punishing Archie for what happened.'

'I'm not.' Am I? Lots of people don't want pets.

A rush of heat engulfs me. George places his hand on my shoulder. I angrily shrug him off.

'How can you do this to me?' I ask.

‘I’m doing this *for* you. If nothing else the dog will be protection.’

But the only thing I feel I need protecting from in this instant is my husband.

There’s a smattering of reporters outside the house and for once George agrees that Archie and I should stay home.

Today.

I keep checking the doormat but no letter has arrived.

‘I’ll go to Tesco’s and do a shop,’ he offers, ‘and pick up some bits at Pets at Home.’ He stalks to the bottom of our drive and informs the crowd that the curtains are staying closed and I won’t be going outside. Some of them drift away immediately. Some of them linger in hope.

I ring Tash.

‘How was the dentist?’ Despite everything, I haven’t forgotten my manners.

‘Dentist?’

‘Your emergency appointment yesterday?’

‘Yes. Fine. Are you okay?’

‘You’ll never guess what my husband has done?’ I ask.

‘What?’ she sounds wary.

‘He’s bought Archie a dog.’

‘He’s a good man,’ Tash says. ‘He only ever tries to do the right thing for you.’

‘Whose side are you on?’ Irritation creeps into my voice.

‘Yours,’ she assures me quickly. ‘It’s just that George, George…’ she begins to cry.

‘Tash? What’s wrong?’

‘You’re not going to like this.’ Her voice is thick with tears.

'Tash! You're scaring me. Nothing can be that bad.'

'I wasn't at the dentist yesterday.'

'Right.' I'm not sure what to make of it. 'So where were you?'

'The doctor's.'

'Are you okay?'

For a second there is silence broken by the odd sniff. 'I… I'm pregnant.'

'What?' I'm stunned. 'But you said you didn't… you haven't even got a boyfriend?'

'It was a one-night thing. Listen, Leah. I wanted to tell you but I sounded out George first to see how he thought you'd take it. You know how you are about…'

'Hospitals. Germs. Child safety. Everything,' I finish for her. She knows the details. All that happened. I know she's been thinking of me but it's sad she hadn't felt able to share her news without considering how it would affect me.

'He asked me to wait until after the anniversary. Said you were fragile enough. You're lucky to have him, Leah. He wouldn't have brought the dog home if he thought it wouldn't be good for you in the long run.'

'I don't know what to say. You're doing it alone?'

'Yes.'

'Who will be with you when you give birth?' Selfishly I am worried she might ask me.

'I don't know but, Leah, I'll be okay and hospitals are pretty sterile with their antibacterial dispensers everywhere and… I think… I think I'll be a good mum. I know I said I didn't want kids but since I've found out I feel all… I don't know.'

'Maternal?'

'Yeah. I guess. It feels like a good thing. Not a disaster, you know?'

'Then I'm happy for you,' I say and I am. It will be another person in my orbit to worry about, but that's because I will love this baby as much as I love Tash.

'Thanks. So how are you? Really? Has there been a letter today?'

'No. I keep waiting for something to happen. It is "The Day", but other than the bloody dog nothing has happened.'

'That's good. Hopefully tomorrow you'll feel better.'

'I'll feel better when Marie turns up.'

'Still no word?'

'No. I know this isn't out of character for her but… well, she wanted me and Carly to help with the TV thing and we didn't really listen to her properly. I just hope she has got a tour and isn't off somewhere feeling let down. Or…'

'I don't think she's been taken. It doesn't make sense that she would be. Not without you and Carly anyway.'

But that's what I'm afraid of. That today he's coming for us too.

'Mummy!' Archie calls from the kitchen. 'Mummy the puppy has done a *big* wee on the floor.'

I tell Tash I'll speak to her later and hang up the phone.

By the time I have cleared up and washed the floor three times it is lunchtime. Archie plays with the puppy in the garden. I watch him out of the window while I make us a sandwich. I hope George will be home soon. My phone rings and I brush the crumbs from my gloves before I answer it.

'How are you holding up today?' Graham doesn't bother with pleasantries.

'Pretty much as expected,' I say.

'Look. I did a bit of digging. Not that I think he's a threat to you or anything but...'

'But?'

'I checked the CCTV of the Dog and Duck on the day you think Marie went missing and she was there.'

'There?'

'Outside the pub. She was with a man but he had his back to the camera. There's only one working on that road so you can't see if she left with him but she didn't look scared. Sorry I can't offer anything else. I'll keep looking into it, I promise. In the meantime don't do anything stupid. What you did the last time, paying someone to plant evidence to frame him for a crime he hadn't committed... I can't turn a blind eye to anything like that again. Understand?'

'Yes.' I hang up the phone and sink into my chair, heavy with dread. Closing my eyes, I summon up the image of my twin but instead of seeing her as she is now, I see her as she was then, running furiously towards the man who had me in his grip. Pummelling him with both hands.

Brave.

The memory gives me courage.

She never let me down. I can't let her down now. It crosses my mind that I should ring Carly, but first I need to get my thoughts in order. It's such a lot to process.

Marie was at the Dog and Duck.

He drinks at the Dog and Duck.

The man who arranged our abduction. The only one who went to jail after Doc committed suicide and Moustache was shot in a botched armed robbery. Before Moustache died he told the doctor that he'd been paid to kidnap us by a man and, in between asking for forgiveness, he gave up the name of the man who had arranged it all.

Him.

Simon.

Is it possible she is with him?

The man whose horrible, selfish, unfathomable decision ruined all our lives.

Willingly with him?

She could be. After all, *he* – Simon – is her father.

Mine too.

Part Two

Chapter Forty-Three

Marie

Then

Marie couldn't sleep. It was a muggy night and her Little Mermaid duvet felt suffocating but she worried that if she kicked it off then something might come along and nibble her feet. She pulled her covers up to her chin, taking comfort in the fact that Ariel, with hair as red as hers and Leah's, would keep her safe from the toe-nibbler who she thought lived under her bed, swishing him away with her tail.

Her twin had been asleep for ages. It was rare for one sister to be awake without the other and Marie was bored. She slipped out of bed, padded over to the chest of drawers and wound the projector again. The motor hummed, casting sea creatures across the deep-blue walls. Carly said it was designed for babies and that the twins should have outgrown it at eight but how could you be too old to feel as though you were part of the ocean? She could almost smell the salt, feel the warm sand between her toes. She did hope they'd be going on holiday this year, they had stayed at home all of last summer and she'd missed going on an aeroplane, then playing with kids they'd met on the beach...

Tonight it was as though she was alone in the world except

for the octopus drifting across her wall, the shoals of orange striped fish shimmering across her ceiling. It was disconcerting. Marie didn't like being alone. 'It's the actress in you,' her mum said. 'Always wanting an audience.' She didn't mean it unkindly but still, Marie didn't agree. It wasn't that she craved attention but it was just… better when she was with Leah. Without her twin she felt incomplete. They were two halves of a whole. It was more fun with Carly too. Well, it used to be. Lately she'd been constantly glued to her phone, waiting for that stupid boy, Dean, to text. She had stopped spending so much time with Leah and Marie, instead lying on her bed, staring at the screen as though willing it to light up. She didn't often dance with them any more and some of their routines didn't work with just two people.

Carly was their half-sister, but it had never made a difference before. She had never seemed any less. Now Marie wondered if she'd gone off her and Leah – often she rolled her eyes if they asked her to perform with them. 'It's adolescence,' their dad said, ruffling Marie's hair when she had cried after Carly had again snapped at her to go away. 'It'll happen to you and Leah soon enough.' The thought that Leah might start to prefer the company of boys to her own sister seemed ridiculous, but still a piece of string wiggled around inside Marie's belly until it tied itself in knots.

Why couldn't things remain exactly as they were? She wanted them to stay together forever. She'd even imagined the sisters sharing their own house one day. Instead of a boring dining room they'd have a room with a stage where they'd sing karaoke after a hard day at work.

Marie thought back to the last time Carly had babysat her and Leah. Marie and Leah had leaped around the kitchen, pretending to smooch with the backs of their hands – '*Carly and Dean sitting in a tree, K.I.S.S.I.N.G.*' Carly had burst into tears and pounded up to her room, and when the twins had shuffled in shamefaced to say sorry, she had flung her mobile phone across the room and shouted, 'Get lost.' Later Carly had come back downstairs and microwaved some popcorn before melting butter and coating the kernels. The girls had snuggled on the sofa and watched *The Parent Trap* – a comedy about identical twins being separated at birth that made them laugh but also made Marie sad the girls in the film weren't being raised together.

She wanted a cuddle.

Marie considered waking her twin but if she told Leah her innermost fears she knew her twin would become anxious too and she already worried too much – but then she was the baby of the family; Marie was a whole twelve minutes older. Instead, Marie cracked open the bedroom door as quietly as she could, her socked feet swallowed by the thick-pile carpet as she crept downstairs.

The lounge was in darkness but there was a sliver of light spilling out from under the kitchen door. Marie wrapped her fingers around the handle but before she could press it down she heard the sound of her mum crying.

'There has to be another way?'

'Feel free to think of one.' Marie could tell her dad was trying not to shout but she could hear his crossness nevertheless. It was the stern tone he frequently used for Bruno after the dog had shaken his head, coating the walls with his slobber.

'I can't agree to it. It will be emotionally damaging and terrifying and… it's wrong.'

'It'll be over so quickly. It'll be an adventure… Don't look at me like that. Okay, "adventure" is a bad choice of word, but is it really so terrible if you look at the bigger picture? We know there is no real threat. No one will be hurt. It's for the greater good really. A short-term sacrifice for a long-term gain. Isn't it worth it? To get our security back? For the years of happiness that will lie ahead. I promise you we will *all* quickly forget.'

'Would it be so bad if we had to sell up? Downsize?'

'Steph, I've been over this *again* and *again*.' His words dripped with exasperation. Marie could almost picture him running his hand over his scalp, bristling the ginger hair he kept almost shaved as though he was ashamed of it, despite the fact he claimed he loved the colour on her and Leah. 'We'll be bankrupt. The business I've spent years building up will be gone. We'll have nothing. We'll *be* nothing. What will people think?'

'Does it matter? If we're together.'

'Who says we'll be together? It will put a huge strain on us living in some council house, relying on benefits—'

'It's not that bad—'

'You can't tell me you were happier when you and Carly were living hand-to-mouth? Don't tell me you don't love the holidays, the shopping. You bloody do enough of it. Carly won't remember living like that. You'll be sending her back to a life she'll feel she doesn't belong in. She'll resent you.'

'But the twins are young, they'll—'

'Who's to say I'll let Leah and Marie live in some hovel? They'll stay with me. I've friends—'

'So where are they now? These *friends*? Anyway, why couldn't me and Carly come?'

'It's a big ask to expect someone to house five extra people, three is a push. And that's without the bloody dog. He'd have to go to the shelter, of course.'

'I can't believe you're even considering us living apart.'

'That's the last thing I want. I love you all. I know you don't want to go back to where you and Carly came from. I'm doing my utmost to prevent that.'

'The thought of us separating shouldn't even have crossed your mind. We're a *family*.'

There was a pause. Marie's fingers slipped from the handle. Her palm was damp. She wiped it on her pyjama top. Panic made her feel all funny and light-headed. She didn't understand half of the conversation but she grasped her dad was saying he might take her and Leah away. What was he talking about? Carly and Mum living in a different house to him and Marie and Leah. Would that just be the start? Would Marie be sent somewhere else? She'd played orphan Annie on stage and it was fun, but didn't want to end up in a care home eating cold mush with somebody like Miss Hannigan looking after her.

'Tell me again,' her mum said.

'With the right media coverage, missing children can attract a lot of attention. More and more people are using the internet. You're always on that Friends Reunited. There are sites where we can place digital appeals to ask for money.'

'But surely that money can't come directly to us? It must be allocated to—'

'That's where Stuart would come in. I'd move him over from the business to focus on creating a campaign, both online and through newspapers. Getting people to invest their cash is what he excels at.'

Mum muttered something Marie couldn't hear.

'He's not accountable for the current market. Even if clients aren't dipping their hands into their pockets for products, they *will* pay for a story that pulls at the heartstrings.'

'And he'd know it's all fake?'

'God, no. The fewer people who know the truth, the less room there is for error. Besides, we want him to feel frightened for our family unit. Fear is a great motivator. He's very fond of us, you know, and despite the dip in profits these past couple of years, he is very good at what he does. Potentially, if we hit it hard, I'd expect to raise an easy seven figures worldwide.'

'And that would be ours? No questions asked?'

'It's feasible it would go on our living expenses while the search is on and that could cover a multitude of sins. If we stretched the time we could form a charity and—'

'Absolutely not. A couple of days, you said.'

'A week, tops.'

'That's too long—'

'There'll be no risk. No danger. I promise. Afterwards there'll be a big reunion piece and we can sell photos of the first time we're all together again, and for future anniversaries, milestones. Literally everything in the press is staged. There'll also be interviews. Chat shows. How do you fancy sitting on the sofa on that breakfast TV show you love?'

'It's all a lie. I don't know if I can—'

'You can. For me.'

'But what about the logistics? How would it happen? When?'

'You leave that to me. The less you know, the better. When you stand in front of the camera and plead directly to the abductor, I want the shock on your face to be genuine. The more the public root for you, the more they'll feel inclined to donate.'

'What if it backfires?'

'It won't. It's foolproof. I'm surprised no other families have done this. I'm sure in years to come they will. I've planned it so meticulously nothing can go wrong. We'll be back on our feet financially. I know it's a disruption for the girls but a few days is better than ripping their lives apart long-term. They won't have to change to state schools or live on a rough estate where they'd probably end up on drugs. I know it seems extreme but I've given it so much thought. We can go to Florida afterwards, make it up to them. Even have family therapy if you feel it's needed, but I genuinely believe they'll be fine. They're young. In time they'll forget it ever happened. It will be just one small event in their long and happy lives.'

'You think?'

'I know. Trust me.'

'I do,' said her mum but Marie wasn't sure who she trusted any more. She sank to the floor, tears streaming down her cheeks. Although she didn't know what her dad had planned, she knew it was bad, very bad indeed – and she was the only one who knew.

The only one who could stop him.

Chapter Forty-Four

Marie

One week ago

Marie drifted around her flat after her sisters had left. Although they hadn't been here for long, their absence was noticeable everywhere; from the dip in the sofa where Carly had sat, to Leah's untouched tea on the table, and the pangs in Marie's heart. They hadn't agreed to the TV interview but it hadn't gone as badly as it could have done. Despite their initial outrage – the awkwardness that always seemed to settle around them whenever they met – there was something else. Hope. This year, Marie hadn't tried to justify the unjustifiable – absolving herself of the blame that pressed on her shoulders like a concrete cape – by steering the annual conversation in its usual direction – the *it wasn't as bad as we thought, was it?* and *it's made us into the people we are today* – as though the abduction had been a good thing.

It hadn't.

And that knowing. That godawful knowing – crawling across her skin – that she *could* have stopped it. That she *should* have stopped it. The constant itch of guilt that she couldn't scratch, that alcohol couldn't numb. That couldn't be sated by the stream of men that woke up in her bed. She didn't trust any of them and she wondered if she had ever been really loved by the many hands that had touched her. She didn't believe she had.

But her sisters had loved her once. They still did. She knew this from the way they would drop everything to sit in a freezing theatre while she overacted for a barely-there audience, Leah's hands slapping together like an over-enthusiastic seal, the way they had done when Marie had put on plays when they were small.

'*Again, Marie, again.*'

The way they scolded her when she returned after disappearing on a tour she hadn't told them about, promising them she'd let them know next time. Not telling them that there hadn't been a tour, instead a round of dirty bars and faceless men and a pounding headache that she dulled with vodka whenever her hangover crept back in. Whenever her thoughts crept back in.

Sometimes it got too much, their love – and yet she craved it, but not as much as she craved forgiveness. She tried to be a good sister but she was the shadow twin. The darkness to Leah's light. As much as she needed to be around her sisters, the burden of truth always sent her scuttling away from them again. She wanted them to miss her but equally she wanted them to forget her.

It was all such a mess.

Marie picked up the plate of biscuits before setting them back down again. She was twitchy, unable to settle. Her veins felt empty as her craving built until the thought of a hit was all-consuming, but her stash was as empty as her purse. God, why had she slipped into drugs? It was so much easier, so much more socially acceptable when it was just the alcohol. But she'd gained a reputation as a drunk and once the acting offers dried up she had thought that if she stayed sober but dabbled in substances occasionally just to take the edge off, it would be easier.

She was such a fool.

She'd make herself a cup of tea although she knew her spasming stomach would likely throw it back up.

While the kettle boiled she checked her phone – two missed calls from George. Her body went hot at the thought that Leah could have picked up his call. What had she become? Secrets. Lies. She was an awful, terrible person. Her skin itched. She bounced up and down on the balls of her feet.

What was she going to do?

If she wanted to repair her fractured relationship with Leah and Carly she couldn't push them into doing the interview. Understandably, they were shocked that Marie would even suggest going on a live TV show to rip off the scab they were always picking at, knowing how raw it would be underneath. And Marie couldn't explain it to them, no matter how much she wanted to.

Carly was partly right – initially, Marie had been attracted to the large sum of money on offer. God knows she needed it. She owed her dealer a small fortune. Two weeks ago he'd pushed her up against the wall in the alley next to the Dog and Duck, the slime coating her back, skin grazing her elbows as he pinned her wrists against the rough bricks. Rain plastered her hair to her scalp as he pressed his mouth against her ear. She could smell his breath, coffee and smoke. Panic cut off her air supply. Just being back in an alley again could do that to her, even disregarding what he wanted to do to her.

'Fourteen days. You 'ave fourteen days to pay or I'm gonna break yer legs. Yer face.'

'I can't.'

He shoved his hand roughly between her legs. 'Lucky yer got sommat you can sell then, ain't it?'

To her eternal shame, Marie hadn't fought back. She'd let him shove his fingers inside her knickers before she dropped to her knees, squeezing her eyes shut as she heard him unzip his jeans.

Afterwards he'd tossed a foil wrap on the floor and she'd scrambled for it like a stray dog tossed a scrap of meat.

'Don't fink this means I've knocked any off your debt, yer skank. I were just trying yer out.' Her pinched her cheeks between his thumb and index finger. 'Yer ain't all that.' He pushed her roughly and left Marie face down in a filthy puddle, the feel of his fingers still inside her, the sour taste of him in her mouth.

She dragged herself up and stuffed the wrap inside her bra before stumbling home. Back in the flat she didn't strip off her sodden clothes, she didn't cram her tainted knickers in the bin, she didn't even shower. It wouldn't have made any difference, she'd not felt clean for years. Instead she waited for the hit and wished that alcohol was still enough to numb her.

The following day – despite her good intentions to stay home, ride out the withdrawal symptoms – Marie found herself applying eyeliner with a shaking hand, slicking red gloss on the lips she was prepared to wrap around a stranger for a crumpled note. She stared at herself in the mirror. A stranger stared back. Marie hadn't known who she was since she was eight years old. She was a keeper of secrets. She could do this. She always was an actress.

Everyone knew where the women gathered, the desperate and needy with their short skirts and tight smiles and the promises of heaven. Marie leaned nonchalantly against a wall and tried to act as though she fit in.

She did not.

She was chased away by a tall, thin woman and a short, round girl with frizzy blonde hair who didn't look old enough to be there.

Marie slowed to a brisk walk when she reached the main road; a stitch in her side throbbing, her ankles burning as her feet wobbled in shoes that were too high. Her mind scrambled for possibilities. She'd steeled herself to do the unimaginable, and now she didn't want to go home empty-handed.

A trail of laughter led her to a pub, where three men gathered outside, their breath billowing with cold and smoke. Marie watched as they ground cigarette butts under their boots and stalked back inside. The heavy wooden door swung shut behind them. Marie crossed her arms over her chest to keep the shattered pieces of herself together, tucked her freezing hands into her armpits. Just as she was resigned to giving up – she didn't know who she was but she knew she wasn't this – the door swung open again and a familiar figure stepped outside.

George.

Her brother-in-law had always had a soft spot for her. Marie observed him for a few moments until – as though sensing he was being watched – he turned. His eyes met hers.

And she knew from his expression that he would be the one to save her.

Chapter Forty-Five

George

Now

George doesn't know how much longer he can keep up the pretence. Every single time he got home and washed her off his skin he promised himself he would be a better husband. A better father. A better version of himself but, no matter how steely his resolve, she is like a furnace, bending his good intentions out of shape until they are something entirely different. Until he is something entirely different.

The shopping is defrosting in the boot. He should be getting home to Leah. It isn't fair to leave her with a puppy she never wanted. At the time he thought it was a good idea. As soon as he saw the advert for the dog on Facebook he had called Francesca and asked her opinion. She had warned him that Leah wasn't mentally strong enough for exposure therapy. He foolishly thought he knew better. He'd watched a documentary on Sky about phobias, a man with a fear of spiders held a tarantula and realized they weren't so scary after all. He thought it might be like that – in his own way he thought he might be helping, but the second he'd seen her stricken face pale he realized he'd made a horrible mistake.

Another one.

And he has no idea how to sort it out either.

Archie was in raptures. He'd fallen in love with that puppy the second he had seen him. George could still hear Archie's excited screams ringing in his ears. To take him away now would be cruel, particularly… George swallowed hard – particularly if George was no longer living at home full-time. If he was honest, that was part of the dog's appeal. Something that could protect his family if… when he was no longer around.

'George…' She stirs next to him, drawing him out of his thoughts and back into her bed. He feels the soft curve of her waist, the brush of her breasts on his chest as she levers herself onto her elbow and gazes at him with love. 'What are you thinking?'

'I'm thinking about Leah.'

Her face clouds. George wants to kiss away her worries.

'I can't keep doing this,' he says.

'I know. Me neither.' Her pain matches his, it's hard for her also. She feels it keenly, the sense of betrayal. She cares about Leah too.

'I'm going to leave her.' Voicing the words outside of his head gives them weight and clarity.

'Are you sure?' Her face is both hopeful and afraid.

'Yes. It's you I want to be with. I love you, Francesca.'

Chapter Forty-Six

Marie

Thirteen days ago

As soon as Marie saw George kissing another woman outside the pub, she knew she held another secret in the palm of her hands. When George turned, as though sensing Marie's presence, it gave her a clear view of the woman's face. Marie was shocked and angry it was Leah's therapist, Francesca. She was saddened for her sister that this clearly wasn't some one-night stand.

George's expression as he caught sight of his sister-in-law was a mixture of shame and fear. She knew how he felt, terrified of being exposed for the person you were rather than the person everyone thought you should be.

She waited while George spoke low and urgently to Francesca, who bowed her head and scurried away.

'What… what are you doing here?' asked George as he drank in Marie's too-short skirt, her too-glossy lips that could spill his sordid secret.

Sarcasm sat on Marie's tongue but instead of releasing it, she swallowed it down and pursued a rare course of action.

She was honest.

‘I… I’m an addict.’ This time it was Marie who couldn’t meet George’s eyes.

‘Marie…’ George toed the kerb. ‘We all know you like a drink—’

‘It’s more than alcohol now, I’m afraid.’ She rubbed her arms, whether to draw attention to her track marks or hide them, she did not know.

‘Does Leah know?’

‘Leah doesn’t need to know everything.’ Marie’s eyes flickered in Francesca’s direction.

‘This isn’t what it looks like,’ George said quickly.

‘Good. Because it looks like you’re cheating on my sister.’

‘It’s complicated. Leah’s complicated.’

‘We all are,’ Marie said. ‘But don’t give up on her, George. Please. What we went through has made us who we are today but we can change. Leah wants to. I want to.’

‘Have you tried… to give up?’

‘Yeah. But… it’s…’ Marie tugged down her skirt. ‘To say it’s a craving doesn’t even cover it. We crave food or drink or… love and when we have it we feel satisfied, but this… it’s like I’ll die if I don’t have a hit. I can’t think about anything else. I can’t focus on anything. I’d do anything – I *have* done anything.’

Marie told George about the money she owed her dealer. The way he’d held her head, knotting his hands into her hair as he thrust himself into her mouth. Her sorry tale tumbling heavy and toxic onto the pavement between them, crouching among the dog-ends and the crumpled fag packets, ready to spring again and again.

‘Christ. Marie…’

‘That’s why I’m here. Dressed to impress.’ She fluttered jazz hands and tried to smile but she couldn't. 'I was chased earlier by two women. I was on their spot. George,' – her teeth begin to chatter – 'have you got any cash?'

'Marie. I can't… I can't give you money for drugs. To kill yourself.'

'I wasn't selling myself for that. I was trying to raise enough for rehab. I…' Her voice cracked. 'I want…' she whispered, 'I want to be clean.'

Strangely it was this admission that brought her the most shame, as though it was other people who led good, healthy lives and she had no right to any of it. But how she wanted it. How she wanted her life back. No, not even back. She wanted her adult life to begin in a way it hadn't before. Free from guilt, from secrets.

Free from lies – but now in addition to the dirty untruths she already carried, she was adding to her burden. She eyed George warily. She didn't mention blackmail – Leah was her sister and she didn't want her to be hurt – but she didn't have to say it aloud. George knew what she had willingly done in the putrid alley, on her knees, mouth in a perfect 'o'. He knew what she had come here to do tonight. He'd seen the worst of her and so he assumed the worst and it was this that made her want to cry. Longing to tell him that, despite everything, she had morals and there were things she could not do.

'How much do you need?' he asked wearily.

She did a quick calculation in her head, adding on some for rehab. He winced as she presented her final figure.

'Fuck, Marie. We're not doing that great ourselves…' he trailed off but he hadn't said no.

'There's money coming in. The book royalties are going to be higher this quarter and we've been offered a TV interview – the fee for that is huge if we can come up with a new angle.'

They talked for several minutes more before he turned and left. Francesca was waiting for him in the shadows of the car park. Marie watched as George hugged her close before guiding her forwards, one hand on the small of her back.

More than anything, that was what Marie craved. A touch that came from kindness, from love. As she watched him tenderly settle Francesca in his car, Marie knew that Leah had already lost him and, although Marie felt sorry for her sister, she also felt a pang of envy that Leah had known that kind of love.

And relief. She felt relief that George had ultimately said yes. That he was going to help her.

Chapter Forty-Seven

Leah

Now

The air stills around me, the hum of the fridge fades while I try and process what Graham has told me. Is Marie with our dad and if so why?

That day – all those years ago when the police had turned up on the doorstep – hadn't seemed unusual. We were used to them dropping in. We knew they'd caught Moustache for armed robbery and that he was in hospital.

'Come in.' Mum gestured them inside. In the kitchen she wiped her hands on her apron and asked, 'Sorry, I was just serving up dinner. Do you want tea? Coffee?'

'No, thank you, Mrs Sinclair.'

Dad, Marie, Carly and I were sat around the table. Five plates rested on the worktop, a mound of steaming mashed potato on each. Under the grill, sausages hissed and spat while peas in boiling water bubbled on the hob.

We waited.

Worriedly, I glanced at Carly. She was so pale, her lips devoid of colour.

'Has he… Moustache. Has he escaped?' she whispered.

'No. Goodness. No.' Graham looked at us sadly. He'd become close to our family. 'But he has told us that when he took you girls he was acting on instructions. Simon Sinclair…' Graham approached the table. 'I'm arresting you for—'

Mum screamed over and over. Dad stood, his chair falling loudly onto its side. He slammed his palms on the table, eyes darting left and right. Towards the door. He ran. Graham grabbed his arms, clicked on handcuffs. Mum shouted, 'They must have made a mistake—' Carly wrapped her arms around Marie and I. Shuffling together – an awkward centipede – down the hallway as Dad was dragged, struggling to be free, all the way to the front door.

My sisters and I stood disbelieving on the doorstep as Dad was put in the police car, protesting his innocence. Mum's legs crumpled as she covered her face. '*I can't believe it. I can't believe it.*'

Again, the reporters returned to our street.

Again, we were prisoners in our own home.

'It's a mistake,' Mum told us. 'There's no proof.'

But there was. Dad had been seen with Moustache and Doc. His fingerprints were in their car. He'd withdrawn a large amount of cash the day before Moustache deposited it in his account. The police found a list among Moustache's possessions of things we liked to eat and drink, it was written in Dad's handwriting.

Mum visited him. When she came out her nose was pink, eyes red.

'He's pleading guilty.'

'But… why?' Still none of us could believe it. None of us wanted to believe it, I suppose.

'Because he did it. He thought that financially it was the right thing to do. I don't think he thought it would have a permanent effect on you. Children are supposed to be resilient.' She sounded almost resentful as she said this, but as she spoke she tugged off her wedding ring and never spoke his name again.

While Dad was held on remand we were sent back to school but whereas before we were treated with pity, now the other kids taunted us in the playground.

'The Sinclair Sisters are so ugly their dad paid somebody to take them away.'

'What do you do when you can't pay your bills? Kidnap your daughters.'

'What do you call a father who makes dreams come true? Father Christmas. What do you call a father who makes nightmares come true? Simon Sinclair.'

Whereas before life was difficult, now it was unbearable. Neighbours who had been leaving casseroles on our doorstep, cheesy lasagnes and thick vegetable soups, now crossed the road to avoid Mum. Dad may have been a monster but she was the one who had married him.

We didn't go to the trial. Mum wanted to but the police told her it would give the impression that she was supporting him and there was enough speculation as it was. Some newspapers hinted she must have known something but, of course, she didn't. None of us thought for a second he would be capable of staging the abduction of his daughters. It horrified not just our close-knit community but the country, then the world.

What did the media want us to share now that could be worse than that? Marie reconciling with him?

A new angle.

Suspicions creep from the corners of my mind where they stamp for attention in the centre of all other thoughts.

A new angle.

Marie couldn't be the one sending letters for him, she wouldn't. Would she?

I don't believe it. I can't believe it. And yet she's seemingly vanished without a trace the day after he was released. When she was desperate for a story to sell.

I hurry to the back door to call Archie in. I'll settle him with a sandwich in front of the TV and then I'll phone Carly. See what she makes of it all. Hoping she'll tell me I'm being ridiculous. Even if we were no longer close, Marie wouldn't betray us.

A new angle.

I fling open the back door. Scream as I see them on the step immediately.

Oh God, no.

Mice.

Three dead mice laid out like an offering. Dark, empty spaces where their eyes should be.

Three blind mice.

'Archie?' I look wildly around my garden.

My empty garden.

I am falling. Hurtling through time and space. The past and present strobing. A searing pain in my head. My heart.

The gate is swinging open.

My parents' gate.

My gate.

Bruno is missing.

Our new puppy is missing.

Archie, too. Missing.

Chapter Forty-Eight

Carly

One week ago

Carly was emotionally drained when she left Marie's flat. As she drove home she couldn't stop thinking about the offer of the TV interview. *A new angle*. Knowing that Marie must want Carly to stand up in front of the nation, in front of the world and take the blame caused something to shrivel inside her like a deflated balloon. Twenty years ago YouTube hadn't existed. Neither had Facebook. It wasn't until their book was published that the public felt they had access to the girls and they had lapped up the details like a thirsty dog.

Poor Leah.

Poor Marie.

Poor Carly.

They'd never told about the things that took place before the abduction. The argument. The way Carly had been so fixated on a boy whose name she couldn't recall that she'd been careless with her sisters' feelings. Her sisters' safety.

She could still feel it. The sun on her skin. See the whites of the twins' school socks. The blackness of the scurrying beetle. Inconsequential details she shared with the ghost writer. She never shared that Leah hadn't shut the gate properly. Carly knew Leah blamed herself too.

Carly slotted her car into a space outside her flat and rummaged in her bag for her mobile. Leah should be home by now and she wanted to check she was okay. She wanted to ask whether Leah had any second thoughts about turning down the interview. Perhaps Marie was right. It might be cathartic to share it all, a confession of sorts. Perhaps then they might be left alone, for every year there would be an anniversary, journalists picking over the carcass of their past. If there was nothing left to tell, the meat stripped bare, there'd be no truth left then for them to fight over, would there? And the money? Blood money, but Carly knew that Leah and George were struggling and she hated to think of Archie going without. Her nephew was the light of her life. Sometimes it was more than she could bear that Leah had brought him into a world that was heartless and cruel.

Her fingers skimmed over a tube of Polos, her purse, a packet of tissues but not her phone.

Carly sighed as she remembered she'd been bidding on eBay when Leah had arrived. She'd tossed her mobile onto Marie's worktop so she could hug her sister. She hadn't picked it back up. She restarted the car, a blast of cold air shot from the vents before blowing hot once more, and she pulled back onto the main road. Carly thought it might be a good thing that she was returning to Marie's alone. A chance to talk. *A new angle*. Carly mulled this over. She'd make Marie tell her exactly what she had in mind.

Chapter Forty-Nine

Marie

One week ago

It was less than half an hour after Leah and Carly had left that Marie stripped off her top that was dripping with perspiration. She was instantly freezing in her grubby once-white camisole but she knew to ride it out. It wouldn't be long until heat swept through her body once more. A few months ago she had tried to detox herself. Had shut herself in her bedroom with a bucket for vomit and a bucket for the waste that would spew from her body like poison. Her skin crawled and her veins burned and she hadn't been able to cope. She'd staggered down the street in her pyjamas, desperate for the hit, which she took in the overgrown parking space behind the pizza parlour with the broken glass and the rat that sauntered out from behind a skip, eyeing her as though she was the vermin.

Now she thought that she was better off using the cash George supplied her with to feed her habit until she could get hold of the extortionate fee for rehab – the NHS had already tried and failed her. She needed more than their resources could offer. She needed to be locked in a room for a longer period, with no access to the outside world.

Again.

The irony of this was not lost on her.

Time stretched. Without the earlier distraction of her sisters, the afternoon seemed endless. A check of her watch told her that George was not due for a while. He'd promised her some more cash but Marie knew she couldn't rely on his money much longer. For the first few days after she'd found out about him and Francesca, he'd told her it was a mistake, that he'd end it. Now he didn't say anything at all, although he still couldn't meet her eye. He wasn't proud of himself, Marie knew. The shamed could recognize the shameful like a kindred spirit.

Despite everything, she thought George was a good man. He had a good heart. Leah was a lot to handle. All of them were a lot to handle. Two days ago when he dropped off some money Marie could see Francesca sitting in the passenger seat, pulling down the sun visor and checking her lipstick in the mirror. Marie knew it was only a matter of time before he left Leah to begin a new life, and the thought of her fragile sister alone broke her heart. How would she manage emotionally? Financially? How would Archie cope without his father? It wasn't easy adjusting to life with a single parent. She should know. The selfish part of her unfurled. How would she cope without his money? If only there was a way to do the TV interview alone. But could she betray her sisters?

Could she betray her sisters again?

The doorbell rang. Marie padded down the hallway, gripped the door handle with her slick palm and hesitated, unsure of who was on the other side. She never had unscheduled visitors, no friends that might drop in for coffee.

Who was out there?

Marie didn't think her dealer knew where she lived but it wouldn't have been hard to find out. She swallowed hard, the taste of him rising in her throat once more. This time, there was a banging on the door.

'Marie?' Carly's impatient voice called.

Marie opened the door.

'I left my phone in your kitchen.' Carly pushed past her. Marie stayed rooted to the spot, hoping that Carly would collect her mobile and leave, and yet overriding that thought was a desire that Carly would stay. Marie hated being alone. She was always alone. 'Found it. Can I talk to you a sec?'

Carly crossed into the lounge. Marie closed the door and checked her watch again. She'd have to get rid of Carly before George arrived. Who knew how she'd react if she knew Marie had been blackmailing him? Taking money away from Leah who was always her favourite and Archie who she adored.

She'd probably want to kill her.

Chapter Fifty

Carly

One week ago

Carly tried to put her thoughts in order, rearrange the words in her head while she waited for Marie to join her in the lounge. It wasn't exactly that she felt they should do the interview but, now she'd had a chance to calm down, she had to admit her curiosity was building brick by brick – but the wall of questions crumbled the instant Marie shuffled into the room.

'Marie? You look awful. Are you sick?' Carly began to stand but Marie held out her hands to stop her. At first Carly thought Marie was trying to keep her away from any germs but then she noticed the track marks on her arms.

'Oh, Marie.' Again, Carly felt the weight of responsibility she always bore. She should have noticed before. She could have done *something*. Now she knew, she could help. 'Is that why you wanted to do the TV thing? For money for…'

Carly's eyes flickered towards Marie's forearms. She didn't know what Marie was taking. What did you inject? Cocaine? Heroin? It was a different world to the one Carly inhabited.

Marie sank into the chair, her knees springing up, her hands pushing them back down. 'I want the cash for rehab. I want to be clean, Carly.'

'How much do you need?'

Marie told her the figure. Carly felt her chest tighten. She made enough selling bits and pieces online to cover her frugal lifestyle. She couldn't fund that much. 'Couldn't your GP help?'

'Been there, done that.' Marie seemed to shrink before Carly's eyes until she was eight once more. A wave of maternal longing swept over Carly.

'Tell me what you need us to do. What do the production company want?'

A new angle.

Marie shook her head.

'You must have had something in mind when you asked us here earlier. Tell me.'

'You'll... You'll hate me once you know.'

'I won't. I couldn't. Marie, please, what is it?'

A new angle.

Wasn't it enough that their dad had arranged their abduction to save his business? The community had been outraged when the truth came out, some disbelieving. There had been a smidgeon of reassurance when it was thought the girls had been abducted by a stranger – there was only a slim likelihood it would ever happen again. The revelation that Simon had arranged it had hit the town hard. A monster walked among them and they had sat with him in the pub, stood next to him at football matches, chatted to him as they walked their dogs. They had never guessed and were horrified but, however bad they thought they had it, it had been a million times worse for Carly.

She had *chosen* to love him. Chosen to think of him as her dad. Even now, it was impossible not to label him this way because she thought of Leah and Marie as her whole sisters. They'd never thought of themselves as anything but. Once a journalist had thrust a microphone towards her mouth and demanded to know whether Carly wished her mum had never met Simon so Carly wouldn't have gone through such an ordeal. The notion threw Carly. The small space of her throat had closed and she'd pushed past the woman with her weasel face, her acrylic red nails and thoughtless questions.

Did she wish her mum had never met Simon?

If she hadn't met him then the twins would never exist and how could she ever wish for that? That man had ruined her life with one hand but given her something precious with the other.

Sisters.

And for a time they'd all been happy. A proper family. Leah and Marie had been the closest, of course, but that was because they were twins, not because she had a different dad. She had never felt any less.

A new angle.

What was so bad that Marie couldn't meet her eye?

Half a sister.

Half a person.

Half the truth.

'Tell me,' Carly demanded over and over until Marie falteringly began to speak.

Chapter Fifty-One

Marie

One week ago

'I… I…' Marie's hands were shaking, her teeth too. 'I overheard Mum and Dad talking… planning, I suppose. The abduction… I—'

'Mum didn't know!' Carly said.

'She did… I heard them.'

'When? Where were we?' Carly's eyes narrowed.

'It was late. You were in bed, and Leah was asleep. I was wide awake, worrying.'

'About what?'

Marie scratched her arm. 'You, I guess. I was thinking you'd gone off us, that you preferred Dean Malden to—'

'Oh, for God's sake,' Carly snapped. 'Tell me about Mum and Dad.'

'Well, I crept downstairs and they were in the kitchen. They didn't know I was outside the door. I was about to go in when Mum said, *Tell me again* and there was something in her voice that made me hesitate. Dad explained to her that, with the right media coverage, missing children can attract a lot of attention. People would donate money…'

'Even if he said that, Mum would never agree. Why would she?' Carly cut in.

'She did say no... at first.'

'What changed her mind?' The expression on Carly's face told Marie that she didn't believe any of it.

It was a sharp and jagged truth and, as much as Marie didn't want to share it, it was a relief in a way. She'd carried it alone for such a long time.

'Dad said that... he said that if Mum didn't agree then they would lose the house—'

'So? Big deal. Loads of people move.'

'And... and that we wouldn't be able to stay together. He had a friend who would probably put up him and... me and Leah, but you and Mum would be on your own. Back to the council estate. He said you'd probably end up on drugs or worse.'

'Well, that's fucking ironic, looking at you.' Marie didn't blame Carly for lashing out.

'Dad said it would only be for a couple of days and there wouldn't be any lasting effects.'

'Yeah, right.' Carly jabbed her finger at Marie. 'Junkie.' She pointed a finger at herself. '*Too scared to trust anyone* and Leah...'

'I know.' Marie hung her head.

'Christ.' Carly pressed her fingers into her skull. 'Sorry. I don't mean to take it out on you but... really? That's all it took to persuade Mum?'

'Dad really scared her. He said we'd all have to change schools. That me and Leah probably wouldn't see her or you again. She was terrified. He told her that in time we'd forget it ever happened. "It will be just one small event in their long and happy lives," he said.'

'Yes, because we're all *so* happy.'

'He asked her to trust him,' Marie said. 'And I suppose she did.'

Neither of them spoke. The muscle in Carly's jaw was pulsing, quick and angry. Marie felt it all again. The fear that she might lose her sisters but this time it would be all her fault. She should have said something before. Her stomach contracted, veins screamed, body craving a numbness that she couldn't afford. Right now there was only Carly and the truth.

'Why the fuck didn't you tell us?' Marie flinched as Carly swore at her. 'In court Dad said he'd acted alone. Mum swore she didn't know anything. *They* were lying. *You* were lying. Why didn't you tell us before it happened?'

'I wanted to but I thought I could talk Dad out of it. I tried, I really did.'

Carly rose to her feet and began to pace the room. Four steps to the window, turn. Five steps to the door. Marie's breath hitched in her throat, afraid Carly would leave but equally hoping she would just go. Carly strode over to the bookcase. Giant angry steps for such a small oppressive room. 'Tell me *everything*.'

'Okay.' Marie closed her eyes and she remembered.

Chapter Fifty-Two

Carly

One week ago

Carly thought that nothing Marie could tell her now would be as bad as what had been revealed moments before.

She was wrong.

Chapter Fifty-Three

Marie

Then

Marie closed her eyes as her mum pressed the back of her hand against her forehead.

'You don't feel hot but you are very pale. And it's your tummy?'

'Yes. It hurts.' Marie wasn't lying. Ever since she'd eavesdropped on the conversation between her parents last night, the knot in her stomach had tightened and she felt a constant dull ache. 'I think Leah's sick too. She should stay here.'

'God, if they're both claiming to be ill they've probably got a maths test or something. Mum, we're going to be late,' Carly said unfairly. The twins were often ill at the same time. Chicken pox. Measles. Once Marie had lost her voice although she hadn't felt remotely poorly, not knowing that Leah had gone to see the school nurse, hit by a sudden bout of tonsillitis.

'Leah, are you poorly too?' Mum asked. Marie willed her twin to say she was. If she stayed home Marie could tell her what she had overheard and they could try and work out what it all meant. Leah met Marie's gaze and Marie knew she understood the wordless message.

'I… I'm…' Leah clasped her hands over her stomach. 'Umm.' Her cheeks flushed red. She was always useless at lying.

'Leah?' Mum tilted her head to one side.

'I… I'm okay.' She mouthed *sorry* at Marie as she picked up her rucksack and followed Carly out of the room.

Mum crossed the floor and slotted *The Little Mermaid* DVD into the side of the TV. She handed the remote control to Marie.

'I'll drop your sisters at school and then I'm going out but Dad's working from home today and he'll—'

'Please don't leave me.' Marie grabbed her mum's hand and tried her to pull her back.

'Mum!' Carly shouted from downstairs.

'I've got to go. See you later. Love you.' Mum dropped a kiss on the top of Marie's head. The front door slammed and a sense of separation saddened Marie. She listened to her sisters' chatter as they piled into the car below her window. The engine roared to life and it felt to Marie as if they weren't just driving away from the house, they were driving away from her. Tears poured down her cheeks, soaking into her Ariel pyjama top. Marie had never felt so lonely.

It wasn't long until she heard Dad climbing the stairs. 'I'm under orders to bring you Calpol,' he boomed cheerfully. She was eight and could swallow a paracetamol but Marie still preferred the sweet gloopy medicine that tasted of strawberries. She didn't want to see her dad, though. She certainly didn't want to speak to him. She quickly shuffled under the covers and turned her face to the wall, forced her breath to be slow and even as she pretended to be asleep.

She was good at pretending.

Dad quietly put the bottle and the spoon on her bedside

cabinet and left the room, leaving Marie alone with her fake stomach ache, in her fake life where everything suddenly felt as temporary as the stage scenery in her school production of *Annie*. From the outside the buildings looked real and solid when in fact they were weak and flimsy. Easy to knock down.

Each time the DVD reached the end it would whirr back to the beginning, but Marie had barely registered her favourite film. Her mind was a slideshow of clips from completely different movies, but instead of the usual characters, it was her and her family playing the parts. Herself and Leah separated from their mother and abandoned by their father, placed in the care of a cruel Miss Hannigan, waiting for a Daddy Warbucks who never came – *it's a hard knock life*. Carly, thin and hungry, holding out a bowl – *please, sir, can I have some more?* Bruno forced out of the home he loved, fleeing from the Dog Catcher who wanted to lock him up. Reliant on begging for spaghetti from a kindly Italian restaurant owner so he didn't starve.

It was all too much. She must have got it wrong. She slid out of bed and padded downstairs. Dad was in his study, his back to her as he hunched over his laptop. Instead of pushing her way in like she usually would, clambering on his lap, she hesitated in the doorway, uncertain and afraid. It was Bruno who spotted her first. He was dozing in the corner in front of the bay window where a patch of sunlight warmed the carpet. Immediately he bounded over to her, ears flapping and tail wagging. He delightedly licked her face with his rough tongue.

'Marie!' Her father spun around on his chair. 'You gave me a fright. It must be almost lunchtime. Hungry?'

Marie shook her head.

'How are you feeling?' he asked.

Marie didn't know how to articulate all of the emotions that wriggled around her tummy like worms. She thought very hard about what she wanted to say – the questions she wanted to ask – but there was a part of her, a big part that just didn't want to know the answers. She shrugged.

'Let's get you back to bed.' He stretched out his hand and led the way upstairs. She didn't want to take it, in that moment he almost felt like a stranger to her, but then she thought, *be good and he won't send you away.*

'Daddy.' She looked at him earnestly as he tucked the duvet around her legs. 'I'd never take drugs. Neither would Leah or Carly.'

Be good and he won't send you away.

'I should hope not! You shouldn't be thinking of such things at your age.'

Her stomach growled. She hadn't eaten since dinner last night. She was ravenous.

'Shall I bring up some soup? Beans on toast?'

'Which is cheaper?'

Be good and he won't send you away.

'I don't know. That's a funny question. Why do you ask?'

'I think...' Marie's voice wobbled. 'I think we must all cost a lot to feed and we could eat less, I could and—'

'Why—'

'And I could share my dinner with Bruno so he doesn't have to live in a cage with the other dogs laughing at him because he comes from a posh home.' Tears streamed down Marie's cheeks.

'Marie.' The mattress dipped as her dad perched on the edge. 'I need you to tell me what this is about.'

All the words she needed to say clumped together as one hard mass and rose in her throat but she couldn't spit them out. She couldn't swallow. Breathe.

'Shhh.' Dad rubbed her back. 'Calm down. It's okay.'

'It isn't.' Marie hiccupped. 'I heard you and Mum last night. I know you're going to split us all up and I'll have to eat cold mush and scrub floors and— '

'Enough.' Her dad held up his palm. His shoulders rose before slumping. Marie heard the breath whoosh out of his nose. 'It seems I have some explaining to do. But, Marie, you must give me your extra best promise that you can keep a secret. Can you do that?'

'Yes, Daddy.' His gaze held hers, waiting for more. 'I promise I can keep a secret.'

Be good and he won't send you away.

'We're in a bit of a sticky situation,' he began falteringly. 'Financially… You might have noticed we haven't been on holiday for a long time. The fridge isn't packed full of the usual things we like to eat.'

'Carly babysits us so Mum doesn't have to pay anyone?'

'Yes. That sort of thing. If we don't get back on our feet pretty sharpish I won't have a business and we won't be able to live here any more.'

'Carly and Mum have to go and live in a hovel? And Bruno has to live at the pound. And me and Leah might stay together but three is still a big number to house.' Marie repeated back the things she had overheard, her voice thick with tears.

'No. You shouldn't have… I didn't mean.' Her dad dropped his head in his hands. Tentatively Marie shuffled forward in the bed and stroked his hair. He raised his face, his eyes looking at something just past Marie's shoulder. 'Yes,' he said quietly. 'That's exactly what could happen. We'll all be split up and living in different houses.'

'And we will have to wear rags,' Marie said sadly. 'And eat scraps.'

'Possibly,' he said. 'We might all lose touch and never see each other again.'

'I'll *never* not see Leah – we're twins. And Carly's my sister. We all belong together.'

The Adam's apple in her dad's throat raised and then dropped. 'You might never see Leah or Carly again.'

'No!' Marie's whole body shook as she sobbed. 'Can't you do *something*, Daddy?'

'Perhaps.'

Marie felt a little spark of hope.

'I do have an idea but I'm afraid it's not very nice, but Mummy agrees it's the only way to save our family. It would mean a couple of horrible days but then it would all be over and we'd go on holiday—'

'To Disneyland?' Marie remembered what she'd heard.

'Yes.'

'And I'd meet the real Ariel!'

'Yes.'

'Well, do your idea then, silly!'

Dad took Marie's hands in his. 'It's not that easy. One, because it has to stay a secret or it won't work. Even afterwards. If anyone ever finds out, you will all be taken away and put in separate homes and never be allowed to see each other again.'

'Okay. Daddy, I have something to tell you…'

'Yes?'

'It was me who knocked that m-mink vase and smashed it. When you and Mum asked I blamed Bruno because he was only a puppy then and I've kept that a secret for years and years. You must keep it too now and not pass it on to Mummy, or shout at me. I'm only telling you so you know I am *good* at keeping secrets.'

'You are indeed, Marie. There's a second problem, though. To carry out the plan I need a really brilliant actress to make sure everyone is in the right place at the right time.'

'That's me! Don't you remember I was Annie! And I was so good that Mrs Walters said she thought I'd go to Hollywood!'

'She did indeed. But, Marie, you're only eight.' He shook his head sadly.

'I may be small but I love you all big and if there's a way we can all stay together I want to do it. I do.'

Her dad tilted his head to one side and studied her. 'Okay, you've worn me down! I will share my idea with you but only because you're my best girl and I trust you. Remember, it might sound awful but it's not for long and it isn't real.'

'It's like a game?'

'Exactly like a game but only you and me can know.'

'Or we'll all be split up and hungry.'

'Yes. And it's worth a tiny bit of being uncomfortable for the rest of our lives together as a family, isn't it?'

'Yes.'

'Right. We'll make it happen tomorrow. You must promise to do exactly what I say and don't tell anybody?'

'I promise, Daddy.'

Be good and he won't send you away.

If she needed to lie, she would.

Chapter Fifty-Four

Carly

One week ago

'You're *lying*!' Carly couldn't accept what she was hearing. She couldn't accept she'd been betrayed by her mum as well as her dad. By her little sister. 'You just want a new angle so we can sell our stories again. How could you make—'

'I'm not making it up. Yeah, okay, I need the money, but I do think it's time the truth came out. It's been killing me keeping it to myself all these years.'

'There's no way—'

'It's true.'

'True? You wouldn't know the truth if it—'

'It's true,' Marie said softly.

'You didn't think to warn us? When we were pissing in a corner and terrified… of course *you* wouldn't have been terrified, would you? Always the fucking actress, weren't you, Marie? Well, that must have been your biggest role. Bravo.' Carly began to slowly clap.

'Stop it! You don't understand.'

'No, I don't understand. Have you got any idea what I've been through? How awful Mum made me feel all these years.

She couldn't wait to get rid of us. I thought it was because she couldn't cope with what we'd been through but what she couldn't cope with was the fact she'd known all along. She must have been terrified of being found out.'

'She couldn't help it, she loved him. She loves him. Still.'

'How do you know that?'

'I know that she still visits him.'

Carly didn't know what to say. She couldn't understand why her mum would stand by her dad, even now. What would she do when he was released again? Take him back?

'Do you know what this has done to me?' Carly dropped her head in her hands.

'Yes! I know what you went through. I *was* there.'

'Not there. Since. I have felt responsible for what happened *every single day*. I was supposed to be the one in charge, watching you both. God… Leah? Does Leah know?'

'No. I never told her, I swear. She'd never have coped.'

'And now? You think she'll cope now if this all comes out?'

This time a flicker of indecision crosses Marie's face. 'She's stronger than we think.'

'I don't think she is. She'll fall apart. Remember what happened last time she thought he was back? The Fregoli? The ways she was convinced he was everywhere she turned. She was nearly sectioned, for God's sake, and yet you're willing to sell her out for cold hard cash.'

'But don't you see? Once it's all out there. The truth about the way I was persuaded by our dad—'

'*That man is not my father*. Fuck, my whole life has been ruined by that fucking man and I'm not even related to him. Barely related to you and Leah.'

'That's not fair.'

'How can you talk to me about *fair*? You knew he'd planned it but even when were locked in that stinking room you didn't tell us, Marie.'

'I couldn't. I was terrified we'd be split up. I thought it was for the best. Dad sounded so convincing. We'd have gone on holiday afterwards and everything would be okay.'

'I can't believe someone would be cruel enough to put their daughters through that and think a holiday to Disneyland would make up for everything.'

'I didn't know it would be so awful, Carly. I was terrified but I thought if I told you what was going on then we'd all be separated and the trauma of being tied up and shoved in the van would be for nothing. I didn't know what to—'

'You should have told us.'

'I was eight! And if I'm honest, there… there was a part of me that… that was scared of him. Although he never threatened me, it was unspoken that if I ever told, he'd do something bad to me. And… and the thought that my own father might… might…' Marie dissolved into tears.

Carly thought about how betrayed she had felt when she found out Simon was behind their fake kidnapping. How hurt and unloved – but ultimately she wasn't his biological daughter. How must Marie have felt all these years, knowing that her natural dad had set her up? Carly felt herself softening.

'I think you should have told me – someone – but it can't have been easy for you knowing your dad was prepared to put you and Leah through such an ordeal… What?' Marie had turned away, hanging her head as she swiped furiously at her cheeks.

'Marie?' Carly touched her sister's shoulders. 'What is it?' But then it hit her.

The truth.

'Oh God.' Carly clasped her hands over her mouth. She was going to be sick. She shook her head from side to side. Marie sobbed, knowing that Carly had worked it out. Carly tried to breathe but her throat was burning with bile, nausea rising up as she kept swallowing it down. 'Oh God.' She couldn't find any other words. She sank to a crouch. Her head in her hands. She was going to faint. 'Oh God.'

It was all so blindingly obvious. The way there were only two men to snatch three girls. The insubstantial amount of food. One mattress. The single blanket. A lonely teddy bear. She began to cry.

Minutes passed until Carly raised her tear-stained face. Marie's expression confirmed what she already knew but she had to hear her say it. 'It was only ever meant to be me that was taken, wasn't it?' Carly had thought she'd closed herself off to hurt, but the pain she felt was unimaginable. She wiped her nose with her sleeve. 'You and Leah? You were never part of the plan.' She thought back to when they were reunited at the police station. Simon balancing a twin on each hip – *thank God, thank God, thank God.*

'I was supposed to get you out of the garden and into the alley where I knew they'd be waiting. I threw the ball over but you wouldn't fetch it. I didn't know what to do when you made us go inside the house for tea so I pretended I'd left my fleece outside, opened the gate and let Bruno out. You were supposed to go and look that way on your own but—'

'I had Leah with me, and you didn't want to put her through

it.' Carly gave a wry smile, although inside her heart was breaking. 'That's understandable, she is your sister.'

'*You're* my sister too,' Marie said. 'But yes, when you took Leah I panicked and followed you. When the men grabbed you both I couldn't let you go through it alone. I thought… I thought I could make it fun.'

It's a game, isn't it? Marie had kept saying. Perhaps she really believed that, Carly thought. Perhaps that's the only way her mind could cope with it.

But Carly's mind couldn't cope with what she was hearing now. She just couldn't process it all. Her body was ice. Her teeth rattled together.

'Carly, please. Now you know we can—'

'There is no *we*.' Carly picked up her bag from the floor.

'Carly, please don't leave.'

Carly turned to look at the girl she once thought of as her sister. The desperation on her face. She sighed. 'Get your coat. Your coming with me.'

'Where?' Marie's face creased with anxiety.

'To the cashpoint. I'll give you some money. Not enough, but some, but we're *not* doing the TV interview. We have to think of Leah.'

It took three attempts for Marie to push her arm into her sleeve, she was trembling so hard. 'Thanks. Afterwards, can you drop me somewhere?'

'Where?'

Marie told her. Carly wished she had never asked.

Chapter Fifty-Five

Leah

Now

Archie is missing.

I don't stop to lock the back door as I run through the kitchen and grab my mobile.

Archie is missing.

If I call the police now they'll want me to stay home so they can send someone out, and how long might that take? With my track record of reporting things that aren't real they probably won't rush with sirens blaring and blue lights flashing. Anything could happen to Archie, could be happening to Archie. He was taken in the same way as we were. It stands to reason he'll have been taken to the same place.

A new angle.

You can't get more dramatic than this. The open gate, the missing dog, my son being snatched. Part of me wants to think it's a stunt Simon and Marie have planned together for money. How much would the TV and newspapers pay for an exclusive of this story? A lot, I bet. If Marie is involved she wouldn't hurt Archie, would she? I may have drifted apart from my twin but deep down I believe she wouldn't hurt anybody. Yet... I remember the mice on the doorstep.

Three blind mice.

Killed. Their eyes brutally gouged out – and there's another part of me, a bigger, louder part, that is screaming, *Archie hasn't been taken for money*. He's been taken for revenge.

Simon spent all those extra years in prison for a crime he didn't commit. What if he had found out I was behind it and...

My heart actually hurts. Not a dull ache but as though someone has pierced it with a knife, is dragging the sharp blade through it, slicing it in two.

My darling, darling boy.

I'll do anything to get him back.

Anything.

My car tyres screech as I accelerate off the driveway, onto the road. Thankfully the reporters George had chased away haven't returned.

What will I find when I get there? I am second-guessing Simon just as he will be second-guessing me.

See how they run.

Well, I'm not running now.

The traffic thins. I'm on a country road, punching out a text on my mobile as I drive. A horn blares. I have drifted over the white lines. I toss my phone onto the passenger seat and concentrate until I am almost there and then I slow. Pick up my phone once more.

Archie taken to Norwood. I'm going to get him back. Call police.

I send it to George, Tash and Carly. One of them will see it straight away, if not all. I complete the last few hundred yards of my journey, wondering who will be waiting for me inside. Marie? Simon? Both of them together?

Norwood looms out of the shadows. I feel myself shrink.

I'm back.

Memories crush down upon my chest. The feel of rope around my wrists. My ankles. Eyes blindfolded, mouth taped shut.

I'm back.

Sometimes when you revisit a place as an adult that you've only ever seen through a child's eyes it seems smaller, you feel bigger. This isn't the case now. Norwood is still huge and horribly, horribly frightening.

I'm back.

Now I'm here, it seems inevitable. The camp has been waiting for me to return. Any smidgeon of doubt I had that Archie might not be here vanishes.

Daylight is beginning to fade. Grey clouds sucking away the light.

I abandon the car on the grass verge we had crawled along to make our escape that harsh, stormy night. A new security fence was erected after we'd been found in a bid to stop the ghouls and the true-crime addicts gathering at the site as though it was a tourist spot.

It didn't.

As I jog towards it I can see place where the wire has been snipped, rolled back to create a space big enough for an adult to crawl through.

WARNING – GUARD DOGS signs are cable-tied to the fence, along with a 24-HOUR SECURITY notice, but I know it's a lie. There hasn't been anything here for years to protect. Until now.

Archie.

He must be terrified. I don't hesitate before dropping to my knees and crawling across the ground. I don't care about germs or contamination or anything except the small boy who will be scared and confused and longing for his mum. Sharp edges of wire drag at my hair. Scrape my cheek, which dampens with blood.

My legs are shaking, my knees rubber, but I force myself to stand. The police aren't yet here but I hope they won't be long. George and Carly will be out of their minds. Tash too. They'll likely all come, but for now there is only me.

I'm back.

And I'm not leaving without my son.

Chapter Fifty-Six

George

Now

The screen lights up on George's phone. Leah's picture grins at him. He doesn't need to read the text to know what it will say. His stomach turns.

It's all come to a head, lightning fast and just as frightening.

Chapter Fifty-Seven

Leah

Now

The world seems to hold its breath once I'm inside Norwood's grounds. The silence perfect.

'Archie?' Fear tears his name from my throat. 'Archie!' A flock of birds rises from the trees, black wings beating, cawing out a warning. The back of my neck tingles.

Is someone watching me?

I turn a slow 360. There's nobody visible but still I feel eyes on me. Waiting to see where I'll go. What I'll do when I get there.

It's easier than I thought to get my bearings. The camp is huge – hiding places everywhere – but Simon will want me to find him. There's little point to coming back here otherwise. Archie will be in the room we were held in.

Determinedly, I run over to the building where I was once carried inside, gagged and blindfolded, terrified, but the horror I felt then pales in comparison to the horror I feel now. I'd sacrifice myself a million times over to save my child.

The building is gloomy. Darkness swallows me as I step inside. I need a torch. Too late I realize I have left my mobile in the centre console of the car.

I'd been so young when I was here that I wasn't sure whether I'd know which room had been our prison, but evil is thick in the blackness, beckoning me forward. Broken glass crunches underfoot as I edge down the hallway.

Something touches my face. I stifle a scream and bat it away.

A cobweb.

I can do this.

My body feels like one of the paper dolls Marie and I used to dress up, flimsy and insubstantial. I place my hands on my thighs to reassure myself that my legs are still there, solid and able to support me.

I can do this.

My teeth chatter as I reach the room.

Our room.

In the muted grey light spilling in through the patchy roof, my eyes scan the door. There are six nail holes where the bolts used to be. Crudely painted in faded red on the outside is *RIP Sinclair Sisters* as though we had died that day. I suppose in a way we had. We had come out of here altogether different children to the ones who had been dragged in. I squint as I search the corridor for a weapon. There's a wooden post with rusted nails jutting out from its splintered sides.

I raise it above my head.

I can do this.

Archie is all I can think of as I kick the door open, pelting to the room as fast as I can.

The element of surprise.

But it is me who is surprised.

Chapter Fifty-Eight

Carly

Now

Leah's at Norwood.

Norwood.

Carly thrusts her phone into her pocket and begins to run.

Chapter Fifty-Nine

Leah

Now

Archie isn't here.

Nobody is here.

That's not strictly true. There are the ghosts of the young Sinclair Sisters who once sang and danced and tried not to be broken by all that happened in this room.

It looks the same and yet different. The piles of rubbish have been cleared but it still stinks here. The bars that once striped the windows have gone. Probably taken as crime memorabilia. After our book came out, Carly saw the blanket we had supposedly been given by Doc for sale on eBay. Whether it was the actual one or not was impossible to tell.

The grubby mattress we had lain upon is also missing. It makes my skin crawl to think that somebody might lie on it and get a kick out of imagining three small, terrified girls, huddled together, fearing for their lives. Morbid fascination for the macabre is something I'll never get to grips with. I turn and my heart stutters at the face I have never forgotten.

The shock of orange hair and bright red nose. The red mouth slashed into a grin. The graffiti clown laughs.

You're back! he seems to say.

Fuck you, I reply.

There's a creak.

The door begins to close.

Chapter Sixty

George

Now

George passes his mobile from palm to palm, as though it is as hot as the shame that burns inside him. Leah's text still unopened.

What has he done?

Chapter Sixty-One

Carly

Now

Norwood looms larger than in her nightmares. Carly can't believe she's here but she'll do anything for Archie. He really is the light of her life.

Will you ever go back? a reporter had asked her once.

Only in my nightmares, she'd replied but here she is, wide awake and utterly terrified.

A shadow. A movement.

'Leah?' she whispers. Scared to shout. Scared to move. Scared about what's going to happen next.

Chapter Sixty-Two

Leah

Now

I push open the door that had begun to close in the breeze and step into the hallway. Outside, the staircase is patchy and rotten. The bannisters dangle precariously from their fixings. When we had escaped the room before we didn't go upstairs, so I almost dismiss the idea, but what-ifs gnaw at me.

Archie could be up there?

Distributing my weight evenly, I begin to crawl up to the second floor, avoiding the holes. All the while holding my breath, as though that will somehow make me lighter.

I'm almost at the top when there's a crack, a shift. I plummet to the ground.

Rockets of pain shoot through my spine. My lungs struggle for air. I roll onto my side, waiting for the dizziness to subside. I think of Carly's tattoo. A comma, not a full stop. This isn't over. I push myself to my feet. The muscles in my lower back spasm as I move, slower than I'd like but I can't give up. I won't.

A comma.

I wish Carly were here.

From outside I think I hear someone whisper my name. I listen but the only sound is my blood whooshing in my ears.

Picking up the wooden post that now feels heavier in my hand, I limp forwards, my thoughts racing, my body slow, following our invisible train of sorrow over to the main building.

The NORWOOD ARMY CAMP sign is still there. My breath rasps as I heft myself up the five steps I once pounded up, terrified Moustache and Doc were close behind.

The reception is pretty much as it had been, with the curved desk, the *Welcome* graffiti faded from black to grey. Curved above it, like a rainbow is another word, and this one causes a whimper to break free from my lips, which are clamped together in fright.

Today.

I am in the right place.

Up ahead, a noise. Not the police sirens I am so desperate to hear, but something else.

Somebody else?

In the cinema room some of the benches have been burned, ash heaped on the floor. The wind gusts through the empty window frames. A crisp packet crinkles from the direction of the ballroom.

Spicy Tomato Snaps.

All at once I can taste them in my mouth. Bile rises. I have never felt so scared. I push myself onwards. My back screams with every small step. The ballroom is in a worse state than before. To my left a heap of grubby blankets. I tiptoe around broken glass, discarded syringes, but I'm sure my pounding heart is audible even if my footsteps aren't. The gaping holes in the ceiling from which the chandeliers once hung watch me. Every few seconds I look up, half expecting to see someone above me, but there's no one here. I inch forward as quietly as I can.

There is still a huge mound of rubbish in the centre of the room. I remember the smell of it as I cowered inside with Carly and Marie. A bonfire waiting to be lit. I skirt around it, my memories causing me to tremble, when out of the corner of my eye I spot them.

Feet.

Instantly I clamp my hands over my mouth to contain my scream. The feet are too large to be Archie's. But that doesn't mean he's not here, huddled inside the stinking pile. I creep towards the feet, unable to tear my eyes away from them. They don't move. Do they know I'm here?

Thoughts ricochet. I don't want to drive my post into the pile in case Archie is inside. Instead, I angle the corner of the wood and lift the rubbish so I can properly see the legs, the body, the face.

Oh God, the face.

Nausea rises hot and sour as the blank, lifeless eyes of my sister stare back at me.

Chapter Sixty-Three

George

Now

George can't bring himself to open Leah's text. He is lost in thought. Lost in shame.

And regret.

He has always felt at home at Francesca's, his body falling into a level of relaxation that didn't happen anywhere else, but now it feels different.

It feels wrong.

The cream fabric couch pops with yellow cushions, a light grey carpet swallows each footstep with its deep pile. George tries to imagine Archie in this room, but he can't.

'You okay?' Francesca places a tumbler of water on the glass table in front of him. She doesn't like hot drinks near the couch. Will it really be so different living with her to living with Leah? Suddenly, it all feels frighteningly real. No longer only the distraction of sex, a loving touch from a gloveless hand, but in a bills-to-pay, meals-to-make kind of way.

'I got a text from Leah.'

'What does she say?' Francesca's eyes are bright with tears. She's finding this as difficult as George.

'I haven't opened it.' George knows Leah will have found the goodbye note by the bed, opened his wardrobe to find only empty hangers. He'd taken the coward's way out and he was ashamed. Leah deserves better than this. Archie deserves better than this. Already he misses them both with a ferocity that hurts. He loves Leah. He loves her so much.

'I think I've made a mistake.' George begins to cry.

Chapter Sixty-Four

Leah

Now

Oh God, no. Please no.

She's dead.

I know this with certainty but it doesn't stop me shaking her shoulders.

'Wake up,' I whisper loudly. 'Please. Wake up.'

She doesn't.

She can't.

My fingers stray to her wrist, fumble to find a pulse that isn't there. My head drops to her chest but there is no *thump-thump-thump* of her heart.

Yet I still can't quite accept it.

'Wake up. Please. You have to.' I shake her shoulders once more before I sit back on my heels, my eyes trained on her face that still looks beautiful to me.

It's as though my heart has been ripped from its cavity and I claw it back, clutching it to my chest, not ready to give into the numbness that whispers that it's hopeless. That everything was always leading up to this. I was too late to save her and I am too late for...

'Archie!' I openly scream his name now, picturing him hiding somewhere, eyes screwed up tight the same as when he has a middle-of-the-night nightmare. The lifeless face of his aunt forever etched on his tender young mind. How will he ever recover from this?

'Archie!' My arms windmill wildly as I rummage through the rubbish, terrified I'll feel a limb. A skull. Hair. But there's nothing. He isn't here. It is both a relief and a disappointment.

I stand, but I catch sight of her again and my paper-doll legs veer out of control. I sway wildly.

'I'll be back,' I whisper to ears that can no longer hear. Reluctant to tear my gaze away from her glassy eyes that will never again see the beauty in the world.

Or the horrors.

'I'll be back,' I say once more but, even to me, my promise is gossamer-fine, easily broken.

I trail after the wisp of memories of three girls hand in hand who were as desperate to stay hidden as I am to be found.

'Archie!'

His name echoes through the windowless rooms. The ghosts of the past whisper, *You know where he is.*

And I do.

The decontamination chamber. Where everything ended last time.

Where everything will now begin.

Chapter Sixty-Five

George

Now

George vows he will make it up to Leah somehow. He swerves in and out of traffic, slicing through lights on the cusp of turning from amber to red. He screeches onto the empty driveway. Leah's car is missing.

Where is she?

It isn't like her to take Archie out in the evening, she must be distraught to upset his bedtime routine. He can picture her face crumpling after reading his goodbye letter.

Why had he written it? He's such an idiot.

He needs to call Carly and Tash. Leah must be with one of them. She has no other friends. George is her best friend and he has let her down.

The house is cold and dark. He slinks inside like a scolded puppy with his tale between his legs. There is no scramble of paws.

Where is the dog? Has Leah taken him with her to keep Archie amused while she pours her heart out to her sister or her best friend?

It doesn't feel right.

Why haven't Tash or Carly come here?

George strides up the stairs two at a time. The envelope he addressed to his wife still stands against her bedside lamp. He picks it up and runs his fingers across the unbroken seal and thinks how lucky he is that he got here first. That she hasn't read it. He can make it right.

All of it.

But still. Where is she? Archie? The puppy? Something is off. He sinks onto the bed. Their bed. Pulls out his phone to call her and sees her unopened text.

Archie is missing.

The bed rocks beneath him as he reads, seasickness swirling in his stomach. He pounds down the stairs and throws himself into his car.

Archie is missing.

George hares towards Norwood, calling the police as he drives.

'Please hurry.' He garbles out the details. The operator tells him to stay where he is. Not to put himself in any danger. He cuts the call and tosses his phone onto the passenger seat where his wife should be. His eyes flicker to the rear-view mirror. The sight of Archie's empty booster seat is a punch to the gut. He should have believed Leah that Simon was back. He's going to kill the bastard with his bare hands.

I'm coming-I'm coming-I'm coming.

He grips the steering wheel tightly.

He hopes he's not too late.

Chapter Sixty-Six

Leah

Now

Twenty years ago I had made this trek, the security of my sisters dulling my panic. Now there is only me. Injured by my fall, my back shrieks with protest but I don't care. I don't care about anything except finding my son. I burst out of the main building. It seemed inevitable that I would be greeted with a clap of thunder, a flash of lightning, but the sky is a flat, cloudless grey and it's worse somehow. The silence. A storm would no longer faze me. I am incredulous that I was ever scared of the weather. This sharp-tongued fear relentlessly licking at my organs, coating my insides sour, is like nothing I've ever experienced.

My baby. My boy.

At least the hammering rain would make me feel I wasn't quite so alone. That I was recreating the past that, if not granted a happy ending, was at least satisfactory.

We were all alive.

Then.

My stomach roils. I push the image of the ballroom away. Glassy eyes staring up at me. Grey skin. Blue lips. I can grieve later. Now is not the time to fall apart. It is as though my feet remember where to go. This time there is no circling around back to the main building. The decontamination chamber looms in front of me. The rusting DANGER sign still in place. I have left the wooden post back in the ballroom and feel small and vulnerable but filled with an unmatchable fury. My mother's instinct roaring louder than the beat of my heart, which I know thuds in sync with the life I created. The life I will save, even if it costs me my own.

Abandon hope all ye who enter here. I hadn't noticed that last time but I notice it now.

Simon, I am coming for you.

I step into the entrance where I once huddled with Marie while Carly covered our footsteps in the wet earth outside. This was where Carly had dropped her shoes and Moustache and Doc had found them. Holding the door open for light, I scan the floor. My body jolts as though it has been shocked when I see two small trainers I recognize. Thomas the Tank Engine's face beaming from the heels.

Archie is here.

I try to calm my breath before I move on. Then, Carly had fumbled for our hands and I'd held tightly onto hers as we edged our way into the next room. Now mine are empty. I ball them into fists.

I am ready.

The smell of the shower room rises, slime still thick on the walls. I search through the gloom for a piece of the pipes that had littered the floor last time where they had been wrenched from the walls. There is nothing I can use for a weapon. The graffiti is everywhere.

This is the building it all ended in!!!

This is SO cool!

Creepy as fuck

I know what I'd do with three girls in here!

Wanker, someone had written underneath.

Lastly, by the open door, a sign. THIS WAY next to an arrow.

Ghouls and ghosts are everywhere. I rub my arms to feel my flesh, the warmth of my blood coating my bones.

I am here.

I am here again.

Following the arrow, I try not to think of the true-crime fans' mounting excitement when I feel nothing but dread. In the corridor, the hole in the roof has stretched wider. I raise my face and can see both the sun and the moon vying for dominance, casting their glow into the place that I do not want to step into but must.

The morgue.

Although I am trying to be strong, I am crying as I tentatively open each of the lockers that are too small to hide an adult but would easily house a small child the way they had before. The memory presses down on me, heart-wrenching and overwhelming. Carly pushing Marie and I inside. The feel of dust and grit on my skin. The soft click of metal on metal as she closed the door. The sense of suffocation despite the stagnant air being plentiful.

Three blind mice. Three blind mice.

Has Simon locked Archie here?

See how they run.

Please don't let my boy be here.

He isn't.

That leaves only one place.

It feels as though I am walking towards the gallows as

I approach the chutes – contaminated clothes, contaminated shoes. They are bigger than I remember but I still doubt that I will fit through the way I had before, the way Archie would now. Momentarily I wonder whether I should instead locate the end of the tunnel and work my way inwards, but my gut feeling is that I'd be wasting valuable time. There was no marker and it might be impossible to find. It might have caved in by now.

I pull open the hatch. Above hang large metal hooks. I jump and catch one in each hand, my shoulder sockets burning as I dangle there helplessly, feet scrambling for traction as I try to hoist up my weight so I can slip my legs inside the chute.

I can't get the angle right.

My arms aren't strong enough. I lift my legs once more. My hands slip from the hook. I have no choice. I'll have to dive in head first.

Archie.

The thought of plummeting into blackness with nothing to break my fall is terrifying but not as terrifying as the thought of my baby being down there with the dark, and the cold, and the beetles. I steel myself, hands clasped together as though I am in prayer, ready to dive into a waterless pit. I am gripped by utter terror.

Archie.

I am free-falling through time and space. It takes an eternity and it takes no time at all. I crash to the ground. I can hear the snap of my wrist before I feel the searing pain. My mouth pressed to the ground is full of dirt.

I roll over.

My ears are ringing from the fall and my mouth is full of blood where my teeth clamped around my tongue, but I can see. There is a circle of light pooling from a torch. My head feels heavy on my neck as I look around the room. The ground is strewn with empty spirit bottles, shards of glass where some of them have smashed, crushed cans, cigarette butts. Quite the party. I can almost see the true-crime fanatics, torch pointed under their chins, faces waxy and pale as they recount our final steps. I shift my gaze and see something that lights me with happiness until fear dampens my fleetingly joyful glow.

Curled into himself is Archie. But he is too still. Too quiet.

And he isn't alone.

Chapter Sixty-Seven

Carly

Now

'Leah,' Carly says. 'You found us.' She begins to cry.

Chapter Sixty-Eight

Leah

Now

'Thank God. You're alive. Marie is… Is Archie…?'

I begin to scramble over to him but Carly shouts, 'Stop' in a voice that doesn't quite sound like hers. Confused, my eyes find hers. They are full of fear and regret, but something else.

Anger.

Chapter Sixty-Nine

Carly

Now

Carly watches as Leah's confused expression morphs to fear when she sees the glint of the knife Carly is brandishing in her hand.

'What are you doing?' Leah's voice is high.

'Did you know?' Carly demands as she bundles Archie onto her lap. He is warm and soft. She loves him so very much.

'What's wrong with Archie?' Leah inches forward, stopping when she sees the blade swish dangerously close to Archie's beautiful waxy face. 'Carly!'

'I gave him one of your sleeping tablets. Answer me.'

'Answer what?"

'About Marie. Did. You. Know?' She shouts now, but it doesn't really matter what Leah says, Carly knows she won't believe her.

Chapter Seventy

Leah

Now

'Marie?' I repeat. Does Carly know that our sister is dead? It's the only explanation I can think of that might go some small way to explaining her erratic behaviour but if there's a chance, however tiny, that she doesn't know I don't want to tell her right now. She's already teetering on the edge, I can't be the one to push her over. I don't know why she's given Archie a sleeping tablet. I don't know why she's brandishing a knife. All I know is that the longer I can keep her talking the better. George must have read my text, he's always glued to his phone. The police have to be on their way.

Don't they?

Chapter Seventy-One

Carly

Now

'Marie knew about the abduction,' Carly says, her voice monotone.

'I don't understand. Knew?'

'Before it happened. Mum was in on it too, apparently. She must have hated us even then.'

When Carly first found out the truth she had believed Marie's assurances that Leah hadn't known their parents' plan, but the more she had thought about it the more she became convinced that was a lie.

Another one.

They were twins. They shared everything.

Leah takes a sharp intake of breath. In the dim, milky light Carly can see her face is the colour of flour. Carly thinks she might have got it wrong. Leah might not have known. She's always worn her heart on her sleeve. It was Marie who was always the actress. It appears she might have fooled them both.

'Your dad—'

'Don't call him that,' Leah says sharply.

'Simon was planning it with Mum. Marie overheard him and Mum talking.'

'I can't… I don't…'

'It's true. That was the *new angle* she was alluding to when she told us about the offer of the TV interview.'

'No… She was my twin. I would have known. No…'

'Yes.'

Leah buries her hands in her hair. Carly feels her anguish. Carly has always known how her sisters felt, or she thought she had. She was always the one who wanted to make it better for them but she can't make this better. No one can. Carly gives Leah a minute. Her heart twists at her sister's distress. In the silence she hears a scuttling. A burying insect. The memory of the beetles, in her hair, in her mouth returns to her with a punch. So much she has been through because of one man. So much that could have been stopped if Marie had just told the truth.

She feels angry again.

She places her palm flat against Archie's chest to calm herself. Feels the rise and fall of his rib cage. She grapples for the words to continue. 'Remember the day before we were snatched when Marie was off school sick? It was because she'd overheard them planning it and she wanted to talk Simon out of it. He… he told her that it wouldn't be real. It would be like a game. He warned Marie that if it didn't work we'd all be separated and sent to different homes. He was broke. Remember when she used to say, "This isn't real. This is just a game. Just pretend."'

Leah opens her mouth and closes it again. Instead of speaking she nods.

'She was scared. I get that but…' Carly's voice cracks. 'Our parents betrayed us. Doc and Moustache were the worst kind of people. The world is full of them. But Marie… We were all supposed to have each other's backs. Sisters. You can't trust anyone. You really didn't know, Leah?'

Leah shakes her head violently. 'I swear, Carly. I swear on Archie's life.' Carly believes her but it doesn't change the way she feels right now.

'Please.' Leah stretches out her arms. 'Please give me Archie. Let's go home, Carly.'

Carly is torn in a million different pieces. She knows what she's about to do is the right thing, but it still hurts all the same.

Chapter Seventy-Two

Leah

Now

'I can't give you Archie,' Carly says. 'He's too good for this world. Too pure.'

My blood freezes. Ice heavy in my veins. I watch Carly's hand caress the handle of the knife. Panic bulldozes into me. She wouldn't, would she? She loves him. She loves me. Marie.

'Marie.' All at once my throat is hot and swollen at the thought that has just occurred to me. I'm wrong. I have to be. 'Marie… is dead.' The words burn my tongue. I study Carly's face through my clouded tears. She doesn't look surprised. 'I… I found her in the ballroom.'

I fall into silence. So much hinges on Carly's reaction.

'I *know* she's dead,' Carly speaks slowly. 'She's been dead for days.'

'How…' I want to ask how Carly knows that but I'm scared of her answer. I don't recognize her, this woman with wild, staring eyes and flat robotic voice. She shifts Archie on her lap. The blade is horribly close to his perfect, unblemished skin. What has happened to my sister? Our protector. Marie might have made a mistake by not telling us but she was *eight*. We were all just *children*. How can Carly have known that Marie is dead and not tell anyone? To stand shoulder to shoulder with me in the police station, her lips straight and silent, while I tried to report my twin missing. I know Carly's not coping. I've barely seen her this past week. I know she's been avoiding me but *this*?

This?

Surely I'm wrong.

I don't want to ask, but I have to. 'Carly…' Just how unbalanced has my sister become? 'Did you kill Marie?'

Chapter Seventy-Three

Carly

Now

Carly nods her head – *yes, I killed Marie* – and then she shakes it before nodding it once more. Did she kill her? She really doesn't know. Something is sandpapering her memories, smoothing away the blunt edge of reality. She pushes her tongue into the gap in her mouth where the tooth that had been knocked out the day they were taken used to sit. Is it her fault? Is it her fault again? She thinks it is.

'Get your coat. You're coming with me,' Carly had told Marie that day in her sister's flat when she had expected to leave with her forgotten phone but instead was handed the cold, hard truth. Her stepdad had tried to set her up, her alone. Her mum had known. Marie had known. Probably Leah, too, she had thought. The world in which she had always felt unsafe now felt even darker, more dangerous, as though she'd be better off without it. As though the world would be better off without her. All along it had been Leah that Marie had wanted to save. Leah. Not her.

Never her.

'Where are we going?' Marie's face creased with anxiety.

'To the cashpoint. I'll give you some money. Not enough,

but some, but we're *not* doing the TV interview.' Carly had felt shock and confusion but rising to the surface a deep sense of shame. She'd loved her sister completely. Both her sisters. She was such a fool. She'd give Marie what she had in the bank and then she was cutting her off. Her and Leah.

'Thanks. Afterwards, can you drop me somewhere?'

'Where?'

Marie told her where she wanted to go and Carly wished she had never asked.

'Carly. I do love you. Sisters.' Marie offers her little finger: '*A pinkie promise can't be broke, Or you'll disappear in a puff of smoke...*' Carly didn't join in, leaving her arms by her sides. Marie trailed off.

Sisters.

But they weren't, not really. Her and mum. Leah, Marie and Dad. Two jigsaw pieces forced together to try and complete a picture of a happy family but they didn't fit.

Marie dropped her hand but still wore the trace of a smile on her lips. Anger burned among Carly's confusion. Marie looked different. Lighter somehow. Relieved to have shared her secret or relived she was getting her fix. Once again, Carly felt unimportant and alone.

'Shall we go?' Marie was bouncing on the balls of her feet, eager to leave. There was no more conversation. No explanation. No further apology.

Although a thousand *sorry*s couldn't eradicate the utter despair Carly felt as she trailed Marie down the stairwell.

Her.

It was only ever meant to be her who was taken.

Carly remembers the teeming rain as she had pulled up

outside the bank. She remembers withdrawing her daily limit of five hundred pounds. Even if that hadn't been her limit, there was no more money left to give. Back in the car she had followed Marie's directions to a pub, wooden boards criss-crossing its windows, paint flaking from the DOG AND DUCK sign swinging cheerily in the breeze. Marie turned to Carly. There was so much Carly wanted to say. So much she wanted to ask. Marie gave a barely detectable nod and attempted a smile, her eyes bright with tears.

'Say *something*,' Carly screamed in her head. 'Make me understand why I was the one to be sacrificed.' But Marie was already clicking open the door. The wind blustered inside the car, coating Carly's cheeks with rain. Carly didn't care about the weather. Her cheeks were already wet with tears. Marie crossed her arms over her chest and hurried over the road.

From out of the alley stepped a man. He gripped Marie's chin with his thumb and forefinger before spitting on the pavement beside her. The rain plastered Marie's hair to her scalp, her thin jacket soaked through. Carly watched as Marie plucked notes from the bundle Carly had given her. He counted them with one hand, the other he thrust between Marie's legs, laughing as she flinched and backed away. He held out a small parcel and she snatched it before backing off again. He followed her further down the street.

Carly looked around, wondering if anyone would help Marie, but the man's eyes flickered upwards and Carly saw he'd glanced at the CCTV camera. They continued talking but this time he kept his distance. Carly couldn't bear to watch any more. Marie had made her choice just as Carly had made hers. She shifted the car into first gear and pulled away. In her rear-view mirror she saw the man hold out something to Marie who snatched it and put it in her pocket before walking away. Carly braked. Her fingers drumming on the steering wheel. If she reverses it would never end. She would never break free. Marie was a mess. They all were a mess.

Family.

Except they weren't now. Not really. They had made their choice to single out Carly. Her parents. Her sisters.

Marie raised her arm at a passing cab. Carly took comfort that she was off the streets at least.

She released the handbrake and drove away but as she was passing a lay-by she pulled in, rested her forehead on the steering wheel and wept.

By the time Carly arrived home, anger was again her overriding emotion. She picked up the phone and, pacing the lounge, she called the only person who could make her feel better.

'Hello.'

'Mum' was all she could say before she was crying again. One word. Three letters that should mean so many things – love, protection, stability, strength – and it didn't mean any of them.

'Carly? What's wrong?' There was concern in her mum's voice but this only made Carly cry harder.

She wiped her nose with her sleeve and tried to stem her tears. 'Marie has told me.'

'Told you what?'

'Everything.'

There's a pause. The sound of her mum's breath coming faster. 'It's not true,' she said at last.

'So you know what I'm talking about?' Carly slumped onto her sofa.

'What? No, of course not. Just... just that Marie drinks too much and whatever she's told you is probably a lie. What did she say?'

'You knew,' Carly said softly.

'I didn't... I swear...'

'You. Knew,' Carly said, louder this time.

'It was complicated. We were in a terrible situation. I thought we were doing the right thing for you all. If you were a parent you'd understand—'

'And whose fault is it I don't have a family of my own? That I can't bear the thought of ending up like Leah. Terrified that every time Archie is out of her sight someone will take him, and I *would* be like that. Scared that I'd brought a child into a world that is full of monsters. You, Mum. You're a monster.'

'Don't say that. I...' Her mum was crying. It was the first time in years Carly had felt any emotion from her.

'Was it really only ever meant to be me that was taken? Not Leah or Marie?'

'Yes. Just you.' Her mum's voice was thin.

Carly waited. Prepared to listen. Desperate to understand.

'Are you going to tell anyone? The police?' her mum asked. Questions not apologies. Worried for herself, not for her daughter. Carly let the phone drop from her hand. She scrunched herself into a ball of sorrow.

Later, Carly's phone buzzed with a message. She unfurled herself and rubbed her sore eyes before picking up her handset, convinced it would be her mum.

It wasn't.

The text was from Marie.

So sorry for what we put you through. Back to where it all started. My final dance. You don't have to worry about me again.

Carly didn't hesitate. She scooped up her car keys and raced to Norwood. It was dark when she arrived. Shining her mobile ahead of her for light, she made for the room they'd been held captive in. Carly felt fevered. Detached. As though she was having a hallucination. The room was smaller than she remembered but empty. Dizziness engulfed her and she realized she wasn't breathing. She didn't want to breathe this filthy fucking air. She ran back outside.

'Marie!'

Where could she be? Had she got it wrong and she wasn't at Norwood at all? Her eyes scanned the text. Two words sprang out: *last dance*.

'Marie!' Carly raced towards the ballroom. Her feet slip-sliding in the mud. Skidding on the steps. She crunched over broken glass, hurdled over upturned benches in the cinema briefing room.

Marie was in the ballroom, slumped on a pile of blankets. Her belt tightened around her arm, needle protruding from her vein. The expression on her face was peaceful, happy almost. Carly dropped hard onto her knees. Fingers fumbling for a pulse, but the blood in Marie's veins was still. Carly held her for a long time. Loving her and hating her all at once. Envying her too. She had found the peace they'd all craved.

She didn't know what to do. Again, she was left feeling to blame. Carrying the burden of guilt. If she hadn't given Marie the money she'd still be alive. It was always her fault.

Always.

She was furious that again one of the Sinclairs had done something else to try and ruin her. She felt like she was broken.

As angry as she was, she couldn't just leave Marie. Carly was gentle as she eased her hands into Marie's armpits and dragged her over to the centre of the room. She walked slowly, collecting cardboard, broken pallets, building a pile over Marie much like the one that had been there before. It was there she left her.

Forever hiding.

Forever safe.

'Oh Carly,' Leah said softly. 'It wasn't your fault. If you hadn't given her the money, she'd have found it somehow. Addicts always do. She loved you. Please never doubt that. We all love you. You *are* our sister and we never thought of you as any different.'

'Everyone lied to me.'

'Mum lied to me too.'

'It's not the same. Did you know it was only meant to be me?' Carly hated how small her voice sounded. How needy.

'What was?'

'The abduction. Marie was supposed to get me into the alley on my own. Two men to take one girl. One mattress. One blanket. One teddy.'

'Carly, I didn't… I can't imagine…' There's a beat. 'Look, I'm sure it was because you were the oldest…'

But Carly knew it was because she was the least loved. Her fingers played with Archie's hair. 'It was only meant to be me,' she said again sadly. 'It all has to end. Now.'

Chapter Seventy-Four

Leah

Now

My heart breaks for Carly. Finally I am free from the guilt that it wasn't my fault – that I likely had shut the gate properly but Marie had opened it again – but instead I am burdened with the knowledge that my dad – Simon – had formulated his plan around Carly as if she didn't matter. After all his talk about family, about treating the girls the same despite Carly not being his, he didn't care. The knowing that, after years of thinking otherwise, he *had* perhaps loved Marie and me doesn't bring any comfort.

We were sisters. We felt what each other felt. The horror. The burden. The grief. The fear.

'Everything that has happened the past few days, was it all you?' I ask Carly – for the first time it occurs to me that Simon wasn't behind any of it. 'Did you send me the countdown letters?'

'Yes. I wrote myself the same letters so you wouldn't suspect me.'

'I'd never have suspected you… Was *all* of it you? The mice? The teddy? The cross around his neck?'

'Yes,' she says simply. 'I didn't know what to do. I couldn't think clearly after Marie had confessed. There was the buzzing in my head. I wasn't thinking. I just went home and went to bed. The next day when you took us to Marie's flat and let us in with the spare key, it seemed easier to scribble a note from her in the kitchen, saying that she'd gone on tour. You were in the bedroom. I didn't think it through, it just *happened*.' Carly had always been good at forging handwriting, faking letters from Mum to the school to get herself out of PE. 'There was this feeling, Leah, that if I called the police they'd blame me for Marie's death. Everyone would blame me for Marie. You were always the nation's favourites, the cute pigtailed twins. I was... an awkward teenager. Now I'm an awkward adult. I couldn't face it all around the anniversary. And...' Carly wipes the tears from her cheeks with the hand that still grips the knife. 'I don't know. I thought you knew. I hated you both for... for being born, I suppose. Ruining Mum's life. My life. I wished it was just her and me again in our tiny flat, eating chicken nuggets.'

'I don't blame you for wanting revenge, Carly. But this... this isn't right. Archie...'

'I'm so very sorry but Archie has to now die, Leah. It's the only way.'

Chapter Seventy-Five

Carly

Now

Leah doesn't cry but Carly can feel her onslaught of panic as her mind scrambles for a way she can save her son.

She can't.

It tears Carly apart to see her little sister – the person she has always tried to protect – fall apart. She can almost hear Leah shatter. See pieces of her scatter to the floor.

'Carly…' she says, her voice a wail. She looks at Carly with mistrust and hurt. She looks at Carly as though she is a monster.

She isn't.

Is she?

'Leah…' Carly wants to explain. To ease Leah's pain. 'I'm sorry I've frightened you the past few days with the letters and everything.' Carly feels such remorse that she'd behaved so badly. 'It's as though I wasn't myself and that's the problem, don't you see? I don't know who I am. Who I would have been if it weren't for Simon. If I hadn't been abducted.'

'I know who you are! You're a good—'

'You don't even know who you are, Leah.'

'I do.' Leah grabs at the straw she thinks she is being offered. 'I'm Archie's mum. George's wife. Your *sister*.'

'Those are all labels. Names don't define us. Our actions do. Our feelings do. Since Marie got sick in that filthy room, you've put yourself in a bubble with your incessant cleaning. Those bloody gloves.'

Leah raises her hands and stares at them as though she has never seen them before.

'The rituals you carry out. Everything has to be done three times because you should have banged the gate shut three times. You don't *live*, not really.'

'I do live—'

'You live in *fear*. Remember when Archie was born and you wouldn't take him out of the house. You wouldn't let him go to toddler groups in case he caught an infection.'

'Yes. But he goes now and—'

'And you worry about him every single second he's out of your sight, don't you?'

Leah's silence is her agreement.

'But it's not germs and illness and all those other things you say, is it? Not really. You think someone might take him. Hurt him, because… because you *know*, Leah. You and I both know that there are bad people out there. The worst people out there. We've lived with them, you and I. We've *loved* them. How long do you think it will be before Archie learns the world is not what he thought? When he starts school and the children tease him about you, because the children will find out through their parents who you are.'

'But… but…'

Leah can't think of an argument. Carly hopes she is convincing her. It would be so much easier if she agrees to this. They could all just slip away from the world now. Together.

'Look at him.' Carly strokes Archie's hair. 'He's so innocent. So pure. Remember when we felt like that? Before the day we were snatched? Wouldn't it be nice if he stayed like that? Stayed asleep? We could join him, you and I. Join Marie. No more fear. No more pain. No more—'

'No!' Leah shouts. 'You're wrong. I know you want to protect him but this isn't the way. It isn't. There is good in the world. Kindness. Love. We teach Archie all of those things. We can *show* him all of those things and he'll have a good life. A long life.'

'What do you show him, Leah? Really? That you're always looking over your shoulder. That it isn't safe to touch anything without your skin being covered. That—'

Carly is stunned into silence by what happens next.

Chapter Seventy-Six

Leah

Now

I pull off my gloves and push up my sleeves before rubbing my bare hands over the earth. I smear the dirt over my arms, my face.

'I don't care about germs, really I don't. It hasn't ruined me. It hasn't ruined us.' Carly doesn't respond and so I scoop up handfuls of soil and cram them into my mouth, trying not to retch as the earth clogs my throat. Trying to block out the thought of beetles scurrying down my windpipe, laying their eggs in my stomach, their babies bursting through my skin.

'See.' I try to speak but my words are muffled. I swallow hard. Something jagged tears at my throat. I think I've swallowed some glass but I don't care. I lift another palmful and again stuff it inside my mouth. Feeling it coating my teeth, my gums. 'It's not too late. It's never too late. Please, Carly, don't hurt him.'

Carly cradles Archie's head in her lap and pulls off her jumper while I am calculating if I should dive at her during the split second that her face is covered but my moment has passed. She rolls her jumper into a ball and holds it above Archie's mouth.

'Please.' My heart is breaking. I scan the distance between us.

If I lurch towards her she'll have time to snatch the knife and plunge it into Archie's small body. If he has to die, suffocation is the kinder death but I can't let her do it. I just can't. 'Carly, don't! You *love* him.'

'Haven't you been *listening*? It's *because* I love him. The world is too cruel. Too awful. You should never have had a child. You know what can happen to children. We're vulnerable.' She begins to rock back and forth. 'All these years. All these years, Leah, and I thought it was my fault. I haven't been able to let it go. I haven't got any friends. I haven't got a family—'

'We're your family. Archie. George and me.'

'George has been having an affair, Leah.'

'What? No—'

'Marie told me. See, people are bad. The world is bad. We're better off somewhere else. Somewhere better.'

I hesitate. Is she right? I thought I could trust George, but then I trusted my mum. My dad. I trusted my twin. I glance at Archie. He is stirring. Do I really want to put him through all the pain I have felt? Am feeling.

'Carly…' I swallow hard.

Chapter Seventy-Seven

Carly

Now

Carly has seen something change in Leah's expression. She thinks she has convinced her.

'You know I'm right, don't you?' Carly asks.

Chapter Seventy-Eight

Leah

Now

Carly thinks she has convinced me. She knows what it's like to feel betrayed. To feel fear. But she doesn't know what it feels like to be a mother. The lengths I would go to in order to protect my boy.

My fingers skim the earth until they brush against something sharp and pointed. I manoeuvre the shard of glass into my hand.

From afar, I hear the muffled sound of sirens. If I can just keep her talking.

'Archie is so young. So innocent,' I say.

'But that's the point. Don't you *see*?' She pleads with me and I do see. We were just like him once. Trusting. Malleable. Full of hope. But if I admit to understanding her logic, she might think I'm condoning what she's about to do and I'm not. Despite the world sometimes being a broken, ugly, hateful place, it's also full of warmth and kindness and laughter. The good outweighs the bad, every single day.

Again, Archie stirs on her lap. She presses the jumper down over his mouth. I move suddenly, startling her. She scoops up the knife with her other hand and brandishes it. 'Let him go.

It's kinder this way. You can't protect him out there… I can't protect him out there.' Tears stream down her face.

I hold the shard tightly in my grip, my palm now sticky with blood. I don't care about contamination or infection.

I have to do something. I don't want to hurt her but I have to shock her into releasing Archie. She loves him completely but I know that deep down she loves me too.

'Carly,' I say sharply. She raises her eyes to mine.

I lift the shard. Only once, not three times. There is no time, no need for rituals. I drive it as hard as I can into my stomach. There's a pop. A give. A rush of blood.

The sirens are growing louder. A trace of a smile passes across my lips as I think it isn't too late for Archie, even if it is too late for me.

'Leah!" I hear Carly scream. She shoves Archie from her lap and scrambles over to me, just as I knew she would. I feel her grasp my hands. She doesn't go near the torch, but everything darkens all the same.

I see nothing.

I feel nothing.

I am nothing.

Chapter Seventy-Nine

Leah

Now

George holds my hand, his faced creased with concern. He rubs his thumb over mine. Skin on cotton. I know he's the one who eased my fingers into clean gloves while I was unconscious. I'd like to say I don't need them now. That everything I have been through has made me stronger. Resilient. But when George mentioned bringing Archie in to visit me I felt a rush of panic, heat prickling my scalp. As much as I was longing to see my boy, the thought of him here among the germs and the illness and the threat of MRSA sent me teetering to the edge until George pulled me back with his soothing voice and kind words. So while I'd like to say I'm cured, I'm not. I want to be, though, and wanting is always the start of something, isn't it?

Disinfectant clogs my throat while the police ask me questions. Endless questions.

It is difficult to answer them. Through the haze of medication the *then* merges with the *now*. We were taken. Archie was taken. It is all a bit of a blur.

'When was the last time you saw Marie?' PC Godley asks.

'You know when.' I can't keep the bitterness out of my

voice. 'I came to the station to tell you she was missing. I knew something was wrong and you dismissed it as a *feeling*.'

'It's estimated that Marie's overdose took place before you reported it, so even if we had located her it would have been too late.' He looks ashamed. 'I am sorry, though.'

'Thank you.' I know it isn't his fault.

'And where is Carly now?'

This time it is me who feels ashamed. How could Mum have agreed to Dad arranging Carly's abduction? Knowing that Marie and I were never supposed to be taken is too awful for me to process. No wonder Carly unravelled the way she did.

'She said she was going away, for a while. It's all been very traumatic.'

Whatever happens I will protect her. My sister, the way that in the end she protected me. I knew she wouldn't let me die. George says when he arrived, at much the same time as the police, she was standing outside, balancing a conscious but groggy Archie on her hip, waving and screaming for help. That image is comforting. She could have left me alone and gone underground, but she didn't. Our family nearly destroyed her and I hope wherever she is, she can be happy.

I hope that she'll come back.

'So tell me again, Leah. Why did you go to Norwood?'

'It all got too much. The letters. The journalists. I thought that if I revisited the place that has never really left me I could begin to put it behind me somehow. I wasn't thinking straight.'

'So…' he consults his notes, 'you threw yourself down the contamination chute?'

'Yes. It's where it ended before. It was unfortunate there was broken glass. It was such a shock to land on it. I don't know what I'd have done if Carly hadn't come and found me.'

'And you think she guessed where you were?'

'Yes. We're sisters. We have a special bond.'

'And you say she brought Archie along because she was babysitting?'

'Yes. She'd never have left him alone. She loves him.' That much, at least, is true.

Thankfully, Archie doesn't remember anything that happened. Once I'd been taken to the hospital George had called Tash. She'd picked up Archie and had taken him home while I was operated on. The glass had missed my liver by millimetres. I am lucky, I was told.

'Right.' PC Godley puts away his pen. 'I suppose we'll leave it at that then. The owners of the land could prosecute you for trespassing but it's not something we'll encourage them to do. Hopefully now the anniversary has been and gone we'll hear no more from you.'

I think he's glad to see the back of me.

It is the first day I have been out of bed. The pain in my side is sharp and slicing but, with George's help, I make it to the bathroom and a nurse helps me wash my hair while I tremble and try not to cry at the thought of all those who have used the shower before me. The skin they would have shed. Traces of bacteria. We don't have to be able to see something to fear it. The invisible is always the worst. Afterwards, my hair is wrapped in a stiff and yellowing towel. The nurse supports my elbow as I shuffle back into the corridor.

'Turn the light off,' she asks.

Hesitantly I stretch out my fingers and flick the switch, fighting the urge to repeat it twice more.

Small steps.

I am settled in the day room with George. A dark brown tea sits on the table before me. It's in my own mug, which George has brought in. He looks tired. His jeans hang loose on his hips. Stubble shadows his chin.

I have something to tell him.

'The doctor has suggested that I don't come home when I'm discharged. That I admit myself to Mulberry.' I like that they give it a one-word name. It doesn't sound like the psychiatric unit it is. 'The staff are experienced in compulsive OCD and panic disorder and can help me deal with… with the root cause. I think I need… I want to get better. Be better. I don't know if I should go. I'll miss Archie… and you. I'll miss you.' My words tumble out. 'I know it hasn't been easy for you, George, and you deserve a wife who's… who's…' Tears well and before I can swallow them down and speak again, George has reached for my hand.

'Never doubt that I love you.' He doesn't smile as he says this; dread curdles as I wait for the but. And when it comes it is hard and painful. A double betrayal. I had pushed Carly's revelation about George's affair to the back of my mind. Not wanting to believe it, but George says:

'I've been having an affair… with Francesca.'

It's true. I've been betrayed by two of the people I trusted most in the world. Betrayed by two of the people I trust most in the world *again*. Perhaps it's not as shocking as the deceit of my parents, but all the same I feel an overwhelming sadness. This isn't only George's fault though. What have we done to each other? Simon – I never call him Dad – has shaped our lives, is *still* shaping our lives. It has to stop.

'Is it over?' I ask.

'Yes.' This time he looks me directly in the eye.

'Why?' I wonder if he's giving her up for Archie's sake.

'Because... You.' He tries to take my hand but I bend my fingers so he can't hold them. 'You are everything to me and when... when you started slipping backwards again all I could remember was the rituals, the panic, the OCD, and I forgot,' he says simply. 'I forgot how good we can be together and how much I love you.'

'Do you love her?' It's the only other thing I need to know right now.

'I thought I did.' He looks stricken as he says this but I am glad he has. If he had just taken comfort in another body without caring I think it would hurt more. The fact I wasn't enough for him – that anyone else could have done. Knowing he had real feelings makes it at least understandable if not forgivable.

'And now?'

'What I feel for Francesca is... something. But it's not even close to love. Leah, when I saw you carried out of the tunnel, barely conscious and bleeding...' He takes a moment to compose himself. 'During the hours I sat in the waiting room while you were in surgery, I had so much time to contemplate life without you. The future looked so bleak but the future I kept imagining – if the worst did happen and you didn't make it – was always me and Archie. Never with her.' He reaches for my hand again and this time I let him take it, although when he squeezes I don't squeeze back.

'I don't know what to say to you. It's such a lot to process.'

'I know, but I can promise you, Leah, that I know I've been an idiot and nothing like this will *ever* happen again. You and Archie—'

'I'm going to go to Mulberry and we can sort the rest out when I'm back.' I don't say *home*. I can't. Home suddenly feels house-of-cards precarious. On the brink of collapse.

He nods. There is nothing more to say yet. The difficult conversations will come later. He presses his lips against mine. They are dry and his breath smells of coffee. He walks away and my heart is breaking.

It feels like the end and the beginning of something all at once.

Chapter Eighty

Leah

Now

My clothes are as dark as my mood as I reluctantly dress for Marie's funeral. Today I am burying my twin; the other half of me who I had always thought, despite her drinking, to be lighter, happier. I hadn't known then her endless *what happened made us into the people we are today* and *it wasn't as bad as we thought, was it?* wasn't the outlook of a more optimistic person than me, but a desperate need to be absolved of blame, freed from the terrible guilt she carried.

'Let me help you with that.' My caseworker at Mulberry fastens the buttons on my dress that my shaking fingers can't quite manage. 'Your husband is waiting for you in reception. He's bringing you back afterwards?'

'Yes.' My voice is hoarse with the tears I have already shed this morning.

'Are you sure you're up to it, Leah?'

This I don't answer. I'm not up to it. Is anyone ever ready to let go of someone they love?

George doesn't ask if I'm okay. He knows I'm not. We don't talk on the way to the church, my head is too full of worries for words. Should I have let Archie come even though he's only four and barely knew his aunt? Should I have travelled in the procession behind the hearse? Endlessly I think of Carly. Where is she? Is she okay?

Will she turn up today?

The car crawls along the High Street, through the lunchtime traffic. I've only been at Mulberry for a few days but the world outside, it feels too big. Too overwhelming. Brighter and louder than I had remembered it.

I clasp my gloved hands tightly together on my lap and keep my eyes lowered. Already I've started Acceptance and Commitment therapy at Mulberry and I don't want to negate the scant progress I have made with a sighting of *him,* real or imagined.

Simon.

My father.

I haven't spoken to Mum but when she wrote to tell me she'd like to be the one to make the arrangements today, she reassured me that Simon wouldn't be at the funeral out of respect for me.

Respect.

We park. It takes several deep breaths before I can climb out of the car and walk towards the church. The sight of Marie's name in white flowers is a blow to the abdomen and I fold into myself. If my arm wasn't linked through George's I would have fallen to the ground.

I can't cope.

I'm caught between panic and utter despair.

'Let's do this,' Marie had said, hands on her hips, preparing to dance.

I count in my head *five, six, seven, eight* over and over again as I shuffle forward, staring at my feet, until somehow I am in the church. The smell of beeswax and roses fills my nostrils. I raise my face and my eyes meet Marie's. She's smiling out of the photo resting on her coffin. It's an old picture, her hair is still red. We look identical.

I have lost a piece of myself.

Sorrow is a solid weight in my chest. It's hard to move.

George grasps my hand as we take a slow walk past the pews – not as empty as I'd feared; hordes of theatre people have come to pay their respect.

Marie was loved. She just hadn't known it.

Carly is loved but she doesn't know it.

And me? I slide into a row beside my husband. He hasn't once let go of me.

The vicar speaks of Marie's life. Her achievements. The roles she played, but he doesn't mention the most important role of all.

The sister that she was.

It is unspeakable to me that everyone might leave not knowing that, but the thought of standing up, walking to the lectern is unimaginable. I can't.

Let's do this.

I can't, Marie. I'm not brave enough.

Acting is easy. You just pretend.

And so I pretend to be braver than I feel. My legs are paper-doll precarious as I shuffle to the front, feeling the tear-bright eyes of the mourners on my back.

'I just…' I clear my throat. 'I want to say a few words about my sister. Marie. We were twins but she never stopped reminding me that she was twelve minutes older than me. She took her role of big sister very seriously, as did Carly who…' – I scan the faces in front of me hopefully, just in case – 'who… isn't… can't be here today. You all know what we went through twenty years ago. The Sinclair Sisters. The Stolen Sisters, the press called us – but we were so much more than that. Marie was so much more than that. I was frightened. Terrified… much as I feel today, but Marie… Marie made up games while we were trapped in that room. Made up stories of dragons and princesses.' Grief is my dragon with fiery breath and scorching heat. Beads form on my top lip. I wipe them away. 'In Marie's stories we always ended up with medals for courage, and that is what I wish her to be remembered for. Her courage. Her kindness. The way she always tried to protect the people she loved.'

In my head I promise her that this will be her legacy. That no one will ever find out that she knew what my parents had planned. I almost feel her little finger linking around mine.

A pinkie promise can't be broke

Or you'll disappear in a puff of smoke

This is my vow to you,

I'll keep my promise through and through.

A whispered breath of thank you, against my neck.

I stumble back to my seat. The music begins. Annie promising us that the sun will come out tomorrow.

Later, the last of the mourners have retreated to the pub. George is waiting in the car to give me some space while I say my final goodbye. It's hard to believe that Marie is under the heaped earth. Once more trapped in a small, dark, space.

'Is this all my fault?' Mum slips into the space beside me.

I am about to say yes when I turn my head and register the

anguish on her face. She has lost a child. I can't even begin to imagine.

'I don't know. There are many paths that lead us to the same place.' Who's to say Marie wouldn't always have turned out an addict? I think of the small girl with her big dreams of stardom who just wanted to be universally adored and I want to weep.

'I didn't think Carly would miss this,' Mum says.

'Carly's broken. She coped with so much. If it wasn't for her...'

'Tell me,' Mum cut in.

'What?'

'Tell me what it was like. What you said about Marie's stories. Her games. I want to hear it. All of it.'

So I tell Mum the details that she'd never wanted to know. That Carly escaped but she came back for me and Marie. She fought men three times as big and a hundred times scarier to set us free. That when we were cold and scared we sang and danced. Together.

'When Marie was ill Carly kept her calm, held back her hair and cleaned her up. I was beside myself, thinking she was going to die, but Carly never showed us she was scared, not once. When the door was left open Carly could have left us, she'd have been quicker on her own, particularly after I twisted my ankle but she was always... there.' Tears gather but I don't let them fall. 'She never let us down. Not once.'

'I am sorry,' Mum says. 'For all of it... so is your dad.'

'I don't want to talk about *him*. How could you even bear to visit him? I know that you did.'

'Because... Because he's sorry. Because part of loving is forgiving and because—'

'How could you forgive him?'

'He's forgiven you.'

'For what?'

Mum holds my gaze. 'For all those extra years he served in prison. For being beaten almost daily by the other inmates. For being put on the Sex Offenders Register, effectively ruining all his future job prospects, meaning he'll always have to look over his shoulder.'

'When did he find out it was me?' There is no point denying it. There have been enough lies.

'Within a couple of days of being arrested. You can find out most things in prison. Criminals know other criminals. It only took a few packets of fags for him to find out your name.'

'Why didn't he tell the police it was me?'

'Because... Because you'd have been arrested and... he felt he deserved it. All of it and worse. Like I said, he's sorry.'

I can't speak for a minute.

'Mum?' I ask. 'Are you seeing him again? That day I came to your house... the steak? I thought I saw somebody inside.'

'Yes. I am. I know you won't approve or understand but we're moving away. To Scotland. I don't want you girls to have to worry about seeing him around.'

'Again. You're putting him before us again?'

'Leah...' Mum's eyes glisten. 'If you want me to stay, I'll stay.'

I think about the unhappiness we have all suffered. The potential for happiness that is within her grasp. I don't know if I will ever stop resenting her for what happened. If I stop her being with *him* – Simon – she might never stop resenting me.

'Go,' I give her my blessing.

She doesn't speak but opens her arms and, although I hesitate,

I step into them for the first time in years. It is both a hello and a goodbye.

She releases me. I blow my nose and dry my eyes as I watch her leave. She doesn't look back.

On the way to the car I notice a shadow slip behind the trees. A halo of glossy blonde hair.

I think it's Carly but I can't be sure and by the time I get there, she is gone.

Chapter Eighty-One

Leah

Now

George rings the doorbell when he comes to see Archie, which feels odd. He still slots in here. The last puzzle piece of our beautiful, broken, healing family. Since I left Mulberry he has been renting a small place in town on a month-by-month basis. During our time apart I've been building on the work I started at the hospital. I've a new counsellor – a man this time – and slowly I'm learning to live again. I am choosing who I want to be and I want to be happy. I hope Carly is too, wherever she is.

I miss her.

She hasn't been in touch, not once.

I think about her every single day.

These past few weeks George's visits have stretched beyond the time Archie is tucked up in bed. Often, evenings find George sitting in one armchair, and me in the other. Steaming mugs of coffee and a plate of biscuits on the table between us, forming a barrier. At first we skirted around the real issues, clinging to the superficial that was less painful. Firing minor irritations across the room – the loo seat being left up, is it fair it's always one person who empties the bin or does the shopping. We talked in circles – tag; you take the blame now – until one of us yawned and I'd show him to the door like the visitor he'd become, watching as he strode down the driveway, shoulders hunched, breath clouding from the mouth that hadn't kissed me goodnight.

Eventually we talked about Francesca, of course we did.

'Have you had any contact with her?' I asked.

'No.'

'You would say no. How can I trust you?' It was my stock reply.

'I don't know.' George looked sad. 'I can't tell you how, I can only hope that one day you can.'

'Did you think about me when you were with her?'

'Every time. I felt horrible.'

'Did you think about her with you were with me?'

'Leah…'

'Well, did you?' I wanted to know everything; when it started, how often he saw her, how it felt. I cried every single time, and at first so did he.

I had spoken to Francesca on the phone. Just once. She couldn't have been more sorry. At first I thought she was worried I'd report her for professional misconduct but as her apologies tumbled down the receiver I realized she was genuine. In her own way she cares about me, as does George. He was just at a loss to know how to help me. I get that. I had no idea how to help myself.

But now I do.

Once I had thought women who take men back after affairs were weak but, although I think sleeping with somebody else is inexcusable, it has taken strength for me to admit my share of responsibility for our problems.

Just like being happy, I could choose whether to forgive or not. I had already lost so much. Mum, Dad, Marie and Carly.

'You're stronger than I have given you credit for,' George told me after I'd explained what had happened in the decontamination chamber with Carly. How my injuries were self-inflected.

'We have to fight for the ones we love,' I told him, and that's what we're doing. Fighting for love. For each other. The thing I have learned is this: nothing is irreparable. My sense of safety, my trust, my hope. It may feel spiderweb-fragile, easily swept away, but it can be rebuilt if I want it enough.

And I do.

We became gentler as we picked at the cracks in our marriage, peering in to see if there was any way we could possibly fill them, and we are. With hope and understanding, and love. We're filling them with love. Little by little we're healing from the inside out.

There's been a change, a shift. Our conversations are not only deep and heavy but more and more peppered with lightness. Laughter. The *do you remember when* tales that everyone with a joint history has. The ones that are nice to share. We sip our wine. Hands wrapped around glasses, itching to touch each other. I wanted to take it slow.

We sit on the sofa together now, me with my legs tucked under me, leaning against one arm, him with his elbow resting on the other, still a distance between us, but perhaps not quite so far. I want to bridge the gap entirely.

'George.' His eyes meet mine, there's an unspoken question in them, and then an understanding. Relief. He comes closer, leans in.

Our lips meet and I can almost hear Marie chanting, 'Leah and George sitting in a tree, K-I-S-S-I-N-G.'

We break away. He tenderly tucks a strand of hair behind my ear; it's still long, still red.

I'm still me.

We're still us.

Epilogue

Leah

Eight months later

'Mummy!' My son's face is pure joy as I walk into the kitchen. Archie is my warmth on this biting autumn morning. 'My rucksack is all packed.'

'Great.' I crouch and clip the lead onto the dog's collar while George zips up Archie's coat before tugging his bobble hat over his head. 'You can come along for the ride, pooch.'

'Are you sure you want to do this?' George looks at me with concern. 'You know we don't have to.'

'It'll be exciting for Archie and good for me to see it.'

'Can we get a hot chocolate afterwards? With cream. Please!' Archie pleads.

'Yes.' I ruffle his hair. I wouldn't normally encourage such a hit of sugar in the morning, but then this is a special occasion.

It's the day I've been waiting for.

The sky is dull and grey, which seems fitting. The windscreen wipers swish intermittently, although it's more moist air than drizzle dampening the windscreen. I watch the scenery flash by, absent-mindedly running my fingers over yesterday's new tattoo;

a comma. I was terrified of infection and threw up beforehand, but I did it.

'Can you pull in here?' I gesture to a lay-by next to a café. 'I think we could do with that warming drink to take with us, don't you?'

Archie squeals in excitement and launches himself out of the car. I think how wonderful it would be to see the world through a five-year-old's eyes. Finding the joy in something most of us would take for granted – complain about even, I think as I look at the queue.

Eventually it is our turn.

'Three hot chocolates, please.' Archie beams his biggest smile.

'I think we only want two,' George turns to me. 'You haven't brought your cup, have you?'

'No. But I'll have one, thanks,' I say to the barista. I can feel George still staring at me in shock. Inside I am a mass of delight and pride with a hint of trepidation. The Acceptance and Commitment therapy I've been using seems to be working for me in a way that other methods haven't, which isn't to say I'll drink the chocolate that's now being topped with a heap of swirling cream, but I'm willing to try.

Small steps.

It is properly raining when we get there.

'We'll stay in the car and watch,' George says to Archie. 'Snuggly and warm.'

There are only a handful of spectators. An elderly man in a wheelchair in full army uniform, medals pinned on his chest. Someone – I'm guessing his daughter – holding a black umbrella over his head.

A reporter from the local newspaper scowls from under his hood, his cameraman shielding his lens with his hand.

There's a clutch of people gathered at the wire fence. I'm not sure why they are here but I'm sure they have a reason. We all have a history, don't we? Tonight, a party has been planned in one of the local pubs. The community will celebrate the demolition of the site that attracts the true-crime ghouls. The demolition of their guilt that Simon was one of their own.

It is time.

Archie scrambles into the front of the car, dragging his rucksack behind him. He settles himself on George's lap and unzips his bag.

Carefully he unpacks his bright plastic toys: Scoop, Muck, Dizzy, Roley and Lofty, lining the construction vehicles from *Bob the Builder* on the dashboard.

'Are you ready?' he asks them sweetly. 'Those big machines out there are going to flatten this site.' He claps his hands excitedly, making me jump. 'And then they're going to build some houses. The soldiers don't need this place any more, do they, Mummy?'

'No, Archie. No one needs it.'

The wrecking ball begins to swing.

'Can you see, Dizzy?' Archie asks his orange cement mixer, leaning forward to listen for the answer. 'He says he can see.'

I can see.

I can see three young girls kicking and screaming as they are carried inside. I can see a filthy room where the girls sang and danced, watched over by a clown with a shock of orange hair. I can see three sisters huddled together on a mattress, promising to always be there for each other.

I can see it all.

'I'll be back soon.' My eyes find George's and I shake my head before he asks. No, I don't want him to come with me.

'Do you want your gloves? It's freezing outside?' He lifts them from the centre console.

'No.' I don't want my gloves today, or any day. Now, I like to feel.

Outside the car, the noise and the vibrations from the wrecking ball are immense. The main building is almost rubble, the NORCROFT ARMY CAMP sign hidden under a cloud of dust. As I pass behind the soldier, I reach out a hand and squeeze his shoulder, wondering if in his mind he's back in that ballroom – a blue-eyed boy with cropped blond hair, hovering by the refreshment table and summoning up the courage to ask a girl to dance while Vera Lynn sings 'We'll Meet Again', just the way Carly had described.

There's no one around the side of the base. The site is so vast it could be days, weeks even before the machines trek where tanks had once trundled. I link my fingers through the chain fence as I stare at the decontamination chamber, not caring who might have touched the metal before me, the germs I might be picking up. My stomach twists as I remember Carly bundling Marie and I inside those lockers I had thought were for rucksacks but later found out were for bodies. I remember her sending us down the chute, through the tunnel. Marie weak and sick, me with my swollen, twisted ankle. So many times Carly could have left us, but she didn't.

She wouldn't.

Even now.

The air chills around me as I wait. The rain lashes against my face.

I don't hear footsteps. There is no sun to cast a shadow, but I feel her all the same.

My back instantly warmer as she shields me from the wind.

'I knew you'd come,' I say as her arms slip around my waist.

'I'm—'

'Shh.' Now I'm the one taking charge. 'It doesn't matter. None of it. I've lost one sister, I won't lose another.' It's my turn to look after my big sister. To find her the help she needs. She can heal. We both can.

I lean back against her and her chin rests on my shoulder.

Simultaneously I see it. Carly draws in a sharp breath. I know she has seen it too.

A small figure through the sheeting rain, twirling with her hands above her head.

I imagine it's the ghost of Marie, singing and dancing and dreaming of her big future in Hollywood.

And for the longest moment I imagine we're all together again.

The following letter contains spoilers

Hello,

Thank you so much for reading my sixth psychological thriller, *The Stolen Sisters*. If you enjoyed it and have a spare few moments to pop a review online I'd hugely appreciate it. It really does make such a difference to an author.

I remember, with clarity, the moment the seeds of this story were planted.

It was a Saturday. *The Date* was newly published, and I was engrossed in writing *The Family* when my youngest son came hurtling into my study.

'Mum!' he clutched his laptop to his chest. 'Do you know what Fregoli Syndrome is?'

I didn't.

'Watch this,' he said.

We settled down on the sofa and he showed me what he'd found online. I was both intrigued and saddened by this unusual condition that I hadn't heard of, instantly knowing it was a fabulous basis for a novel.

Too excited to wait until Monday, I called my agent and explained the concept to him.

'You must write a book about it,' he said.

I spent much time thinking about how frightening it would be to suffer from Fregoli, to be convinced you are seeing the face of your tormentor everywhere you turn. How terrifying it would be if you really were seeing them but, because of a medical diagnosis, nobody would believe you.

Leah, Carly and Marie Sinclair came to me time and time again and I pushed them away. As a mother of three children, I didn't want to read about missing children, and I certainly didn't want to write about them.

Blocking them out was fruitless. Those small girls became permanent residents in my head. Whispering their heart-wrenching story.

By the time I was ready to begin a new book, I knew Leah, Carly and Marie weren't going to leave me alone. I also knew that the only way I could write about missing children was if we discover at the beginning they are adults, alive, physically unharmed, but mentally, emotionally damaged – that's what I wanted to explore. To the outside word they had survived a horrific ordeal but Leah with her OCD, Carly with her inability to trust, and Marie with her drinking weren't okay at all.

Since I've finished writing this book, I've written two more, but the Sinclair sisters are still very much in my head. In my heart.

They will stay with me. Always.

I'd love to hear what you thought. You can find me at www.louisejensen.co.uk and https://twitter.com/Fab_fiction and https://www.facebook.com/fabricatingfiction/

Do join me next autumn for the publication of my next thriller.

Louise x

Acknowledgements

My sixth thriller and it never gets any less exciting. As usual, there have been masses of people involved in bringing my story to life. As ever, thanks to my agent, Rory Scarfe, for his continued support. My fabulous editor, Manpreet Grewal, who loved the Sinclair sisters right from the first draft and helped me develop it to its fullest potential. Lisa Milton and the entire HQ family, in particular Melanie Hayes, Janet Aspey in marketing and Lucy Richardson in PR and the production team. Thanks to Jon Appleton for the copy-edit.

Big thanks to all the book bloggers whose cheerleading immensely brightens up my day and to everyone who speaks to me on social media. Writing can be a lonely process. It's great to have a friend who is also in the business so, even though I drink too much coffee and eat too much hummus with Darren O'Sullivan, it's great to be able to chat about our writing lives. My non-writing friends: in particular, Hilary, Sarah, Natalie, Sue and Kuldip. Emma Mitchell – thanks for your friendship and support.

To my family: Mum, Karen, Bekkii and Pete, thanks for supporting me through another book. And to Glynn, who we miss dearly.

My husband, Tim, the Sinclair sisters' heartbreaking tale affected me emotionally at times so thanks for the end-of-the-day hugs.

My children, Callum, Kai and Finley who remain my entire world.

And Ian Hawley. With so much love.

Book Club Questions

1) The story features an unusual medical condition. Had you ever heard of this? What did you make of it?

2) '*A comma not a full stop. This isn't the end*,' Carly says. There was a time she could have escaped and fetched help, leaving her sisters behind. Do you think she was wrong to stay?

3) Part One of the story closes with a dramatic twist. Discuss.

4) In the Sinclair family, secrets are kept. Is it ever okay to keep things from those closest to you?

5) '*I would do anything to protect my child. Anything*,' Leah says. Do her actions shock you?

6) What theories did you form throughout this book?

7) Did any of your theories turn out to be correct?

8) Who is your favourite Sinclair Sister and why?

9) '*I can choose to be happy. I can choose to forgive*,' Leah says. Are our emotions, to a point, a choice?

10) What do you think the future holds for the girls?

Turn the page for an exclusive extract from the nail-biting and gripping thriller from Louise Jensen

The Family

Available to buy now

PROLOGUE

Now
LAURA

It all unfolds with cinematic clarity; the gunshot, the scream. Every detail sharp and clear. Time slows as her eyes plead with me to help her. In my mind I bundle her behind me, shielding her body with mine, but she is too far away and I know I cannot reach her in time.

But still I try.

My legs are weighted with dread as I run towards her; the fist around my heart tightening.

A second shot.

Her knees buckle. She crumples like a paper doll.

The ground falls away beneath my feet and I crawl towards her like the animal I have become. My palms are sticky in the arc of blood that is staining the floor red. Blood is thicker than water they say, but hers is thin and beacon-bright. Adrenaline pulses through me leaving numbness in its wake, as I press against her wrist, desperately seeking a pulse. With my other hand I link my fingers through hers the way we used to, before I brought us to this place that has been our ruin. A lifetime of memories strobe through my mind; cradling her close in the maternity wing; Easter eggs spilling out of the wicker basket looped over her pudgy arm; her first day of school, ribboned pigtails swinging as she ran across the playground.

She can't be gone.

Can she?

Fingers of panic press hard against my skull. The colour leaches from the room. A black and white hue descending upon me. I tighten my fingers around hers, afraid I'm going to faint. Afraid I'm going to let her go.

But then.

A flicker of eyelids. A murmur from her lips.

I lay next to her, gently rolling her towards me, holding her in my arms. I can't, I won't leave her. Family should stick together. Protect each other. Instead, I chose to come here.

This is all my fault.

The drumming in my head grows louder – the sound of footfall. I don't have to look up to feel their anger, solid and immovable.

The acrid smell of gunpowder hangs in the air along with my fear.

Looking up, my eyes meet the shooter's; they are still holding the gun and sensations return, hard and fast. The pain in my stomach is cutting and deep and I am no longer sure if the blood I am covered in has come from her.

Or is coming from me.

Her top is soaked crimson, as is mine.

The pain increases.

Terrified, I tug at her clothes, my clothes. Praying. Let her be okay. Seventeen is no age. Let it be me.

At last I find the wound but before I can apply pressure to stem the flow of blood there are hands on my shoulders. My elbows. Pulling.

Darkness flickers at the edge of my vision but still I fight against it. I fight against them.

My hands are restrained, feet kick out, teeth sinking into flesh, but it's fruitless. I am growing weaker.

Her fingers twitch. Once. Twice.

Nothing.

'Tilly!' My scream rips through me as I am yanked to my feet. 'Tilly!' I scramble for traction, every fibre of my being straining to reach my daughter.

I can't.

I am still wrestling to be free as I am dragged, my feet scraping the ground.

I know they'll never let us leave here now.

Not alive anyway.